'All I can say is, Holy yowza, Batman! [...]
into the 'What to read after *Fifty* [...]
my opinion – and pay attention t[...]
blows *Fifty Shades* out of the wa[...]
I unabashedly adored this bo[...]
(full review at www.ravingb[...]

Quotes from Goodreads.com user reviews:

'Sexcapades delivered with a bit o' pain by a beautiful
Irishman. Yum! Everyone should roll around a bit in
The Pleasures of Winter. Wickedly Delicious!'

'What can I say – it took my breath away . . . It was a truly
intimate love story . . . I laughed, I cried, I got frustrated with
Abbie because of the way he was treating her . . . but as the
story went on I got to understand Jack a bit more and realized
why he was like this. [He] truly loved Abbie . . . It was an
awesome read and very well written.'

'Awesome book! If you are a fan of *Fifty Shades of Grey* or
Bared to You, you must read this book!'

'The book was deliciously titillating! I loved the characters and
the story. I also love the sex scenes, they were seriously
steamy . . . I do not believe I will ever be able to look at
a feather again without feeling dirty!'

'Wow, did this book take me by surprise. I've been looking for
something similar to *Fifty Shades* and *Bared to You* for a while
and this book is definitely up there with them.'

'Reading the description of *The Pleasures Of Winter* one may
just assume it's yet another *Fifty Shades/Bared To You*
bandwagon book, but it is so much more. I honestly found
myself enjoying this book way more.'

The Pleasures of Summer

EVIE HUNTER

PENGUIN BOOKS

PENGUIN BOOKS

Published by the Penguin Group
Penguin Books Ltd, 80 Strand, London WC2R ORL, England
Penguin Group (USA) Inc., 375 Hudson Street, New York, New York 10014, USA
Penguin Group (Canada), 90 Eglinton Avenue East, Suite 700, Toronto, Ontario, Canada M4P 2Y3
(a division of Pearson Penguin Canada Inc.)
Penguin Ireland, 25 St Stephen's Green, Dublin 2, Ireland (a division of Penguin Books Ltd)
Penguin Group (Australia), 707 Collins Street, Melbourne, Victoria 3008, Australia
(a division of Pearson Australia Group Pty Ltd)
Penguin Books India Pvt Ltd, 11 Community Centre, Panchsheel Park, New Delhi – 110 017, India
Penguin Group (NZ), 67 Apollo Drive, Rosedale, Auckland 0632, New Zealand
(a division of Pearson New Zealand Ltd)
Penguin Books (South Africa) (Pty) Ltd, Block D, Rosebank Office Park,
181 Jan Smuts Avenue, Parktown North, Gauteng 2193, South Africa

Penguin Books Ltd, Registered Offices: 80 Strand, London WC2R ORL, England

www.penguin.com

First published 2013
001

Copyright © Eileen Gormley and Caroline McCall, 2013

The moral right of the authors has been asserted

Set in 12.5/14.75pt Garamond MT Std
Typeset by Jouve (UK), Milton Keynes
Printed in Great Britain by Clays Ltd, St Ives plc

A CIP catalogue record for this book is available from the British Library

ISBN: 978-0-241-96664-8

www.greenpenguin.co.uk

MIX
Paper from
responsible sources
FSC
www.fsc.org
FSC™ C018179

Penguin Books is committed to a sustainable
future for our business, our readers and our planet.
This book is made from Forest Stewardship
Council™ certified paper.

ALWAYS LEARNING   **PEARSON**

To our families

Prologue

December

Summer O'Sullivan's heart pounded when she checked her rear view mirror again. The blue van was still following her. Usually she wouldn't notice anything less exotic than a Bugatti Veyron, but it was after 4 a.m. and she'd had two unpleasant encounters already that night. Why couldn't the paparazzi leave her alone?

She accelerated away from the van, only to be stopped fifty yards down the street at the pedestrian crossing. Summer tapped her fingers on the steering wheel as the remnants of a hen party staggered across the road singing 'Merry Christmas Everyone'. The bride carried a traffic cone. How could they take so long?

She glanced at the mirror; the blue van was still on her tail. The creep wasn't acting like a pap, but he was driving close enough to send a trickle of sweat down her spine. Summer fumbled in her bag for her mobile phone. *Bugger.* It was dead. She must have forgotten to charge it.

As the lights changed, she slammed her foot down on the accelerator. Her BMW shot forwards with a screech and she raced away. She didn't care if she got a ticket. In fact, she would be delighted to be stopped by a policeman anytime now.

London's finest weren't inclined to oblige her.

Praying that she had lost him, Summer took the turn for Hampstead. She glanced in her mirror, relieved when there was no sign of the van. Exhaling a breath she hadn't realized she had been holding, she eased back on the accelerator.

Summer switched on the radio, hoping the late-night jazz would calm her. Maybe she was overreacting, but since the break-up with Adam, her life had turned crazy.

It's over. Don't think about him now.

Lights flashed behind her, taking her by surprise, and a van overtook her at speed, causing her to swerve on the icy road. Bloody lunatic.

She relaxed when she saw the turn off. Almost home. She rounded the final bend with relief.

'What the –' Headlights blinded her and for a split second she couldn't see a thing. She blinked. There was a vehicle blocking the road. Instinctively, she jammed on the brakes and the rear wheels lost traction. Her nails dug into the leather-covered steering wheel as she turned into the skid, struggling to regain control, but it was too late. Her car hit the kerb and she jerked forwards. The seatbelt whipped her back against the seat like a rag doll, knocking the breath from her lungs. The airbag engaged before she had time to scream.

Blackness. Fuzzy vision. Everything hurt and there was blood. Hers, she realized with a hysterical laugh. The sound of wheels spinning uselessly grated on the silent winter road. The radio continued to play a Melody Gardot song about a man with a heart as black as night.

A light flashed through the windscreen. Summer scrunched her eyes shut and then forced them open.

'Hold on. I'll soon have you out.' The voice was muffled.

'Oh, thank god,' she gasped.

It rattled, but the driver's door wouldn't open. The man walked around to the passenger door and tugged hard, cursing when he realized that it was jammed.

He knocked on the window. 'Open it.'

'Ca-a-an't,' she managed. 'I think my arm is . . .'

'Open the fucking door.' He banged on the roof of the car.

Why was he shouting at her? Summer squinted, trying to focus on the road. There was no patrol car, no ambulance, just a dark van. A sharp blow on the window made her jump. The glass in the passenger window shattered, the cracks spreading out like a spider's web. What the hell was he doing? Was he crazy? Was this a robbery? A car-jack?

'Please don't,' she whimpered. A trickle of moisture blinded her. She wiped it away, sickened when she realized that it was blood.

The man struck the window again and it collapsed into the passenger seat in a shattering rush. She shrieked as he reached through the broken window and tugged at the handle. He ignored the Chanel tote on the passenger seat. It wasn't a robbery. He wanted her.

'You fucking little bitch.' He grabbed her sleeve, wrenching her arm as he pulled it, and a bright arc of pain shot through her. Oh god. Oh god. Her heart thudded until she thought it was going to explode. Somehow, she dragged her arm free and grabbing a handful of the broken glass on the passenger seat, she flung it in his face.

'Whore,' he spat, recoiling. 'You'll fucking pay for that.'

She needed a weapon. Shoes. She had the needle-spiked Louboutins she had worn at the party. Her fingertips brushed the soft suede, but she couldn't get a grip. Again, and this time she caught something. Her shoulder screamed in protest as she dragged the shoe free. When he reached through the window again she slammed the heel into his hand as hard as she could. He roared with pain.

Summer pressed her hand on the car horn and held it down. *Somebody hear me. Somebody please hear me.*

After that, everything went black.

I

Six months later

'Summer!'

Summer opened one eye. The other eye was glued together with the remains of her false eyelashes. She groaned into her pillow. Lifting the duvet, she took a quick inventory. She was still wearing the slinky pink dress from the night before but there was a stain on the front that looked remarkably like . . .

'Summer!'

The roar came again, louder this time.

'Ugh.' If her father found her in this state he would go crazy.

'Summer!' The roaring was getting closer now.

She tumbled out of bed and hurried to the bathroom.

Her blonde hair extensions were clumped together and the remains of last night's mascara stared accusingly at her from the mirror. She looked like a hung-over raccoon. Somewhere in the deepest recesses of her brain stirred a vague recollection of dancing on a table singing 'The Fields of Athenry'.

'You are never drinking cocktails again,' she told her reflection.

She stripped off her dress, scrubbed her face clean,

rinsed her mouth with mouthwash, pulled on a bathrobe and wound her hair into a turban.

'Summer.' This time the roar was accompanied by pounding on the bathroom door. Her dad had finally lost it. She opened the door reluctantly.

Tim O'Sullivan's face was scarlet. 'What the hell did you do to my car?'

'Me? Nothing.'

'Don't lie to me. If you took my car . . .'

Summer's own face flushed. 'I wasn't anywhere near your cars. Natasha gave me a lift yesterday. You can ask her if you like.' And he probably would. Her dad would believe anyone before he believed her.

His face crumpled. 'God, I was hoping it was you.'

She stared, shocked.

'If it wasn't then some feckers broke in and did it.'

'Calm down, Dad. Remember what the doctor said –'

Her father turned away, already heading for the door. 'Feck the doctor,' he muttered under his breath.

Shoving her feet into a pair of mules, Summer followed him down the stairs, through the open door and around to the side of the house where he garaged his collection of vintage cars. She winced. It wasn't just any car that was damaged. It was *that* car. Sitting on the gravel driveway was her father's pride and joy, the one that she had been driving yesterday. The silver Aston Martin DB5 – no wonder he was ranting.

She had listened to the story a zillion times. How Tim O'Sullivan, son of a poor fishing family, dragged himself up from nothing to build an international airline, *yadda yadda yadda*. This particular car was the symbol of his meteoric rise to success. It was one of only six built for a James Bond movie. Now it was splashed with red paint and there were deep grooves in the passenger door.

'What the hell am I paying security for?'

Her father was shaking. The last few months had been terrible for him. The plane crash, the hate mail, the endless newspaper coverage, and now this. She patted his arm. 'It will all blow over. The inquiry found it was an accident.'

He clenched his hand into a fist. 'Do you think any of them care? If it's not the media following me around like a pack of hyenas, it's some crackpot who thinks I'm responsible for every plane that drops out of the sky. You'll be better off back home until things settle.'

He couldn't be serious. Boarding school had been bad enough. Then, when she was doing her MBA, he had insisted that she share a flat with her strait-laced cousin Sinead. But Castletownbloodyberehaven with her grandmother watching her like a hawk?

'Sorry, Dad. There's no way I'm going there.'

'You listen to me, young lady. It's Castletownberehaven or you're getting a bodyguard. After last year, you can't possibly think it's safe for you to be on your own.'

Calling her young lady was a sure sign that he had made his mind up and he would never change it. Summer had other plans while she was in London, but they weren't the kind she was going to share with her father. She had to calm him down. 'Please don't send me away. You need me here. Please Dad.'

He gave her a measuring look. 'Sometimes you remind me of your mother, lord rest her. I'm not going to risk losing you as well.'

He pulled his phone out of his pocket and tapped the speed dial. 'Brian, I need you to organize security for Summer. Yes. Until I get back from Atlanta.' He eyed the vandalized car and shook his head. 'And tell the garage to send someone over ASAP.'

Summer forced a smile onto her face. This was a temporary setback. She could handle a bodyguard. Her dad would be away for most of the month and when she got rid of the bodyguard, she could carry out her plans.

In the breakfast room, they helped themselves to food from the covered dishes on the sideboard. There were sausages, bacon, eggs cooked four ways, fried pancakes, mushroom, beans, black pudding and toast. She would have to speak to the new chef and tell him that he wasn't feeding an army. No wonder her dad was overweight.

How was she supposed to run the household and keep her dad healthy when people kept leaving all the time? She had no idea why there was such a high turnover of staff.

Summer helped herself to yoghurt and fruit and sprinkled it with granola. Her stomach lurched. She was still queasy from the night before. Pouring herself a cup of coffee, she picked up the morning paper. Her own face looked back at her from the third page. Damn. There was a photo of her holding Maya's hair as she puked out the door of the limo. How the hell did the tabloids get these stories? She would have sworn no one else had seen that nasty little incident. Summer read on: 'Irish eyes were certainly smiling last night when socialite Summer O'Sullivan hooked up with hunky Australian half-back Mike Chester.'

'Oh bugger,' she muttered.

8

'What's that, Summer?'

'Nothing, Dad.' She forced a smile and dropped the paper under the table. Her dad had enough to worry about without having to read about her latest exploits.

She took out her Xperia to check her messages.

Her father opened his laptop and they read through their emails in silence, broken only by the occasional expletive from her father when something annoyed him. He never stopped working. She couldn't remember when they had last gone out for dinner together or done anything that wasn't connected with business. It must have been when her mother was alive.

'So when do you fly to the States?' she asked to distract him from his latest rant about share prices.

'Next Tuesday at noon. But don't worry. Brian said they're sending someone round at eleven.' He said that his assistant was a godsend, efficient and organized. Summer hated him.

'Great.' Summer poured another cup of coffee. 'I can't wait.' *To get rid of him.*

At precisely 10.55 a.m. a nondescript grey Nissan made its way sedately up the driveway. Summer let the curtain slide back into place. She couldn't see the driver clearly but he looked middle-aged. Perfect for what she had in mind. Grabbing her towel, she hurried downstairs to the pool.

By the time they found her, she had swum four lengths at a fast crawl. The uniformed maid stumbled when she saw that Summer wasn't wearing a swimsuit. With a blush and an apologetic glance at the visitor, she hurried away.

Through her tinted swim goggles, she watched as the

bodyguard stood at the side of the pool, shifting from foot to foot. She kept him waiting while she swam another length and then she climbed out, took off her goggles and shook her hair.

'Towel,' she said in a clipped tone, stretching out her hand in his direction.

After a moment's hesitation, he fetched the towel from the sun-lounger. Keeping his eyes averted from her naked body, he carefully handed it over.

Summer deliberately didn't thank him. She wrapped the towel around her hair, rubbed it dry and dropped the wet towel at her feet. Stepping closer, she stared him down. He was in great shape for his age, but no match for her.

'I swim three kilometres every morning at seven and I expect you to join me. Oh, and be a darling and make sure that there are no leaves or insects in the pool before I arrive.' She strolled away, leaving him staring open mouthed at her ass – and walked straight into her dad.

That was the end of Bob.

After that, operation *Defeat the Bodyguard* became her favourite game. Tyler, the driver, arrived the following day. She managed to clock up two speeding tickets during the afternoon she spent with him. Her dad had gone crazy about that one.

Then there was Joe. He was a real sweetie and a strict vegetarian. Serving braised liver for lunch and steak tartare for dinner two nights in a row had ended that particular assignment. The poor guy had been almost barfing while he watched her eat and she wasn't sure if she could keep that much protein down.

Thursday brought the charming Tony who had a penchant for expensive Italian suits. Luckily he was gay. A heated kiss in her father's office while she was giving him a tour of the house ensured that he was sent packing before his first hour was up. She really should have mentioned the hidden security cameras.

The last guy was bald, monosyllabic and built like a brick house. He had been a tough nut to crack until she had taken him lingerie shopping for three hours, insisting that he sit outside her dressing room and view each outfit she tried on. Asking the assistant to take their photograph was probably a bit mean, but then so was sharing them on FB. He hadn't returned the next day.

No new bodyguards had arrived since Friday.

Summer stretched and yawned before she got up. She would be a sweet, dutiful daughter until her dad left for Atlanta. Casual clothes and no make-up except a quick slick of her favourite lip-gloss. She had almost reached the landing when she heard her father's voice in the hallway below.

'What do you mean, you have no one available? You're on a retainer, Niall. Make someone available, for Christ's sakes.'

She sat down on the stairs. Operation *Defeat the Bodyguard* obviously wasn't over yet. When her dad's voice dropped, she tilted her head to catch the rest of his words.

'I want the best. I don't care what it costs. Just get him here by this evening.'

Summer heard the door to the breakfast room slam. Her dad sounded worried, and that was unlike him. She rested her head against the banisters while she twisted the ring on her right hand. The plain gold band had once belonged to her mother. It was the only piece of jewellery she had been allowed to wear at school and now it wouldn't come off.

She wondered what her mother would think if she saw her now. The Hampstead mansion was very different from the one-roomed flat where her parents had spent the first few years of their marriage. What would her mother say if she knew about all the naughty things she had done during the week? Worst of all, she wondered if her mum knew that she was planning to go to an exclusive fetish club with her friend Molly?

Out of habit, Summer kissed the ring. She was being foolish. Her mum was dead. Climbing to her feet, she hurried down the rest of the stairs.

The blonde's parted lips were moist and glossy. She was kneeling at his feet, her position in contrast to her prim office uniform of black skirt, white blouse and hair in a neat chignon. 'Please, Sir, allow me to pleasure you,' she begged.

Flynn looked down at her, appreciating the angle of her neck in that position. He would strip her later and mess up that efficient hairstyle, but not yet. 'You haven't earned that right yet. Has she, Lottie?'

The raven-haired siren shook her glossy bob. 'No, Sir. I should be the one to pleasure you.' Lottie wore a skin-tight latex outfit that showed off her generous curves. She was tall enough that her six-inch heels brought her close to his height. And put the collar she wore right into convenient grabbing distance.

He smiled slowly. 'I'm inclined to agree. Lottie, you can show her how to worship me with your mouth.' He turned to the blonde. 'Bella, remain kneeling there and watch. Pay attention. There will be an exam later, and you won't like the penalty if you fail.'

He settled himself back on the couch while Lottie dropped to her knees in front of him and unfastened his leather trousers.

A buzzing sensation against his hip distracted him. He hadn't given her permission to use the vibrator, so what was it? The pulsation continued, accompanied by the sound of the Tardis.

'Fuck!' Reluctantly, Flynn opened his eyes, allowing the vision of the two gorgeous women to dissipate, and groped for his phone. The boat rocked as he rooted through the outer pocket of his fishing waders to find it and fumble it out.

'This had better be good,' he growled. 'Lottie LeBlanc was about to give me a BJ.'

His boss's voice was disgustingly cheerful, but not at all sympathetic. 'Tell her to take a rain check. I have a job for you. An interesting one.'

'Yeah?' Flynn was wary but intrigued. Niall knew that his idea of an interesting job involved an H&K semi, a dozen bad guys and blowing things up with C4. He wasn't back at full strength yet after the last, and hopefully final, round of surgery, but he was prepared to fake it. 'What is it?'

'Security detail. Nothing too taxing, don't worry.'

Damn, how did Niall Moore do it? He hadn't told his boss about his injuries, but somehow he had found out.

It was creepy how he did that. Niall went on, 'It's easy work, but the fringe benefits are stunning.'

'Go on.' This he had to hear.

'You know those blondes you see in glossy magazines and wonder if they're real?'

'I read *Jane's*, *An Cosantóir* and the *New Yorker*.' The last time Flynn had used a glossy magazine, he was jamming it into a toaster to use as a detonator.

'In that case, you might have missed her. Summer O'Sullivan. She's under threat from some dipshit moron with a grudge against her father, Tim. You're just the man to keep her safe.'

That was a name Flynn knew. 'O'Sullivan Airlines? I didn't know the mouthy little git had a daughter.' Then a memory clicked. 'Hold on. You're talking about the blonde airhead?'

The photo on the front page of the *Daily Star* of Summer O'Sullivan, naked except for a Garda jacket, screaming abuse as she was being dragged along Grafton Street, had sold lots of papers.

'You've got to be fucking kidding me. I'm not baby-sitting that brat. Get someone else.'

'There is no one else.' For the first time, Flynn caught a hint of exhaustion in Niall's voice. 'Come on, Fug, do me a favour. O'Sullivan is the sort of windbag who will ruin the agency's reputation if I can't deliver. And I've no one else left.'

Flynn didn't bother getting pissed about being called Fug. He knew damn well that when anyone from the Wing called him that, it stood for Fucked Up Guy, not Flynn Ulysses Grant. In a way, considering the source, it was almost a compliment. He focused on the important question. 'How come you have no operatives? Last time we talked, you had half a dozen qualified men.'

'Civilians.' Niall sounded disgusted. 'Not one of them can cope with the little madam. They're too polite. So I thought, who's the least polite person I know?'

'And fuck you too, you bastard,' Flynn said, but it was half-hearted. He couldn't argue with the truth. 'It's pity work.'

'Okay, it's not East Timor, but it's real work. It's only for a few weeks; you can get back to fighting form and take a more challenging job afterwards. I promise I'll find you something more to your taste.'

'Something with a lot of C4?' Flynn asked.

'Could be. There's a nice little covert-ops job coming up, something that calls for your special skills. If I'm sure you are up to the job.'

'That's blackmail!' But it was a half-hearted protest.

'Suck it up, Fug, and get your ass down to the O'Sullivan place in London ASAP. I'll send you the details.' Niall disconnected the call before Flynn could protest any further.

'Well, fuck!' He stared at his phone in frustration, but knew he'd been had. Somehow, his old CO had conned him into babysitting a blonde brat for a couple of weeks.

2

Dunboy House, the O'Sullivan mansion near Hampstead Heath, reminded Flynn of one of the big houses in the midlands of Ireland. It was a huge Regency-style building, with colonnades, marble steps and a beech-lined avenue. But it was surrounded by a demesne wall that wouldn't keep out a child. He was going to have his work cut out for him.

He announced himself at the security gate.

For an instant, he considered how out of place he was going to look, still rough from his fishing trip, but he didn't allow it to bother him. They needed his expertise, not *GQ* looks. He'd leave the pretty boy stuff to Niall. He checked his watch; yes, he was on time.

When the gates opened, Flynn sped up the driveway. He stopped the Venom, a bike that was more powerful than it looked, outside the front door and grabbed his rucksack. Out of long habit, he hefted it as if it didn't contain an arsenal's worth of weapons. It took more effort than usual. Damn his injuries. He was determined to be back at his fighting best as soon as possible.

The front door was slightly ajar. The security was so sloppy it was scary. 'Al Qaeda could waltz in here,' he muttered. Even at the best of times, this was stupid. When a nutcase was making death threats against your family, it was criminal.

He didn't bother ringing the bell to announce his arrival, but pushed the door open and walked inside. An open door was an invitation in his book. Hell, anything not secured with laser and a triple deadlock was an invitation to Flynn.

The hall was cool and dim, with oak panels and black and white marble tiles that looked original. A wide wooden staircase drew his eyes upwards and a movement at the top caught his attention.

A blonde, wearing only a skimpy towel tucked around her breasts and which barely covered her hips, fussed with her damp hair as she descended. 'Malcolm,' she called over her shoulder. 'I'm going to the sauna. Send someone with towels.'

Flynn whistled in appreciation. The legs revealed by that inadequate towel were spectacular, long and shapely and lightly tanned. Her feet were elegant and high-arched, with nails painted silver and pink. Those luscious thighs were the stuff of fantasy, and Flynn allowed himself a brief vision of how she would look without the towel.

She stopped on the last step, artfully widening her eyes as if she was surprised to see him there. Yeah right, as if she hadn't been aware of him from the moment she turned onto the landing.

She looked him up and down, examining him, and then turned away dismissively. 'The servants' entrance is around the rear,' she said, pointing to the front door.

He laughed and moved closer, onto the step where she stood. This close, he could see the individual lashes around her dark blue eyes. She wore no make-up, but smelled of something exotic and expensive.

She took a half step back before she halted, staring up at him defiantly.

'I usually have to pay someone to say something that corny. But don't worry, I won't forget.'

On impulse, he moved in and gave her damp hair a slight tug. Something about the texture was wrong; it wasn't vibrant enough for her personality. For an instant, she softened, swaying slightly in his direction, before indignation stiffened her spine and she snapped, 'Take your hands off me.'

Flynn let go. He'd had the answer he needed.

'Just checking if the curtains matched the carpet – since you so kindly gave me a flash of the carpet on your way down.'

She gasped in outrage, yanking the towel tight around her. 'How dare you?'

He laughed. 'You can ask that after parading in front of a strange man wearing only a towel? You must be kidding.'

'I'll have you fired, just like the others.'

'I'm disappointed. I didn't think you'd give in so easily. That's blondes for you, I suppose, even fake ones.'

The flash in her eyes made him chuckle.

'You stink!'

He hadn't had a chance to shower since leaving the boat, so it was true. 'That's the best you can come up with? What are you, five?'

A cough from the side of the hallway interrupted him. 'Ahem. If you two are finished flirting, I need to speak to Mr Grant.'

Flynn gave her a half smile, one that promised interesting things in the future, before turning away.

'Teflon' Tim O'Sullivan was shorter than he had expected. On television, where he was frequently seen exhorting the government to get out of the airline business and stop interfering with him, he was larger than life. In his office, surprisingly modern for such an ancient building, he was small and wiry, full of nervous energy and an air of ferocious intelligence.

He waved Flynn to a seat, a large leather armchair that looked at least a hundred years old, while he sat behind a heavy mahogany desk. Instead Flynn took a modern wooden chair, one that would allow him to spring up without fighting his way out of a pile of horsehair. O'Sullivan said nothing, but his shrewd eyes took note.

'I'm sorry about that little episode,' he began. 'But I'm glad I saw it. As you'll have gathered, Summer is a bit of a handful and she resents having a bodyguard. She's developed a talent for getting rid of them. I'm glad to see that you're not so easily intimidated.'

Flynn smiled briefly. 'No, I think it's safe to say that I don't scare easily.'

O'Sullivan flicked a glance at his laptop screen. 'Niall Moore gave me some of your background. You sound more than capable of taking care of my daughter.'

'I'm happy you think so.' Of course, Niall hadn't told O'Sullivan everything. If he knew just how lethal Flynn was, he would never have invited him into his house.

While other elite Special Ops divisions boasted about how tough the training was for Navy SEALS or the SAS, the Irish Army Rangers Wing said nothing, but just got on with business.

O'Sullivan sighed. 'It's the worst time to have to be away, but I can't help it.'

'Can you brief me on the situation, sir?' Flynn had some details from Niall, but it was good practice to make sure there were no gaps in his information. Besides, everyone lied, and it would be useful to see what O'Sullivan lied about.

The older man leaned forwards, spinning the computer screen around so Flynn could see it. 'That bloody crash. The OS723 from Atlanta crashed coming in to Heathrow and seventeen people were killed. The BAA inquiry has already cleared us; it was caused by a wheel which fell off an earlier plane, but do you think the crackpots will believe it? Oh no, it must be my fault. Just because it was a budget flight does not mean we cut corners. Damn it, our pilots are better paid than average. Do you –'

O'Sullivan was all set to continue his rant, but a look from Flynn pulled him up. He calmed down slightly. 'Anyway, I have to go to Atlanta for a meeting with the Federal Aviation Authority. I want to expand my operations stateside, but I'm worried about Summer. Especially after that incident last year.'

Flynn went on alert. 'What incident?'

'Some guy side-swiped her car less than a mile from here and he didn't even stop. Not so much as a call to 999. There are a lot of bad feckers around so I don't want Summer on her own.'

'Why not take her with you?' It seemed the obvious solution.

'She wants to stay here.'

'With all due respect,' Flynn was doing his best to be diplomatic, but not sure if he could succeed. 'This house is a security nightmare. Take her with you or send her somewhere that is safer.'

O'Sullivan sighed. 'She won't come with me. Says she hates Atlanta. And nothing will make her go back to Ireland.'

'You're her father. Make her do what she's told.' It seemed simple enough to him.

The older man gave him a look of pity. 'Easy to see you don't have children. She's set on staying here so I need someone to keep her safe. Can you do that?'

Flynn nodded. 'As long as it's understood that only Niall Moore can fire me. She can't. And I get carte blanche to do whatever it takes to keep her safe.' O'Sullivan nodded, so Flynn continued, 'I need the plans for this house, the security system, the staff rota, passwords, list of everyone who has access, any other information you have.'

O'Sullivan got busy pulling files from his computer, grumbling under his breath about the details Flynn demanded. 'There'd be less fuss for the President.'

Flynn heard. 'That was easier. At least she did what she was told.'

There was a second of shock, and then O'Sullivan laughed. 'Now I know my little girl is in good hands.'

Summer slammed the bedroom door behind her. The nerve of him. Marching through the front door as if he owned the place. And he was scruffy. His leather jacket was worn. His dark jeans were stained with oil and he smelled of fish. What way was that to turn up for a job interview?

'Fish,' she snapped at her reflection as she tugged her fingers through the tangled mane of hair extensions. For the money they had cost, they should have come with their own personal hairdresser. What had possessed her to go blonde in the first place? She thought it would make her look cute and bubbly, not haggard and high maintenance.

'Curtains and carpet indeed.' Who the hell did he think he was to speak to her like that? It was none of his business that she hadn't been to the beauty salon this month. And for him to comment about it like that.

'Arrogant idiot.' As if he had the slimmest chance of getting up close and personal with her. She wouldn't touch him with a ten-foot pole. And what was that thing with the hair pulling? He had taken hold of her as if he owned her. It was a pity her dad hadn't arrived on the scene sooner. He would have sent him packing.

Summer suppressed a shiver as she recalled just how close he had been to her. Underneath the dark stubble, his unshaven jaw was firm. His facial features made a strong masculine statement. His cheekbones were razor sharp and the slightly crooked angle of his nose gave him a hint of menace. This was no pretty boy for her to play with. And those eyes. Hazel flecked with green and gold under heavy eyebrows. Intriguing and a little dangerous. It would take her more than a day to get rid of this one and time was running out. She needed to be bodyguard-free by the weekend or there would be no *Noir* for her.

Her dad would be away for almost a month. Surely he wouldn't consider leaving her with him? She would have to make sure that he didn't.

Summer reached for the hair iron, transforming her thick mane into casual cascading curls. She applied a little make-up. Not too much, she wanted to look innocent. She barely brushed her lashes with mascara and added a coat of pink lipstick until she had the subtle effect she wanted. A pair of pale jeans, a pretty floral top and she was daddy's sweet little girl.

She pouted at her reflection. 'Please don't leave me with the nasty man.'

Slipping on a pair of sandals, she took a last glance in the mirror. She had managed to get rid of the others without too much difficulty. There was no way that her dad would leave that scruffy, arrogant guy in charge while he was away. She was panicking unnecessarily.

Summer hesitated for a moment outside the office door. No one was permitted to enter without invitation. She had raised her hand to knock when she heard laughter from inside. That wasn't encouraging. They were getting on far too well for her liking. She tapped on the door and went inside.

Her dad's tie was loose and the top button of his shirt was undone, a sure sign that he was relaxing. Across from him, on the chair where she usually sat, was Fishboy. His easy smile vanished when he saw her and he stood up.

'Miss O'Sullivan.' He inclined his head. She caught a faint hint of a Scottish burr. It wasn't fair. The one accent in the world guaranteed to melt ice and set her pulse racing.

He scanned her from head to foot, taking in everything

from her glossy hair to the painted tips of her toes before he caught her gaze and held it.

Summer didn't flinch. She was used to men staring at her. It was part of the game. She smiled sweetly at him. 'It's Summer, and I'm afraid you have me at a disadvantage. What am I to call you?'

'This is Flynn Grant.' Her father said. 'He's going to be taking care of things while I'm away.'

She sat on an upright chair and folded her hands demurely. 'By "things", I presume you mean me? Don't you think that I should have some choice about who I'm going to be living with for the next three weeks?'

'You've already had plenty of choice. Now I'm choosing. Mr Grant is the best there is. You won't even notice he's there.'

Considering the slight twitch of that arrogant mouth, Summer wasn't too sure about that. In fact, she was willing to bet that Flynn Grant was capable of being a complete pain in the ass.

Her father had made his decision. She had another bloody bodyguard. This little skirmish might be lost but there was still time to make Flynn pack up and go back to where he came from. She flashed him a bored glance. 'I'm sure you're right. Now, if you gentlemen will excuse me, I'll just check and see how the chef is getting on with dinner. I presume you'll be staying, Mr Grant?'

'That's most kind of you, Summer.' The smirk was back.

'Any allergies or conditions that we should be aware of? We wouldn't want to poison you accidentally.'

'I'm sure you wouldn't,' he agreed evenly. 'No conditions. No allergies.'

Summer stepped into the hallway. 'Pity,' she murmured under her breath.

Flynn watched with appreciation as Summer left the study. That was a backside worth his attention: firm, rounded and enticing. Mind you, the entire package was a temptation. The sweet-girl-next-door look was such a contrast to the siren on the stairs when he arrived that he wondered who the real Summer was.

He turned back to O'Sullivan. 'If you're happy, I'll move in right away and start work.' When sending the holdall of essentials he hadn't had time to pick up, his brother David could also send enough smart clothes that he could pass muster while he was here. This was a civilized house; he should dress to fit in. And it had nothing at all to do with wanting to correct Summer's first impression of him. Nothing at all.

An hour later, he was clean and starving. A bell rang, announcing that dinner was served. Flynn wondered what he could expect. If the food was prepared by Summer's fair hands, he had no doubt that it would contain a generous helping of arsenic. But where were the odds that little Miss Sunshine knew her way around a kitchen? Pretty low, he'd bet.

He followed his nose down a long corridor lined with double doors and with a huge picture window at the end which looked out over the park. The cost of a house like this, in one of the best parts of London, made him whistle. This was a family with serious money.

The walls of the dining room had portraits of eighteenth

and nineteenth century people that Flynn was willing to bet were no relation to the O'Sullivans. Summer and her father were already sitting at the antique mahogany table. Flynn sat down at the third place. It was remarkably formal for a family dinner. Flynn wondered what Summer was up to.

Nothing, it appeared. She was politeness itself, urging him to sit down and make himself comfortable. The meal would be served as soon as he was settled.

She had dressed for dinner, wearing a sophisticated black dress that left her neck and arms bare apart from the diamond bracelet that circled her right wrist. Her hair had been swept up into an elegant style that revealed her delicate neck.

Flynn stifled the urges the sight of that vulnerable neck raised in him. This wasn't the time or the place. Summer wasn't the girl and her father was watching them both. *Down boy*, he ordered his unruly libido. Still, the stirring was welcome. After that last round of surgery, he had been on so many meds that he worried about chemical castration.

'Oh, did I forget to mention? We dress for dinner,' Summer told him with a charming smile.

He smiled back, refusing to let her get to him. 'I am dressed. If you prefer, I can go naked.' He started to undo the buttons of his shirt.

'Stop!'

Tim sniggered at Summer's instinctive reaction. But Flynn thought there had been a flicker of interest in her eyes. David had sent on his all-purpose holdall. He supposed he could have dug out something formal for dinner, but he was willing to bet that the whole 'dressing for dinner' thing was one more attempt by Summer to make him uncomfortable. He had a brief vision of how he would like to make her uncomfortable. Ass-up over his knee. *Down boy*, he told his libido. That was never going to happen.

Summer recovered herself. 'You can wear whatever you like.' She picked up her napkin and touched it to her mouth.

The meal was served. They started with consommé served with tiny pieces of Melba toast. It was beautifully flavoured and Flynn could have drunk three bowls of it. Summer ate it in tiny spoonfuls while chatting away about the weather, the picture of the perfect hostess.

The next course was a herb soufflé, light and airy and insubstantial. It was followed by a green salad with slivers of almonds and toasted pine nuts. Tim poked it with his fork. 'What the hell is this stuff?'

'Salad,' Summer said calmly. 'You've been eating too much greasy food. This is much better for you.' She turned to Flynn. 'Wouldn't you agree, Mr Grant?'

'Oh, very healthy. If you're a rabbit.' Flynn shoved a forkful into his mouth and chewed vigorously. 'It's a waste of canine teeth, but I suppose you're easy.'

She stiffened. 'I beg your pardon!' Her air of offended outrage would have done credit to the Queen.

He gave an evil grin. 'I mean you like easy food. Nothing that you have to hunt or kill.'

'I like healthy food. So should you if you have any concern for your heart.'

He chewed the last bit of salad. 'My heart is just fine, thank you. Can you say the same?'

She turned her shoulder on him, leaving him with an interesting view of her bare back. He wasn't concerned with getting the cold shoulder. It gave him the chance to watch father and daughter together.

They truly did love each other, he decided, but there were all sorts of undercurrents going on there. He honestly couldn't work out which one was manipulating the other.

As he ate his sorbet, Tim issued a list of instructions to both of them, starting with telling Summer to do what Flynn told her. Her expression was priceless. Flynn had to stay with Summer at all times and make sure not only that she stayed alive, but also that she didn't get into any trouble. 'I don't want to read about you in the tabloids again, understand?' he told Summer.

'Of course, Dad. I'll be an angel.' Flynn trusted her docility and sweet smile as much as a mosquito in a nudist colony. 'And you won't object if I invite a couple of friends to keep me company while you are gone?'

Flynn's 'No!' was automatic, but Summer ignored him, speaking only to Tim.

'Please Dad. I'll be so lonely when you're away, and if I have no one to talk to, I'll be bored.' Flynn recognized a threat when he heard one, but Tim wavered.

'Very well. Just a few friends. But you still have to obey Flynn.'

She beamed at him. 'Thank you, Dad. We'll have so much fun.'

Flynn groaned. He had a bad feeling about this. He patted his belly. 'I'm still starving. Where's the nearest chipper?'

3

Flynn ate a silent breakfast with his charge. Well, he was silent, but O'Sullivan made up for it, complaining about airport security, the fact that liquid limits applied even to the man who owned the airline, the decaf coffee Summer insisted he drink instead of his normal gut-rot brew and the guests that Summer was inviting while he was away.

'Mike bloody Chester! What the hell are you doing with an Australian rugby player? Are there not enough Irish ones to suit you? You know that man is only after one thing, and by god, he's not getting it from you.'

'Of course not, Dad.' Her earnest tone didn't fool him, and Flynn wondered how a father would allow himself to be so easily misled. At least breakfast at Dunboy House was substantial, and he helped himself to a fourth egg to fortify himself for the day to come. On the evidence of last night's dinner, he could be hungry for the rest of his time here.

'And as for that pair of airheads you've invited – I didn't know they let girls with minus IQs out in public,' O'Sullivan continued.

'I thought Maya and Natasha were the sort of girls you wanted me to be friends with. Good family, posh schools, Royal Ascot, that sort of thing.'

'I want you to have friends with a good background, but at least pick ones with a couple of brain cells to rub together. Those two have no talent except for spending money, drinking and making fools of themselves in the tabloids.' O'Sullivan broke off his tirade to take a mouthful of coffee and pull a face at it.

'Who are they?' Flynn asked, bringing two pairs of identical blue eyes in his direction. He didn't care if he was interrupting a family dispute.

'What business is it of yours?' Summer demanded.

'I'm in charge of keeping you safe; I need to know who they are so I can run a background check on them.' He did his best to keep his voice level, remembering all Niall's warnings about not pissing off the principal.

There was a flash of something that looked like fear on her face, but she answered readily enough. 'Maya Wilson-Smythe and Natasha fForbes.'

'You're kidding me!' No one had names like that in real life, did they?

She gave him a frosty glare. 'Do you have a problem with that?'

'No, should make them easy to track down. I'll know everything about them, back to the time of their conception.' There was that flicker of uneasiness again. Summer O'Sullivan was hiding something.

He hadn't been in Dunboy House for an hour before Malcolm had given him the polite version of how Summer had got the other bodyguards sacked. Any details the painfully polite butler had left out, the new maid and the chef had filled in for him. The chef had added a number of choice epithets about bossy little madams who thought he didn't know how to do his job. Jean Carrier didn't like Summer's attitude any more than Flynn himself did.

'Pair of bimbos,' continued O'Sullivan. 'You know what, I'm going to invite your cousin Sinead to come and keep you company.' He ignored Summer's protests and picked up his phone to send a brief message. 'There. She'll probably join you tomorrow or the next day.'

'Dad, that's not fair. I had to put up with her for years in boarding school and at college. It's too much to expect me to endure her pulling a sour face at me now.'

O'Sullivan ignored her and turned to Flynn. 'You know what you have to do? Not only are you to keep Summer safe, you are to keep her out of trouble. The last thing I need when I'm in America are reports that my daughter is dragging my reputation through the mud again. There are to be no scandals, no photographs in the tabloids. Nothing! Understood?'

Flynn nodded while Summer pouted mutinously. 'I've already arranged for an improved security system on the house. That will be installed today. And I'll get Mr Moore to send a couple of female bodyguards along as backup.'

'What? No!' Summer's outrage was genuine. 'That's not necessary.'

'It's the bare minimum required to keep her safe if she goes anywhere,' Flynn said calmly. 'Your choice, sir.'

With her face flushed with indignation, Summer looked younger and prettier and very fuckable. This morning, she was all sweet little girl next door. 'No, Dad, please, I don't need more strangers in the house. I promise I won't get into any trouble or do anything to make Mr Grant's work difficult.'

'You'll obey my rules?' Flynn asked.

She nodded mutinously.

'And do what I tell you?'

Another nod.

'Everything I tell you?'

Those stormy blue eyes flashed, but she nodded. 'I won't be any trouble.'

Flynn didn't believe a word of it, and wondered exactly what Summer O'Sullivan was up to. He'd bet his best H&K sub-machine gun it was trouble.

Tim agreed that the female bodyguards were unnecessary and then departed amid a flurry of cursing, last minute instructions, hugs and what looked like genuine tears from Summer. Looks like the little madam really would miss her father. Or maybe she would just miss having someone she could wind around her perfectly manicured fingers?

Summer checked her watch again. Natasha and Maya were on their way and darling Mike was bringing his Australian friend Gavin. She had put the girls and guys in guest rooms on different floors – no point in spoiling them. She hadn't told Flynn or her dad that she had invited other guests – Molly and her new boyfriend, Robert. Molly sounded really excited on the phone and said that she had lots of news. Robert was an actual Dom and he was going to vet Summer's application to attend *Noir*. Her heart raced at the prospect.

The only fly in the ointment was Flynn. Without asking her permission, the arrogant Scot had moved into the adjoining room and organized a locksmith to break open the sealed-up doorway between the two suites. His excuse was that he needed access to her quickly in case of danger.

She was still fuming over that one. The only danger she was in was the prospect of living like a nun for the next few days. She and Flynn needed to have a heart-to-heart. It was time to put him in his place.

Without bothering to knock, she opened the newly restored door. The short hallway between the rooms was lined with cupboards. Well, she could always do with more wardrobe space. She hesitated at the closed door and decided not to bother knocking. He was staff, for god's sake.

Summer pushed her way inside. The door of his bathroom was closed and the bedroom was empty. There was no harm having a quick peek through his things. She riffled through his clothing. Lots of plain things. Dark coloured, but good quality. A toilet bag beckoned and she unzipped it. Standard stuff. Razor. Soap that smelled like vetivert. She quite liked that. Condoms – two packs, neither of which had been opened. She scowled. Hardly surprising, given his complete lack of skill in the charm department.

She picked up a bottle of Etro and sniffed. Flynn knew his stuff, but what was he doing with expensive Italian cologne, when he insisted on going around dressed like a tramp?

Summer stubbed her toe on something under the bed. What could he be hiding? Kneeling down, she found a dark, heavy carryall. She tugged hard and landed in an ungainly heap on her ass.

'You idiot,' she muttered. It felt like weights. Maybe he had brought his own gym. There was a fully equipped one in the basement. Served him right for not asking first. She pulled the zipper down and congratulated herself when she heard the clank of metal. She was right. It had to be gym stuff.

The metal bar was dark and long and had a funny end on it. Hardly something she could hang weights on. She reached inside and found a handle. Well, not a handle exactly. It was cool and heavy to the touch. Summer pulled it free. It was a gun. An honest-to-god, scare-the-knickers-off-you gun. Sweet mother of Jesus. Flynn had brought weapons into the house.

Summer was glad she was kneeling down. She wasn't sure if her legs would have held her up. The door opened and she had no place to hide.

'Do you make a habit of riffling through everyone's luggage, or just the stuff belonging to the hired help?'

Flynn's eyes narrowed and she wasn't sure if it was disapproval at finding her with enough weapons to start a small war, or the fact that she was showing quite a lot of leg. She itched to tug her short skirt down but she gritted her teeth and suppressed it. She was more than a match for Flynn and this wasn't the time to show weakness. 'Were you planning to rob a bank this weekend?'

A grin quirked his mouth before he broke into a genuine smile, softening the harsh planes of his face. 'No. If I were robbing a bank, I would have brought the C4. It's quicker,' he said.

'What's C4?'

'My favourite explosive,' he said with a grin.

'So all of this is for me?' Summer stroked the dark metal barrel, pleased when she caught a trace of nervousness on his face.

'All for you, darling.' The face was stern again, the hint of humour gone.

She didn't know what to say. A small shiver raced down her spine. Flynn had guns. This wasn't a joke any longer. Her dad was gone, and she was stuck here with Action Man. This was *so* not happening. She scrambled to her feet and brushed past him. 'Just keep them out of sight,' she said brusquely.

The alarm alerted Flynn when the first car arrived at the outside gate. 'Who is it?' he demanded.

'Er, it's Maya and Natasha,' an uncertain voice replied. 'This is Dunboy House, isn't it?'

Through the CCTV camera, he could see two blondes in an open-top red Mercedes. One was touching up her lipstick in the rear view mirror. The driver was looking around as if she had no idea where she was.

He took a photo of the car's number plate and pressed the button to open the gate.

Summer rushed downstairs when the coupe swerved to a halt in a spray of gravel, and the two girls climbed the steps to the front door. 'Natasha, Maya, I'm so glad you made it.'

They squealed in delight at the sight of her and waved twin jeroboams of Moët. 'Party time.'

Yep, they were a pair of airheads, no doubt about that.

The first bottle was barely open when the next car arrived. It was a muscle pick-up truck with Australian flags all over it. The sounds of a Muse guitar riff preceded the two men inside. Summer rushed out to welcome them,

35

followed by Airhead One and Two. 'Mike, Gavin, I'm so glad you made it.'

Mike, the big blond, lifted her off the ground and spun her around, kissing her loudly and enthusiastically. 'My gorgeous girl, you're looking better than ever.' He gave her another loud kiss before he put her down. Flynn decided he didn't like this guy at all.

The second man, equally big but with shaggy dark hair and a tan so dark his white shirt looked electric, gave Summer a quick hug and she pulled his head down to kiss his cheek. 'Gavin, when did you get to be such a stranger?' She dragged both men into the drawing room without making any effort to include Flynn in the group.

He took a quick look around the pick-up truck, checking it over, before he followed them inside.

Summer was busy getting everyone drinks, directing one of the staff to carry bags upstairs, and making introductions. She was a practised hostess with a knack for putting people at ease. Except him.

The gate alarm alerted him to more visitors. He checked the camera and saw a green Jaguar outside. 'Who is it?' he asked.

'Robert Fielding and Molly Ainsworth,' said a female voice. 'Summer is expecting us.'

'Wait there.' He'd had no warning about this. Summer had questions to answer.

'Oh yes, didn't I mention them?' Summer said innocently, but the quiver in her voice gave her away. This was why she had been on edge all day. 'They're old friends.'

With Summer vouching for them, Flynn let them in, but he was going to check them out later.

These visitors were a surprise. Molly Ainsworth was a petite sprite, with a pixie crop and pointed chin. She bubbled with nervous energy and hugged Summer enthusiastically. 'I can't believe we are finally here. The traffic was terrible.' Her smile lit her face, revealing dimples in her cheeks.

Robert Fielding was tall, at least six foot two, with wide shoulders and a swimmer's body. He was poised and confident, with an aura of power and old money. He even dressed like old money, in a navy blazer which set off his fair hair and blue eyes.

He shook Summer's hand formally. 'Miss O'Sullivan, it's a pleasure to meet you.'

'You mean, meet me again, don't you?' Summer said. 'You can't have forgotten about Hickstead?'

He gave her a half bow. 'Of course.'

Summer led them into the drawing room with Flynn bringing up the rear. 'Come on, everyone; let's have some drinks before dinner.'

Summer was relieved that Flynn stayed out of her way as she checked the kitchen and put the final touches to dinner. Although she had been her father's hostess for years, she had never been so nervous. It was vital that she impress Robert Fielding. Molly said that he loved good food so she had agonized over the menu. But by the time she had quaffed her second glass of champagne she was no longer worried.

Robert was handsome, and there was definitely something about him. An air of command? An expectation that he would always get his way? Something that made her shiver. Or perhaps it was just that she knew he was a Dom. Her first real-life Dom. Just like the ones in the novels she downloaded to her Kindle.

They took their places at the table. Annoyingly, Flynn, who hadn't bothered to turn up for the pre-dinner drinks, arrived at the last minute and insisted on sitting beside her. She gulped another mouthful of champers.

The plates were presented to oohs and aahs of delight from the girls. Ravioli of Cornish crab, slivers of artichoke heart and a lemongrass sauce.

It was beautiful – and tiny. Barely a mouthful of food decorated the oversized plates. After the previous evening when he had grumbled about the salad, Summer was suddenly nervous about Flynn's reaction to the starter. He didn't disappoint her. Picking up the single ravioli between his fingers, he popped it into his mouth and swallowed it whole. Gavin and Mike followed suit with hoots of laughter.

Affronted, Robert glared at them and proceeded to cut into his parcel of pasta, pronouncing it perfectly al dente. He savoured the sauce like a connoisseur. Summer was relieved when the plates were collected and hoped that the next course was ready. *Plaisirs du Mer* – wild brill, oyster, scallop, shaved cucumber and wasabi.

The confection arrived in an exquisite tower and she felt a small thrill when Robert's eyes lit up.

'What's the green stuff?' Gavin asked.

'That would be the salad,' Mike replied, eying the single leaf of chervil. There was another guffaw of laughter and Summer glared at them.

'Mmm, green,' Flynn said with relish. He swiped his index finger through the tiny green mound and raised it to his lips.

'Don't.' The word was out of her mouth before she could stop it. 'It's hot.' She tried to sound reasonable. 'No sense in burning yourself.'

She forced a smile. Secretly, she would have been happy if Flynn had eaten the whole dish of wasabi. She hoped that he might spend half the night in the loo. It might keep him out of her way for a while.

Ignoring her, he sucked his finger without a hint of discomfort. The elegant fish course was speared and swallowed in seconds. When Gavin asked for a beer, Flynn announced that he had some cooling in the kitchen. She took a deep breath and tried not to glare at him.

Robert carefully dissected his fish into individual pieces before placing them into his mouth one by one. 'I see you like a little spectacle, Summer. I admire a woman who uses her imagination.'

She heard what sounded suspiciously like a snort of laughter from the chair beside hers and she ignored it. Flynn was so going to pay for this.

Natasha clapped her hands when the main course was presented. Roasted fillet of rosé veal. Summer wouldn't admit that she didn't like veal.

Gavin swigged his champagne as if it was water. 'A bit of meat for the guys. About time.'

Summer could have cheerfully stabbed him with a fork. She sliced into the meat and pushed it around her plate, pretending to eat. She hated to think of the baby calves being taken away from their mothers.

'Not hungry?' Flynn asked before spearing her veal and popping it onto his own plate.

Robert stared speculatively at them. 'I didn't realize that you were –'

'Her boyfriend,' Flynn countered without blinking.

'I was going to say hungry.' Robert laughed at his own joke. Fuelled with champagne, Mike and Gavin joined in.

The evening was turning into a disaster. How dare Flynn act like this? And Mike and Gavin were almost as bad. A pair of drunken . . . Australians.

It was bad enough that Flynn had barely left her side all evening, but to announce that he was her boyfriend? She glanced across the table at Robert. If she made a scene now and admitted Flynn was really her bodyguard, she could kiss her invitation to *Noir* goodbye. With an angry swish of her napkin, Summer stood up. 'Dessert will be served on the terrace.'

4

A knock came on the bedroom door. 'Are you decent?'

'No. But I'm dressed,' Summer replied. 'Come on in.'

Molly surveyed the opulent bedroom and whistled. 'Wow, I thought our room was fab but this is . . . wow.'

Summer glanced around her at the antique furniture, the pristine bed linen and heavy silk drapes. Her father had spared no expense in the renovation and decoration of the property. She supposed it was 'wow' if you didn't sleep in it every night. She patted the bed beside her. They chatted so often online that it was hard to believe that she hadn't seen Molly since they left college. 'So, tell me about Robert. I want to know everything, you dark horse.'

Molly giggled as she sat down. 'I know. I still can't believe it. Isn't he gorgeous?'

'I'll say, and is he really a . . . you know?'

'A Dom? Oh yes.'

'You can't just say "oh yes" and stop. I want details. How did you meet him?'

'We met at *Noir*. You know, the club I told you about –'

'And?'

'Well, I did a scene with him.'

A scene. Summer was torn between wanting to know every intimate detail and being afraid to ask. 'What kind of scene?'

'Oh, nothing crazy.' Molly shrugged. 'I'm no rope

bunny and Robert isn't into humiliation or anything. I mean, as if.'

Summer nodded as if she understood. *What the hell was a rope bunny?* 'Of course you're not.'

'Anyway, I was at the bar watching the latex boys – some of them are really buff – and then Robert came over and we started chatting.'

Chatting. That was it? It didn't sound any more danger-ous than a night out in Chelsea. When was Molly going to get to the good stuff?

'And then Robert said, "You'd look stunning on the St Andrew's Cross." So I followed him to the main play area.'

Molly's eyes misted and she patted her chest. 'Oh. My. God, it was so intense. I mean, I'd never done a public scene before. With all those people looking at me. I thought that I wouldn't be able to . . .'

'To what?' Summer asked, impatient for her to get to the point.

'To go into subspace.'

Summer sat up. She didn't care if her mouth was hang-ing open. Subspace. She had thought that whole thing about submissives going into a trance state during a scene was just a myth. 'And did you?'

'Oh, yeah.' Molly lay back on the bed and stretched her arms over her head.

Summer was about to beat her if she didn't share soon. Molly was describing BDSM nirvana. 'And?' she prompted.

'Well, I suppose subspace is a bit like being stoned. You know when you're really shit-faced and you see some perfectly ordinary thing, and it, like, suddenly becomes the most fascinating thing in the universe?'

'Um, no.' Summer had never bothered with drugs. She had seen enough junkies in the streets when she was at college. No one wanted to look like one of those *Shaun of the Dead* creatures, did they?

'I mean, I don't think I had an actual conversation with anyone. Robert kept asking me if I was okay. But all I could do was giggle. Then he started laughing too and told me that I was his best little girl.' She rolled over. 'That was when I knew.'

If Summer had a sharp stick, she would have used it to poke Molly. 'Knew what?'

'What I was. What I've been looking for all my life. I mean, Robert just seemed to understand exactly what I needed.'

'Which is?'

'To belong to him.'

Summer hadn't expected that. 'Belong to him? You mean like you're his slave?'

'Oh no.' Molly was horrified. 'It's way more than that. Robert knows me. I mean, it's like having the best boyfriend ever. He just wants to take care of me all the time. He even tells me when to go to bed.'

'Right,' Summer said. That sounded worse than her dad.

'Isn't he wonderful? And the sex is just . . .'

'Yes?' Summer perked up. Finally Molly had something interesting to say.

'Amazing. You have no idea. Multiples of multiple orgasms every night. God, I'm exhausted from coming.'

'Really?' Summer hated to admit it, but she hadn't had

a boyfriend since the debacle with Adam. She shuddered at the memory of how close she had come to marrying a fortune-hunting weasel. Her attempts to get back in the game afterwards had all been a bust. She had even struck out with the gorgeous Mike that night at the club. Maybe it was time for a re-match.

Molly grabbed her hand. 'You have to talk to him. Robert is so interested in getting to know you. It's all he's spoken about since he got here.'

She wasn't sure if she liked the sound of that. She could just imagine Flynn's disapproving scowl if he discovered what she was planning. 'I will. It's just that . . .'

'You haven't changed your mind about *Noir*, have you? I was so looking forward to showing you around.'

'Don't be silly, I'm really looking forward to it, but what should I wear?' The idea of Flynn following her around the stores while she was shopping for fetish wear was terrifying.

Molly giggled. 'As little as possible. Half the members wear next to nothing. Some boots, a collar and chain . . .'

'You better be joking.'

'Relax, Summer. You've got a great body. It will be such fun. Do you remember that time in Grafton Street when we posed naked for that PETA protest? You weren't so shy then.'

Summer laughed at the memory. A dozen students posing outside one of Dublin's top department stores to protest about the furs displayed in the window. They had been marched into the back of a Garda van and taken to the local station. Her dad had a fit when he heard. 'And then you had a date with one of the guards later?'

Molly dissolved into laughter and then stopped suddenly when she caught a glimpse of her watch. 'Oh, I am so late. Robert will be cross. And I haven't asked you about your new boyfriend or your dad yet. How are things with him?'

Summer didn't know where to start. She had felt like slapping Flynn for his stupid remark at dinner, but she hadn't wanted to make a scene in front of Robert. She couldn't let Flynn mess up her trip to *Noir*. Everyone would think she was an idiot if she had a bodyguard trailing around after her in a fetish club.

'Please don't tell Robert, but Flynn's not really my boyfriend. He's just a bodyguard Dad employed. You know what he's like – same old Dadzilla. I hope it won't affect Saturday night?'

Molly winked. 'Don't worry, my lips are sealed. We'll find some way of ditching him for the evening. I meant to ask. How have you been since . . .'

'To be honest, I'm really fed up. I haven't had a job for almost a year.' Even now, the memory of being hauled into HR and dismissed still hurt. Summer shrugged the memory away. 'I asked Dad about joining the airline – he always promised I could work for him when I finished my MBA and I was the only one in my class who studied Transportation and Logistics. But none of that seems to matter now. Every time I mention it, he just tells me not to worry about working.

'All he wants me to do is host dinner parties for him and look pretty. I don't know why I thought that things would be better when I got back from Vietnam.'

A flash of sympathy crossed Molly's face. 'You went on

honeymoon on your own? I mean, ouch, Summer. Why didn't you just cancel it?'

Summer shrugged. 'I needed to get away from here. I couldn't face people. You know. Not after . . . everything. Anyway, you better go. Robert's waiting.'

Sliding off the bed, Molly straightened her skirt and glanced at her reflection in the mirror. She ran her hand through her short, spiky hair. 'Do you have any lippy?'

'Top drawer.' Summer watched Molly repair her make-up. Her friend had changed so much since college and she wasn't sure if she approved. The thing with Robert sounded both scary and fascinating. She couldn't imagine what it would be like to belong to someone like that. There was no way that she would let a man make decisions for her. How could she bear the loss of independence?

Molly smoothed on some lip-gloss and smiled at her reflection. 'Promise me you'll chat with Robert?'

'I will, I promise.'

After Molly left, she lay on the bed, thinking. Her friend was right: if she wanted to go to *Noir*, she had to talk to Robert. But how was she going to manage it with Flynn watching her every move? It was a wonder he hadn't insisted on moving into her room.

Her mouth curved in a smile. Mike and Gavin. Surely they could distract him for a little while. Maybe they could talk to him about rugby or something. Pleased with her decision, she slipped off the bed and riffled through her wardrobe. Just what did one wear for an interview to join a fetish club?

She knew that she had picked the right outfit when a

shrill wolf whistle announced her arrival in the sitting room. Robert and Molly were playing Wii, the Australians had opened a couple of beers and Flynn was sitting apart from the others on an antique chair with a disapproving look on his face.

'Mike, can I have a word please?'

'No worries.' He handed his beer to Gavin and hurried over. 'What seems to be the problem?'

'No problem.' Summer whispered. 'I just need you to do me a little favour.'

Mike gave a low laugh. 'Just name it, darling.' He really was rather cute.

Gavin cheered loudly when Molly scored and Summer seized her chance. 'Come with me.'

Grabbing his hand, she hurried down the hallway, past the office. There was a small sitting room at the back of the house that they used during the winter. It was cosier than the gigantic lounge. It would have to do. She pushed open the door and pulled him inside. When she reached for the light switch, Mike covered her hand with his and planted a quick kiss on her neck.

'That couch is a bit small, if you're thinking what I'm thinking. Why don't we take this upstairs?'

'Will you stop that?' Summer giggled, trying to evade his searching hands.

Mike ignored her protests and, lifting her up, he pressed her against the wall and moved in for a lingering kiss. She caught the scent of soap and hair gel. She had a vague recollection of kissing him outside the nightclub the night she had got so sloshed with Natasha and Maya. It had been a bad idea then and it was a worse one now. She didn't need a hook-up; she needed him to distract Flynn. Grabbing a handful of his hair, she tugged hard. 'I said, stop.'

The door opened. 'You have two seconds to put her down or you'll be sitting on the sideline for the next couple of seasons.'

From anyone else, the words would have sounded like an empty threat. Mike was an inch taller than Flynn and built like a house. But there was something about the expression on Flynn's face that made Mike hesitate. Releasing her, he let her slide to the floor and raised his hands in mock surrender. 'Sorry mate, I didn't realize that she was taken.'

'I am not . . .' Summer began, but a warning gaze from Flynn made her close her mouth.

Mike edged past him. 'Catch you later.'

Summer's attempt to follow him was rudely interrupted when Flynn's arm blocked the doorway. 'Back inside, Summer. You and I need to have a little chat.'

Flynn couldn't believe it when he saw Summer dragging that Neanderthal out of the lounge and down the hallway. Was she out of her fucking mind? Here she was, under threat from lunatics, and she ignored every bit of common sense by going off with that hormone-driven meathead.

He followed, his mood worsening with every step. What was particularly annoying was that he didn't have a legitimate gripe. Summer O'Sullivan was in her own house, one that he had personally checked over for security. Only a special-ops team would get in without alerting him and he was pretty sure that was one threat Ms O'Sullivan didn't have to worry about.

It was her business who she kissed or caressed – or fucked, for that matter. He was the babysitter, she was the principal. It wasn't as if he normally paid much attention to what his principals did, but this was different.

Summer was the sort of brat who would get herself into trouble because she couldn't help it. Apparently, his new client had a unique talent for pissing everyone off and driving men up the wall. First there was the flirting with Fielding and now he was going to have to listen to Chester groping her as well.

But when he got to the sitting room and heard the sound of a struggle and Summer's voice saying, 'I said stop,' Flynn lost his legendary cool.

He slammed the door open and took in the sight of his principal pulling Chester back by his hair, while he tried to push one hand down her dress. It took every ounce of Flynn's training and discipline not to rip the fucker's head off his shoulders. At least the stupid bollix had enough sense to know when to cut his losses. After one good look at Flynn, he backed away, muttering apologies, and fled.

Summer tried to follow him, but he put one arm across the doorway to stop her. He was going to put an end to this nonsense once and for all.

She stood back and glared at him. 'What do you think you're doing? You have no right to stop me going wherever I want in my own house.'

'Don't you mean your father's house?'

For an instant, she flinched, but she recovered herself. 'When he's not here, it's my house and I'm in charge.

49

You're my bodyguard, not my father. You can't tell me what to do.' She put her hands on her hips and attempted to stare him down.

He had to give her marks for courage – there were members of the SAS who had backed down from his glare – but her sheer pig-headedness flipped a switch in him. No matter how much he reminded himself that she was the principal, he couldn't help seeing her as a woman. He just wasn't sure if he wanted to fuck her or spank her. Or both.

He locked his knees and shoved his hands into his pockets to keep from grabbing her, but the intensity of his desire to lay hands on her must have shown on his face. She sucked in a breath which made her breasts tremble – and which called attention to her outfit.

'What the hell do you think you are wearing?'

She looked down in surprise.

How could she have forgotten putting on that excuse for an outfit, never mind got up the nerve to wear it in public? He remembered where he usually saw clothes like that, then slammed his mind shut on the thought.

'This old thing?' She tried to sound bored as she ran her hand over her hip, but the slight tremble in her fingers gave her away. 'I had forgotten I put it on.'

The silky top and skirt were conservative enough, but the corset pulling in her waist was the real thing. Steel-boned and rigid and difficult to lace up. It pulled her in so tightly that his hands itched to check if he really could make them meet around that impossibly tiny waist. She had a figure that could raise a sweat on a statue, but that corset did illegal things to her.

'Liar,' he growled, stepping closer to her. 'No one puts on a corset by accident. Since I'm sure you weren't trying to entice me, who does that leave?'

Another subtle flinch. She was hiding something. 'It's not like that.'

He ignored her protests. 'If it was Chester, you changed your mind very quickly. And I'm betting it's not the other gorilla, which leaves Fielding.' Her breath hitched and he pounced. 'Ah, so you're making a move on your friend's lover. Very edifying.'

'No!' The protest was immediate. 'It's not like that. I swear.' Then she recovered herself. 'Not that it's any of your business what I do.'

He moved closer. Summer held her ground, so that he could smell the subtle perfume she wore. From here, he could see the way every breath she took caused a fine quiver in her breasts. Her pink-glossed lips beckoned him.

He leaned in closer. Her rapid breath fanned his face. 'It is my business. Everything you do is my business. When you wear an outfit that's designed to tempt every man here to strip it off you. When you go off on your own with a loser with two convictions for violence –'

'What?'

He gave her a nasty smile. 'You didn't know lover boy had beaten up two previous girlfriends?'

'No.' She was genuinely shaken.

'No, you went off with him without knowing the most basic information, just because he looks good with his shirt off.'

She opened her mouth to answer, but stopped. Whatever she had been about to say, she thought better of it.

Flynn had a burning desire to know what she was thinking. But she recovered her aplomb. 'At least he does look good with his shirt off. Tell me, are you jealous, surrounded by all those tall, gorgeous men? I haven't seen you without your shirt yet. Are you afraid you'll look bad in comparison?'

He blinked, unable to believe his ears for a second. 'You little shrew,' he said with appreciation. 'You have no idea how much you need to have your arse tanned.'

There was a second of stunned shock, and the pupils of her eyes dilated, betraying her excitement. 'You wouldn't dare,' she breathed. 'I'm your client.'

'And that's the only thing which is stopping me putting you over my knee and teaching you a few things that you need to know.' Somehow, he was so close to her that their lips were almost touching. He had to fight to keep from grabbing her. 'But you won't always be the principal. And I will remember.'

She dragged in a shuddering breath and moved away from him, putting several feet between them. 'I'll have you fired.'

Flynn laughed. 'Try it. But remember what I said. I meant it.' Then he made a half bow to her. 'Shall we re-join the others? Or would you like me to consider your presence here an invitation?'

She glared at him and marched out of the sitting room. 'You'll live to regret that,' she told him over her shoulder.

He dragged his attention away from the illegal things the corset did to her arse and grinned. 'Well, one of us will.'

5

Summer and Robert swam side by side, stroke for stroke, and for once Flynn wasn't around to interrupt. Robert was a good swimmer, strong and graceful. His skin was completely smooth, at least everything that wasn't covered by his black Speedo trunks. There wasn't a hair anywhere on his body that she could see. Molly had said he waxed.

She couldn't imagine Flynn doing that. From the little she had seen of him, his body hair was dark and a little dangerous. Summer shook the thought out of her head. One almost-kiss from him and she was obsessing about a bodyguard. Summer reached the end of the pool and turned. She really needed to burn off some energy. Kicking hard, she struck out for the other end and Robert was surprised when she passed him, beating him by several metres.

She heaved herself out of the pool and sat gasping on the edge.

Robert's head popped out of the water. 'That's some frustration you've built up. Are you always like this?'

'Not usually. I've been a bit on edge lately,' she admitted.

His eyes crinkled with laughter as if she had cracked a joke. 'I know something that will cure that.'

'You do?' She had been wondering how to raise the subject of the club, but it looked as if Robert was taking matters into his own hands.

'Yes. You have no idea of how effectively a touch of pain can relieve stress.' Robert drew his finger along the length of her forearm. His touch was hot against her skin. There was something mesmerizing about it. She didn't try to pull away, but slowly slipped back into the pool.

'Good girl,' Robert crooned approvingly. 'I'm sure we can take care of you at the club.'

'Take care of me.' She repeated his words like an idiot.

'Of course, that's what a good Dom would do. Would you like that, Summer? Someone to take care of you. Someone who was utterly focused on you, on your needs and desires.'

Despite the coolness of the water, Summer flushed. Would she like that? No one had taken care of her since her mum died. Her dad showered her with gifts and money but was always too busy to give her the attention that she craved. Sure, there was fame – or infamy, depending on which gossip column she appeared in – but it wasn't the same as being cared for.

'Molly seems happy,' she offered, 'but I'm not sure if I'd be into that sort of thing. In public, I mean.'

'I understand your concerns. *Noir* is full of people who value their privacy and we work hard to protect them. That's why the club is careful about who they admit as members. We don't want any nasty gossip. Do we?'

'No, I –'

The French doors opened and Flynn appeared, carrying two cups of coffee. His mouth tightened when he saw Robert's hand on her arm. Summer swallowed hard. Flynn's expression was openly challenging, but Robert didn't move away. It was as if a battle had been declared and each side was waiting for the other to make the first move.

'Is that coffee I smell?' Robert asked, breaking the silence.

Flynn raised his cup and smiled. 'Yes. I just brewed some. Yours is in the kitchen.'

Robert laughed and, releasing her arm, he pushed away from the side of the pool, moving through the water in a slow backstroke. He got out of the water and, picking up his robe, he headed for the kitchen.

Trying to ignore the quaking in the pit of her stomach, Summer climbed out of the pool. Flynn strolled towards her with the easy grace of a panther, looking for all the world as if he was going to pounce on her, rather than deliver a cup of coffee. His eyes raked her from head to toe, taking in her stylish one-piece, sending a shiver down her spine.

She quickly wrapped her towel around herself. Flynn watched as she dried off, making her feel more self-conscious than ever. What was wrong with her? He hadn't actually kissed her. She dragged a comb through her tangled hair before accepting the cup and taking a sip of her coffee.

'He seems very attentive,' Flynn said. She caught the disapproval in his tone. If she didn't know better, she would have mistaken it for jealousy.

'Robert?' she asked innocently.

'Just how well do you know him?'

'I . . .' there was no point in lying. Flynn could probably find out anyway. 'We've only met briefly once before, but I've known Molly since college.'

'And she doesn't mind you flirting with her boyfriend?'

'We were just talking.'

'Like you were talking to Chester last night?'

She was tempted to snap back at him, but there was no point. Flynn's opinion of her was obvious. He thought she was a shameless flirt. Maybe that was why he had challenged her last night. She had been foolish to think that it had been anything else.

Summer tried to sound flippant. 'What's the matter? Afraid of a little competition?'

His eyes narrowed. 'I'll do whatever is necessary to get the job done.'

'Great. We're having an archery contest later. Let's see how competitive you are then.'

Grabbing her robe, she hurried into the house. As she passed the sitting room, she heard Maya laughing. At least someone was having a good time. She opened the door and was just about to wish her good morning when the laughter was suddenly silenced.

Summer backed out of the room quietly, trying not to disturb the kissing couple. Maya and Gavin? How had she missed that one? Gavin broke the kiss and stroked Maya's face tenderly. Her friend hadn't hooked up with anyone in months. She couldn't wait to tell Natasha.

Racing up the stairs two at a time, she hurried to the guest room and pushed open the door. 'Natasha, you'll never guess . . .'

The rest of the words froze in her throat. Her friend was still sleeping, but she wasn't alone and Summer recognized that particular mop of blond hair. She wished she had pulled it harder when she'd had the chance the previous night. Mike bloody Chester. He hadn't wasted much time. She wasn't sure if she was jealous or relieved.

Back in her room she showered quickly and riffled through her wardrobe. This was turning into the weekend from hell. The humiliation of it. Her first house party and everyone had paired off except her. She could just imagine the knowing smirk on Flynn's face when he realized.

Summer heard a truck coming up the drive and she pulled back the curtains. The entertainment had arrived. 'Mircat Archery' had brought everything they needed for an afternoon of archery including an expert to tutor them. It was expensive but luckily her dad didn't bother looking at her credit card bill. He wouldn't spend time with her, but he paid her Visa bill each month without a quibble.

Gavin and Mike had boasted about how good they were at sports and the girls loved a chance to dress up. She pulled out a silk dress she had bought when she was in the Far East. It was pretty and feminine and floated about her ankles. The perfect thing to cheer herself up on a less than perfect day. When she had organized the party, she had visions of herself wandering around like a princess. Now, she would be more like the ugly sister.

She hung around her room for as long as was decently possible, pretending that she was catching up on emails. Outside, she could hear the sound of hammering from the lawn. They were obviously setting up the targets. She was just being silly. She couldn't mope about here any longer. It was time to face her friends.

Preparations for the party had already started. A bare-chested Gavin had unearthed the barbecue from one of the storerooms and was busy cleaning it. 'Hey,

Summer,' Gavin shouted. 'We're going to cook you some real food for a change. Mike and Natasha have gone to the village for steaks and more beer.'

'Great.' She tried to sound enthusiastic.

Maya arrived with an ice-cold can of beer. Sneaking up behind him, she pressed it against Gavin's back. The Australian roared with surprise before he turned to revenge himself on his attacker. Maya fled, squealing. She was no match for Gavin's speed or his flying tackle. The pair ended up in the pool, sending water flying everywhere. Maya made her way to the surface, spluttering and laughing at the same time.

Gavin caught her in his arms and gave her a hungry kiss. 'You are going to pay for that.'

Summer wasn't jealous of Maya; she had no interest in Gavin, but she envied that they were together and that they appeared to be happy. Like she had been? She shook away the memory. Adam Bayliss had no place in her life now.

'Penny for them?'

She hadn't heard Flynn arrive. The man defined the word stealth. 'My thoughts? I doubt if they're worth that much.'

'What's the matter? Are you annoyed that you've lost your admirers?' He watched with amusement as Maya wriggled from Gavin's hold and tried unsuccessfully to swim away. Gavin was after her in an instant and the pair disappeared beneath the water.

Poor little rich girl left on her own again. How Flynn would enjoy that one. Summer shrugged, feigning boredom. 'You have no idea, Flynn. You don't know me at all.'

*

To her surprise, the expert teaching them about archery was a woman. Summer felt a moment of guilt for assuming it would be a man, then forgot it as she found herself being included in the class. So much for her vision of herself as a fairytale princess, ready to bestow a kiss on the victor of the competition. Eleanor Grimes, middle-aged, petite and brisk, assumed that everyone was going to shoot.

Before she handed out bows, however, Eleanor took them through the basic movements and muscle groups used in drawing the bow. Summer caught Molly's eye and the pair of them tried not to giggle. It felt like they were doing bust exercises at the gym.

It felt good just to have fun, Summer realized. It was too long since she had wanted to laugh. The sight of Flynn, a long-suffering look on his face, stoically copying the instructor, did make her chuckle.

They followed Eleanor through a series of exercises which she insisted would improve muscle memory, before they were handed their bows. Molly got a dainty one, but Eleanor checked Summer over with an experienced eye and handed her a much bigger one.

Robert looked at his weapon in disgust. 'A pyramid bow? Really? I have shot before, you know.' Without a word, Eleanor handed him a traditional medieval longbow.

Then she gave them more co-ordination movements to tie the techniques together. 'Tilt the bow,' she told them. 'You need to be able to see the target with both eyes.' Summer was mortified when Eleanor told her to hold her bow at an even more pronounced angle. 'It has to come up under your armpit or it will hit your breasts. You don't want the string catching you.'

Mike chortled and made rude gestures with his hands. What had she ever seen in him? Summer wondered.

'Now, draw back on the string as the bow comes up. Anchor your hand against your cheek,' Eleanor told them. 'Don't look at the bow or arrow, look at the target.'

The targets were about twenty feet away. They had looked a perfectly reasonable size when she had helped set them up. Now they looked tiny and distant.

Flynn was going through the motions, but his attention was on the others. Even so, Summer couldn't help noticing the definition of his arm and shoulder muscles when he drew the bow. His loose T-shirt had tightened enough to reveal that his torso was solid bone and muscle. There was nothing elegant about him, but the raw strength had a unique appeal.

The Australians were paying more attention than Summer had expected, and Molly was a picture of concentration. But Natasha and Maya were complaining about the damage to their nails, and Robert looked bored.

Robert's iPhone cheeped. 'Excuse me, I have to take this.'

'Turn it off,' Eleanor snapped. 'You should know better than that.' Robert closed his phone with a bad grace.

Summer nocked her arrow under Eleanor's direction, surprised at how solid it felt.

'Make sure you have the cock feather pointing in the right direction. Otherwise you'll find you're making a cock up.'

Gavin snorted with laughter, and even Maya cracked a smile. Robert winked at Molly and ran a possessive hand down her back. She leaned into his touch, purring with pleasure.

Flynn leaned in towards Summer and murmured, 'Bet I know who's going to have a cock up soon.'

She glared at him before turning her back on him.

He laughed.

They finally got to shoot, and although her first few arrows missed the target, Summer was delighted when she was the first of the beginners to hit the target. 'Women are often faster than men at picking this up,' Eleanor told the disgruntled Australians. After that, every one of her arrows hit the target and Summer was disappointed when Eleanor told them to take a break and go for a walk.

'But I'm just getting the hang of it. Can't I keep going?'

'You'll shoot better after a break.'

Fielding took advantage of the break to make a series of phone calls. Summer didn't intend to eavesdrop, but she couldn't help overhearing. He was as charming and authoritative on the phone as he was in person, she decided.

'I'm sure that can be arranged, Uri. No problem, and the best to your family, too.' He stroked Molly's hair as he talked on the phone and Summer felt a tiny twinge of jealousy. Even when Robert was busy, he was still paying attention to Molly. She'd love to have someone do that to her.

She sneaked a glance at Flynn who, as usual, was right beside her. But his attention was never on her, and he only touched her when he wanted to make a point. She was glad of that. He wasn't the sort of man she needed. She wanted a Dom, a real one, someone who was focused on her and who knew exactly what he was doing.

The prospect of becoming involved again scared the

hell out of her. You're not getting involved, she told herself. You're just . . . oh hell, she didn't know what she was doing.

Flynn's expression caught her attention. God, the man never stopped working. He was listening to Robert's phone calls, Maya and Natasha chattering about manicures, and Mike talking about the chances of Australia taking the Ashes.

Robert finished his call and sent Molly off to adjust his target. Eleanor stopped her with a raised hand and a frown. 'You were told in the safety briefing never to do this. Do not go in front of the shooting line unless all bows are down. Ever.' Molly meekly went back to her own bow.

When Eleanor gave the signal they started again. Now they were firing more arrows, and faster. Robert hit the target again and again with careless ease. Even though she didn't have his style, Summer felt relaxed and managed a respectable number of hits. She decided that archery was something she could learn to do well.

After a while, everyone had the hang of the basic technique and a competition was breaking out among the men. The only one not competing was Flynn. His arrows never seemed to hit, except as a fluke. Summer took great pleasure in gloating at his lack of expertise.

Robert's phone rang again. He answered it, frowning. 'I told you, Uri, it's under control. No, I have it all in hand. Another week and it will be sorted.'

Finally, the lesson was over, with Robert the winner of their impromptu competition. Summer didn't bother trying to hide her joy when she came a surprisingly close runner-up. They handed the bows back and Summer led the way into the house, promising champagne to celebrate. All in all, this had been better fun than being a fairytale princess.

She realized that her shadow was missing and looked around for Flynn. Through the dining room window, she could see that he was still at the range, chatting to Eleanor. He was smiling at the other woman, a warm smile that lit up his face and caused a peculiar twinge in Summer's stomach. Then, in one fluid motion, Flynn raised his bow and released an arrow. It hit the very furthest target dead centre. Reaching into his quiver, he pulled out an arrow and shot again, striking the target with ease. He nodded and handed the bow back to Eleanor.

'Summer. Where are the champagne glasses?'

She turned away from the window, and forced herself to attend to her guests, but her thoughts would not obey so easily. Flynn had been hiding his ability to shoot. Why? And what else was he hiding?

Flynn grinned as the arrow hit the target with a satisfying *thunk*. During the lesson he had been concentrating, as usual, on Summer, her playmates and the open space around them. He hadn't bothered trying to show off and possibly alert the others to his capabilities. But when he was chatting to Eleanor, he hadn't been able to resist one decent shot.

His reputation as a short-sighted wimp was a small price to pay to watch Summer when she was concentrating on her shot and forgetting to be a spoilt society princess. He was only a few days into the job, but sometimes she drove him so mad that he had to clench his fists not to shake her senseless. According to Niall's background check, her father had spent a small fortune on her education and Summer had come top of her class in business school.

Someone with her talents and connections should be out there working in the real world. But the way she acted, it was hard to believe that there really was a working brain under the cloud of blonde hair. Could one bad experience have really had such a devastating effect on her?

Despite the fact that she acted like a first class airhead, he had to admit that she was stunning. Those eyes, beautiful as a dark sky, and usually fluttering flirtatiously at every man except him, occasionally gleamed with intelligence.

Out of habit, he watched the perimeter as he helped Eleanor pack up the targets. The security system was good, but nothing could replace a pair of watchful eyes and an alert brain.

His phone rang. He checked the number and winced – it was his personal phone, the one only his family used. He answered anyway. 'Hi, Mum. What's up?' he asked.

'Flynn, you bad boy. Why haven't you rung?' His mother's voice, thick with a Scottish burr, was the sound of home.

'Come on, Mum, I rang last week.'

'No, I haven't heard a word from you for three whole weeks. And I doubt I would have heard then if the hospital hadn't rung me. Were you planning to tell me you were injured?'

No, he hadn't planned to tell her a single word, and

cursed the meddling hospital pen pusher who had taken it upon herself to ring his ICE numbers. Flynn resolved to put Niall Moore in as his In Case of Emergency contact in future.

'Of course I would, Mum, but it was nothing, just a scratch.'

There was a brief outraged silence on the other end. 'You consider getting your ribs broken and spleen ruptured a scratch?'

'When you say it that way, of course it sounds bad, but it was minor. A quick keyhole op and I'm good as new.' Except for the pains that hit him when he twisted in certain directions and the fact that he was lifting half his usual weights in O'Sullivan's well-equipped gym.

Eleanor finished packing up. He waved goodbye to her and missed his mother's next words. When he paid attention again, he heard, 'Isn't it great about David?'

Flynn went on high alert. 'What has he done now?' he asked warily.

Anything involving his half-brother was rarely great. David had a unique ability to get into trouble. When he was younger, it had been cars, gangs and the police. When he grew out of that phase, it had been women. Flynn still shuddered when he remembered David's last terrible choice. It was one reason he had not been home in a long time.

'He's getting married. Isn't it wonderful?' There was no mistaking the joy in his mother's voice.

He clutched the phone tightly. 'Who is he marrying?' Surely David wouldn't –

'Lorna, of course.'

Of course it was Lorna. Flynn closed his eyes for a second. Of all the women in Scotland, in the world, David had managed to pick the most unsuitable one. The one woman guaranteed to break his heart and tear the family apart.

'They're getting married?' He tried to keep his feelings under control but his mother had no trouble hearing the lack of enthusiasm.

'Now Flynn, I don't know what you have against her. Give her a chance. Lorna is a lovely girl.'

'I know.' And he did. But how could he watch her marry his unsuspecting brother?

Lorna, his former sub. The woman who had smashed his heart when she had walked away from him. He had always known that she would, that she needed a full-time Dom, someone who was there for her all the time, not a Ranger who was away for months at a time and who came home with injuries he couldn't talk about. She had asked him to tear up her contract and he had. He hid his broken heart and wished her well.

That had been hard enough. Watching her when she started to date David had been a special kind of torture, especially when he was certain that there was still a spark between them. Now he waited, wondering when David would find out that his angelic new girlfriend was a submissive with a need for what she called 'Lovely ouchies'. And that Flynn was the man whose collar she used to wear.

'When is the wedding?' Please let it be a long engagement, one that would give David time to come to his senses.

'The thirty-first of July, in the Canongate. You're best man. Don't think you can get out of it by saying you don't have a tux, David said you can wear your kilt.'

He murmured something incoherent before he hung up. Fuck, what a disaster. He had no idea what to do about this.

With an effort, he dragged his attention away from his personal problems and back to the professional ones. He dialled a familiar number.

'Hey Niall, check out a Robert Fielding for me, would you?'

6

'Girly day?'

Summer watched as Flynn gave an almost impercept-ible shudder.

'Yes. You know, salon, waxing, facial, nails. Molly is coming with me. You're welcome to tag along if you want.'

'Which salon?'

She rattled off the address and the phone number. Flynn would check. Summer was counting on it. She had booked the works. A range of appointments which would last an entire day. It would give Molly enough time to slip out and buy her something suitable for the club. And by the time she was finished, none of the paparazzi would recognize her.

'I'll drive you there.' Flynn's expression reflected his suspicion. His desire to keep her within his sights warred with his aversion to spending the day hanging about a beauty salon.

'Great,' she agreed readily. 'I'll grab my bag.'

Flynn didn't look happy but she pretended not to notice. At least he hadn't tried to prevent her from leaving the house. As she hurried up the stairs, she could hear him on the phone to the salon. He didn't trust her an inch.

He was quiet on the drive into the city. Flynn was back in bodyguard mode. He kept within the speed limit and checked his mirror constantly. Her dad had said that he was used to looking after important people but he wasn't like the other men her father had employed. There was a quiet sense of efficiency about Flynn that made her feel protected.

'Give me your phone,' he said as they pulled up outside the salon.

'Why? I'll need it for later.'

He gave an impatient sigh. 'I want to programme my number into your speed dial. If anything, and I mean anything, unusual happens, you will phone me immediately.'

She almost said 'Yes, sir'. 'Fine, I promise.' Handing over her phone, she watched as he flicked through the menus.

'All done.' He smiled and returned the phone. 'I'll call you later.'

Summer tugged a sunhat from her bag and pulled it over her hair.

'Good idea.' He nodded approvingly. 'Your hair is very distinctive.'

Summer suppressed a smile. If her day went according to plan, no one would recognize her at *Noir* tonight. Flynn waited until they entered the salon before moving away. She was willing to bet that he wasn't going back to the house. In fact, he was probably heading to the nearest coffee shop.

'I thought he was never going to go,' Molly giggled. 'Are you sure this is going to work?'

Summer crossed her fingers. 'It better. Now, go find me something to wear and make sure you're back before 3 p.m. for your facial.'

*

It was almost 5 p.m. when the stylist sprayed enough hair-spray on her to put another dent in the ozone layer, before spinning her chair around to face the mirror. Summer touched her hair. Her long mane had been replaced by a sleek, shoulder-length style in her natural brunette.

'You like?' he asked as he ran his fingers through it, smoothing the strands until he was satisfied.

'Yes, I like.' She really did. Gone was the blonde bomb-shell. She looked almost like her old self again. The way she was before she met Adam. Her dad would be pleased.

Her phone buzzed and she checked the display. It was a message from Flynn. *I'm outside.*

No greeting. No please or thank you. She was tempted to type something rude in response, but there was no sense in annoying him. She tapped the display. *Coming.*

Molly was waiting for her in the lobby. Her mouth dropped when she saw her. 'I almost didn't recognize you. Wait till you see what I've bought for you. You'll wow them at *Noir* tonight.'

She wished she was so sure, but she couldn't back out now. 'Are you ready for the next part of the plan?'

'Absolutely,' Molly agreed. 'I can't wait.'

Summer pulled on her hat. Operation *Defeat the Bodyguard* was on.

'Have a good day, ladies?' Flynn was remarkably cheerful for someone who had spent the day hanging around waiting for them.

'It was okay,' Summer shrugged, 'but I think I'm coming down with a migraine.'

Flynn was all concern. 'Do you need medication?'

'No. I've got some at home.'

'It's such a pity you'll miss the show,' Molly said.

'What show?' Flynn asked, darting a suspicious look at Summer.

'Robert called. He has tickets for the theatre – *Phantom*. He'll be so disappointed that you can't come with us.'

Summer did her best to look disappointed. 'I'll have an early night. I'm sure I'll be fine tomorrow.'

Back at the house, she picked at her dinner silently before disappearing up to her room. She pulled the heavy drapes across the window and hurried into the bathroom to try on the clothes that Molly had bought for her.

Sweet mother of god! It was lingerie! But not like any she had ever worn. The electric blue latex tube was designed to cover her butt or her boobs, but not both simultaneously. She would be more decently covered in a swimsuit. Summer tipped the contents of the bag onto the floor. Hold-up stockings and some leather cuffs with studs. There was a length of silver-coloured chain with a clip on one end like a dog leash. And a tube of her favourite lipstick, called 'Vamp'.

Summer carefully applied her make-up, paying particular attention to her eyes. The girl who stared back at her looked as if she belonged in a fetish club, even if she was shaking inside. Hearing a knock on the bedroom door, Summer hastily pulled on a bathrobe. She was relieved when it turned out to be Molly, already wearing her coat.

'Well what do you think?'

Summer slipped off the robe and adjusted the dress, trying to cover her nipples. 'I think I've worn more clothes to the beach.'

'Oh don't be silly. You'll be wearing more than anyone else there. It's sexy, but modest.'

'Modest? I'd hate to see your idea of outrageous,' she muttered. 'Where is Flynn?'

'He's downstairs watching TV. I've told him that you usually sleep for hours when you have a headache and that I'd check on you before I went. Robert's already moved the car to the front of the house and he'll distract Flynn while we leave.'

They giggled as they tucked the pillows beneath the sheets until they had a body-like figure. Summer produced a handful of hair extensions from the bag she had brought from the salon and put them on the pillow. 'I knew they'd be useful for something.'

'Let's go,' Molly said. She opened the bedroom door and peeked down the corridor. They could hear the latest Wii battle going on downstairs and Robert's voice.

They tiptoed down the stairs and opened the front door. The car was parked outside. 'Get in and stay down. I'll fetch Robert.'

Heart racing, Summer slid into the back seat and lay down. If she was caught now, Flynn would have a fit. She heard the door opening again and the crunch of gravel underfoot.

'Please don't let it be Flynn.' She could just imagine his expression if he caught her wearing nothing but a trench coat and underwear.

The car doors opened and Robert and Molly climbed in. Summer didn't stop shaking until they were out on the open road.

'You can sit up now.' She could hear the amusement in Robert's tone. 'I don't think I've had quite so much fun since I smuggled an ostrich into Eton.'

'An ostrich?' Molly giggled. 'Why an ostrich?'

'Because it was the most outrageous thing I could think of at the time. I was fifteen,' he added. He glanced in the rear view mirror. 'Open your coat, Summer. Let me see you.'

Summer moved instinctively to obey him and then stopped. She wasn't sure if the dress had stayed in place while she was lying down and there was something weird about flashing her boobs at her best friend's guy.

'Behave.' Molly gave him a mock slap. 'You can be so bad.'

'Of course, my darling. But you can hardly expect me not to be impatient at the thought of bringing two lovely ladies to my favourite club.'

'Charmer! Ignore him, Summer. He's just teasing.'

Summer caught Robert's glance in the mirror. For a brief second his usual urbane expression was replaced by something dangerous. Nonsense, she told herself. He's Molly's boyfriend, not an axe murderer.

As they drove through the night, she wondered what Flynn would do if he discovered that she was missing. Send out a search party? Hardly. He would probably give her a stern lecture in the morning. She was an adult. She didn't need his permission to attend a club.

They turned into a side street and Robert reduced speed. Outside a nondescript doorway, two dark-suited security men wearing earpieces waited. One waved to Robert as he pulled up outside. 'Good evening, sir,' he said as they climbed out of the car.

'Good evening, Stan,' Robert replied. 'These lovely ladies are my guests.'

Through the thin fabric of her coat, Summer could feel the warmth of Robert's hand on her back. He opened the door and ushered them inside.

Summer wasn't sure what she had been expecting. Something dark and gloomy, maybe a little seedy. She had been to plenty of clubs before, but the quiet luxury of the entrance lobby to *Noir* was impressive. Several people waved to Robert.

A dark-haired lady offered to take their coats. Summer's fingers trembled as she opened the first button. Now that the moment had arrived, she wasn't sure if she wanted to go through with it.

Molly slipped off her coat and handed it over. Summer didn't know where to look. She was wearing nothing but a red satin thong. A silver chain stretched from a matching collar around her neck and dangled between her breasts. On her nipples were tiny jewelled clamps.

'Here, let me help you with that.' Robert unbuttoned Summer's coat deftly and slipped it off her shoulders. She resisted the temptation to tug at the dress. Molly had been right. She was wearing more than most of the women here.

'Beautiful,' Robert said admiringly. 'The colour matches your eyes.'

He glanced at her neck, bare of adornment. 'Haven't you brought the chain and collar?'

'No,' Summer replied. 'I'm fine without it.' There was no way that she would let anyone put a collar on her.

'Of course.' He inclined his head. 'If you prefer. You're such a pretty little one. I thought it might make things a little easier.'

He picked up Molly's leash. 'Come along.'

Summer followed them through the door into the main club area.

She stayed close to Molly as they moved through the crowd. A dark-eyed man dressed in green surgical scrubs winked at her as she passed. She dropped her eyes and hurried after Molly.

Indiana Jones and his sexy sidekick were chatting quietly in one corner, while a man in a soldier's uniform licked the boots of a red-headed woman. 'Is she a . . .' Summer couldn't get the word out.

'A Domme?' Molly replied. 'One of the best. She earns a fortune for private consultations. You have no idea how many captains of industry want to be told that they've been naughty boys. Come on, let me show you around.'

Something was wrong. Flynn knew it; he just couldn't put his finger on it. Well, there were a lot of things wrong; starting with the knowledge that David was all set to marry Lorna. Once he had seen Summer safely into her salon, he had settled himself in a café across the road where he could see anyone going in or out, and had phoned his half-brother.

He still winced at the memory of that call. David had not been impressed by Flynn's interference. 'Who the fuck do you think you are to tell me who I can or can't marry?' David demanded.

'I don't want to tell you who to marry; I'm just saying that you don't know Lorna all that well.'

'Better than you do. Asshole.'

'I doubt it.' Flynn was torn between trying to keep David, and Lorna as well, from making a colossal mistake, and wanting to keep his former sub's secrets. 'She's not what you think.'

'Oh?' David sneered. 'I suppose you are going to tell me she's not a virgin? Well, prepare for a shock, bro. Neither am I.'

That pulled a reluctant laugh from Flynn. He knew that David was far from being a virgin, but Lorna was a different matter altogether. She had a taste for extremes that he couldn't imagine his brother ever satisfying. Not only was it likely to crucify David when he discovered the truth, it wasn't fair to Lorna either. She shouldn't have to settle for vanilla when she was used to dark chocolate with extra chilli. She deserved better.

'Like you?' whispered the little voice in his head which urged him to cut David out and put his collar back on Lorna. He knew all her buttons and he knew he could bring her back to him. It's better to break them up now, not wait until they're married.

The last time he had met her, Lorna had watched him, not David.

But first he had a job to do. And a spoilt little rich girl to protect from her own actions.

How much longer would this job take? The last phone call from Niall had told him to get back to full strength and wrap up the O'Sullivan job as soon as possible. When he was fighting fit again, Niall had a gig waiting for him, one that involved the sort of work Flynn liked best.

So what if I love to blow shit up? That's not a crime, is it?

He focused on the job at hand. Summer was up to

76

something. He knew it. The knowledge was like an itch he couldn't scratch. Flynn had become convinced that the airhead heiress act was just that, an act. The woman who had been so competitive on the archery range was not the sort to spend all day lazing around getting her hair and nails done. She was up to no good, he would bet a month's pay on it.

He checked the security camera, but there she was, curled up in bed. As he studied the grainy image in the small screen, he frowned. Normally, just looking at Summer caused an unwelcome surge in his libido. A flutter of those ridiculously long lashes, a flick of her hair, the sway of her hips, all were guaranteed to send the blood heading southwards.

Summer alone in bed should have done something to him. God knows he had imagined her in his bed often enough. Why was the picture of her sleeping like a baby not turning him on?

He looked closer. She was very still. The mic should have picked up something. Maybe there was a malfunction. He headed upstairs to check for himself. He would just stand at the door, he assured himself. He absolutely would not go into the room and check her for fever. That would be unethical and damnably stupid. Just stand at the door.

The room was silent. Too silent. As soon as he eased the bedroom door open a crack, Flynn knew he had been tricked. The room was empty. The little bitch had given him the slip.

A certain reluctant admiration for her cunning mixed with fury and aggravation.

Now he had to find her.

He knew it was wasted effort, but he tore through the house, searching for her. No sign. He rang her mobile phone and wasn't surprised when it immediately went to voicemail. Didn't matter, he had his lead.

'Niall? Check the location of a phone for me, would you?' He rattled off Summer's number. He had only seen it once, but he was good with details.

He drummed his fingers impatiently while he waited for his friend to come back with the co-ordinates, then realized what he was doing and stopped. What the fuck was wrong with him? His icy coolness under pressure was legendary. It wasn't as if Summer had been abducted. She had deliberately given him the slip so she could play hooky. But a nagging sense of urgency would not be denied.

'Here you go,' Niall's voice was as calm as usual. Nothing ever ruffled that guy. 'The phone is at number 13 Bruno Street in London. It's listed as a private club, but there are no details. I'll get back to you as soon as I find them.'

Fuck, fuck, fuck. Flynn found his voice. 'Don't bother. I recognize that address. I've been there before. Give me ten minutes to change and I'm on my way.'

7

Summer's eyes were like saucers as she looked around *Noir*. Her imagination had not done justice to the club. For one thing, it was much bigger than she had been expecting, and much more luxurious.

Robert had changed his clothes and now he looked every inch the Dom in black leather and boots, with his hair slicked back to show the noble lines of his face. He held Molly's leash in one hand and a long leather bag in the other. Summer swallowed. She had an idea what was in that bag, and wasn't sure if she wanted to encounter any of it.

She'd already noticed that most of the Doms carried a similar bag. Some of them had floggers or paddles in their hands. One corseted Domme also had a tool bag, but hers was being carried by a tall man whose rubber suit left his buttocks exposed.

Summer meekly followed Robert and Molly, and found herself in a large room, with thick carpets and dramatic artwork on the walls. The music was techno but at a lower volume than she was used to, so that conversation flowed freely.

'I like it,' she whispered to Molly. 'I'm not being deafened.'

'It's so you can hear a safe word.'

Safe word. Summer swallowed again. This wasn't a joke.

People clustered in groups, talking and laughing. It could have been any cocktail party, except for the outfits. James Bond held a glass to Miss Moneypenny's lips. She couldn't drink without help as she was kneeling with her hands cuffed behind her back.

There was a group where everyone wore a rubber version of a military outfit, and a red-haired woman wearing only a pair of outrageously long studded boots served drinks.

Summer felt overdressed, and was glad of it.

Robert led them to the bar, where he ordered a glass of vintage champagne for himself and two club sodas for the girls. Summer took a gulp, and then had to fight the urge to sneeze. She gripped the glass tightly as she continued to gaze around.

A large screen television on the opposite wall showed a black and white vampire film. A man in a leather skirt was tying a woman up, and then attaching the ropes to a ring in the ceiling. Between one breath and the next, she was in suspension, spinning around, and he was encouraging her twirl with a flogger.

A priest appeared to be hearing confessions on a bench. Whatever the penitent had said obviously called for a lot of contrition, because the 'priest' hauled her over his knee and spanked her soundly. Her squeals were ignored by the laughing group.

A tiny flicker of excitement spread through Summer at the sight. She'd always had fantasies about being spanked, just not by a priest.

'Robert, introduce me to your charming companions,' said a voice belonging to a tall highwayman.

Summer froze. Oh no, what if he gave her name? Summer wasn't such a common name that people were likely to forget it. And her face was famous enough.

'Ladies, allow me to introduce Peter, the scourge of the local heath. Peter, this is Lola and Wild Child.' Thank god he had used their online names.

Peter swept his tricorne hat off his head and bowed deeply to both of them. 'Enchanted. I'm delighted to meet you. I hope we get an opportunity to play at some stage.' He beckoned over another man, whose costume seemed to be mostly chains, and introduced him as well.

Summer took another mouthful of soda, her worries easing slightly. The formality and politeness were at odds with her expectations. She had been afraid that as soon as she got into the club, wearing this excuse for a dress, she would be grabbed and groped by strange men. Instead, she was being introduced with a degree of formality that wouldn't have been out of place at an embassy reception. Although people were doing things which made her feel like a nun at an orgy, it appeared to be by invitation only.

She could cope with this, she decided. It wasn't as if she was going to do anything but watch.

Robert ordered another glass of champagne and chatted for a few more minutes. 'Now girls, I think it's time we went to the play area.'

Molly squealed with delight.

This wasn't the play area?

She followed them deeper into the club. Back here, it was equally luxurious, but was stocked with equipment that made her catch her breath. Old-fashioned stocks. A cage. A medical table with straps for wrists and ankles.

A large frame with ropes. A wooden X-shaped cross, already equipped with cuffs.

'Do you want to go first?' Robert asked her.

He rifled through the case David had sent on from home. There must be something in here that he could wear. Ah! That should it. It had been years since he had been at *Noir*, but he was certain that the dress code would still be rigidly enforced. He stuffed his favourite flail and leather strap into their holsters and grabbed a leash and collar. He'd like to see Summer's expression when he produced them.

Within minutes, he was on the Venom heading for London. As he set off at an illegal speed, he voice-dialled Niall, briefing him on where he was going and telling him to keep him posted on any changes, particularly on the position of Summer's phone.

Then he had nothing but Summer to occupy his thoughts.

She was on the scene. How had she disguised it so well and how had he not picked up any of the subtle clues that he normally caught within minutes of meeting someone? He would have sworn she was vanilla, though a 'nilla with potential.

He swore. Well, he had been wrong before, but never by this much. No wonder O'Sullivan was so paranoid about keeping Summer out of trouble. He obviously knew that his daughter spent her spare time playing in one of the world's most notorious fetish clubs. It was only a matter of time before the paparazzi got wind of it and she ended up spread over the front pages of the tabloids.

The fact that he'd entertained a few fantasies about Summer O'Sullivan spread out for his delight just added fuel to his anger. What the hell was she doing at *Noir*, and even more infuriating, who was she doing it with?

The obvious answer was Robert bloody Fielding. Flynn had recognized the dynamics of a D/s relationship between Fielding and Molly Ainsworth right away, but hadn't expected that he'd try to include Summer in that relationship. Just shows how wrong he was, he'd have bet good money that Summer was too proud to be second string in a ménage.

He opened the throttle a little more, fighting to get the last ergs out of the engine. The thought of Fielding putting his hands on Summer made him clench his teeth in rage. He was going to rip Fielding's fucking head off his shoulders.

When he got there, the place still looked the same, sedate and respectable. There was only a slight echo of music to be heard outside and no clue to what went on inside. He knocked on the door and the security screen slid back. 'Let me in. I'm Fug, you know me.'

A masculine voice said, 'Come in, mate. We haven't seen you for a while.'

Flynn crossed the lobby and headed straight for the club area, only to be stopped by a tuxedo clad security guard who gave his biking gear a look of disdain. 'You know the dress code.'

'Come on, give me a break.' His sense of urgency was riding him hard.

Fuck. Flynn hurried into the changing rooms, stripped off his bike leathers and pulled on his costume. He always felt like a wanker when he first put it on, but it would do the job.

The main socializing area was busy, and there was no sign of Summer. Damn it. Where was she? He spotted a familiar face. 'Hey Steve,' he said. 'Have you seen a new girl with long blonde hair? She might be with Fielding.'

The priest grimaced in thought. 'No, don't think so. Fielding had a couple of pretty little fillies with him, but it was his regular girl and a brunette.'

Damn it. Could he have made a mistake? Was Summer here at all?

Summer forced a smile onto her face. This is what she was here for, wasn't it? This was what she had been discussing with Molly for months. So why wasn't she eager? Why did she have a sick feeling in the pit of her stomach that no amount of soda could take away?

'Please, Sir. Me, Sir.' Molly pouted at Robert, her large eyes pleading with him for attention.

Robert dropped a kiss on her forehead. 'How remiss of me. Of course, my pet. Let me take care of you first.'

The eagerness in her friend's attitude surprised her. This was Molly? Molly, who could out-drink and out-flirt an entire rugby team. They had backpacked across Europe together. Molly was a free spirit, wild and independent. She didn't say Sir or let a guy drag her around on a leash like a pet. There was something wrong with this picture.

'I want you to sit here, Su –. You are not to move and

84

you are not to accept an invitation to play. Do you understand?'

Summer nodded. She had no intention of playing with anyone. Satisfied, Robert turned and bent down to open his tool kit. He pulled out a riding crop and tapped it firmly against his palm. Oh dear god, he wasn't going to beat Molly with that?

'Another time.' Replacing it in the bag, he drew out a leather flail.

She watched in shocked fascination as he led Molly to the X-shaped cross. Her friend stood obediently while Robert attached leather restraints to her wrists and ankles. Molly's eyes were bright with anticipation. She really wanted this. Robert dragged one hand through her hair and pulled her head back before taking her mouth in a rough kiss. His other hand roamed her abdomen before plunging into the front of her thong. Molly stood on tiptoe, leaning against him, eager for his touch.

Summer blushed. Were they going to have sex in front of her? She didn't know if she could watch. As he continued to kiss her, Robert opened his eyes. His hard stare held a hint of dark promise. This scene wasn't for Molly. This was a demonstration of his power over her.

Robert stepped away, staggering slightly. His face was flushed from the two drinks he'd had since they'd arrived at the club. She had thought you weren't supposed to drink if you were going to play. Summer looked around. She didn't know anyone here. There was no one she could ask. She sat frozen to her seat as Robert swung his arm for the first blow.

The leather made contact with Molly's skin and she flinched and cried out. 'Oh!'

Summer sat rigid, fascinated and shocked by the scene in front of her. Robert wielded his flogger with skill, whisking it around and around, hitting Molly with a hypnotic rhythm. At first she gasped and flinched with every stroke but after a dozen or so, she stopped fighting and something changed. Her body softened, relaxing against the wood of the cross.

Robert changed his stance, so that he could flash up and down her body with the leather flail. He broke off to change it for a different one, and Molly grunted when he laid it across her buttocks.

Robert's arm flashed at lightning speed, across her legs and back.

Twenty, fifty, one hundred, more. Summer lost count. She could almost feel each stroke of the lash. Her nails dug deep into the velvet chair. Her palms sweated, even as goose bumps popped up on her skin.

Robert paused, to wipe the sweat from his brow with the sleeve of his shirt. He stroked the reddening skin, pleased with his work. He pulled down Molly's thong, leaving it around her thighs while his fingers played with her. 'Good girl,' he praised her. 'What do you say?'

When Molly nodded weakly, Robert administered a sharp slap. Her eyes snapped open. 'Thank you, Master.'

Removing his shirt, he reached for the bag again and removed the crop. He slapped it hard against his palm. The sound of it made Molly straighten up and Summer wasn't sure whether it was with eagerness or fear. He traced a path down her back with the tip of the crop. 'Do you want this?'

'I want to please you,' she said in a hoarse whisper.

'There's a good pet.'

Robert's back was dripping with sweat. Ignoring the bottled water on the tables, he reached for his champagne glass again and took a deep gulp. A few drops dribbled down his chin and he wiped it away with the back of his hand.

One of the staff approached Robert and whispered to him. Summer couldn't hear what was said, but he spoke quietly to Molly for a moment and she nodded her head. The man pressed an open water bottle to her lips and she drank greedily.

'Do you want to stop?' he asked Molly. She shook her head.

With a disapproving glance at Robert, the dungeon monitor left. Summer was tempted to follow him. She couldn't watch this anymore, but she couldn't leave her friend here. The sound of a crop against flesh startled her.

'Count them, and thank me,' Robert growled. His temper had taken a turn for the worse following the interruption.

Six blows landed in quick succession on Molly's already reddened flesh. Each stroke left a mark. Molly panted and gasped as she forced the numbers out. At each blow, Molly cried out in pain. Summer rose to her feet. She knew that you weren't supposed to interfere in a scene but she had to do something.

Robert grunted as he whipped her. He smiled as she flinched and writhed against the restraints. A small crowd of men formed a circle around them, their eyes watching eagerly as Robert worked himself into a frenzy.

Sickened, Summer hurried from the room. She had to find someone to help. Where was that dungeon monitor who had been there before?

8

Summer hurried through the crowded rooms. There were so many people here now and each of the rooms looked the same. She spotted the man dressed as a surgeon heading her way and turned left to avoid him. That guy was creepy.

Another dimly lit corridor. Behind each closed door she could hear the sounds of women and men groaning with pleasure. Occasionally someone screamed. Her heart raced. What the hell was she going to do? Where were the dungeon monitors? There should be staff in a place like this.

She headed for the cloakroom. She needed to get her phone. She had nodded when Molly had told her to leave her bag with her phone in the cloakroom. 'No phones allowed. Nothing that could take photos of or record a scene.' At the time it had made sense, but now she desperately wanted that phone so she could phone for help.

Maya or Natasha? She couldn't call them, they were too far away, and the Aussie guys were probably out partying. She suppressed a hysterical giggle as she imagined Mike and Gavin pushing their way through the club as if they were heading for a try at Lansdowne Road.

Her dad. Oh yeah, that would be sweet. Hi, Dad. I'm in a fetish club with Molly watching her boyfriend beat the crap out of her.

Flynn. She had Flynn's number. If she could get to her phone and call him, he would protect her and get Molly out of here. Yes, she would have to explain. Admit that she had lied to him and face his anger and his disgust. His opinion of her was already low enough. Spoilt little girl. No job and a mega-rich daddy. Flynn couldn't possibly understand that money wasn't always enough to protect you.

But it would be worth it. Flynn would rescue her. She wasn't sure why she was so certain, but she was. All she had to do was get to her phone.

She took a breath and left the ladies room. She remembered the way. Summer set out, weaving her way through the crowd in the main area as she headed to the cloakroom. Yes, there it was.

It was closed. Summer wanted to cry. She banged on the wooden shutter. 'Open up. Please, I need my phone.' There was no reply. The cloakroom was deserted.

Okay, O'Sullivan, time to put your big girl panties on. You have to do this yourself. She would find the man who had given Molly the water and get him to help her. And if she couldn't find him she would do something herself.

There was no sign of creepy surgeon guy, but she did see a familiar figure in the crowd. Peter the Highwayman. Heaving a sigh of relief, she hurried across the room and tapped him on the shoulder.

'Well, if it isn't the little wild child?' He inclined his head in a small bow. 'Is there some service that I can perform for my lady?'

'As a matter of fact there is. It's my first time here and I'm afraid I'm lost. I need to find my way back to the playroom.'

Peter offered her his arm. 'It would be my pleasure, my lady.'

Clutching the sleeve of his greatcoat, Summer allowed him to lead her through the club. Peter seemed nice. Maybe she could ask him to help her. 'Um, have you known Robert long?'

'Just at the club and some private parties. Robert is quite a showman. He is always worth watching when he plays.' He slanted a speculative look at her. 'I wouldn't have pegged you for one of his girls. You don't strike me as the sort who likes group play.'

Group play? What was he talking about?

His eyes raked over her skimpy dress and Summer wasn't sure if she should pull it up or down. 'Something tells me that you're a virgin.' He gestured around him. 'To this scene, I mean. But don't worry, Robert will fix that.'

'No!' The exclamation burst out of her before she thought.

The highwayman's eyes gleamed. 'Well, if you are looking for someone else, I'd be happy to oblige you. I bet that pert little arse would wriggle a lot if I had you over my knee.'

Oh god. She had no idea how to get out of this. She needed someone to help Molly. If she promised the highwayman he could spank her, would he help? Even now, the thought of what would happen if she made enough of a fuss to attract attention made her shudder. She had to do this quietly, without calling too much attention to Molly or herself.

A new player had entered the room. His white pirate shirt was open to the waist, displaying tight abs and a V of dark hair. A black leather kilt with a studded belt covered his thighs. Slung over his right shoulder was an arrow quiver. Dark stubble decorated his strong jaw. His mouth was set in a stern line that spelt danger for anyone who crossed him, but it was his eyes that caught and held her attention. The gold-flecked hazel was almost black with rage. It was Flynn.

Flynn was here.

Summer cringed, waiting for his anger to focus on her. She had lied to him, deceived him. She deserved every bit of it, but she didn't care as long as she could get Molly out of here. Standing at the edge of the crowd, Flynn had the stillness of a predator waiting to pounce. His eyes scanned the room, taking in everything. Nothing escaped his attention. She knew that he had been a soldier. Was this what he was like before he went into battle? There was an aura of suppressed power about him that was incredibly sexy.

Others apparently thought so too. A Dom leading two white-shirted schoolgirls by their school ties approached him. Flynn politely declined before resuming his scan of the room. His eyes passed over her. He hadn't noticed her. The hair. She had forgotten about her hair.

'Come along, my dear, I promised Robert that I'd take care of you.' Highwayman Peter took her arm.

Summer flinched. She couldn't let him take her out of here. 'I can't. I've just seen my Master.'

Highwayman gave her a disbelieving look. 'Your Master? And which one would he be?'

Summer glanced towards the doorway. Her change of appearance had only fooled Flynn for a moment. He was striding through the crowd with an expression as dark as a storm cloud. Flynn inclined his head to Highwayman politely before shooting her a glance that would melt steel.

'She says that she is yours,' Highwayman offered.

Flynn's eyes narrowed. 'Aye, I'm afraid that she is. She's new and untrained. I apologize if she's been troublesome.'

'That's quite alright. She's a pretty little thing, although I imagine that she needs a firm hand.'

'Indeed,' Flynn agreed. 'She can be quite the brat at times.' He reached into his sporran and pulled out a length of silver chain and a collar.

Oh, he wouldn't. Flynn wouldn't dare put a collar on her in front of all these people. She thought she caught a hint of a smile as he fastened it around her neck. He inserted a finger between the collar and her bare skin before attaching the chain to the collar.

She flashed him a mutinous glare but remained silent. It was her own fault that she was in this mess. She might have to put up with it now, but she would make him pay for this later.

'She's had enough excitement for one night,' Flynn said. 'Have you seen her companions? I'd like to say good-night before I take her home.'

'Robert and Molly? I'm afraid you've missed them. Two of Robert's eastern European friends turned up and they left together.'

'But was Molly okay?' Summer asked.

Peter laughed. 'She was barely warmed up. Molly has a remarkably high pain threshold.'

They left her? Molly and Robert had left her here alone? Summer swallowed hard. If Flynn hadn't arrived when he did . . . She didn't want to think about that. This night wasn't turning out as she had planned. She had to get out of here. Summer moved towards the door, only to be pulled up sharply by the leash.

'Going somewhere?' Flynn asked mildly.

Hell. She had forgotten that she was supposed to be his sub and Highwayman was still hanging around. 'No . . . I . . .'

'No, what?' he said sharply.

The words stuck in her throat like shards of glass. When they got home, Flynn was going to suffer. Really suffer. 'No, Master.'

'Good girl,' he praised her. 'I've had a long, thirsty ride to fetch you. I need a drink.'

She followed obediently behind them, praying that no one she knew saw her. The ignominy of it. Summer O'Sullivan on a leash and chain. She would make Flynn pay for this.

Through an ornate pair of doors was another bar. This one was quieter, more formal. Groups sat quietly chatting. They could have been in the lobby of a five-star hotel. She glanced around her, gritting her teeth when she realized that the subs were expected to sit at their masters' feet. They had to be kidding. Flynn chose a quiet alcove with two wing-backed leather chairs. He was going to do it. This was his petty revenge for making him drive into the city to rescue her.

Flynn ordered two single malts and a sparkling water, while Highwayman located a low footstool and placed it beside Flynn's chair. She smiled gratefully at him; at least she didn't have to sit on the floor. When the server arrived with their drinks, Flynn offered her the whiskey. 'I don't . . .' she began.

His warning glance silenced her and she accepted the glass without further protest. The men chatted about the club. Flynn seemed to know many of the members, which was surprising. But then, a lot of things about tonight had shocked the hell out of her. She took a sip, savouring the warming flare of the whiskey as it slipped down her throat.

She was suddenly desperately tired. Would this night ever end? As if she had spoken out loud, Flynn stroked her hair and he gently pressed her head against his knee. She rested her cheek against his thigh.

Highwayman rambled on. Underneath the wig and the flamboyant costume, he was an old gossip. 'Dreadful business about the property crash. There were rumours that Robert got himself mixed up in some deal in Bratislava. And I heard that Maurice was hit so hard he had to move back in with his parents.'

'Very unfortunate,' Flynn agreed.

The highwayman put down his drink and got to his feet. 'Break time is over.' He looked at Flynn and smiled. 'I wonder if I might play with your pet?'

Summer squeaked. 'No, I'm fine, thanks.'

Highwayman ignored her. 'I noticed that she hasn't played all night.' Was there a flicker of suspicion in his eyes?

She pressed closer to Flynn. Surely he wouldn't let anyone touch her.

'Your choice, pet,' Flynn said. 'Would you like to play with me or Peter?'

What? This wasn't what she had expected. She glared

94

from one to the other while Flynn grinned at her. She was going to kill him for this. Kill him stone dead and scatter his body parts over the manure heap.

Summer unclenched her teeth and forced the words out. 'Please, Sir, would you like to spank me?'

Highwayman gestured at Flynn. 'In that case, go for it, sir. I love watching you in action.'

'Of course.' Before she could blink, Flynn had caught her around the waist and flipped her so that she was ass-upwards over his knee. Instinctively, she put her hands down on the carpet to balance herself. Her toes barely reached the ground, but Flynn's strong arm held her securely in position.

Almost before she could register her position, his hand flashed down in a series of quick spanks. It stung, bright and hot. She wanted to yell in outrage, but the sound of his hand hitting her latex dress was shockingly loud and attracted the attention of everyone in the room. If she called him the names she wanted to, everyone would notice.

She set her teeth and silently vowed to kill him.

A dozen spanks later, he let her up and helped her to her feet. 'What do you say?' The unholy grin on his face showed he knew her dilemma.

'Thank you, Master.' Killing was too good for him. She was going to have him tortured for eternity.

'You may rub.'

On those words, the heat in her rear end blossomed and she couldn't help rubbing to relieve it. Oh yeah, the man was mincemeat.

Highwayman tipped his tricorne to her, and departed.

'He's gone. You can stop pretending now,' she told Flynn

His demeanour had changed too. Gone was the playful Dom. The efficient bodyguard who despised his principal was back. 'Why? Isn't this what you wanted? Some cheap titillation for a bored little rich girl.'

'It wasn't like that,' she snapped. 'Molly and I have been planning this for months.' She had said too much. She could almost see Flynn filing that particular piece of information away for later.

'What was it that you wanted?' His eyes raked the minuscule dress. 'A chance to dress up like a tart? Being a Saturday night submissive so that you could gossip with the girls over Sunday brunch?'

That was it, she'd had enough. Summer tugged the leash from his hand and stood up. Ignoring his order to halt she hurried through the club and into the lobby. The cloakroom lady was back on duty, returning coats and bags to those who were ready to call it a night. Still fuming from her encounter with Flynn, she handed over her ticket and grabbed her coat and bag.

She was in a part of the city she didn't know well. She didn't have enough cash to take a taxi home, even if she could get any driver to take her, and she could hardly get a room in a decent hotel in the middle of the night dressed like this. Damn. Damn. Damn.

Flynn appeared in the lobby. The kilt and white shirt were gone. In their place were jeans and a leather jacket. A dark T-shirt stretched across his chest. 'Do you need a ride?'

His knowing smirk was the last straw.

'No, thank you. I'd rather walk.' Ignoring his laughter,

she stormed out of the club. She would find her own way home.

An unseasonable rainstorm had made the night sky even darker. The side street was longer and gloomier than she remembered. Her heels clicked noisily on the wet pavement, the sound echoing against the shuttered buildings. A Jeep drove past on the narrow street, sending a wash of rainwater onto the pavement. Within seconds, her feet were soaked.

Up ahead, the scaffolding of a renovation project blocked the path. She would have to walk on the road. Summer stepped between two parked cars, straight into the path of an oncoming motorcycle. She stumbled against one car as the bike screeched to a halt.

Flynn pulled off his helmet. 'Are you trying to get yourself killed?'

'Why? Are you worried about being unemployed? Go to hell and leave me alone.' Ignoring the revving of the engine behind her, she set off again. If she couldn't walk on the road, she would have to walk beneath the scaffolding. At least Flynn couldn't follow her there. A footfall behind her told her that her prayers hadn't been answered.

His rough hand pulled on her shoulder and Flynn spun her around. Bright drops of rain clung to his hair and his eyes glinted dangerously. 'Don't you ever walk away from me.'

'Or what?' Summer knew that she was provoking him but she no longer cared.

With a muttered oath, he pressed her against the rough brick wall. His hard frame caged her. 'Why were you at that club tonight? Tell me.'

She couldn't meet his gaze. Summer turned her head away and remained stubbornly silent. How could she confess to him that she didn't know what she wanted? That there was an ache inside her, an emptiness that she didn't know how to fill.

His chest rose and fell, his breath came in angry rasps as he waited for her response. 'Perhaps you need a little encouragement?'

The first press of his mouth against her neck was barely a whisper. A more insistent nip dragged a soft cry from her throat. Flynn continued to torture her, a kiss here, a nip there, never twice in the same spot. When he caught the lobe of her ear between his teeth she groaned and arched against him.

'I'll ask you again. Does the thought of being sexually submissive to a man turn you on?'

It was none of his business. 'I don't know.'

'Oh, I think you do.'

His warm hands slid the length of her latex dress and he cupped her butt, dragging her against the hard length of him. God, that felt so good. She squirmed, seeking more pressure against her clit.

'Ah-ah. Who's doing the driving?' Releasing her, he eased away. 'Or maybe you just like it a little rough.'

His hands peeled down the latex of her dress to expose her breasts. The chill of the damp air made her nipples pucker into hard peaks, aching for him. He bent his head. She gasped at the shock of his hot mouth fastening over one nipple and he laved and suckled until she was breathless before he turned his attention to her other breast. When he nipped hard, she cried out.

Flynn pushed his thigh between her legs and she arched against him like a cat. She rocked against his leg as he turned his attention to her neck again, finding all the sensitive little spots that made her dizzy with need. His knowing hands played with her breasts, plumping and squeezing them until her pleas became an incoherent jumble. She wanted to come. Needed the release that he could give her.

Then everything stopped.

Despite the rapid rise and fall of his chest, Flynn was still very much in control. His hand fisted in her hair, tilting her head back, holding her in place. Summer couldn't meet his eyes, afraid of what she might see there. Instead, she stared at his mouth, realizing for the first time that despite everything they had done, he hadn't kissed her yet.

Flynn hadn't kissed her and she very much wanted him to. Her whole body tingled with anticipation. If he didn't touch her soon she would die.

'I'll ask you one more time. What do you want, Summer?'

Despite his self-control, his voice was hoarse. This wasn't a lesson. He wasn't her Master. Flynn was as affected by her as she was by him.

'I want you to fuck me.'

'Fuck me.' Those words hit Flynn like a blow. He stiffened, all his defences down, and all his attention on the woman in his arms. She wasn't the principal; she was Summer, the woman he wanted more than his next breath.

He had spent the last three hours obsessed with finding her safe and healthy, and when he did find her, his focus was getting her out of *Noir* without a scene. During all that time, he hadn't allowed himself to think of her as a desirable woman who drove him nuts. She was the principal, he was the minder and he was determined to keep it that way. Even seeing her in that excuse for a dress, one that showed every succulent curve in more detail than if she were naked, hadn't derailed him completely. But those words, 'I want you to fuck me'. That was all it took.

God help him, he was going to fuck her. Nothing would stop him now.

He shoved both hands into her hair, relishing the new smoothness of it, and held her head still while he took her mouth.

He had dreamt of kissing her, had awakened from sweaty dreams of her mouth. The reality surpassed all his expectations.

Summer's lips were soft and parted sweetly for his tongue. As he plundered the softness of her mouth, she made a tiny noise at the back of her throat. It enflamed him. He pulled her tighter against him, impatient to feel every one of her curves. She fitted against him as if she had been made to his exact specifications.

He couldn't get enough of her. He slanted his head and plunged deeply, tasting her and drinking in the essence of Summer. She moaned again and brushed her tongue tentatively against his. The touch was magic, easing something inside him that he wasn't aware had been wound too tight, while sending all the blood in his head southwards. He thought his cock was hard before; now it was so rigid that only the feel of Summer's soft stomach prevented it being painful.

He didn't care. Kissing Summer could easily become an addiction. He shifted his feet, widening his stance so he could hold her more tightly, and kissed her again.

Her kiss was oddly tentative. For someone who was notorious for her sexual exploits and who had been plastered all over the tabloids at frequent intervals for the last five years, she was surprisingly hesitant. That in itself was an aphrodisiac to him. Flynn took charge, tilting her head back so he could ravish her mouth.

He could have kissed her for hours, undeterred by the rain pouring down on them, but when she raked her fingers down his back, he jerked against her and his cock grew more demanding. She wanted to be fucked? By god, he was the man to do it.

He grabbed the hem of her little latex dress, pulling it up, eager to get his hands on that world-class arse.

'What the hell?' He broke off to look at what she was wearing.

In a club where the women competed to prance around in the most minuscule thong, Summer had dressed in the opposite extreme. No teeny-weeny thong for her. Instead, she was wearing a garment that could only be described as big knickers. They were latex, true, but they were solid and high waisted.

'You're wearing granny pants?'

'Oh!' She wiggled, embarrassed, and in spite of his frustrations, he wanted to laugh. 'My dress is so short; I didn't want to flash by accident.'

'The Bailey Lighthouse couldn't flash in those things,' he told her. 'Even my cock wouldn't get through them without bolt cutters.'

'Hey!' She punched him, right on top of the last surgery site. He winced. Usually her best punch would have been only a love tap to him, but that hurt.

She noticed and her expression changed. 'Oh god, I'm sorry, did I hurt you?'

He shook his head. 'It's nothing. Come on, grab a helmet and I'll take you somewhere dry where we can decant you from the granny pants.'

For once, she didn't argue as he led her to the bike. He gave her a quick kiss before he pulled the helmet down over her head and adjusted it. God help him, he had to get her naked and underneath him soon or his dick would explode.

Judging from the way she wiggled on the seat behind him, and gripped him so tightly that he could feel her stiff nipples boring into his back, Summer felt the same.

There was no question of riding back to Hampstead. With the few functioning brain cells still in operation, Flynn remembered the Baker Street apartment Niall kept for guests and clients. He had the code. He'd take her there.

9

The scent of his leather jacket was an aphrodisiac she didn't need. Summer was already unbearably aroused. The sting from the earlier punishment had turned into a luscious heat that made her wet and needy. She clung on tighter as Flynn drove through the rainy streets, staying within the speed limit, always watchful, always careful. But the tension in his shoulders and back betrayed him. Flynn was as taut as the string on a bow, ready to fire its arrow, and she had done this to him.

Her ass still burned from the spanking. She could still feel the tingling of her heated flesh. She had gone to the club to explore and Flynn had more than satisfied her curiosity. Her erotic romance novels were nothing like this. None of them had mentioned how the feelings of arousal and humiliation and pain could morph into searing lust. Her encounter with Flynn had shattered an emotional wall inside her, broken a dark taboo, and the evening wasn't over yet.

Sliding her palm beneath his T-shirt, she stroked the planes of his abs. Flynn had a six-pack, maybe even an eight-pack. God, how could she have missed it? He muttered something then that sounded like, 'Oh shit.'

Behind her helmet, Summer giggled. She was really going to do this. She was dizzy with excitement. She was going to make love to a man for the first time since Adam.

Summer waited for the stab of pain that usually accompanied his memory and was surprised to find that it was missing.

Flynn was determined to take every short cut that he knew. For her. He wanted her. They passed the tube station on Baker Street and after a short ride, Flynn pulled up and parked the bike. A discreet brass plate announced that they had reached the Granard Serviced Apartments.

Flynn dismounted. Taking off his helmet, he stowed it in the carrier before turning his attention to her. His warm fingers brushed her neck in a way that she knew was no accident. The memory of his kiss, of his hands and mouth on her skin, made her tingle. What would it be like to be with him?

He carefully removed her helmet and ruffled his fingers through her hair. 'I like this. It's more you, somehow.'

'Thanks. Where are we? I mean, do you live here?' She gestured to the building.

'God no. It's a company place. I use it sometimes when I'm on a job.'

On a job. Something about his words made her spirits plummet. She was a job. She was his employer and she had almost let him take her against a brick wall in a side street. Her heady sense of wonder evaporated.

'Don't,' he said in a warning tone. 'Don't let your mind fuck up what your body wants.'

'And what does my body want?'

'Me,' he said with total confidence. His heavy-lidded expression told her that it wasn't an idle boast. There was no subterfuge with him. Flynn would say what he thought and take what he wanted.

'Did anyone ever tell you that you're an arrogant bastard?'

'I may be arrogant, but I'm usually right.' His mouth quirked into a smile, softening his words.

Summer took a deep breath. She was going to do this. She climbed off the bike and adjusted her trench coat to cover the latex dress. No sense in announcing where she had come from. 'Lead the way,' she said.

He took her hand and they walked up the steps. Flynn punched in the code and they stepped into a marble-floored lobby. It was as luxurious as a boutique hotel. He entered another code to summon the lift.

'It's like Fort Knox,' she whispered.

'Fort Knox is a bit bigger.'

She didn't want to know what he had been doing there. Knowing Flynn, it was something dangerous. The lift door closed and he punched the button for the penthouse. If he didn't touch her soon she would burst into flames. Slowly, she unbuttoned her coat. The latex dress had moved again and it didn't quite cover her breasts.

'Don't,' he groaned, closing her coat again. 'Watch out for the cameras. You've no idea what people get up to in lifts.'

'Trying to protect my reputation?' That would make a nice change. Usually guys couldn't wait to run to the newspapers with an *I snogged Summer* story.

'No, I'm trying to stop you giving the security guard a heart attack. Now, behave.'

'Or what?' She couldn't resist challenging him. An aroused Flynn was something she wanted to see.

The look he gave her was frankly dangerous. 'I can

think of a few things you might like and some things you won't like at all.'

'Such as?'

The bell announcing their arrival on the fifth floor saved him from replying. Grabbing her wrist, Flynn pulled her from the elevator and she stumbled alongside him as he strode for a door at the end of the hall.

Another code. The door swung open. 'Inside.' Flynn's gruff command sent a shiver down her spine.

The apartment was large. She caught a glimpse of neutral walls decorated with original art. A pair of mocha-coloured couches looked inviting. The heat in Flynn's expression was more inviting still.

Grasping the shoulders of her trench coat, he dragged it down her arms and let it drop to the floor. He captured her face between his palms and took a slow tentative taste of her mouth. God, he smelled good, like musk and leather and a faint hint of cologne. Summer traced a path along the seam of his lips with her tongue, pleased when he opened to her.

Her tongue delved into its hot depths, swirling against his. She could kiss him for hours. Maybe later. She had another goal in mind now. Desire coiled like a spring, sending out sharp darts of pleasure. Summer tangled her fingers in his hair and was rewarded with a muffled hiss. Months of loneliness and frustration rose to a steady boil. Flynn was in deep trouble. She only hoped that he was up to handling the accumulated hunger that was threatening to devour her.

His hands cupped her butt, dragging her against his hard length. She rubbed against him in a reprise of their encounter on the street, enjoying the friction. This was better. Much, much better. But she wasn't sure how long she could last. She wanted it hard and fast, but how to ask was beyond her. This was too new, too raw. 'Flynn, I –'

'No talking.'

Dragging her mouth away from his, she moved to explore his neck, savouring the salty taste of sweat on his skin. She nipped hard, drawing out another groan. With eager fingers, she pulled the cotton T-shirt free of his jeans and tugged at the zipper.

Flynn's hand covered hers, squeezing lightly. Summer twisted and wrestled her hand away and Flynn hissed loudly as her arm came into contact with his ribs. Shocked, Summer stopped her attack. 'Are you okay?'

'Fine,' he muttered. 'Just a bit of post-op stuff. Nothing to worry about.'

'Post op? What happened to you? Let me see.' She reached for the hem of his T-shirt and yelped as her wrists were captured in one of his hands. Summer tugged hard, but she couldn't move them. Flynn had a grip of iron.

'I'm in charge.'

Their eyes held and a silent message passed between them. If she wanted him, it would be his way or not at all. She nodded her acceptance.

He bent his head and took her mouth, his kiss turning hot and open mouthed. Flynn's tongue thrust against hers. Like sex, just like sex. She wanted to touch him, to rake his back with her nails, to feel his mouth and hands on her bare skin. 'More,' she pleaded.

He reached into his pocket and produced a Swiss army knife. The latex was no match for the sharpened blade.

With single-minded precision, Flynn sliced through the dress from top to bottom until it fell away, leaving her in nothing but heels and – oh no. She had forgotten about the granny knickers.

His fingers gripped the waistband and he yanked them down. When she was completely bare, the heat in his eyes intensified. His slid one long finger into her aching wetness and pumped slowly, watching her reaction through passion-filled eyes. She squirmed against his hand

'Tell me you want this,' he said hoarsely.

'Yes,' she whispered.

His fingers worked her hard, plunging in and out as her inner muscles sought to clamp them in place. It was too much. She couldn't take any more. 'Oh god,' she cried.

Withdrawing his fingers, he pressed them to his mouth and licked them. The sight of Flynn tasting her almost sent her over the edge.

He pulled his wallet from his jacket and produced a single condom. 'Thank god,' he muttered.

Their fingers clashed as they fumbled at his zipper. She wanted him now. She couldn't wait any longer. Flynn sheathed his cock with the condom and reached for her again. He lifted her, caging her against the wall and his mouth took hers once more. Hot and hungry. Teeth clashed, tongues duelled in a frantic endless kiss.

The crown of his cock nudged against her clit and she moved against him, needing Flynn inside her. With a grunt he thrust deep and she gasped.

He stilled.

'Summer, are you –'

'I'm fine. Don't stop.'

She clung to him as he took her. Each hard thrust, every ragged breath, shattered something deep inside her and freed her from the past. There was nothing but Flynn and her and their overpowering need. Bright arcs of fire streaked through her body. Flynn's insistent pounding never faltered. When the first waves of pleasure hit, she cried out his name.

With a groan, he thrust again and followed her into ecstasy.

Long moments of gasping shudders followed. Summer clung to him like a limpet, weathering the storm. He found her mouth and kissed her gently. She returned his gesture of affection with tenderness. His limp cock slid from her and he eased her slowly to the ground.

She was suddenly shy of him. Flynn had taken her like that, naked against the wall, while he was still almost fully clothed.

He dropped a kiss on her forehead. 'The bedroom's through there. I just need to make a phone call.'

Conscious of his eyes on her, Summer walked slowly to the bedroom wearing nothing but a pair of heels. She closed the door behind her and kicked them off. Oh my god, she had done it. Summer hurried to the en-suite on trembling legs. A wild woman stared back at her from the mirror. She had a serious case of bed-head hair. Her mouth was swollen from his kisses and her neck and breasts were marked from the stubble on his chin.

She could still feel the unfamiliar ache between her thighs. Sex with Adam had never been like that. In fact, she had never had sex like that. Flynn made every lover she had slept with seem like a boy. The way that he had touched her. The rough command in his voice that made her want to obey him without question.

He was so much more masculine than any of the men at the club. Even Robert. How could she have not known? *Stupid stupid Summer.* She had gone to *Noir* looking for a Dom and she'd had one living at her house all along. Summer heard the bedroom door opening and the sound of whistling as Flynn undressed and hung up his clothes.

Clothes. She had no clothes. She would have to walk in there naked and get into bed with him. The memory of his quiet deliberation as he cut the dress from her, made her shiver. Seeing Flynn naked was a treat she was looking forward to, but how was she going to walk out there and be naked with him?

'You've just had sex with the guy,' she told her reflection. 'It's a bit late being nervous now.' She flushed the loo and washed her hands. Summer took a deep breath before opening the door.

Flynn was lying naked in the centre of the bed, the very picture of masculine indolence. His legs were long, the muscles of his calves and thighs well defined. A light dusting of hair trailed down his chest to his groin. His abs were as sharp as the ridges left on a sandy beach when the tide went out. A small, but livid, scar marred the portrait of masculine perfection. Summer found it as sexy as hell. She had an uncontrollable urge to kiss it.

She watched Flynn's nostrils flare as if he was scenting her, but he didn't move, he simply waited for her to come to him. His hooded expression gave her little confidence. She had never felt so naked.

'Do you like what you see?' he asked.

'Yes.' Her voice sounded throaty to her ears.

'Good girl,' he praised her. 'Never lie to me, or I will know and there will be consequences.' There was no anger in his words, just a quiet confidence that she would obey him.

She swallowed, trying to stop herself from replying, 'Yes, Sir.'

'Now, come here.' He patted the bed beside him. 'I want to see you.'

She sat on the edge of the bed and waited nervously. Flynn reached out his hand and cupped her breast. Her nipples peaked into hard points almost immediately.

'Responsive wee thing, aren't you?' Flynn trailed a finger between her breasts and down along her abdomen. 'Open for me.'

She blushed as she parted her thighs. She had never felt so exposed. He traced a slow tortuous finger around her clit and she almost came on the spot. He plunged one finger inside her and she cried out when he touched one deliciously sensitive spot and then trembled when he withdrew it.

He held her gaze as he licked it clean. 'Mmmmm, hot and sweet and so very wet. Now, lie down, Summer. I'm going to take care of you.'

She lay down.

'Put your arms over your head and grip the headboard. You are not to move your hands or I will stop immediately. Is that clear?'

She nodded, and gripped the headboard. He placed a pillow beneath her hips and Summer closed her eyes. What had she let herself in for?

'Ah ah, no. Eyes open. I want you to watch.'

The heat in his gaze made her shiver, but not as much as the feel of his touch. He pumped his finger slowly inside her; the exquisite torture made her bite down on her lip. She clenched her inner muscles seeking more pressure and received a sharp tap on her thigh.

'Naughty,' he said. 'Not yet.'

He added a second finger and then gently made a *'come here'* movement, curling his fingers inside her.

'Oh god,' she cried out. 'That's . . . that's . . .'

'Your G-spot,' he said with a smug expression on his face. 'Like it?'

'Oh. Oh.' A warm feeling built inside her as he continued his sensual massage. Flynn pressed down lightly on her lower stomach and the sensation of pressure seemed to increase. His fingers moved faster, ramping up the intensity. Her breath came in short, panting gasps and she gripped the headboard tighter as the first wave of a massive orgasm shot through her. This wasn't like before; it went on and on, so intense that she felt that she was going to pass out. She couldn't control her wails. They could probably hear her in the next apartment.

As the wave ebbed away, Flynn turned his attention to her clit, rubbing the already tender nub until she was begging him to stop. 'Don't. Please. I'm too sensitive.'

Flynn ignored her. With impossible speed another orgasm built into a sensory overload that she couldn't control. Mindless with pleasure, she screamed out his name as her body wracked with the aftershocks of pleasure. There wasn't an inch of her that didn't tremble. Still, she clung to the headboard. The indentations of her nails would leave a permanent scar there.

'You're the one who wanted an erotic adventure tonight. What's the matter? Is it too much for you?' Flynn asked with the barest hint of sympathy. He was enjoying this far too much.

'Bastard,' she gasped out. Flynn was going to torture her all night. Death by orgasm. 'I hope you have a hard-on for a week.'

'I suggest that you think about the consequences of that remark. I can always guard you in bed.' The devilish glint in his eyes suggested he was only half joking. After a month in bed with Flynn she wouldn't be able to walk. She would be a helpless sex-crazed zombie.

'I think one more, before I let you sleep.'

'No.' She clenched her thighs together. Her poor tortured flesh couldn't take any more pleasure.

'Open.' The slap of his hand against her thigh made her jump.

Flynn would brook no disobedience. She parted her legs and he settled between them. The first lick made her arch off the bed. Summer clenched her eyes shut and writhed against him, but he held her thighs apart while he took his time, tasting her with long slow licks while she begged him to stop. His mouth fastened over her sensitized flesh and she cried out when he took the tender bud between his teeth and bit lightly.

Starlight exploded behind her eyelids and she came again, helpless against the pulses of sensation that surged through her. She couldn't control the throaty screams of pleasure that came from her mouth. Even the sensation of his breath against her skin was too much. It was long minutes before the last shudder stopped.

'Poor baby,' Flynn murmured.

She felt his kiss on her forehead and the sensation of a cool sheet being draped over her skin. She couldn't have moved, even if the building went on fire.

Summer woke during the night and watched the rise and fall of Flynn's chest. This wasn't like a fantasy from one of her erotic novels – where the heroine went home after a fantastic sex-filled night at a club. Flynn was beautiful and it would be so easy to fall for him.

Her body still burned from his touch. She had never had so many orgasms in one night. If she let this continue, she would be his slave by the end of the month. His sex slave. Flynn wouldn't be content to let this be a romantic fling, he would dominate the hell out of her and then he would be gone. She couldn't do this. She couldn't risk her heart again. Tomorrow morning, she would have to pretend that this night meant nothing to her.

The old Summer was coming back and Flynn Grant better watch out.

10

Flynn woke up, fully alert as always. After more than ten years in the Rangers, he knew he would never master the art of the slow start. But the warm body cuddled at his side was a great incentive to stay in bed.

He smiled. He had no idea that Summer O'Sullivan was such a cracker. She had a fire that she somehow managed to keep well hidden, but now that he knew about it, he'd make sure she made the most of it.

Morning sunlight filtered in through the louvred shutters, illuminating Summer's skin with light and shadow. The straight lines of the shadows against the roundness of her hips and waist was an erotic contrast. Her newly-brown hair gleamed, even as it hid most of her face. He allowed his fingers to comb through the soft strands, enjoying the feel of it curling with a life of its own.

His morning hard-on twitched, eager for a replay of the night before, but he remembered ruefully that he had used his last condom. Ah well, there were other ways to deal with that particular problem. He stroked Summer's back, marvelling at the smoothness of her skin. She really was amazing.

Summer moaned in protest at being woken, even as she arched into his touch like a cat. Sensual little creature. Flynn grinned. He was looking forward to exploring every inch of her curvy wee body again.

Who'd have guessed she was a snuggler? He usually didn't like clingy women, but in this case, he reckoned he could make good use of it. If she wanted to cuddle up to him, he was all for it. It would make his job so much easier if she wanted to stay with him instead of constantly trying to run away. And the fringe benefits would be stunning. Despite himself, he stroked her skin, his fingers caressing the side of her breast.

'Go 'way. It's not morning yet,' she muttered, even as she cuddled in closer, burying her face against his neck. He shuddered as the tip of her tongue flicked out, tasting the skin of his collarbone. God, she would kill him.

'You're salty,' she complained, then opened her eyes.

Seeing her expression of sleepy satisfaction turn to horror would have been entertaining in other circumstances, but not when it was directed at him.

'You!'

'Me,' he agreed. 'Who were you expecting? Or do you not keep track?'

She dragged the sheet from around her waist and hauled it up to her neck. 'I didn't . . . We didn't –' She floundered to a stop.

'Oh yes, we did. I did and you did. Both of us did.' Flynn couldn't conceal a sardonic smile at her horrified reaction. 'You were begging me to keep doing it. To strip you naked and –'

'Stop! I didn't mean –' She took a breath and composed herself. 'If you were a gentleman, you wouldn't mention it.'

'Would a gentleman mention that he could see your gorgeous arse in all its glory?' he asked.

She whirled, eyes rounding as she noticed that the ornate mirror on the wall reflected her entire back view to Flynn's observant eyes.

'You, you, you –' Lost for words, she wrapped the entire sheet around herself and stalked off to the bathroom. Moments later, Flynn heard the sound of a bath running.

By the time she emerged, wrapped in a fluffy bathrobe, Flynn had showered in the small guest bathroom, dressed, had his breakfast and was on his third cup of coffee. He poured her one and passed it over to her. 'Would you like eggs or yoghurt for breakfast? We need to eat and be on the road soon.'

Summer glared at him. 'I am not going anywhere.'

He had been about to take another mouthful of coffee but stopped. 'Oh, you like it here?'

'I have nothing to wear.' She waved a hand over her white bathrobe. 'It's this or my trench coat.'

He grinned. 'I'm easy with whatever you choose.' The thought of the body under that robe brought his cock to full attention. Fortunately the table hid it, so he could continue to pretend to be a gentleman.

She looked at him with loathing. 'I'm not leaving this apartment until I have proper clothes.'

He grimaced, but could see her point. A ride on his motorbike would be a bit draughty wearing only a trench coat. 'Fair enough. What size are you? I'll go out and buy you a pair of jeans and a T-shirt.' After all, he had been the one who cut off her latex number.

'Are you mad?' She glowered at him. 'I'm not letting you pick out anything for me. God knows what you'd come back with. Probably something slutty with a collar and leash.'

'Something slutty with a collar and leash looked damn good on you,' he said, but didn't object when she pulled out her phone and rang Harrods.

An hour later, he wasn't smiling. The apartment was awash with clothes. Summer and a tall stylish woman were arguing about cut and colour. Flynn fumed silently. What sort of woman had her own personal shopper in Harrods? And seemed unable to get dressed without trying on six different versions of everything first.

'These ones bind at the crotch,' Summer insisted, holding up a pair of ridiculously expensive jeans. 'I'll be raw by the time I get off the bike.'

Flynn couldn't understand what was wrong with a pair of Levi's.

'But they are so gorgeous on you. They do amazing things to your bum,' the other woman said as she stood back to admire yet another pair.

'Her bum is amazing naked. Now buy a pair and we'll go.' Both women glared at him, though there was a trace of colour in Summer's cheeks. Then they turned their backs and went back to the fascinating subject of fabric, cut and stitching.

For fuck's sake, how could an intelligent woman like Summer waste her brains on this kind of stuff? He didn't blame the woman from Harrods, she was only doing her job, but they were acting as if they didn't have a brain cell between them.

Ten minutes later, he ran out of patience. 'Okay, Princess. It's time to go.'

'Did I just hear you call me Princess?' Summer's voice dripped ice.

'You did. Or to give you the full title, Princess Precious Poodle.' She gasped, and he went on. 'This is ridiculous. Pick a pair of jeans and a top and we're going. Or you can go naked on the back of the bike. See if I care.'

'Naked?' She looked around, as if she was seriously searching for something to throw at him. Then, remembering the personal shopper, she contented herself with a glare that could strip paint off a wall. 'I need a word with you, alone.'

Hugging the bathrobe around her, she marched to the bedroom and closed the door behind them. 'May I remind you that this is all your fault? You interfered so that I had to sneak out without a change of clothes. You turned up at the club and spoilt my fun. You put a bloody collar on me.'

She was working herself up into a fine rage now. 'You made me sit at your feet, almost screwed me in the street, and then cut my dress off. And then you fell asleep, you big Scottish . . .'

'Half Scottish,' he said mildly, and was rewarded by the sight of Summer practically frothing at the mouth. 'And let's not forget the part played by your charming friends.'

'Oh! You . . . !' She was practically incoherent. 'And for what? I don't need you, and I don't need a bodyguard.' She spaced out the last few words and prodded him in the chest to get her point across. He appreciated the view of her flashing eyes, and the glimpse down her robe that showed her enticing cleavage before she left the room, slamming the door behind her.

If she wasn't such a bad-tempered shrew, Summer O'Sullivan would be a very tempting package.

By the time they were heading back to Hampstead, it was almost noon, and Summer was finally dressed. She was also so pissed at him that she refused to speak, and tried to hold herself upright on the back of the bike to avoid touching him. Flynn found he missed the contact.

The house was strangely silent. Natasha and Maya came running as soon as they pulled up outside the front door, with Mike and Gavin following after.

'Thank god you're safe,' Maya sobbed. 'I was so sure you were dead.'

Flynn was instantly alert. He picked out the most controlled person in the crowd and addressed him. 'Malcolm, what's wrong?'

Even the butler appeared rattled. He was his usual stately self, but his voice shook slightly as he said, 'We found something in Miss O'Sullivan's room this morning. I wanted to call the police but knowing Mr O'Sullivan's aversion to publicity, I thought I would ask you first.'

He led them upstairs to Summer's room. It looked almost the same as when she had left it, with clothes tossed on the floor, the curtains drawn and a life-like blonde figure in the bed. The difference was that the body in the bed now had a knife in it. The knife, a Sabatier if Flynn was any judge, was sticking into where, had it been a real person, the heart would have been.

Summer moaned in distress. Flynn turned to her. She had turned white, but as he watched, the shutters went down, shielding her emotions. Just how much was she hiding? Malcolm cleared his throat.

'There's more, sir.' He led them into Summer's bathroom. Scrawled across the mirror in bright red lipstick were the words, 'DIE BITCH!'

'Bugger. That was my last tube of Vamp.'

'How can you think about lipstick at a time like this?' Maya wailed. 'Someone tried to kill you.'

'Nonsense. It's just a silly joke,' Summer said, but Flynn noticed her hands were shaking slightly as she picked up the now empty tube. 'I'm just annoyed they used it all up.'

'You're vamp enough without the lipstick,' he told her brusquely. The last thing they needed was Summer having hysterics. He turned to the butler. 'I'll check the security system. Don't worry, I'll soon find out who did this.'

Twenty minutes later, he cursed, using a string of foul words in creative combinations. So much for his hope that it was a practical joke by one of the houseguests. Whoever had done it had not only managed to sneak in undetected, they had also disabled the entire security system for over twenty minutes. He had to acquit the guests – they were all playing Wii in the lounge when the system went down, and were still there, with a much higher score, when it went back online. Besides, they had all hooked up. Neither of the guys had a reason to be mad at Summer, and he'd bet money that this was a man's work.

He would question all the servants, but he knew what he'd find. A big fat nothing.

Before he started, he put his head back into Summer's room. 'Start packing. I'm taking you to a safe house.'

11

A safe house? Flynn had to be kidding. They had a state-of-the-art security system. Her dad still winced when he remembered the cost of it, and Flynn had upgraded it when he arrived. And she had a bodyguard. Just how much more security did she need? 'I'm not going anywhere.'

His mouth formed a hard line. She could tell that he was going to be stubborn about this. She couldn't live her life like some kind of prisoner. Just because she'd slept with Flynn didn't mean that he was in charge.

'Fine.' He reached into his pocket, pulled out his phone and scrolled through the display. 'You can tell your father what happened while I make transport arrangements for Castletownberehaven.'

Bloody stubborn Scot. He wasn't going to ship her off to her grandmother's. She would rather chew her own toenails than go back there. Summer ignored the phone he was holding out. If she rang her dad now he would be worried. It was the last thing he needed when he was in the middle of negotiations with the Americans.

Maya put her hand on her arm. 'Maybe you should go, Summer. Mike and Gavin are packing. They need to get back for training tomorrow, and I'd hate to think of you here on your own.'

She had a choice of being stuck here with Flynn and a psycho or stuck somewhere else with Flynn. Neither prospect appealed to her. She didn't want to think about last night, or how he had made her feel. If she was honest, the sex had been pretty amazing. It had far surpassed any fantasy she had ever had. But in the bedroom, when he had tortured her with pleasure, she had seen another side of Flynn.

He would use her own needs to control her. She had a sneaking suspicion that Flynn would demand more from her than just obedience in the bedroom. Unlike some of her friends, she had never been able to separate the physical from the emotional in relationships. One always followed the other, as surely as night followed day. Look at the awful mess with Adam. There was something wrong with her that she couldn't do casual. When she fell in love, she fell hard and she wanted everything.

Yes, she would have to be careful with Flynn. She was never getting emotionally involved again. Not in a million years.

She sighed. 'Okay then. Where are we going and for how long?'

'I'm afraid I can't tell you that.'

'But what am I to tell my friends?'

'For your own safety, as little as possible. Now, throw some things in a bag. The sooner we get on the road, the better.'

It was like dealing with a brick wall. 'Fine,' she snapped. 'As you won't tell me where we're going or for how long, I'll leave you to do the packing.'

Maya's giggle was silenced by a stern glance from Flynn. Ignoring him, Summer strode past him and down the corridor. Let's see how Mr I'm-in-charge coped with that one.

'You are so bad, Summer.' Maya was still giggling. 'You're just going to let him riffle through your lingerie?'

'Why not? It's not as if he hasn't . . .' The words were out of her mouth before she realized what she had said.

Maya grabbed her arm. 'OMG! You haven't? Tell me you haven't bonked the bodyguard?'

'Who's bonking the bodyguard?' Natasha emerged from the bedroom carrying her bag.

'Will you both shut up?' Summer hissed. She was going to kill Molly. She had warned her not to tell Robert about Flynn, but her friend had obviously taken it literally and told everyone else.

'It was a one-time thing and it's not happening again.'

Natasha ignored her. 'I bet he was hot. That accent, mmmm. And I bet he's ex-military. Those guys are really buff and –'

Summer put her hands up to her ears. 'Not listening.'

Maya nudged Natasha. 'Summer's back on form. Everyone stand back.'

She left them laughing like a pair of demented hyenas while she went to phone Molly.

The number rang and rang. She was just about to give up when a sleepy voice answered the phone. 'Hello.'

'Molls?'

'Um. Summer? What happened to you last night?'

'What happened to me? You left me in that bloody club alone and now Flynn's found out.'

'Oh shit. Peter said he'd take care of you. You're mad at me, aren't you?' Molly's voice trailed away miserably.

Summer closed her eyes. If Molly had been within two feet of her, she would have slapped her. How could she have done that and then act as if nothing had happened? 'If you're referring to the fact that you left me with that cretin in a tricorne and no way of getting home, yes, I am mad at you.'

Silence stretched between them. 'Sorry about that,' Molly eventually replied. 'Some of Robert's business people turned up. They were –'

The phone line suddenly went dead. Summer hit the redial button, but the number was engaged. What was up with Molly?

The lounge door opened. 'Are you ready? We've a long ride ahead of us.'

Summer put her phone into her pocket so she could ring Molly later. She followed Flynn outside. The Aussies were already in their truck. Gavin waved and they sped off with a scatter of gravel. Maya hugged her and Natasha smirked at Flynn and winked at her before they followed the Aussies, honking the horn as they drove away.

The party was definitely over. Summer eyed the battered rucksack at Flynn's feet. She hadn't used it since she had Inter-railed across Europe. How had he unearthed it? 'Which car are we taking?'

Flynn gave a disapproving snort. 'None of those flashy cars are suitable,' he replied. 'They'll attract too much attention. We'll take the bike. Niall will meet us with transport.'

Transport. What did he mean, 'transport'? She glanced at the small carrier on the back of the bike. Flynn's bag was already stowed. 'But what about the rest of my luggage?'

Another snort, this time accompanied by a twitch of

his mouth. Flynn picked up her rucksack and tossed it on top of his. 'This is your luggage.'

Two hours later she was ready to kill him and she had a pain in her butt from sitting on the bike. Flynn had finally pulled in at a service station because she insisted that she had to pee. He hadn't allowed her to remove the rucksack from the carrier. Phone at his ear, he had paced the forecourt like a caged beast until she returned from the grubby ladies room. She'd hate to be on the other end of that particular conversation.

Who did he think he was? She wasn't a soldier to be bossed around like this. Given the amount of luggage he had brought, they couldn't be going far or staying long. The rucksack would barely hold her make-up and hair care products.

'Are you hungry?'

'Well, I suppose I could manage lunch.'

'That's what I thought.' He pulled two cereal bars from his pocket and handed one to her. He munched his cheerfully while she stared at the wrapper, which promised lots of oaty goodness. He was trying to starve her. She hadn't eaten dinner the previous night when she was pretending to be ill and all she'd had for breakfast was yoghurt.

Flynn was doing this deliberately. Why on earth had she agreed to go with him? She could have been at home having a nice meal prepared by her chef. Instead she was parked on the side of the A1 with a truculent Scot.

Summer bit into the cereal bar and tried not to gag. She wouldn't feed this to a horse. There wasn't even any chocolate on it. She managed another mouthful and shoved the rest into her pocket. The sooner they got to their destination, the sooner she could have a bath and a decent meal.

'Ready?' Flynn asked before pulling on his helmet.

'I can't wait.'

After two more hours, she knew she was going to have bruises, but Flynn rode on, ignoring her taps on his shoulder that she needed another loo break. Just when she was ready to throw herself off the bike, he took a turn off the motorway and followed the sign for York.

She almost cried when she saw the spire of York Minster in the distance. They had been on the road for hours, surely they were stopping here. Flynn pulled into a car park outside the medieval city walls and switched off the engine. Summer wasn't sure if she could get off the bike. Her thighs were sore from holding on and she had long ago given up her attempts to avoid touching Flynn. For the last hour she had clung to him shamelessly.

Flynn pulled off his helmet and stretched his arms above his head and yawned before turning his attention to her. 'Good girl,' he said to her. 'You did well. I'll have something better for the rest of the journey.'

That made her want to cry and she couldn't understand the churning feeling she got from his approval. Her stomach growled. She was hungry. It was nothing more than that.

The sound of a horn drew Flynn's attention from her. Summer watched as three battered Jeeps entered the car park. They were identical, down to the mud flaps. It couldn't be a coincidence. The Jeeps were old, probably ex-army issue, and Flynn's eyes lit up when he saw them.

Flynn had never been so glad to see anyone. Although he hadn't said anything to Summer, he was sure that they had been followed on the way to York. A dark blue van had appeared at regular intervals on their journey, staying just far enough behind to avoid attracting attention from anyone. Unless they were dealing with a Ranger.

It could be a coincidence. Flynn didn't believe in coincidence.

'Niall,' he called. 'How's it hanging?'

His boss's attention was already diverted by his pillion passenger. With a grace at odds with his large frame, he lifted Summer off the bike as if she weighed no more than a kitten. A spike of what might be jealousy prodded low in Flynn's abdomen. Niall had turned on the charm and Summer was smiling at him as if he was Santa with a bag full of goodies. Summer fled to the restrooms.

Niall whistled under his breath. 'You, her and a month in the country? Why did I farm out this assignment?'

'Because you're an idiot.' Flynn gave him a smug smile. Although he never settled with the same woman for long, Niall was something of a connoisseur when it came to the ladies and he was glad that his friend wasn't looking after Summer.

'Sorry we had to pull you out like that, Miss O'Sullivan,' Niall said as soon as Summer got back, 'but I have strict orders from your father. Still, you're in good hands with Flynn.'

If only he knew. Niall would kill him if he suspected that he had laid a hand on a principal. Flynn struggled to keep a straight face as Summer blushed.

Niall shot a quick glance in his direction but didn't say a word. He waved to the drivers of the other Jeeps. Within minutes, the men had stowed Flynn's bike in the back of one of the Jeeps. It might help to keep the tracker off their scent until they could get Summer to the safe house. Niall escorted Summer to the passenger side and handed her the rucksack.

'A word, if you please, Flynn'.

Damn. Niall didn't miss a thing. He followed him to the rear of the Jeep.

'What the fuck do you think you're doing? Christ, man, I could put you guarding a beauty pageant and you wouldn't look twice at any of them. Why do you think I gave you this gig?'

'It isn't like that, Summer and I –'

'If this gets out, you won't get work as a lollypop lady.' Niall poked him in the chest and Flynn tried not to wince when his finger strayed too near his healing scar.

'Your job is to protect her, but you keep your hands off her. Do I make myself clear? You may not fuck the principal.'

Niall was right. What had happened between them was a mistake. How could he protect Summer if they were emotionally involved? It was number one on the list of bodyguard sins. Flynn was tempted to salute but contented himself in responding, 'Aye, sir.'

'Now move out. Andy will take point, you follow. If our friend shows up, we'll drop back and box him in.'

Flynn nodded.

'And here.' Niall withdrew an envelope from his pocket. 'You're booked into Dalhousie Castle for tonight. That should keep her ladyship happy.'

'Great.' Flynn climbed into the Jeep and ignored Summer's quizzical look.

'What was that about?' she asked.

'Nothing,' he responded. 'Just a security briefing.' He followed Andy's Jeep out of the car park and back to the motorway.

The next two hours were uneventful. Either they had lost their tracker, or he was being over-cautious. Oblivious, Summer dozed. He smiled to himself as he listened to her make soft snuffling sounds in her sleep, much as she had done when she had slept wrapped around him.

The memory of it warmed him. Her skin was so soft and she had lain in his arms as if she belonged there. Even now the thought of her like that distracted him more than he would care to admit. This is a job. Nothing more. *Focus.*

He focused for less than five minutes before his mind drifted back to the night before. The image of Summer stark naked against the apartment wall while he fucked her senseless woke a part of his body he wished had remained asleep. Flynn groaned. What was wrong with him?

He had guarded beautiful women before and never had this reaction to any of them. They were simply a job, a task, a puzzle, no matter how sexually attractive they were. Anyway, Summer wasn't his type. He liked bright, intelligent women, not needy little daddy's girls who never had to work a day in their lives. Summer was his worst nightmare. He wouldn't have a relationship with her in a million years, even if he wasn't guarding her.

She moaned softly in her sleep. Flynn took his eyes off the road for a second to check that she was okay. Her luscious mouth was partly open. The gloss on her lips made them appear soft and inviting. He wondered what that mouth would feel like wrapped around his shaft.

Would it be hot? Eager to taste him? Would those blue eyes darken with passion as they had done in the apartment, sending a spark of lust straight to his groin? *Stop it, Flynn. You are not doing this.*

His erect cock ignored the message from his brain and he shifted in his seat, trying to ease the pressure. It was a long way to Edinburgh and the first thing he needed when he got there was a long, cold shower.

I 2

'Wake up, Summer. We're here.' The setting sun glinted off the pale pink sandstone of a Scottish castle. Around them were acres of woodland. In the distance she could see a winding river. She almost cried with relief. Civilization. There would be real food and a bath.

She gave Flynn a quick hug. 'It's perfect. I love you. Thank you.'

She was surprised when his cheeks darkened in what was almost a blush. Clambering out of the Jeep, she hurried around the back to grab her luggage. He probably hadn't packed anything that she could wear to a restaurant. Never mind. She could eat in her room if necessary. She almost ran to the doors of the castle. Flynn followed behind.

The dark, wood-panelled reception was empty of guests. In the distance she could hear the sound of bagpipes. Well, she couldn't hope for complete perfection. 'Good evening, sir, madam. You must be Mr and Mrs Smith,' the receptionist said.

Smith? Summer raised an eyebrow. Could he not think of anything more inventive than that?

'That's correct.' Flynn replied evenly as he scrawled some fictitious details in the register.

'I'll have Tommy help you with your luggage. The restaurant's closed tonight for a wedding, but I can have dinner served in your room.'

'That's fine,' Flynn said.

Tommy was a short, grizzled-faced man who must have been pushing seventy. He picked up the rucksacks with the same care and attention he would have used for a matching pair of Louis Vuittons and headed for the stairs. 'You'll be in the Walter Scott suite. Follow me.'

On the first floor landing, a door opened and Summer heard the sound of music and laughter.

'Ian McDonald and Flora Campbell. Her third and his second wedding.' Tommy shook his head. 'Still, we can't complain if it keeps us busy. You're on honeymoon yourselves?'

'Yes,' Flynn agreed, ignoring her outraged glare.

'I can always tell a honeymoon couple, and it's not because of the room they book.' Tommy laughed at his own joke.

'This part of the castle is yours.' He opened a door and they followed him along a pale-carpeted corridor. At the end of the hallway, they climbed three steps and opened another door.

Summer looked around her and took back every single bad thought she had about Flynn all day. They were in the castle tower. The circular room held an enormous four-poster bed with red woollen curtains around it and rose petals scattered on the green silk cover. A fire blazed in the hearth. Beside the narrow stained glass window, a small table was set with fine silver and crystal and a bottle of champagne sat in a bucket of ice.

'Ring reception when you want to order dinner and if there's anything else I can do for you, just give me a shout. I wish you and your lady a good night.'

Summer could hear whistling as he made his way down the corridor and then the sound of the outer door closing. She threw herself onto the bed and grabbed a handful of rose petals. 'Oh, thank god. I was afraid you were going to bring me to some seedy little flat.'

Flynn pulled his shaving kit from his rucksack. 'I didn't book this place. Niall did. Now, if you'll excuse me, I need a shower.'

What was up with him? She clambered off the bed. The ice bucket beckoned. It was time for a drink.

As she passed the fireplace, she spotted Flynn's phone on the mantelpiece. She wondered who he had been so angry with earlier. She glanced at the room door. Flynn was still in the shower. It wouldn't hurt to take a quick peek.

'Messages.' She flicked her thumb across the screen. There were lots from someone called David. *Lorna doesn't love you anymore. Stop doing this.*

'Oh.' Summer closed her eyes. She remembered being on the receiving end of a similar text. Flynn was in love with someone who didn't love him. No wonder he was so bad-tempered.

She hadn't allowed herself to think about the previous night. She had been the one who had initiated everything and look how that had turned out. And she had slept with him. There was something about sleeping with a man that was much more intimate than sex. And tonight she was going to do it again. Mr and Mrs Smith on their wedding night in a romantic Scottish castle.

Summer almost laughed at the irony of it. Tonight would be her second honeymoon without a husband.

Once in Vietnam and once here. She was never getting involved again and Flynn obviously loved someone else. Maybe they could just be there for each other. It didn't have to mean anything more than that.

She opened Flynn's bag. At least he had remembered to bring the condoms. Her mind made up, Summer peeled off her clothes. Mr Smith was in for a surprise. Hurrying down the corridor, she tapped on the bathroom door. 'Room Service,' she announced.

There was no reply, just the sound of running water. Opening the door, she stepped into a cloud of steam. Summer could just about make out the large roll-top bath beneath the window and an enormous glass shower unit. Through the mist she saw his lean form. There was no doubt about it. Flynn was a hottie.

One of his hands was braced against the tiled wall, while the other moved rhythmically. Summer froze to the spot, not knowing whether to slip away or open the glass door. The muscles of Flynn's shoulders rippled beneath his skin. Above the sound of the rushing water, she heard his ragged breathing. With a sick fascination, she continued to watch him masturbate himself towards a climax. He threw his head back and groaned.

It was one of the most erotic things she had ever seen. Despite the warmth of the room, her nipples hardened into peaks. Remembering Flynn's controlled passion of the night before, heat bloomed low in her belly, as his hand still pumped his shaft. Sensing her presence, he turned swiftly. Shock mingled with a flush of embarrassment on his face. They stared at each other for a long moment while water continued to pound down on his back. Rivulets ran down his handsome face. Finally, he spoke. 'Get out of here, before I . . .'

'Before you what?' her words came out in a husky whisper.

Shame and hunger fought a battle in his eyes. He turned off the water and opened the shower door. He grabbed a fluffy white towel from the rail and wrapped it around his hips before handing her a bathrobe. Flynn drew an unsteady breath. 'Go back to the room, there's a good girl.'

Good girl. Her temper bristled. What did he think she was? Some kind of pet?

Before he could say anything more, Summer turned on her heel and slammed the bathroom door behind her. She prayed for a sudden ice age in the bathroom and enjoyed the thought of him freezing his balls off. Served him right. Mr Flynn bloody Grant could go to hell in a basket. Tomorrow she would ring her father and request another bodyguard. She couldn't stay with Flynn.

A knock came on the outer door. 'Room Service,' a female Scottish voice called from outside.

Summer prayed that it was food. Pulling the robe tighter around her breasts she opened the door.

The red-haired bride's mouth dropped open when she saw Summer. 'Who the fuck are you? And what have you done with my Ian?'

Flynn leaned against the tiled wall of the bathroom, panting. That had been the most intense orgasm he had experienced in . . . he couldn't remember. A long, long time. Perhaps ever. It was all due to Summer. And he hadn't even touched her.

He had been thinking about her as he showered and the memory of her in that excuse of a latex dress and writhing on the bed as he brought her to orgasm had made him so hard that he had to take the matter in hand. He had been imagining that his soapy fist was her luscious mouth wrapped around his cock when he looked up and saw her standing there.

For a moment, he had stopped, as startled that she had managed to slip into the bathroom as by what she had caught him doing. Then the curiosity on her face had urged him to continue. For long minutes, he had stroked himself under her shocked and fascinated eyes, deliberately showing himself off for her.

His reward had been her half-parted lips and her small, pink tongue nervously licking the top one in a way that hardened him even more. Her breath had sped up. He wanted to believe that the flush on her cheeks was not solely due to the heat of the bathroom, and the dampness on her neck was not because of the steam from his shower.

Her gaze had been riveted to his cock at first, but then had risen to meet his, and he had been trapped by the endless blue of her eyes. The dilated pupils had been more arousing than her hand would have been.

He had wanted to draw the moment out as long as possible but Summer's response to him had tightened his balls and pushed him towards his climax. He had held her gaze while his body jerked in the most intense orgasm he could remember.

Flynn forced his trembling legs to work, but before he

could open his shaving kit, the sound of raised voices brought him charging out of the bathroom.

His principal was fighting with a red-haired woman in a wedding dress. The bride was screaming, 'You whore, where is he?' and trying to pull Summer's hair. There was a slur of alcohol in her voice.

Summer was using both hands to prise her grip from her hair. This left her bathrobe gaping open in a way which was guaranteed to enflame the angry bride still further, but probably in a different way from how it affected Flynn.

'Let go, you bitch,' she panted.

Flynn was tempted to enjoy the view, but he was her bodyguard, and right now, her body needed guarding. He grabbed the bride's wrist, pressing down on a pressure point which caused her to gasp with pain and release her grip on Summer's hair.

Flynn put himself between the two women, facing the enraged bride, and demanded, 'Who are you and what are you doing?'

She took a breath which caused her breasts to swell above the bodice of her tight dress. The sight didn't do a thing for Flynn. 'I'm Flora Campbell. No, I'm Mrs Flora McDonald, and I want to know what this tart is doing in my bridal suite.'

'Tart?' Summer's outrage was genuine. 'Tart? Miss My-boobs-are-too-big-for-my-dress is calling ME a tart?'

Flynn stifled a grin and concentrated on keeping the outraged bride away from his principal.

But Flora Campbell McDonald had shifted her attention. She took in Flynn in all his towel-clad glory and smacked her lips in appreciation. 'My, my, what have we here?' She reached out to touch his chest, but before she could make contact, her hand was knocked away.

'That's my husband you're groping, you ginger bitch,' Summer announced.

Flora clenched her fist, all set to start the catfight again, when a stout and anxious man knocked on the open door. 'Flora? Sweetheart? I've been looking for you.'

Flora swung around, managing to stay upright more by luck than judgement. 'Ian, they're in our room.'

Ian put a steadying arm around his bride. 'No, Flora, this is their room. Our room is on the next floor.'

'Are you sure?' Ian nodded. She took a breath which strained the bodice of her wedding dress dangerously. 'She said they were married,' Flora added in a tone of accusation.

Summer slid an arm around Flynn's naked back and leaned in against him. 'Yes, we're on our honeymoon.' Even through the bathrobe, he could feel her curves pressed up against him.

'You and him?' Flora was like a dog with a bone. 'Married?'

'Oh yes.' Summer trailed her other hand down his chest, from his collarbone to his abs. That tantalizing hand rested on the edge of his towel. 'We're working on his little problem.'

'Problem?' Both Ian and Flora were fascinated.

'Yes, his LITTLE problem. It's so small we don't know what to do with it, but I'm sure we can come up with something creative.' Flynn fought to keep his face impassive, but could feel the tips of his ears turning red. The little minx. She so badly needed to be put over his knee and spanked again.

Flora's eyes had rounded and Ian had turned bright red. The colour clashed horribly with his freckles and sandy hair. 'Yes, well, none of our business, eh Flora?'

She ignored him, her gaze locked onto Flynn's groin. Thanks to his recent activity in the shower, it didn't respond to her visual stroking, and Flora gave Summer a sympathetic look. 'You poor dear. I apologize for earlier. I had no idea . . .' Her voice trailed away.

'Why don't you two join us for the reception? It will take your mind off things,' Ian said.

Flynn opened his mouth to refuse, but Summer beat him to it. 'We'd love to, wouldn't we, dearest? All those gorgeous Scottish women might even help you get over your LITTLE problem.'

He wasn't sure exactly how it happened, but thirty minutes later he and Summer were in the middle of a rowdy Scottish wedding reception, and she was having the time of her life.

After the meal, the evening was a bodyguard's nightmare. Surrounded by strangers, no back-up and no way to check out the possible threat to his principal. His instincts said that this was not a dangerous situation, but his training wouldn't allow him to relax. The best he could do was keep as close to her as possible, literally guarding her with his body.

Summer was the life and soul of the party. The girl he had glimpsed in the bathroom, the one who had looked at him with hungry eyes, was gone. In her place was a party animal. Within half an hour of entering the reception, Summer was best friends with everyone in the place. She had made friends with the DJ and the barman, and they kept her supplied with a steady stream of her favourite drinks and music.

When she climbed on the table and started dancing, Flynn dragged her down, but she pouted and announced to the fascinated guests, 'He's just grumpy because he's got a teeny weeny.'

He gritted his teeth and pulled her hard against him for a slow dance. 'Feel that? Teeny enough for you?' His cock hardened in a rush at the contact and the smell of her shampoo.

She rubbed against him tauntingly. 'I don't know. Room for improvement, I think, don't you?' Then she left him while she danced with the bridegroom.

Ian beamed a fatuous smile, his face flushing an unattractive shade as Summer danced close against him. How could she, the little tramp? She had managed to fool him for a few minutes into thinking Summer O'Sullivan wasn't the most photographed bimbo that ever came out of Cork. But now she was reminding him.

Flynn stayed close to her for the rest of the night, but though he was able to prevent her dancing again with the bridegroom – hey, he didn't want Flora Campbell McDonald to commit murder with the cake knife she was holding – he couldn't stop Summer eating the fruit sculpture in the middle of the table, the only thing left of the wedding breakfast, or flirting with all of the groomsmen.

While he was distracted by a question from one of the bridesmaids, a hefty girl who did not suit pink satin, Summer had climbed onto the table again and called for limbo music.

That was the end for Flynn. He grabbed her by her hips, now conveniently located just above his head height, and threw her over his shoulder. 'Good night, everyone, I'm taking my darling wife to bed,' he called as he marched out of the great hall. There were boos from the men and cheers from the women.

Summer kicked and cursed and called him names he hadn't heard since he was in the Wing. But he refused to pay any attention, and by the time he got to their room, she had quietened down.

In fact, she had passed out.

With a grimace, Flynn slipped off her shoes, unzipped her dress and admired her barely-there underwear.

He managed not to gawk like a teenage boy in a strip club as he pulled the sheets over her and made sure she wouldn't fall out. A small drunken snore was his reward.

He grinned. Then he picked up his phone. 'Hey Niall? Change of plans. I'm bringing little Miss Spoilt Rotten to the old croft instead. Can you make sure we get some food occasionally? Thanks man.'

13

'Summer.' A rough hand shook her awake.

Her head was pounding like a bass drum. Was there a fire? Why was he shouting at her? She pushed his hand away.

'You have two minutes to get out of bed or . . .' Flynn sounded like a drill sergeant.

'Okay, okay.' She lifted her head and promptly dropped it back onto her pillow. She stretched her bare legs against the smooth cotton of the sheets. When had she lost her clothes? And with Flynn – after he rejected her. Oh, sweet god, no.

She was suddenly wide awake. 'Where are my clothes?'

'On the floor. Where you dropped them.'

Summer closed her eyes. 'Please tell me that we didn't . . .'

A smile tilted the corner of his mouth. 'You're surprisingly affectionate when you have drink on, but no, we didn't. I prefer my women sober.'

Oh god, it was too early in the morning and she was way too wrecked for this. She rolled over in the bed, pulling the covers over her head. 'Call me when Room Service brings breakfast.'

'Fine.' Flynn tugged the sheets from her and picked her up. Marching swiftly down the steps, he strode in the direction of the bathroom.

The breath had been knocked out of her. Was he made

of solid titanium? 'Put me down,' she squealed. She was not at all turned on by his casual strength or the way he manhandled her.

'With pleasure.' Kicking open the bathroom door, he set her down in the shower stall and turned on the water.

Summer screamed. She was going to kill Flynn. The warm spray rained down on her as she leaned against the tiled wall. Her recollections of the night before were fuzzy. There had been singing, and dancing and whisky. Lots of whisky. Oh dear god. The wedding. And Flynn had put her to bed.

When she felt almost human, she wrapped herself in a towel and returned to the room. Flynn was gone. On the bed he had laid out her clothes with a brief note instructing her that she was to be in the breakfast room by 7.30 a.m. and that they were leaving by 8.15. After the evening before, it felt like the middle of the night.

Summer looked at the clothes. Flynn had picked her oldest things. A faded pair of jeans and a long-sleeved pink T-shirt that had seen better days. Interestingly, he hadn't done the same with her underwear. A matching set of cream silk and lace was laid out beside them. So Flynn liked sexy lingerie?

Her old hiking boots and a pair of thick socks were sitting beside them. 'Ah, come on.' It was summer. Why would she need those?

Grumbling, she dressed quickly and looked around the room for her make-up bag. Damn. Flynn had taken both rucksacks. She would look a complete fright. The hairdryer in the bathroom wasn't up to the job of styling her hair.

'Bloody men.'

Summer took one last look around the room. The champagne bottle was empty. The bed was rumpled and the cleaning staff would assume that the honeymoon couple had enjoyed a wild night. She wished. The only thing left was a single orchid – her favourite flower. She picked it up and rubbed the waxy petals between her fingers. It was beautiful. Summer wrapped it carefully in a tissue and put it in her pocket.

Downstairs, the castle was silent. Not surprising when most of the guests hadn't gone to bed until dawn. Only one table was occupied in the massive conservatory breakfast room. Summer blinked. The light was too bright. She wondered if Flynn had packed sunglasses. She carefully sat down in the chair opposite him, wincing at the noise when it scraped against the tiled floor.

A smiling waitress brought a dome-covered dish and laid it before her. 'Porridge with cream,' she announced cheerfully. 'Your husband ordered it specially.'

It was in a delicate porcelain bowl with gold-tinted roses painted on it. The porridge was garnished with slivers of strawberry and it was served with a small jug of cream. But it was still porridge.

The sight of it made her stomach turn. She shot Flynn a look that would melt the polar ice caps. 'I'm not very –'

'And we'll have some black coffee,' Flynn announced cheerfully.

'Certainly, sir.' The waitress disappeared in the direction of the kitchen.

'It's good for you,' Flynn said. 'Oats neutralize acidity levels in the body and help absorb toxins.'

She flashed him a poisonous glance. She hated porridge. Was he psychic, that he had managed to order the one thing in the world she most hated? But she'd had barely anything to eat the previous day, and she was too hungry to wait for the waitress to come back with a menu. She'd eat a couple of spoonfuls while she ordered a proper breakfast. She sprinkled some brown sugar on top and tried not to remember breakfast at her grandmother's.

'I hate you,' she mumbled as she raised the first spoonful to her mouth, before the aroma hit her nostrils. Summer dropped her spoon into the dish. She couldn't eat it. There was no way that she could get it past her lips.

The waitress returned with a pot of coffee.

'I can't eat this.' Summer ignored Flynn's disapproving glance and pushed her bowl away. 'I don't suppose you have any wheatgrass juice?'

The last statement caused the waitress's mouth to drop open. 'I'm not sure if we have that, madam.'

'She'll have scrambled eggs and toast,' Flynn said in a tone that brooked no argument.

The waitress disappeared in the direction of the kitchen, leaving them alone. 'I should tan your hide for that little performance.'

'Just try it.' She was sick of his he-man attitude. Who did Flynn think he was?

Her eggs had barely arrived before Flynn checked his watch and drummed his fingers on the table. 'You have exactly ten minutes to eat your breakfast. After that we're leaving and you'll have nothing till lunchtime.'

He was as good as his word. Precisely ten minutes later

he stood up, not caring whether she was finished or not. The man was a barbarian.

The coffee kept her awake until she reached the Forth Bridge and after that she drifted in and out of sleep. Each time she opened her eyes, the Scottish countryside raced by at dizzying speed. Flynn allowed her to suffer in silence. Summer let her eyelids drift down again and watched him through her eyelashes.

With each mile they travelled north, he seemed to relax more. The tight expression around his mouth was gone. Maybe it was being back in his home country, although he said that he was only half-Scottish. Flynn was a puzzle she hadn't figured out yet. But she would.

'We're almost at Fort William,' he announced. 'We can take a short break.'

Flynn glanced over at his sulking companion. She was finally coming fully awake after dozing most of the way. When she opened her eyes, it was only to glare at him, before pointedly turning her head away and gazing out at the Scottish countryside.

After that little episode this morning, as arousing as it had been for him, there was no chance that they'd be cuddling happily before a wood fire in the croft tonight. Just as well, he decided reluctantly. Summer O'Sullivan might be sex on legs, but she was the principal and she was trouble.

Those legs looked remarkably good in a pair of faded jeans, and her bountiful breasts filled out that pink T-shirt in a way that should be illegal. So much for his plan to make her look ordinary. Nothing would make Summer look like the girl next door. He suspected that even wearing a bin liner and boot blacking, she would still look spectacular. It didn't help that he knew what was under those jeans. What had possessed him to set out those lacy bits of silk for her to wear?

She shifted her legs, and he imagined how she would look in just her panties. The Jeep was warm and he caught a trace of her fragrance, all natural and uniquely Summer. His cock stirred. *Down boy, you're joining the ranks of the unemployed for the next month.*

Next time he was putting out clothes for her, he would make sure it was plain white cotton. No point torturing himself.

Damn it. The image of Summer presenting herself to him in plain white cotton panties refused to go away. He groaned. There was nothing she could wear that wouldn't turn him on.

She turned at the sound, slight though it had been, and her blue eyes glittered with resentment. 'Are you at least going to tell me where we are going?'

'Turlochbeg.'

'Where the hell is that?' she demanded.

'Sorry, that's on a need-to-know basis,' he said, enjoying her look of frustration.

'I need to know,' she snapped.

'No, you don't. If you don't know, you can't tell.'

'Who do you think you are – the bloody secret service? You work for me; you do what I tell you.'

'No, I work for your father.' He enjoyed reminding her. 'I promised him that I would do whatever it took to keep you safe. Whether you like it or not. The reason we are out here heading for a safe house is because you took a stupid risk.'

She glared at him, a glare worthy of the nastiest instructor in the Wing. No doubt about it, Summer had the bossy-boots routine down pat. He longed to take her in hand and show her exactly what happened to little girls who behaved like brats.

He kept his eyes on the road, now a narrow secondary road that wandered between the hills, and only allowed himself to watch her with his peripheral vision.

She huffed in irritation, and then pulled her Xperia out of her pocket. Before she could switch it on, Flynn seized it out of her hand.

'Hey!' she protested. 'That's mine. Give it back.' She reached over to grab it, but he held it out of her reach. Steering with his knees for a few moments, he disassembled the phone, taking out her SIM card and battery with one hand and pocketing them.

He handed the corpse of the phone back to her. 'Be my guest.'

She stared at it in disbelief. 'What did you just do? How dare you?'

He flicked a quick glance at her. She was furious.

'What's the point of taking you to a safe house if your mobile phone tells them where you are?'

'Don't be stupid. I'm not going to phone the psycho and say "Here I am, come and get me", am I?'

'After seeing you in action, I wouldn't put money on that. But it doesn't matter. Your phone will give your location away. How do you think I knew you were in *Noir*?'

That silenced her for all of three minutes. Then she opened her mouth again. He had to give her credit. Nothing kept Summer down for long. She had a remarkable ability to bounce back, ready to go another round. He squashed the thoughts of what he could do with that ability.

'About that,' she said carefully. 'You looked very at home there. You seemed to know lots of people.'

'Yes.' He could see how hard she was working at keeping her temper.

'Have you been there before?'

'Yes.'

Her eyes flashed. 'What, are we playing twenty questions now?'

Flynn laughed. 'If you like. Keep going.'

'Are you a member?'

'I may have let my membership lapse, but yeah.'

She sucked in a breath. 'Are you a Master, like Robert?' she asked in a rush.

He flicked her a glance. 'No. Robert's an asshole. I'm a Dom. And I'm not the only kinky one in this Jeep, am I?'

'I have no idea what you mean.' Her prim tone didn't fool him for a moment.

'Summer.' She looked around at his change of tone. 'That spanking at the club was just a warm-up. If you do anything so dangerous again, you can expect worse.'

She stared at him as if he had sprouted horns. 'Are you saying that you would spank me again?'

'If necessary.'

'You wouldn't dare.'

'I would.'

She flicked her hair at him. 'You are so full of it. Do your worst.'

Whatever she saw in his eyes silenced her. Ignoring him, she stared out the window and developed a strong interest in the passing scenery.

The road climbed as they reached the Highlands, and the stark countryside was softened by grass, gorse and heather. Flynn took a deep breath. The air up here was clean and fresh. Even though he had been born in the Rotunda hospital in Dublin and served in the Irish Rangers, he still felt that sense of homecoming when he reached the Highlands. The wildness of the landscape echoed something inside him.

The turn-off wasn't signposted, but he didn't need it. He knew where he was going. Summer's eyes widened as they turned off the road onto one that was even narrower, a single lane dirt track with grass going up the middle. 'You're joking, right?' she said.

He shook his head and concentrated on negotiating the rutted track. He knew Niall had put a few bottles of scrumpy into the back of the Jeep along with basic supplies, and Flynn didn't want them to explode from being shaken.

When Flynn pulled up at the croft, Summer blinked, then turned to stare at him. 'Now I know you're kidding me. This is like the worst joke of all time.'

He shook his head. 'No, this is it. Home sweet home.'

Flynn climbed out of the Jeep and strolled around to

the back, whistling as he walked. He was unpacking. This wasn't a joke. They were really going to stay here?

The rough stone cottage looked as if it hadn't been occupied for years. The paint on the door was badly chipped and one of the windows had a crack that zig-zagged from top to bottom. He couldn't mean it. They would be living on top of each other. The pool house in London was bigger than this . . . this heap.

'Grab a box, will you?' Flynn shouted over his shoulder.

'Carry it yourself. I don't want to break another nail.'

Flynn turned. 'Summer, I'm your bodyguard. I have to keep my hands free at all times. Now, fetch the box.'

Muttering under her breath, she went to the back of the Jeep and hefted out a cardboard box. She watched as Flynn pushed his way into the cottage. It wasn't locked. How could it be a safe house if it didn't even have a lock on the front door? She followed him inside. A large cob-web brushed against her hair and she screamed and shook her head, trying to brush it away. Summer blinked, trying to adjust to the lack of light.

Flynn grabbed it, and dropped her on a rough-hewn table and a cloud of dust rose into the air. 'Make yourself at home.'

'Home? This is your home?' She could barely get the words out. Flynn was joking. Any minute now he would laugh.

He wasn't smiling.

Summer stared into the dim recesses of the cottage. The ground floor consisted of one room. A large stone fireplace took up half of one wall. An iron hook was sus-pended over the hearth and on it hung a blackened cauldron. She had seen one just like it in photographs of her great-grandmother's house. There was no cooker. No shiny microwave oven. No stainless steel floor-to-ceiling fridge, just a deep Belfast sink with a single tap. A rickety wooden ladder led to a loft.

Flynn looked around as if seeing it for the first time. 'You're probably thinking that it needs a bit of work,' he said, without a trace of irony.

'Work? It needs to be demolished.'

'My great-grandmother gave birth to four children here. This croft has been in the family since 1745.'

'And it obviously hasn't been redecorated since then. Take me home.'

The look he gave her was frankly dangerous. 'For the next month, this is your home. Now get the rest of the stuff from the Jeep while I get the fire started. It gets a bit chilly here at night.'

Jeep. The Jeep! Why hadn't she thought of that? Flynn could play at being king of the wild frontier; she was heading for the nearest five-star hotel. She allowed her shoulders to slump in defeat. 'Fine, but I need the bathroom first.'

His mouth was twitching again and that usually meant that something nasty was coming. 'Be my guest. It's this way.'

She hadn't noticed the other doorway behind the ladder. It creaked as he opened it outwards onto an overgrown path behind the cottage. Twenty feet away was a small tin hut. Some wit had painted the word 'spa' in red paint on the door.

With a murderous glance in his direction, she strode up the path. Kill him. She wanted to kill him.

Flynn whistled. 'Hey, Princess, you might need this.'

A roll of toilet paper sailed through the air, landing in a patch of nettles beside her. As she scrambled to retrieve it, she could hear Flynn's laughter echoing in the hills behind. He was going to pay for this.

Summer waited until she was sure he was inside the cottage then she retraced her steps, crouching low when she neared the window. He probably wouldn't see her through the glass anyway, it was so filthy.

She opened the door of the Jeep and slid into the driver's seat. It had been a while since she had driven something this ancient. She eyed the gear stick, hoping she remembered how to drive stick shift. Summer reached for the ignition. There were no keys. She looked around her, checking the glove compartment, behind the sun visor. They weren't here.

'Looking for these?' Flynn dangled the leather key fob in front of her.

'Did anyone ever tell you that you were a bastard?'

'Frequently.' Flynn grinned at her. 'It's almost a term of affection. Now, stop messing around and get the rest of the stuff.'

He sauntered away, carrying the dark holdall she remembered from London. Could life get any better? She was stuck in the wilds of god knows where with a man who wouldn't travel anywhere without his gun.

She struggled into the croft, carrying a cardboard box of what felt like weights. Summer huffed a breath as she slid the box onto the table. Curiosity got the better of her and she opened the lid. Tins of soup, meat and vegetables stared back at her. She pulled out one tin. The cheerful yellow label announced that it was alphabet spaghetti in tomato sauce. Great. All she needed now was a white rabbit.

'I need to set up the perimeter alerts,' Flynn said. He took a handful of short metal posts from his bag. They had something electronic on top of them.

'What is that?' she asked. She had never seen anything like them before.

'They'll warn us if anyone approaches.'

She must have looked puzzled.

'They're a bit like breaking the electronic line when you win a race. They'll trigger an alarm.' He headed outside with them.

'I need to lie down,' she said to herself.

Summer looked around her. Bedroom. She hadn't thought about sleeping arrangements. There was barely room to swing a cat down here. That only left . . .

She eyed the rickety ladder. It was too much to hope that there was a king sized bed with an en suite up there. There was no point in putting it off.

The open platform overlooked the room below. A large wooden chest sat against the gable wall of the house. On top of it was a dusty china basin and matching jug; the cheerful red roses were at odds with the rest of the cabin. A cracked shaving mirror completed the facilities. Worst of all was the iron frame resting against one wall. It gave the phrase 'making the bed' a whole new meaning. Flynn would have to put it together before they could sleep.

Downstairs she heard him whistling cheerfully as he stacked the tins on a shelf beside the sink. Summer sank down onto a low, three-legged stool. She was in the middle of a nightmare. A month in the country? More like a month in hell. Tears pricked behind her eyelids but she wouldn't cry. She wouldn't give him the satisfaction.

Flynn probably thought it was hilarious. Well, he could laugh on the other side of his face. Compared with what she had been through the previous year, this was nothing. She could almost hear her father's voice. This was a skirmish, nothing more. The war was still waiting to be won.

14

She was still planning her strategy for getting away from Flynn and back to civilization when he called from below. Downstairs was too grand a name for it. 'Dinner is served.'

Was he serious? He hadn't had time to cook. She peeked down and saw that he had scrubbed down the table and there was something on it. She considered staying where she was just to make the point that he couldn't push her around, but it had been a long time since breakfast.

Summer climbed down the ladder, holding her breath at the creaking of the rungs, and very conscious of Flynn's eyes on her ass as she descended.

Flynn whistled. 'Very nice. You have great legs. And a great arse. And —'

'If you're quite finished.' Summer gave him an icy glare, channelling her father, who could make grown men shrivel with a glance. She wondered if she should have let him say what the other great thing was, then pulled herself up. She had no intention of spending a month here with this oaf, but for whatever short time she was here, she was going to make it clear that she was in charge.

'I haven't even started, sweetheart,' he assured her.

She refused to react to the promise in that statement. He was *so* not her type, and he was going to learn that. It didn't matter a damn what he looked like naked, or that he could reduce her to quivering jelly when he —. She cut off that line of thought. Not the time or place. He had been horrible to her. He had thrown her into a shower and tried to make her eat porridge this morning. It would never be the time or place again.

'I hope you're hungry,' he said.

She was, and could have cheerfully eaten live bugs or whatever rotten things they served up on reality jungle shows. But the sight of the table laid out in front of her almost killed her appetite. There was crispbread, tinned tuna, vacuum-packed ham, a couple of slightly shrivelled apples and a bottle of scrumpy. That was probably warm.

'That's it?' She stared at the meal in disbelief. 'This is the best you could come up with?'

He shrugged, unperturbed. 'Most of that stuff needs cooking and I reckoned you wouldn't want to wait while I chopped wood, cleaned the chimney and lit a fire. Think of it as a picnic.'

'That's your idea of a picnic? I bet you never get a second date, do you?'

He grinned. 'Oh, I get some, but it's not the food they're after.'

She ignored that – damn it, she had already had a sample of why a girl would come back for a second date with him, and she was not going to go there. There was one chair whose wickerwork seat still looked usable. It would be all the better for a good scrubbing, so Summer picked up Flynn's jacket, laid it across the seat, and sat down.

Flynn pulled up a stool and sat on it. He should have looked ridiculous, but still managed to generate an air of danger.

Ignoring the tuna and ham, she bit into an apple and

158

chewed with relish. Even warm, it was the best thing she had eaten all day, and she closed her eyes in appreciation of the scented sweetness.

She opened them to find Flynn staring at her through half-closed lids. His mouth was set in a sensual line that caused her stomach to do an unexpected flip. He had no right to be as handsome as he was. Bodyguards were supposed to be unobtrusive, not look like a teenager's fantasy.

To cover her reaction, she picked up the bottle and took a slug. The rough bite of the scrumpy took her by surprise, catching the back of her throat and setting it on fire. She coughed. 'What is that?' she wheezed, her eyes watering.

'Niall's homemade scrumpy. Nothing will convince him it's not haute cuisine and will be a huge seller.'

For a moment, she met his eyes in appalled understanding. The idea that anyone would like this rotgut was hilarious. She took another bite of her apple to scrub the taste from her mouth. The combination of scrumpy and apple worked surprisingly well.

'Are you not going to eat your ham?' Flynn asked.

She pursed her lips. 'I'm vegetarian. I can't eat this.'

He stared. 'Since when? I saw you eating veal.'

'You're imagining it. I have always refused to despoil my stomach by eating dead animals.' She tried to look saintly and pious. 'We have a duty to look after our fellow creatures as we travel through this world.'

Flynn snorted and helped himself to three slices of ham from her plate. 'I've seen you look after your fellow man, all right.'

'Oh!' She had no illusions about what he meant. She took another swig of the scrumpy. This time it wasn't so rough, and she managed to get it down without choking. She tried again, and it was almost pleasant.

'That stuff is full of processed crap and chemicals. You'll die early from eating it, you know that?' She hadn't intended to say that, but the habit of years of watching her father's diet was kicking in.

'Better than MREs,' he said. She wasn't going to ask him what an MRE was. It sounded nasty. She tossed the core of the apple at the huge fireplace and picked up a second one. It was almost as delicious as the first one and she ate slowly to make it last. She was not going to eat that awful stuff on the table.

'Are these the sort of culinary delights I can look forward to at every meal?' Summer used her most polite voice. She was going to cut him to slices when he came up with excuses.

'Oh no, you are going to provide the culinary delights from now on.'

'What?'

'You'll be doing the cooking. After all, you're the female.'

'No, no, you did not just say that.'

He grinned at her outrage. 'I'm the bodyguard. My contract clearly says that the principal is responsible for providing all my meals. I like my eggs sunny side up.'

'You expect me to –' She spluttered to a halt. 'Do you know I have an MBA? That I have an IQ of 150? And you expect me to –' She stopped at his knowing expression. He was just trying to annoy her.

'Then you know how to read a contract. Mine says that you provide my meals. And obey any orders I give you to preserve your safety.'

'I hope you like tinned tuna then,' she snapped. She looked at the fireplace and wondered how anyone could possibly cook on it. It was impossible. She had to get out of here. She was not going to be some sort of slave to this . . . this . . . Scot. As soon as he was asleep, she was going to steal his keys and sneak out of here.

Summer considered her options. The bed upstairs was still in bits, and she didn't fancy trying to climb that ladder in the dark. That left – she shuddered as she looked around the croft. Oh god, she was going to have to sleep down here.

You can do it. You've slept around snakes before.

'I'm going to bed now. You can bring me my sleeping bag from the Jeep.' She had spotted one when they got in and thought it was a joke. She wasn't laughing now.

Flynn nodded. 'Yes, my lady. Of course, my lady.' She wasn't fooled by his servile tone.

While he was gone, she found an old broom made of actual twigs, and swept a clear space in front of the fireplace.

She shuddered at the thought of going to bed without a proper shower, but needs must. She hurried out to the 'spa' to use the grim facilities and brush her teeth, and then curled up in the sleeping bag, still wearing her clothes. She ostentatiously zipped it up to her neck.

'You can make your own arrangements for where you sleep. I'm staying here,' she informed him.

As soon as he was in bed, she was out of here.

Flynn was determined to ruin her sleep. He hauled a box of tools through the back door and mounted the rickety ladder. Summer couldn't resist a peek at his ass. Well, sauce for the goose and all that, and it was as fine an example as she had seen in a long while. She hadn't really gotten a look at it the night that they . . .

She nibbled her lip. Flynn had given her exactly what she had wanted. A quick fuck; an uncomplicated knee trembler in an anonymous executive apartment and afterwards it had been hot. Really hot.

It was a pity that he was determined to ruin her life. Well, Flynn could join the queue. In the end all men were like that. She closed her eyes again, trying to ignore the uneven floor beneath her back. She could do it. In a couple of hours she would be on the road to the nearest five-star hotel.

Bang. She shot up to a sitting position.

Bang. Bang. The noise came again. Flynn's head appeared over the edge of the platform. 'Sorry about that. I'm afraid that it's going to be a bit noisy for a while.'

Noisy. The insistent thudding continued, until it was banging inside her head. The sound of metal being dragged across a wooden floor made her wince. Flynn was doing this on purpose. More banging. She rolled over. The floor was definitely getting lumpier. How the hell was she going to last for hours lying on this?

Flynn practically slid down the ladder. 'Getting your head down?'

She scrunched her eyes shut, ignoring him as he went outside.

After a few minutes, he tramped through the door

again. The light was beginning to fade, but there was no disguising what he was carrying. A rolled up quilt, and more than one of them. Her back ached in protest on the hard floor. She could be upstairs, on a bed, with a real quilt.

With him. Sharing a bed with Flynn.

Not a bloody chance. She wouldn't give in just because he had a mattress. She was made of sterner stuff than that. Wasn't she? Besides, how could she escape if she was up there? More climbing up and down the ladder, then he disappeared again, carrying a small wash bag. 'I hope you fall into the nettle patch,' she muttered under her breath.

He returned a short while later and Summer caught the faint scent of soap and shaving balm. 'I'm going to bed,' he announced. 'You're a braver woman than I gave you credit for, sleeping on the floor.'

What? He was just trying to spook her.

'I mean with all the mice down here.'

'Mice?' She shot up like a rocket. 'Mice?' God, she hated them. With their little twitchy noses, little pink feet and long tails.

'Aye, I haven't been here for months, and the little buggers get everywhere,' he said as he mounted the ladder. 'Still, they don't bite or anything, but they might nibble at your hair. Just ignore them.'

Ignore them. He expected her to lie here while rodents ate her? A rustle in the fuel basket beside her made her decision. 'It's not terribly comfortable here. Maybe I could bunk up there with you.'

She thought she heard a snort. Bloody-minded Scot. Rolling up her sleeping bag, she followed him up the steps and into the loft. The bed was much bigger than she expected. There was barely enough room to walk around it. There was certainly no room to lay a sleeping bag on the floor. Besides, the bed looked comfy, padded and not at all floor-like. A bare-chested Flynn was already there. His hazel eyes were narrowed, as if he was sizing her up and coming to a decision.

'I'm not going to attack you. I should point out that what happened before was your idea. The bodyguard does not have sex with the principal.' His expression was serious and Summer had no doubt that he believed what he said. Flynn was determined that their encounter wouldn't be repeated.

'Are you sure?' Her voice sounded throaty to her own ears.

He nodded. 'Absolutely. I'm a professional. I don't mix business with pleasure.'

Professional my ass! Maybe she had pushed a little in London, but, boy, hadn't he been enthusiastic? For someone who didn't mix business with pleasure, he had sure enjoyed kissing and sleeping with her. And that 'mission briefing' with the Viking in the car park. They sounded as if they were arguing. Summer's heart raced. She had him. Being nasty to him didn't work, but if he wouldn't mix business and pleasure, she had Flynn. All she had to do was seduce him and this mission was over.

Dropping her sleeping bag on the floor beside the bed, she shimmied out of her clothes and slipped between the sheets. She stretched, luxuriating in the feeling of cool cotton against her skin. 'Mmmmm, lovely,' she purred, before she rolled and dropped her arm over his torso.

She heard his surprised grunt. He wasn't expecting that. She lay on her side, savouring the heat from him, listening to him breathing, waiting until he was almost asleep. Then she moved closer, making sure that her breasts were pressed against his back. Flynn's groan quickly turned into a cough and she stifled the urge to giggle.

Poor baby. Maybe a few days in the country wouldn't be a bad idea. She would stretch this out until she drove him to breaking point. It was his fault she was here anyway. Operation *Defeat the Bodyguard* was still on and she was determined to win.

Flynn lay there, rigid, feeling Summer crushed up against his back, her warmth like a blaze to his senses. What the hell was she up to? He had seen the calculation in her eyes before she slid into the bed beside him. And now, instead of lying as far away from him as possible, which is what he had expected, she was cuddled up like a kitten. A very sexy kitten.

She stretched, moaning slightly, and wiggled, letting him feel the diamond-hard points of her nipples. She was up to something. Flynn would have bet good money that she would have continued to treat him like the hired help, and pretend that nothing had happened between them. Yet here she was, acting as if she wanted him to roll over and give her everything he ached to.

What had he been thinking, inviting her into the bed with him? He had been so sure she'd insist on staying as far away as possible. He should have left her there on the kitchen floor, curled up in front of the fireplace. Looking all soft and vulnerable.

No, bad thought. She's not soft; she's a hellcat in designer clothes. Packing only denim and T-shirts for her had backfired on him. Instead of looking out of place, she had looked far too much at home in those girl-next-door clothes. Approachable and sexy.

Determined to derail his train of thought, he tried to ignore the smell of the woman curled up at his back, and made plans for what he had to do tomorrow. The fire had priority. He would clean out the old fireplace, check the chimney for nests and chop wood. He looked forward to chopping wood. That would test his recovery and enable him to work off some of the sexual energy that was building up.

Lots of wood chopping, then. He'd fill the basket beside the fire, and then he'd start work on repairing the rest of the furniture in the old croft. He and David had spent a couple of weeks here last summer repairing the roof and the water pump, so they were sound, but the table was about the only solid piece of furniture downstairs.

The memory of Summer sitting at that table jumped in front of his closed eyes. Summer pretending she didn't eat meat. Little madam. He had so wanted to make her eat her words. Instead he had politely agreed, when what he really wanted was to spank her boneless.

He would sit on the old chair, and pull her down across his lap. The image of her sprawled across him stirred his blood and hardened his cock in a rush. She'd protest, of course, but weakly. 'What are you doing? I'm not sure about this . . .'

Flynn would ignore it, knowing damn well that she'd be disappointed if he did anything else. He would pull her forwards until she was settled over his thighs. If she struggled a little, he'd hold her wrists with his left hand, leaving his other hand free.

'Comfortable?' he'd whisper softly. 'You won't be for long.' She'd quiver at his words, but would stay where he had put her. Oh yes, he knew her secret; she wanted this even more than he did.

Then he would spank her. Firm, open-handed spanks on her delectable bottom. They would take her by surprise at first. She'd yelp and gasp, try to wiggle away, but his other hand on her back would hold her in place. It's not like she'd be struggling in earnest.

A dozen or so spanks, just to warm her up, until she relaxed a little. Then he would reach underneath her and unfasten those shorts. They'd slide down her legs, those long, tanned legs that haunted his dreams. Then she'd be in her panties. He wondered if she'd be wearing those lace and silk pieces of nothing that he had packed for her. Oh, look, yes she was. He couldn't resist giving a quick stroke to her silk-covered bottom. She moaned and shifted, causing the blood to rush to his cock. Later. For now, he had something much better to think about.

'It's not over yet, you know,' he told her, and spanked her again. This time it was sharper, stronger, without the protection of the denim. She yelped and cursed but he ignored her protests. He spanked her again and again, enjoying the feel of her panties beneath his hand.

She squealed and gasped, but made no real effort to get up.

Then the bit he was really looking forward to. He slid that excuse for underwear down her legs, and instructed her to step out of them. She had to straighten up a little to do this, but went back down onto his knees with no argument.

'Such a good girl,' he crooned, caressing her warm skin. It was only pink, not even red yet. He'd fix that.

Without warning, he spanked again, watching the way her buttocks jiggled with the impact. God, he could look at that all day. He did it again, and his cock rose, fully erect.

If women knew what men were thinking when they looked at a good arse, they'd either wear a nun's habit, or go naked all the time. Why did they persist in thinking that they had to look like stick insects to be beautiful? He spanked Summer again, just for the pleasure of seeing that gorgeous arse quiver.

There wouldn't be a huge difference to her in how it felt to be spanked when she was bare and when she was wearing her panties, but now she would feel exposed. 'Move your feet apart,' he told her, just to increase that feeling of vulnerability.

She did, shuffling her feet in tiny increments, but he waited until they were far enough apart to suit him.

Flynn spanked her again, and she gasped. The new position gave him access to a whole new set of nerve endings. He planned to make the most of them.

'That hurts!'

'It's supposed to. You know you've been a spoilt brat. You deserve a good spanking. I'm going to spank you until you realize how badly you have behaved.'

He kept going, ignoring her gasps, until she quietened and he could see the subtle relaxation in her body. God, he loved this, he could spank her all day. There was nothing in the world like the feel of a hot, quivering arse under his hand.

Flynn stroked his hand down her back and she moaned. He spanked again, altering the angle slightly, and was rewarded by a deep groan. It was a sensual, arousing sound and he ached to hear more. He kept going, and she gasped again, this time more in surprise than pain, and she tipped up her hips so that he could continue what he was doing.

He answered the wordless plea by spanking faster, harder, finding the rhythm that she needed. Her arse was now a deep red, and so beautiful that he caught his breath.

She moaned more loudly, her breath coming faster and faster. Her hands clenched as her body fought to cope with the sensations overwhelming it. With each spank, she tightened further.

'Please Sir, more. More,' she pleaded, and Flynn obliged. Another dozen hard spanks and she broke into orgasm with a wail.

'Ah! Ah! Ah!'

She gasped, trying to catch her breath after he stopped. He continued to smooth his hands gently and soothingly over her bottom. His cock rose demandingly against his belly, aching for release.

'Now that we have established who is in charge,' he told her. 'We can proceed to the main event.'

Oh, the things he wanted to do to this woman.

The noise of a gentle snore stopped him. She had fallen

asleep? The snore was coming from behind him. He opened his eyes and turned his head. Even in the darkness, he could see Summer O'Sullivan curled up in his bed. The real woman looked softer and gentler than the one in his imagination. He knew it was an illusion, but it was enough to break the sensual spell he had been enjoying.

Instead, he forced his mind back to the business of protecting his principal. And reminding himself that he had to keep his hands off her. It was going to be a long night.

15

Summer stretched out her arm. The place where Flynn had lain was still warm, but he was gone. Rolling over, she stared at the cracked plaster on the ceiling. The place had a certain rustic charm if you were into that type of thing, but she was definitely not. The sooner she was out of here the better.

But just how would she appeal to Flynn? He was attracted to her, that was certain, but he was on guard against an overt seduction. Which was probably just as well. Flynn had packed nothing but her oldest clothes and only minimal toiletries. She didn't want to think about her hair. Without the straightening irons she would be curly. Curly! Maya and Natasha would laugh their heads off if they saw her. She didn't do curly.

Since when? A small voice prodded her and she heaved a sigh. She hadn't had a job in almost a year – not since she'd been fired. No one wanted to employ a woman who had been plastered all over the tabloids in a sex scandal.

Since she'd moved back home, her father had indulged her every whim. Well, most of them. But it was an empty kind of existence and she was growing tired of it. Clubs, shopping, the hours of maintenance necessary to be a party girl. She could imagine her grandmother's disapproving glance and blunt remarks. *When are you going to do something with your life?*

After the 24th, she promised herself. One year was enough to mope about anyone, even if Adam had been a first-class opportunistic weasel. But first she had to get out of here. She was getting far too comfortable lying beside the big Scot each night. Even though the cabin had no heating, she had been warm and cosy, but it wouldn't do to get attached to him. Flynn would be gone once this job was over.

The front door opened. 'Summer,' he shouted up. 'It's your turn to cook.'

Cook? Bugger, she had forgotten that she had to feed him. She scrambled out of bed and tipped the contents of her rucksack onto the quilt. At least he had packed some shorts. She dug out a skimpy T-shirt. That would do. Summer picked up a lacy bra and dropped it. Operation tease was about to begin. Her hair was a mess, there was no way she could tame it. She would have to go with the bed-head look.

She could hear Flynn puttering about at the fire below. 'Summer,' he roared. 'It's almost noon. Get up now.'

Suppressing the urge to snap back, she slicked some lip-gloss on and climbed down the ladder slowly. 'I'm here.'

His eyes narrowed at her agreeable tone. Suspicious bloody Scot. She pretended not to notice as his gaze roved quickly over her, taking in the strappy top, the golden tan and the skimpy shorts. 'Do you want to borrow a jumper?'

'No thanks,' she said, trying to keep her expression innocent. It was hard not to smile when his eyes dropped to her breasts and especially to her now erect nipples. It might be June, but obviously Scotland hadn't heard about it. 'Besides, I'll be warm at the fire. Now, what would you like me to cook?'

'Fish,' he announced. 'You said you didn't eat meat.'

A pair of brown trout lay on the table, their gleaming flesh a testament to their freshness. Flynn's expression was frankly challenging. He thought she was a squeamish bimbo who would baulk at the idea of getting her hands dirty. He obviously didn't know that the rest of the O'Sullivans still made their living from fishing. Her grandmother had made sure that every one of them knew the family trade.

She flashed him her brightest smile. 'Great. Do you have any kitchen shears?'

'Hanging over the sink. Are you sure you know what to do with them?'

Ignoring the jibe, she picked up the fish and rinsed it under the tap. Carefully, she inserted the point of the scissors into the silvery underbelly and cut towards the head. Ignoring the Scot beside her, she snapped the bones near the gills on either side of its head before cutting through its mouth. If she did this properly, she could pull the head back and the guts should come in one go. She dropped the slimy mass into the sink.

Before she skinned the fish, she deftly trimmed the fins away with the scissors, then she snapped its neck back and peeled away the skin. Finally, she trimmed off the tail. Done. A bit slower than she used to do it, but still under two minutes. Not a bad job.

As Summer rinsed away the fish blood under the tap, the expression on his face made her want to laugh. She had surprised the Scot and it made her want to dance around the kitchen.

'Where did you learn to do that? Some fancy cordon bleu school?'

The pleasure of his approval died. Flynn would always believe the worst about her. She shrugged, as if his words hadn't stung. 'The stories about my dad weren't made up by someone in marketing. We really do come from a fishing family.' She reached for the second trout. 'My grandmother taught me. I lived with her for a while after my mum died. Dad was away a lot then.'

Flynn had the grace to look ashamed. 'I'm sorry, I shouldn't have . . .'

Summer ignored his apology, concentrating on gutting the fish. It was stupid to want to cry over a snide remark. 'That's okay. Most people think that rich equals stupid. Now, go find me something to cook on.'

For once, he did as he was told. The front door slammed behind him. *Oh, well done, Summer. Way to go on the seduction front. At this rate you'll still be here at Christmas. Now, lighten up and stop being so sensitive.*

When the fish were cleaned, she riffled through the rest of the supplies. Olive oil, a jar of capers, and someone had thought to pack some flour. Flynn baked? The thought of the muscular Scot doing anything in the kitchen but eating straight out of a tin made her giggle.

'Something funny?' Flynn had returned, carrying a sheet of wire mesh which he cleaned under the tap before setting it over the fire.

'Nothing. I don't suppose we have an oven?'

He snorted in reply. 'It's possible to cook a loaf over the fire, but the results are usually inedible. Although I've successfully used one loaf as a weapon.'

Summer couldn't help herself, she chuckled at the thought of Flynn going into battle armed with soda bread. She almost dropped the fish, and that made her laugh more.

His smile made him look younger and less disapproving. When her giggles subsided his expression turned serious. He reached out to ruffle her hair. 'You have a nice laugh,' he said.

Summer was conscious of the warmth of his hand as he stroked her hair away from her face. She could see little golden flecks in his eyes. It might be her imagination, but they seemed to be more pronounced when his emotions ran high. Her cheeks flamed. 'Maybe I'll bake for you while I'm here,' she said, trying to sound nonchalant.

He grinned. 'I might even eat it.'

She drizzled olive oil over a piece of foil and made parcels of the fish and capers. Placing them on a tin plate, she put them carefully on the makeshift grill above the fire. 'It should be ready in fifteen minutes, I think.'

'Would you like to eat outside?' Flynn was armed with a blanket, a bottle of scrumpy and a smile that made her heart flip.

When the fish was cooked she followed him to the edge of the loch. It was a perfect day. The waters of the lake were crystal-clear and a ring of mountains circled the valley, making them feel as if they were the only people left in the world.

She had been to fancier picnics, but nothing beat the quiet beauty of the place, the taste of the simple dish washed down with scrumpy, and the feel of the sun on her shoulders.

Flynn lay back, shielding his eyes from the sun. 'Don't burn,' he warned her.

'I won't.' She lay down beside him and after a few minutes her eyes drifted closed.

'What happened to your mother?'

His question came out of nowhere and she tensed. The memory still hurt. 'A car crash. Mum was picking Dad up from the airport. Some teenagers had stolen a car and –' She swallowed. 'Dad walked away without a scratch.'

Her throat tightened, threatening to stop the words. She didn't want to remember that night. She had never seen grown-ups cry like that before. 'After she . . . after Mum died, Dad was different. He never laughed. Not the way he did when she was around.'

'And then?' Flynn took her hand in his. The warm pressure of his thumb stroking her knuckles encouraged her to continue.

'I lived with my grandmother for a while, and then Dad's business took off.' Literally. The first flight was booked out and after that there was no stopping him. Much to the dismay of the aviation industry, the small regional airline had taken on the big players and stolen a slice of the market from under their noses.

'So you lost both of them.'

Clever Flynn. This was supposed to be her seducing him, not him finding out all about her. She rolled over, resting her head on his chest. She caught the faint hint of soap on his skin. 'Something like that. So, how was your perfect childhood?'

Flynn stilled, and for a moment Summer thought he

was going to pull away from her, then he relaxed. 'Not so perfect. My father was killed when I was young.'

'Killed?'

'A mission that went wrong. My mother was Scottish. She remarried soon after and we moved to Scotland.'

So that's how he got that delectable accent.

'And?' she prompted, waiting for him to continue.

'I joined Dad's old regiment as soon as I was old enough. My family didn't approve.'

The tension that returned to his muscles warned her not to pry further. Flynn had secrets of his own. She needed a distraction. What was it that Molly called it? Shock and awe?

'I'm hot,' she announced. 'I need to cool down.' She kicked off her shoes and strolled towards the loch. The water wasn't exactly warm, but she didn't plan to spend much time in it. Summer looked over her shoulder. 'Coming?'

Flynn shook his head. He was sitting up now, watching her closely. She shrugged out of her shorts slowly. She had his attention now. Summer fingered the edge of her T-shirt and stepped into the water. Taking a deep breath, she took the plunge and dived in.

The cold water hit her with a shock and she had to remind herself to breathe. There was one big difference between swimming off the south-west coast of Ireland in summer and diving into a Scottish loch – there was no Gulf Stream here to warm the water.

With as much grace as she could muster, she emerged from the water. Flynn's attention was still focused on her. His eyes were riveted to the T-shirt which now clung to her body, emphasizing the peaks of her nipples and the lacy panties, which were now virtually transparent. The hunger in his eyes was unmistakable.

Shivering, she dropped down to her knees beside him. 'Flynn, I'm cold. Warm me.'

He didn't wait for another invitation. Flynn reached for her. He dragged the skimpy top over her head and tossed it aside. His first kiss was a searing brand of possession, taking her lips as if he owned them. Thrusting his tongue inside her mouth, seeking, possessing. Summer moaned against his lips. It shouldn't feel this good.

Ignoring the water on her skin, he pulled her down on top of him and rolled, taking her with him. Summer arched as he pressed her on to the rough wool of the rug, his kisses becoming more demanding. His mouth left hers to trail along her jaw and she could feel the day-old stubble on his jaw rasp her tender neck and throat. With a muffled groan, his mouth fastened on one erect nipple.

'Oh god. Oh yes.' Her broken cry rang out in the silent glen.

She ran her fingers through his hair to hold his head in place. She didn't want him to stop kissing her. Flynn's thigh nudged between hers and she parted them willingly. His hard shaft pressed against her clit and she moaned, wriggling against him, seeking more friction. She was so close. She could come right here, with nothing more than this.

With a move that surprised her, Flynn pulled both of her hands above her head. The tempo of his ragged breathing matched the rapid staccato of her heart. He plundered her mouth again in a long, slow kiss that made her tremble with need.

'What do you want, Summer?' The tenderness had vanished from his face.

She wasn't sure if she liked this new Flynn. His stern expression was at odds with the barely leashed passion of a few moments before. She had meant to seduce him, but instead she was the helpless one. This was no longer a game. She wanted him. Wanted Flynn. A cloud passed over the sun and despite the warmth of his body covering hers, she shivered. Why had he stopped? What did he want from her?

Another slow kiss, this time against the tender spot below her ear. 'Say it,' he commanded. 'Say the words.'

'I want you.'

A look of grim satisfaction crossed his face before he rolled off her. 'You deceitful little bitch. Do you think I can't tell what you are up to? Or were you hoping that you could wind me around your little finger with this very delectable body of yours?'

He rose to his feet in one fluid movement. 'Get dressed, Summer. The party is over.'

She watched in shock as he took off in the direction of the small boathouse at the edge of the loch. The stiffness of his gait told her that he was furious. A wave of shame washed over her. How could she have been so stupid as to underestimate him? And how could she stay here and face him after this humiliation?

Summer wrapped the blanket around her shoulders and fled to the cottage. Inside, she climbed the ladder to the loft. She had to get away from him. Surely it couldn't be that far to the nearest village. She couldn't exactly remember the way, but there was a road that led as far as the valley. A few miles, no more.

Summer began to pack and then changed her mind. If she took her things, Flynn would know that she was gone. Summer rolled the quilt into a vaguely human shape. It wouldn't be enough to fool him if he came looking but somehow she didn't think he would want to share a bed with her tonight.

She couldn't take the Jeep. Flynn had hidden the keys and he would catch up with her in no time if she took the dirt track. She would have to find another way. Leaving her damp clothes hanging over a chair, she dressed in jeans, boots and one of Flynn's shirts. Downstairs, she put two apples into her pocket and filled an empty water bottle at the tap. With a final glance around the cottage, she let herself out and closed the door quietly behind her.

Behind the 'spa' was a steep path leading into the woods behind the house. She would find a way through. Somewhere above the valley was a road, and that meant civilization. She didn't care how furious her father would be; there would be no more bodyguards. Not even if she had to return to Castletownbloodyberehaven.

The path narrowed as she climbed, until it was hardly more than a foot wide. Her breath sounded loud to her ears and she paused to take a swig of water. She probably should have brought more of it.

Up ahead, the path forked in two. One fork led downwards, back into the glen. The other was steep, but at least it was going in the right direction. Summer glanced at her watch. It was more than an hour since she had left the cottage. Had Flynn returned? Would he notice that she was gone, or would he just write her off as another pain in the arse client?

She was glad that she wasn't around to find out. Around the next bend the ground dropped away, leaving a ledge that was barely inches wide, the edge tumbling into the forest below. Damn. It was turning into a goat track, but she couldn't go back now.

After a few yards, the path widened again and she was back in the forest. She felt like she had been walking for hours. Surely the glen couldn't be so big? Had she walked in a circle?

A rumble in the distance caught her attention. A truck. She must be near the road and she just might have a ride home. Taking off at a sprint, she raced through the trees. The rumbling grew louder. 'Stop,' she yelled although she knew that he wouldn't hear her.

Concentrating on the sound, she didn't see the gnarled root of the tree in her path. Summer pitched forwards, landing with a yelp. Her heart thudded as she scrambled to her knees and rubbed her stinging palms against her thighs. When the sound of the engine faded away, she wanted to cry with frustration.

Her throat was parched. Maybe she could rest for just a few minutes. Summer climbed to her feet and cried out when she tried to put her weight on her left foot. Limping to the nearest tree, she braced her arm against it and lifted her foot. Already, her ankle was beginning to swell. Should she take the boot off or leave it on? She couldn't remember. All she knew was that it hurt and that she couldn't walk another step. She closed her eyes, trying to shut out the pain. She would rest for a while before she tried to walk again.

16

Flynn watched her go, her body stiff with indignation and anger. Too bad. He had seen the calculation in her eyes when she dived into the lake. Did she really think that she could manipulate him like that? She desperately needed someone to take her in hand and teach her the consequences of her actions.

Summer O'Sullivan was a confusing mixture of naïve little girl, scheming seductress and submissive-in-training. Her beauty, her wealth and her father had protected her from the world she should be experiencing.

He ached to be the man to teach her. She was so fucking beautiful. Those eyes alone could turn him hard as a rock. The mixture of sweetness and calculation appealed to something deep within him. A sweet little innocent didn't do it for him. He wanted someone who was his match, and Summer's eyes said she was every bit as devious as he was. Then there was the rest of the package. That petal-soft skin which just begged for his marks. Her glossy hair, now the right shade for her skin, and just right for holding onto while he kissed her. Or spanked her.

Flynn tore his mind away from Summer's body. His erection was subsiding and he needed to keep it that way. A man who thought with his cock would always make bad decisions.

Turning her down when she was offering herself to

him had been one of the hardest things he had ever done. In comparison, Ranger training, that marathon of torture and exhaustion, was a piece of cake. But she was the principal, and a bodyguard did not get involved with the principal. Ever.

He would give her five minutes to get back to the cottage and put some clothes on. He couldn't watch her doing that in his present mood. Then he would explain exactly how this relationship was going to work. It was time Ms O'Sullivan learned that just because Daddy was rich, she was not going to get everything her own way.

Flynn kept his eyes on the lake, watching the herons diving for fish. A lone boat drifted into view. Flynn narrowed his eyes, examining it carefully. It had a small outboard motor, ideal for fishing, but the boat was drifting.

The sound of a child crying drifted across the water. Flynn could make out muffled words in between the sobs. 'Daddy, wake up. Please Daddy.'

The boat got a little closer and he could see a small red-haired boy tugging at something on the bottom of the boat. The kid couldn't be more than five or six, and he was sobbing.

Fuck. Summer was on her own. Every instinct in his body that urged him to go after her, warred with his concern for the child. Especially if there was a dead or injured man in the boat with him.

'Kid, what's wrong?' he called. His voice carried in the stillness, and the boy's head popped up over the side. His face was red from crying, but a gleam of hope lit his eyes.

'Daddy forgot to take his medicine and now he won't wake up.'

Damn it. His duty was clear. Muttering a string of foul curses to himself, Flynn stripped off his T-shirt and jeans and dived in. The cold was bracing.

He swam over to the boat and hauled himself into it in a wet rush. The boy backed away from the water he brought with him, but pointed at his father. The unconscious man was in his forties, but had prematurely grey hair cut very short and he wore a designer jacket. He was sprawled awkwardly in a heap, but he was breathing. Flynn hunkered down to check him over.

'Do you know what medicine your daddy takes?' he asked the boy, keeping his voice calm.

'He gets injections.'

Flynn searched through the man's pockets and found some glucose sweets and a medical alert bracelet on his wrist. Damn it, the man was a diabetic. Flynn called 112 and asked for medical help. Once he was assured it was on the way, he checked the engine. Out of petrol. He cursed. What sort of gobshite went out without enough petrol? He took a quick glance around the boat. There must be a couple of thousand pounds worth of fishing equipment but no spare petrol.

Fuck it, he couldn't leave them drifting. He grabbed the towrope and slipped back into the water. The swim back to the jetty was a lot harder than the one out, but once he got the boat moving, it was doable.

He had moored the craft by the time the rescue boat came into sight. When it got closer, Flynn cursed. His old school mate, Connor, now Doctor Tait, would recognize him and have the entire lake community aware that he was back in the Highlands. Flynn grabbed his clothes and melted into the shadows of the old boathouse.

He watched in silence, invisible to anyone who wasn't looking directly at him, and smiled as the rescue team praised the boy for his quick thinking in tying up the boat and ringing for help. 'But there was a man,' the boy protested. 'He looked a bit like Wolverine and had muscles like Superman.'

Connor checked over the father and within a few minutes the man was sitting up, groaning and swearing he was never going fishing again. When Flynn was satisfied everything was under control, he pulled his clothes back on, not caring that he was still wet, and headed back to the croft.

It was empty. Damn it. Summer had done a runner. The bed, made up to look vaguely like a human body, was proof. Did she really think he would fall for that trick again? She didn't have much of an opinion of him. But at least it was proof that she had run away, not been snatched. The perimeter alerts had gone haywire with all the rescue personnel, so he couldn't tell which way she had gone.

It was getting late and the light was fading. Outside, the Jeep was still there. Good. He was glad Summer didn't know how to hotwire one. He examined the ground and grinned when he saw tracks heading up the mountain.

Good girl, Summer, lay a false trail before you head for the road. He felt a blaze of pride in her. She wasn't the airhead she pretended to be.

Now he had to track her down and find her before she got into trouble. That woman was a magnet for trouble. Summer would hitch a lift with Jack the Ripper and not expect trouble. He debated taking the Jeep. It would be faster, but on foot, he would see signs he would miss from a vehicle. He set off at a fast jog.

Three miles later, he stopped, frustrated. There was no sign of her. She had managed to leave no tracks and there was no sign of any cars stopping to give a hitcher a lift.

Incredulously, he realized that she must have actually headed up the mountain. On her own. In poor light.

This time, he hit the return at a hard run. By god, he was going to whale on her when he caught her. Was she a complete idiot? He didn't care that she wasn't from the Highlands; she ought to have more sense.

He stopped at the Jeep long enough to retrieve a pair of night vision goggles to combat the dark. The Scottish countryside was transformed into an eerie green, but he could see where he was going. He set off up the mountain, determined to catch up with Ms O'Sullivan and teach her a lesson she wouldn't forget.

It was hard dark by the time Flynn caught up with Summer. Mind you, he thought, hard dark in Scotland in summer was a decent twilight in most of the world. He could probably have managed perfectly well without his NV goggles, but when he saw the route Summer had picked, he decided to keep them on.

What had possessed her to take this path? There's no way she could possibly have thought it was in general use. When he came to the place where the side had fallen away, leaving it unpleasantly narrow, he muttered a string of profanities under his breath. Was she trying to break her fool neck? What had she been thinking?

If a rookie under his command had done this, he'd be out so fast he'd bounce.

She hadn't been thinking at all, he decided. Summer O'Sullivan had been propelled by a mixture of hurt pride and recklessness. She needed a keeper. No, not a keeper. She needed an owner. Preferably one with a strong collar and a whip. For a moment, the memory of Summer kneeling at his feet in the club tormented him. God, she'd looked so at home there, as if she belonged to him.

He shook his head and pushed on up the track. She wasn't his, would never be his, and her escapade in the club was one more example of how she wanted everything her own way.

Flynn half hoped she'd be running when he caught up with her. He'd like to chase her and bring her down in a tackle. It would satisfy something atavistic in him that usually stayed beneath the surface.

When he entered a small clearing and saw her sitting propped against an old oak tree, it was almost an anti-climax. She hadn't run far after all. She was staring up at the sky, still as a rock.

'Summer,' he said. Wherever she was inside her head, it wasn't in the clearing. She shrieked and jerked before scrambling back, trying to get around the tree. She was wearing only one shoe.

'It's okay.' Flynn yanked off his NV goggles and spoke. He was so accustomed to their weight he often forgot how odd they looked to someone who wasn't used to them. 'It's me. It's okay.'

She stilled, her breathing still racing. 'Flynn?' Her voice was rusty, as if she had been crying.

He nodded. 'None other. Always turning up like a bad penny.'

The joke fell flat.

She stiffened. 'You complete and utter bastard.'

'What did I do?' He had eased in beside her, planning to examine her bare foot, but at this he paused.

She stared at him in astonishment. 'This is all your fault. You deliberately humiliated me, then you left me here alone for hours, and when you finally turn up, you look like something out of a horror movie. And you thought I'd be pleased to see you?'

He ignored her outrage to reach for her foot. 'I'm here now and I'll take you home.'

She yanked her foot out of his grasp. 'You don't get to reject me, then grope me. Go away. I'm staying here.'

Despite her objections, he felt her ankle. It was slightly swollen and tender to the touch. Not broken, but she wouldn't enjoy walking on it for a few days.

'I said, take your hands off me,' she snapped and tried to kick him with her other foot, the one still wearing a boot.

'Stop that.' He grabbed her ankle and held her securely. She tried to kick and wiggle free, but he wasn't letting go. No doubt about it, she had hurt it and wouldn't be walking home tonight.

He swung her up into his arms. 'Right, we're going home now.' He headed back towards the croft.

She struggled like a landed trout. 'Put me down. You have no right to put your hands on me.'

He was tempted to leave her on the side of the mountain for the rest of the night, just to see how she liked it, but there was something about her reaction that stopped him. There was more going on here than bad temper.

She tried to wrestle her way out of his arms. 'Stop it, or I'll drop you over the edge of the cliff.' It wasn't a cliff, but the path was narrow and there was a sharp drop off one side where the ground was swallowed up by the dark.

Summer went still and clung desperately to his neck. Her breathing was faster than normal. She didn't even speak for the rest of the journey.

What the hell had she been thinking, running away like that? She needed to learn who was in charge, and learn it soon, before she did something that caused worse than a twisted ankle. The warm weight of the woman in his arms was a temptation Flynn couldn't ignore. He badly wanted to put her across his lap and spank her in retribution, but with an injured ankle, it seemed unfair.

Summer's breathing changed and so did her scent. The hunter in him went on full alert. Those were signs he recognized.

Fight or flight weren't the only reactions to adrenaline. There was also Fuck. Right now, Summer was flooded with a chemical cocktail more potent than any little blue pill. And he was reacting to her arousal.

He pushed in the door of the croft and shifted Summer over one shoulder as he climbed up the ladder, before tossing her on the bed. He reached for her foot, and she kicked him.

'You little hellcat. I'm trying to check your foot.'

She grabbed his hair and pulled. 'Leave it alone. I don't want you touching me.'

'Then let go of my hair.' He leaned into her to break

189

her hold. That position put his head very close to her mouth. He hadn't intended to, but he couldn't resist. Flynn leaned down and brushed his mouth against hers. Summer's mouth was sweet and innocent, a contrast to her sharp tongue and devious smile. She tasted of wild strawberries and he licked at the seam of her lips, desperate for a deeper taste. She opened for him eagerly.

Oh fuck it. One kiss wouldn't hurt. Flynn tilted her head slightly so that he had better access and kissed her back. In the dark and the silence, there was nothing except Summer's mouth, Summer's kiss, Summer writhing beneath him. The taste of strawberries was stronger, now mixed with Summer's own distinctive flavour. God, he could live off this woman.

He plunged his tongue into her mouth, meeting hers in an erotic duel where there were no winners or losers. She sucked on his tongue, and he stiffened, the innocent action arousing him unbearably.

He raised his head. 'Sum –' His movement brought her breasts more firmly against his chest, and she moaned.

He sucked in a breath as the stiff points stabbed him through his T-shirt. She had the most amazing breasts.

Summer shifted restlessly so that her nipples grazed him again. 'More, please more.' Her voice was husky and pleading.

He couldn't help it. She might be the damned client, but she was Summer, lying there, writhing in the dark and begging him to kiss and caress her. He took one generous breast in his hand, loving the feel of it, the way it fit against his palm. He pinched the nipple and she gasped.

He did it again, rolling the tight bud between his finger

and thumb, and enjoyed watching the way her back arched and her breathing accelerated. She was so responsive.

With an unexpected athleticism, she twisted, changing their positions so that she was on top. She pressed her hips against his now straining erection, moving so that every twitch was a new caress. 'Fuck me,' she demanded, now certain she had the upper hand.

He wanted to. His cock was aching, dying to bury itself between those luscious thighs. But not only was she his client, she was a brat in need of a lesson.

'No. You're the principal.'

She rubbed against him again, as wanton as a cat in heat. He almost came in his pants when her tongue darted from her mouth to trace a path along her lower lip. 'You're fired. Now can we fuck?'

'Only your father can fire me.' He pinched the other nipple and watched her gasp.

'Then kiss me. Keep doing what you're doing.'

He braced her against him and rolled over, before swooping down to capture her mouth again. 'Yes, ma'am.' He had no doubt that Summer thought that after a few kisses he'd do what she wanted. But he had other plans.

He kissed her deeply and thoroughly, exploring her mouth at his leisure. For the first time, he would spend as long as he wanted learning her secrets. He was going to make the most of it. By the time he raised his head, she was limp and boneless.

Flynn was smiling as he traced her features, particularly her flying eyebrows, which always intrigued him. Then he found her right ear and explored it with his tongue. For a moment, she recoiled from the unexpected touch, and then she allowed him to continue. She was docile at first but when he nipped the edge of her ear lobe between his teeth, she jerked and gasped. He did it again.

'Flynn? What?' Her hands brushed against his chest, as if uncertain whether to pull him closer or push him away.

What had her previous lovers been thinking? This was a woman who clearly had no idea what she liked or didn't like.

He nipped the top of her ear, enjoying her reaction, and then licked his way down her neck to the point where her neck joined her shoulder, and bit down lightly. She shuddered and groaned, and her legs twisted. Oh yeah, she really liked that.

He did it again, before searching for the other points that turned her from limp noodle to lioness and back again.

Finally, he allowed himself the prize he had been obsessing about for days. He opened her top and feasted on her breasts.

At the first touch of his mouth on her sensitive skin, she gasped. Then she lifted herself against his seeking mouth, trying to get more of the contact.

Flynn kissed his way along the side of her breast, inching closer and closer to the erect nipple, now standing up proudly. He took it into his mouth and sucked.

It tasted of raspberries and salt and musk and Summer. He ran his tongue over the hard point, flicking it back and forth.

Summer gave a muffled scream and clutched his head tighter. 'More, more, please,' she begged.

He sucked a little harder and her back arched, pushing her nipple more firmly into his mouth. Her breathing was racing and the scent which filled his head was ripe with feminine arousal.

He bit down lightly and she shrieked, her hips lifting against his rock-hard cock. He pressed against her for a moment, luxuriating in the contact, before he stopped.

She was an inch away from orgasm. He had heard of women who could climax just from having their nipples bitten, but had never met any. Now he had. Who'd have guessed Summer O'Sullivan was one of them? But she wasn't having it that easy.

He lifted himself away from her and kissed her eyelids. The long lashes tickled his tongue and he smiled.

Blindly, she followed his mouth, trying to get him back to where he had been before. He ignored her, kissing his way around her face and allowing her breathing to calm before he slid down her body to resume his assault on her other breast.

This time he had some idea what to expect, and he experimented, trying out long swipes of his tongue and sharp nips from his teeth to see what caused her to flinch or purr. The delicate texture of her skin fascinated him. If the cosmetic industry could bottle Summer's fine skin, they'd make a fortune.

He played with the right breast while he sucked hard on the left nipple and her reaction was electric. She shrieked and panted. 'Oh god, god, god. Oh god. Flynn!' When he sucked a little harder, she lost her breath altogether. He bit down carefully, waiting for that moment when her body tightened in the beginning of orgasm.

Flynn stopped. 'I'd better check your foot,' he said, as if they were carrying on a conversation.

'What?' She shook her head, dazed. She had been lost in the moment.

'I need to examine your foot, to see if it needs medical treatment.'

'It's fine.' She was snappish now, frustration making her grumpy.

He pressed around the ankle, and she flinched. 'Did you go over on it?'

She nodded. 'But it doesn't matter. Now, where were we?' She slid down on the bed until her breasts were pointing directly at Flynn, and she tugged him down.

'Right about here,' he said, licking his way to the peak of one pink nipple. She groaned with satisfaction and pushed her hands into his hair, encouraging him to find the right one and get busy.

He obliged, using hands and lips and tongue and teeth to drive her on. It didn't take long until she was panting and gasping, 'Flynn, Flynn', and her hips were lifting to him.

He was watching, ready for the moment when her body was right on the edge, and then he stopped. 'Did I mention how pissed I was when I found you gone from the croft?' he asked.

This time it clicked. Summer struggled up onto her elbow, pushing her hair out of her eyes with her other hand. Pieces of twigs and old leaves were still caught in it, but she didn't notice. 'You're doing this deliberately?'

'Yes, ma'am.' Flynn sat up, ignoring his own raging hard-on and enjoying her fury.

'Why?'

'Because you need to learn to do what I say. And I say when you have an orgasm.'

She glared at him, her fury visible even in the single candlelight of the croft. 'Don't bet on it. I can take care of myself.'

'No.' He positioned himself so that he was between her legs, leaning down to kiss her jaw and whisper a promise into her ear. 'Only when I say so.'

His hard thighs held her softer ones apart, but he held himself so that she couldn't press against him. His chest rubbed tantalizingly against her nipples, but without enough pressure to give her what she needed.

'The night is still young,' he told her and to his surprise, she relaxed, allowing him to unfasten her jeans. She even lifted her hips to help him wiggle them off. But Summer was still Summer.

'I'll remember this. You just wait.'

Flynn grinned and resumed his position, but now he had all of Summer spread out before him to feast on. He could play with her stomach and hips and legs all day, and did spend a lot of time indulging his fascination, but the lure of her pussy was too strong to ignore.

The perfume of it, ocean-fresh and sweet, lured him. He ached to bury himself in her depths, but he couldn't make up his mind which part of himself he wanted to bury.

First things first. He nibbled his way down her stomach, laying a trail of stinging kisses as he went. He stopped to play in the neat delta of soft hair, and then moved down again. Summer was panting, eager for him to keep going, desperately trying to tighten her thighs to force him on, but he ignored her. 'Patience. Good things come to those who wait.'

She snorted. 'Good things come to those who get on with it.' She lifted her hips so that her clitoris was right in front of his mouth. He couldn't resist sucking it in like an oyster and savouring the feeling of the little pearl on his tongue.

'Ahhh!' Summer shrieked.

He stopped. 'Oh sorry, didn't mean to hurt you.'

'You didn't. Do more. Please. Do more.'

'Are you sure I wasn't hurting you?' He stayed away from the temptation of her aroused body.

'Yes, now get back to where you were,' she panted. Poor Summer, she was so close.

'I was about here, right?' And he nipped the skin of her stomach. She flinched and gasped, lifting her hips to his mouth.

Fuck it, he couldn't resist any longer. Her moist pussy was calling to him. He tilted her hips to get a better angle, and dived on. Oh god, this was heaven. She was shaking, so ready to explode that he had to work hard not to tip her over the edge. He licked carefully up and down the edges of her lips, enjoying the perfumed saltiness against his tongue.

Summer twisted, trying to get him to where she needed him, but Flynn wasn't going to let her have her way. 'More, please,' she panted. 'Much more.' He licked faster, always keeping away from her tempting clitoris. Now to drive Ms O'Sullivan mad.

His cock was rock hard, rigid against the confines of his jeans and so engorged he wondered if the blood would ever return to his body. But he didn't care. This, pushing Summer beyond her limits, was more enthralling.

He held her still and kept going.

'Let me come, please, please, please.' She was chanting a plea to him, her voice rising higher and higher.

'Only when I say,' he told her.

Summer was beyond dignity now. 'What?'

He licked again, and then raised his head. 'You can't come unless I say so.'

He saw the moment when it clicked, her confusion giving way to understanding, then fury. 'You . . . you. Oh I can't think of anything horrible enough to call you!'

She tried to pull away, but her position with him wedged between her thighs stopped her. 'Fuck you,' she snarled. 'I can take care of myself.'

'No, you won't.' He held her thighs apart firmly with his shoulders and grabbed her hands. She fought his grip but wasn't going anywhere.

He blew firmly on her clitoris.

That was all it took to tip her over into orgasm, but it wasn't all that she needed.

She wailed in fury as the anticipation and tension dissipated, leaving her strung out and disappointed. Her inner muscles, eager for a hard cock, or even a hard body to press against to prologue the pleasure, twitched in confusion.

'What did you do? What was that?'

Flynn raised his head, smiling grimly. 'That, dear Summer, was a ruin. Did you like it?'

Her expression was answer enough. She wasn't going to forgive this in a hurry.

He climbed into bed beside her, and laughed when she turned her back to him.

17

Summer shifted restlessly in the bed. It was dawn, but she hadn't managed to get a wink of sleep all night. Her ankle throbbed, but not as much as other parts of her anatomy and it was all his fault. Her hand strayed beneath her T-shirt, down along her stomach and under her panties.

Beside her, Flynn gave a soft snore and she was tempted to elbow him in the ribs. She didn't even have the privacy to touch herself. If he thought he was going to control every aspect of her life while she was here, he was in line for a severe case of disillusionment. Flynn couldn't break her. No one could.

She dropped her hand away and rolled onto her side to look at him. Even with the beginnings of a beard, he was drop-dead gorgeous and if the tenting in the sheet was anything to go by, almost as horny as she was. A wicked thought came into her head and she smiled. Flynn had deliberately set out to arouse and disappoint her. *Let's see how you like a dose of your own medicine.*

Summer slid beneath the sheets, trying not to touch him until she was ready to play. Poor baby. He didn't stand a chance. By the time she was finished with him, Flynn would be putty in her hands. She stared at his erect cock. It was bigger than she expected. If they weren't in the middle of a battle of the sexes, she might have been full of admiration for such a fine specimen, but this was war, and she was determined to win.

She blew a breath against the silken head and was rewarded with a slight tremble. Slowly she licked it from balls to crown. He tasted salty. Flynn murmured in his sleep and stretched his legs, but didn't waken. He probably thought he was dreaming.

Careful of her injured ankle, she slid between his parted thighs and stroked his sac, rubbing gently behind his balls until he gave another low groan. Summer lowered her head and took him into her mouth. She swirled her tongue around the tip, tasting a pearl of pre-cum. *Oh you are in so much trouble.* She sucked him deeper, licking at the tender spot below the crown, while she continued to stroke him with her hands.

Flynn's hips moved, arching upwards, thrusting, eager for more. Then there was a strangled roar and the sheets were thrown back. 'What the fuck?'

She released his cock with a pop and smiled at the mixture of lust and outrage on his face. Keeping her eyes on his face and her hand wrapped firmly around him, Summer gave him another long, slow lick. Flicking her tongue across the tip. Tasting him.

'Stop that.'

Summer gave him an innocent look before licking him again. 'Why? Don't you like it?'

'Yes. I mean no. Oh, Christ, woman, I don't know what I mean.'

'Let me know when you make up your mind.' She closed her eyes and lowered her head, taking him into her mouth until the tip hit the back of her throat. Flynn's hand fisted in her hair and she didn't know whether he meant to encourage her or stop her.

He tugged her hair, pulling her away from him. 'I said stop.'

With a lingering final kiss, she sat back on her heels and admired her handiwork. He was rock hard and stiff as a board. Flynn would need a cold swim in the loch after this. Now the arrogant Scot knew exactly how it felt to be taken to the edge and left hanging. She lay down beside him, pleased with herself. 'I believe that's called a ruin. How did *you* like it?'

He grinned. 'No, that's a nice way to wake up in the morning. I can thoroughly recommend it.'

She snorted. Her plan to pay him back hadn't worked but there was still potential. She eyed his impressive erection. 'So why don't we put that flagpole to good use? It seems a shame to waste it.'

Flynn climbed out of the bed and grabbed his clothes. 'I don't sleep with my clients and I'm taking my flagpole for a nice relaxing shower.'

He stomped down the ladder as if he was trying to break each rung and she heard the rustle of clothing while he dressed, followed by the door slamming.

Damn. That hadn't gone exactly to plan. Now he was mad at her. Mad and horny. Which made two of them. They would be like a bag of cats trapped in the croft together. Cats in heat.

Flynn would have to give in eventually, but first she had to take care of herself.

With one hand she covered her breast, squeezing and plumping it, just as he had done the previous night. She had never felt so hot. She had heard that some girls could come just from breast play, but she hadn't believed it. But Flynn . . . His hands should be licensed. And his mouth. And every other delicious part of his anatomy. Her other hand strayed to her panties and her fingers traced a path around her clit. She was wet and aroused. It wouldn't take much to push her over the edge and —

The door swung open and she froze as she heard his footsteps on the ladder. She quickly pulled her hand away and covered her breasts, but not before he had caught her.

His hazel eyes were dark. 'Oh no, you don't. If I'm going to suffer, then so are you. Get dressed.'

'But —'

'I said dressed. Now. And don't get any ideas. I'll be watching every move you make.'

His chest rose and fell beneath the dark T-shirt. She had done a good job of getting Flynn worked up, but how long would it take to push him over the edge?

She shrugged. 'Fine.'

Summer climbed off the bed and limped to her rucksack, ignoring the hiss of his indrawn breath as she bent over to grab a clean T-shirt. Oh, she couldn't. That would just be too mean. Schooling her face into an expression of innocence, Summer turned to face him. Flynn was still glaring at her.

With more confidence than she felt, Summer pulled her top over her head. Her nipples pebbled, and she wasn't sure whether it was because of his proximity or the temperature in the cottage. Ignoring the lacy wisp of a bra that he had packed, she pulled the clean T-shirt over her head, smoothing it over her curves, before she stepped out of her panties.

A rumble which sounded suspiciously like a growl came from the other side of the bed. She ignored it. Summer emptied the contents of the rucksack onto the quilt and sorted through them. She risked a glance at his face from beneath her eyelashes. A storm was brewing in his eyes.

'Didn't you pack the pink ones?' she asked innocently. 'Never mind.'

She selected a pair of pale satin boy shorts trimmed with black lace, making sure that Flynn had a good view while she drew them up her legs and pulled on her shorts. Her eyes fell on her wash bag and she grinned. How could she have forgotten? She had a tiny waterproof vibrator in there. Flynn might hover over her while she was in the croft, but he would hardly follow her into that excuse for a bathroom at the end of the garden. Flashing him a bright smile, she picked up her wash bag and towel. 'I may need your help getting down the ladder.'

It was the slowest climb ever. She could feel his breath on her thighs as she limped down the rough steps. Once she pretended to stumble and Flynn was there immediately, holding her close until she reached the bottom step.

'Thank you,' she said in a husky tone that wasn't all pretence. She leaned against him for support she didn't really need.

'Bathroom,' he repeated, while he held her upper arms before he pushed her away.

She gave him a flirtatious smile and took her time as she made her way up the path, conscious of him walking behind her. At the top of the path she opened the door and slipped inside. The light in the spa was dim. The shower was barely a dribble. Summer didn't care. She reached into her wash bag and pulled out the tiny vibrator and blew it a kiss. 'You purple-helmeted love god,' she murmured.

Bracing her hand against the tiled wall of the shower, she pressed the vibrator against her clit and turned it on. Nothing happened. Summer shook it. 'Damned battery.'

She pressed again and waited for the buzz that would tell her that ultimate pleasure was only minutes away. Still nothing happened. She shook the tiny purple vibrator. Maybe the connection was faulty. There was a polite tap on the door and she pulled her towel around her. What did the Scot want now?

She opened the door a crack and a hand appeared.

Flynn's smug expression did nothing to lessen her dismay when she saw the small battery in his open palm. 'Looking for this, Princess?'

Flynn laughed at the fury on Summer's expressive face. She wanted to gut him with a rusty chainsaw, no doubt about that. Well, tough, he was calling the shots around here and for her own good Ms O'Sullivan needed to learn that she had to do as she was told.

She slammed the door in his face and a second later he heard the shower go on full force. But it was a fixed overhead shower so she wouldn't be having much fun with that.

He allowed himself a brief fantasy of Summer slowly pleasuring herself while he watched, then dismissed it. It was too dangerous. Last night had shown him how much she got under his skin. Remembering that she was his client was getting harder and harder.

Still keeping watch on the shed and listening to the noise of Summer splashing as she washed, he nipped down to the point where Niall had left his supplies. It was a well-hidden spot just off the lane but out of sight of the cottage and the main road.

Niall, bless him, had sent fresh milk, eggs, bread, a couple of large T-bone steaks, vegetables, cheese, more scrumpy, a handful of tins and spices, a neat little H&K handgun, a small amount of C4, and a few other goodies. If his boss were a woman, Flynn would marry him. Or at least shag him twice a day, every day. Niall really knew the way to an ex-Ranger's heart.

The shower had stopped by the time Flynn had dumped the box of supplies in the croft and checked out the perimeter alerts. They were all still in position and still working nicely. Nothing bigger than a rabbit would get past them without triggering an alarm, which would give him time to make sure he was ready to defend Summer – the client, he reminded himself – against any intruders.

He felt slightly guilty about the battery – not that she hadn't deserved it – so he prepared breakfast for her. It was almost worth it for the look on her face when she saw the table spread with fresh wheaten bread, butter, coffee and scrambled eggs.

'Ohh!' she breathed. 'I've died and gone to heaven.'

Dressed in shorts and a T-shirt, and with her wet hair already drying into wayward curls, she looked younger and more innocent than he knew her to be.

'No, Turlochbeg,' he said.

'Where did all this come from?' she asked, sitting at the table and diving in.

He shrugged modestly. 'I caught it myself. Foraged for wild food which I prepared with my own hands. I hope you like skylark eggs. I had to climb a lot of trees to get them.'

She paused, her mouth already full of the fluffy yellow eggs and stared at him with wide eyes. 'Really?'

Flynn laughed. 'Of course not. What are they teaching in school now? It's far too late in the season for skylark eggs.'

She laughed, realizing how absurd she sounded, but levelled her fork at him. 'Just wait, I'll get you back for this.'

'Looking forward to it.' And he was. He couldn't wait to see what Summer would come up with next.

Breakfast passed peacefully and was almost over when Flynn put down his mug of coffee and announced, 'There are going to be some rules around here. You are going to learn them, and you are going to obey them.'

True to form, Summer bristled. 'You're going to give me rules?' She sounded as if she couldn't believe her ears.

He nodded. 'Yep. It's clear that you've been getting away with murder for years. Well, that stops now. I'm in charge of your security, and you are going to obey me. Normally, I'd just tell a principal to obey me in matters of security, but since you clearly haven't a clue what is security related and what isn't, we're going to change the rules and you are going to obey me in everything.'

Summer put her cup down very carefully, making sure not to spill a drop. 'Let me understand this,' she said slowly. 'I'm going to obey you. In everything.' She spoke as if he was a particularly backward child.

He smiled. 'Good girl, now you're getting it. I'll give the orders and you'll do what I tell you.'

'I'm not a dog,' she snapped. 'Stop talking to me as if I were.'

'No,' he agreed. 'I keep my dog on a collar and leash.'

She choked, and had to cough before she caught her breath again. 'Let's get this straight. I am your client. I make the decisions. You are the bodyguard. You do what you're told.'

'By your father. And what he told me was to do whatever it took to keep you safe. So I will. And you'll obey all my orders, knowing they're designed to keep you safe.'

'And if I don't?' She raised a challenging eyebrow at him.

'There will be consequences.' He didn't elaborate. She probably had a fair idea of what sort of consequences she faced.

'And what sort of orders will you give? Am I allowed to wear clothes? Will I be required to dance naked for you? Give you a blow job morning and evening?' She was working up a fine head of steam.

'I had more pedestrian things in mind. Rule number one, no more running away. No storming off in a huff. Sulk if you like, but do it where I can see you. You go nowhere without me. Not to the head, not to the lake, not for a run, not to pick strawberries.' He wouldn't forget the tart strawberry taste of her last night. Those tiny mountain strawberries were addictive.

'Are you saying I'm going to have no privacy at all?' She was appalled.

'You can pee with the door closed,' he told her. 'I'll even allow you to shower on your own. That's it. Every other breath you take, I need to be within earshot.'

'You're kidding. I can't live like that. I need privacy.' Her fingers tightened around the cup and it rattled against the table.

He shook his head. 'I'm sorry, Princess, safety trumps privacy. As soon as your father comes back, or Niall catches the nutcase, then you can go back to your private life in front of the paparazzi cameras. Until then, you are stuck here with me.'

She looked around at the croft with dismay in her eyes, and for the first time, he looked at it, not as a labour of love, but with the eyes of a spoilt rich socialite. It was a solid building and the walls and roof had been repaired, but there was no doubt it was short on comforts. The solid table was the focus of the kitchen area, the chairs were mismatched, the old settle needed more work, the fire was primitive and there were no modern appliances. 'Think of it as a break from laptops, phones, television, all that stuff.'

She shuddered. 'I was thinking more of how I've always taken light switches for granted. What the hell will we do here all day?'

'I'm sure we'll think of something. Failing that, there's always your idea.' He grinned when she looked blankly at him. 'Naked belly dancing and blow jobs.'

18

There were few things more boring than watching paint dry and she had experienced all of them over the last few days. Watching Flynn fish – unsuccessfully. Watching Flynn chop wood – well, that hadn't been too bad, especially when he'd taken off his shirt. Worst of all was watching Flynn watching her as she tried to sunbathe without being eaten alive by midges. He was in full bodyguard mode and he had barely smiled at her all morning.

How was she going to survive another three weeks of this? No fun, no conversation, and definitely no sex. It might be a safe house, but that didn't mean it had to be a prison. There had to be some way of charming him, some way of getting under his skin, some way of bringing Flynn over to the dark side.

Maybe she should cave in and go back to Castletownbloodyberehaven. Summer huffed a breath as she swatted away another cloud of flying furies. Bloody things. Not a chance. Granny O'Sullivan wouldn't give her a minute's peace.

The way to a man's heart is through his belly. She could almost hear her grandmother's lecture on how to get your man. Oh yes, be a good little girl and don't worry your silly head about anything serious. Being a surrendered wife had never been on her list of career choices, but a fat lot of good an MBA in Transportation and Logistics was here.

She had always assumed that her dad would welcome her with open arms into the airline business, that they would work side by side. But all he wanted was for her to look pretty and be charming to his important customers. In some ways he was just like Flynn.

She'd bet quite a lot of money that Flynn would love that. A docile woman who would look after his every need and warm his bed at night.

Summer glanced at him from beneath her eyelashes. The bed warming bit wouldn't be a problem. He really was a hottie, if you liked his 'Me Tarzan, you Jane' approach. Was that the key to Flynn? Operation *Defeat the Bodyguard* hadn't been successful. Maybe a charm offensive would work and it was better than spending her days lying around being bored. Summer rose to her feet, conscious of his eyes on her every move.

'Going somewhere?' His tone was suspicious.

'Look,' she tried to sound reasonable, 'I'm sorry. I get it that we're stuck here, so how about a truce?'

'A truce?' Flynn eyed her outstretched hand as if it was a snake about to bite him and he didn't raise his hand to take it.

Embarrassed by his churlish refusal, Summer took a step back. How could she have thought that he was attractive? The man was a Neanderthal. She pitied whatever mindless Stepford wife he ended up with, but she wouldn't give up yet. 'Let me cook dinner tonight.'

'You?'

She might as well have announced that she was joining the space programme. 'Yes.' Summer thumped her chest. 'Jane make dinner for Tarzan.'

She walked away, trying to ignore the snort of laughter coming from behind her. She would show him.

The mysterious delivery man had obviously arrived. The makeshift larder yielded two steaks as well as some fresh vegetables and more dried and tinned stuff. There was even another bottle of scrumpy. They would dine in style today. She foraged outside the backdoor. Someone had obviously tried to start a herb garden at one time and it had gone wild. She pounced on a woody patch of sage and there was wild watercress growing up near the spa. That would do very nicely. Pity there was no fresh garlic but she could still cook up a feast for a king, or a bloody-minded Scot.

Flynn had remained outside, chopping yet more wood, until he had built up quite a sweat and headed for the shower. She guessed that he had been waiting for her to cave in and ask for the tin opener, but if she had to eat another meal that involved tuna or spaghetti she would die.

'Something smells good.'

She was tempted to ask him why he sounded so surprised, but then remembered that she was supposed to be charming him. 'Take a seat and I'll serve.'

His eyes narrowed. Did Flynn think that she would try to poison him? Choke him to death with an overcooked steak? He eyed the rough table which now sported plates, glasses and a stubby candle she had found in the cupboard under the sink. The bottle of scrumpy was keeping cool in the jug she had taken from upstairs.

Summer removed the pan and put the marinated steaks on the metal grid over the fire. The fire sizzled as drops of marinade fell, wafting the aroma of herbs around the room.

'Gnocchi with salvia e burro,' she announced as she laid the first course before him.

The pale potato dumplings glistened in their coating of butter and crisp sage leaves. Flynn stared at the dish. He couldn't have been more shocked if it had been delivered by fairies. He bit into one and gave a moan that was almost orgasmic. Score one for the spoilt heiress.

'How did you . . . ?'

She laughed at his mystified expression. 'I love food, ever since boarding school. I was permanently starving there.'

'You didn't like school?'

'No. College was great, but boarding school was a pain. I missed my dad and some of the other girls were horrible.'

'Is that why you went to the club that night? Do you enjoy pain?'

The club. She had almost forgotten that. That was the night that they had . . . Flynn waited expectantly for her answer. She toyed with her gnocchi, smearing it with the buttery sauce. 'I honestly don't know. Molly said that it was amazing, that I should try it. I guess that I was curious.'

'About what?' Flynn asked.

She had almost forgotten that he had been a member there. Flynn had a few dark corners of his own and she wasn't sure if she wanted to share that much with him yet. She stood up. 'Excuse me; I have to take care of the steaks.'

Flynn's hand whipped out as she passed and he grasped her wrist. 'Curious about what, Summer?'

His voice had an edge that sent a shiver down her spine. Not anger, or impatience, just a simple, quiet command that halted her in her tracks. She stared down at the hand wrapped around her wrist. His fingers looked tanned against her pale skin and he had small cuts on his knuckles from wood splinters.

She could lie to him, but what was the point? In a few weeks, they wouldn't see each other again. 'I wanted to know if I could still feel.'

Summer shook his hand away and went to rescue the steaks, conscious of the sound of his chair scraping against the rough floor. Somehow she doubted that Flynn would let her make a statement like that and walk away. She felt his hand on her shoulder, the warmth of it seeping through the fine cotton of her T-shirt. She straightened and turned into his arms, afraid to look at his face. 'The steaks –'

'Will keep for two more minutes. Tell me what happened to you?'

Why was Flynn pushing this? Surely he knew. The story had been plastered over the tabloids for weeks. She shrugged and tried for levity. 'You must have seen the papers. Where did you spend last June? In a bubble?'

His hand traced the contours of her cheek before curving under her chin and raising her face. 'I spent last June in East Timor. *Hello!* magazine is hard to come by in the jungle.' Flynn's gaze was steady. There was no pity, no judgement. 'I know what happened, Summer. I've read the reports, but they don't tell the whole story. I want you to tell me what happened to you.'

Out of the frying pan, into the fire. She was trapped

between the flames and something hotter, something infinitely more dangerous. Her plan to charm him was unravelling. Flynn was determined to know everything and she wasn't sure if she was ready to tell him.

'Steaks. Please. I promise we can talk later.'

Something in her expression must have appeased him. Flynn relented, releasing her chin, and she breathed a sigh of relief. She had escaped for now, but a reckoning was coming.

The meal's success was measured by Flynn's empty plate, and they finished off the bottle of scrumpy while he talked a little about East Timor. He wouldn't tell her any details about his work, but the things he had seen were shocking and gave her a glimpse into another life, one full of danger and unrecognized heroism. It went some way in explaining why he had been so dismissive when they first met. What a comedown. From life in the jungle to babysitting an heiress.

A hot wave rose up her neck and scalded her cheeks. Flynn was a nice guy and she had been nothing but a brat to him from day one. A horrible, spoilt bitch who had been rude to him, lied to him and pushed him at every turn, when all he wanted to do was protect her. When had she turned into a monster?

Embarrassed, she made a show of clearing the plates and collecting the glasses and put them next to the sink. Maybe she could slip off to bed and . . .

'Come here.'

God, he was turning into Tarzan again. 'The dishes —'

'Can wait until morning. Talk to me.'

She gave him a wide berth and pulled up a chair opposite him.

'What happened last June?'

Summer played with the gold band on her right hand. She had planned to wear it on her wedding day as her *something old*. 'You probably saw it in the papers; last June I was supposed to get married. It didn't happen.'

'Why?'

Trust Flynn to cut to the chase. No platitudes. No cosy, sympathetic words.

'My dad insisted on a pre-nup. I have a shareholding in the airline.'

Flynn whistled. 'Let me guess. There was a problem.'

How could she have been so naïve? All the times Adam was supposed to sign. All the excuses about meetings and business trips abroad. Summer closed her eyes. 'A big problem. Dad put an investigator on my fiancé and . . .'

She remembered the tense meeting with her father and his bespectacled accountant. Adam's stories about his investments and his property portfolio in South Africa and Tokyo. None of it was true. Even with the evidence before her eyes, she still hadn't believed it. Adam loved her. She was certain. But when she tried to confront him, he wasn't in his office. He wouldn't take her calls. He just wasn't there.

And the stupid thing was that she hadn't cared. So what if he didn't have money? She loved him and wanted to marry him.

Flynn moved more quickly than she anticipated. One moment she was sitting on the chair, the next she was lifted up and pulled onto his lap. His muscular arm was tucked around her waist while his other hand stroked her hair. 'Go on.'

His warmth was comforting. She tucked her head under his chin and let it wash over her. She didn't cry about it anymore. She almost never cried. The next bit was harder. 'The wedding was days away. We'd spent over a year planning it. Dad told Adam to sign the pre-nup or the wedding was off.'

Her breath hitched in her throat. 'He didn't. Dad didn't cancel it. But Adam did.'

Flynn gave a sympathetic murmur and she took it as encouragement to press on to the grand finale.

'Then Molly rang me. She was working in PR at the time and . . . There were photographs of Adam and me together. The naked kind. The kind that sell for a lot of money. And that was it. The end of my perfect wedding.'

Flynn watched as she twisted the cheap gold band around her finger. Not the type of jewellery he had expected to see an heiress wearing, but Summer never took it off. The sight of her biting on her lower lip, trying not to cry, made him want to punch something.

He had leafed through Niall's report about the cancellation of the wedding and dismissed it without a second thought. Celebrity relationships broke all the time. Usually within a month they were announcing that they were in love with someone else. But this wasn't a celebrity. This was Summer. And as much as she was the client from hell, she hadn't deserved any of this.

Oh, there was no doubt that she was naïve and that her

father should have screened her boyfriends more thoroughly, but it was too late for that now. The damage was already done. What he hadn't expected to feel was shame, or the fierce sense of anger that raged through him at the thought of someone hurting her like that.

'I'll get Niall to check him out.' It would be nice if the ex-fiancé turned out to be the stalker. It would give Flynn a valid reason for tearing the bastard apart and beating him to a pulp.

She snorted. 'You think Dad hasn't already done that? Believe me; Adam was top of his shit list for months afterwards. For a while, even the rain was his fault.'

'Still. I want to check myself.' Flynn was willing to bet he could dig a lot more dirt than Tim O'Sullivan could. Curiosity overcame him. 'What was in the photos?'

She flushed and ducked her head. 'The usual,' she mumbled. 'Adam set it up. I couldn't understand why he was so keen on me giving him a blow job that evening. He knew I don't like doing them. But he begged, so I did. With perfect camera angles and everything. You could see my face really clearly and hardly a detail of him. He could have been any stray man I had picked up.'

Flynn's fist clenched involuntarily. He forced it to relax before he spoke again. 'You don't like BJs?'

She shrugged. 'I don't like the taste.'

'Really? That's it?'

'I bet most women don't like doing it. They just say they do to make men happy.' She met his incredulous look with a mutinous stare. The way her lower lip stuck out slightly was adorable and tempted him to bite it, but he had to stay focused.

'I'll just have to see about that, won't I?' he said. 'I'm sure if we went about it the right way, we could change your mind.'

'I've heard that line before.' She turned away, backing down from his subtle challenge. 'I bet you've never had a bad break-up.'

Flynn shifted in his chair. He could try to deflect the question, but she had been honest with him and it didn't feel right to lie to her. 'I have. And it wasn't pretty either.'

'Oh?'

He caught a flash of sympathy in her eyes and ploughed on. 'I was involved with someone. It was a D/s thing. We were together when I was home but she wanted more than that. Unfortunately, I was never in the country long enough. When I came back from my next tour of duty, she was dating my brother.'

Flynn remembered David's embarrassment when he tried to break the news about him and Lorna. How the occasional friendly drink and a shoulder to cry on had turned into a relationship. Neither of them had meant for it to happen, but by the time he got home, she and David were already an item.

'So what did you do?' Summer asked.

What could he do? His mother was already mad about her. The prospect of one of her sons marrying and giving her some grandchildren had made her happier than she had been for a long time. He couldn't ruin that. How could he admit that he had met Lorna in a BDSM club and that the pair of them had played together for months? Flynn shrugged. 'There was nothing I could do. They're getting married soon.'

'Ouch. That must hurt. I'm sorry.' Summer placed her hand on his arm in a gesture of comfort. 'Come on, let's get some fresh air. You can walk me to the spa again.'

'Good girl, you're learning.'

She snorted while she grabbed her towel and wash bag.

After she was finished doing whatever it was women did in the shower, and god knows she only had the basics as Flynn had refused to pack any of those oils and potions women seemed to need, he gave himself a speed scrub in the shower and was back at the croft before she had undressed.

The sight of her in those skimpy bits of nothing made sharing a bed with her a bad idea. She was still vulnerable from her early confession and too tempting for his peace of mind. He pulled out the sleeping bag. He would stay downstairs, well away from her. She's the client, he repeated to himself.

And he would wear pyjamas. Well, he amended; he would if he had any. Instead, he pulled on a clean pair of workout pants and tied the cotton drawstring tightly.

Summer had settled in bed, and silence descended on the croft. There was still twilight outside, but it was dim indoors. Flynn stacked his hands beneath his head and stared at the ceiling, trying not to think of her upstairs, all warm and sensual in his bed. The bed he had made with his own hands. The bed he hadn't realized he was making for her to sleep in. The bed he wanted to be in.

He dragged his mind away from her and thought about Adam Whatshisname. It was bad enough marrying a girl for her money, but then to humiliate her like that. These days, once pictures were released, they were out there forever. To the end of her days, Summer was likely to see pictures of herself sucking cock wherever she went. When she applied for jobs, when she was being inaugurated as President, when she was getting married. For some reason, that image annoyed him. He didn't want to think about Summer getting married.

Instead he considered her confession that she didn't like the taste. He really should do something about that. His balls tightened as he considered a course of lessons designed to teach her to love it. And graduation day would be something very special . . . Oh yeah, it was his duty to change her mind. Think of all the sensual pleasures she was missing.

There was a rustle upstairs, and the object of his fantasies poked her head over the edge of the ceiling. 'Are you coming to bed?' She sounded young, uncertain.

'I'll stay down here tonight.'

'Oh! I'm a little bit cold. I thought you might be too.' There was a slight quiver in her voice. Summer wasn't the usual self-possessed princess tonight.

He couldn't resist. 'Yeah, well, maybe I'm a bit cold too,' he lied, climbing out of the sleeping bag and up the ladder. Her bed was warm and smelled like Summer. His cock hardened instantly and he had to position himself carefully so that when she curled against him, she didn't feel it.

She's the principal. He had to keep his distance.

'Of course, that's not the only reason you wanted to go to *Noir*, is it?' he said, almost at random.

'What?'

'You're a kinky little girl, aren't you?'

219

She stiffened. 'What do you mean?'

Good, she was prickly and sounded more like the Summer he was used to.

'I packed for you, remember? I know what you're really like.'

'I have no idea what you are talking about.' She tried to sound indignant.

'Hah! Did you think I wouldn't find your stash? All those books full of kinky sex and spanking? I bet your Kindle is stuffed with erotica, stories full of dark and dangerous desires.'

She had gone rigid. 'You had no right to do that.'

'I'm your bodyguard. I have to know everything about you. And very interesting it was, too.'

She pulled away from him. 'So I'm curious. That's not a crime.'

'No,' he agreed. 'But it was enlightening how you found your way to all the really good stuff. And how well-thumbed your novels were.'

She stayed silent.

He waited for a minute, and then added, 'I assume you used the Rabbit, but tell me, did Adam use that little flail on you? Or those leather cuffs? Or the bondage tape?'

For some reason, the image of Adam playing with those toys enraged Flynn.

She went rigid. 'No!' He waited and eventually she went on, the words coming in jerks. 'No one did. I bought them for him, but we never used them.'

Flynn pulled her against him. 'Why not?' He couldn't resist stroking her back.

'Adam thought it was weird. He said he wasn't into anything like that, but I just wondered . . .' Her voice trailed off.

'Wondered what?' His hand slowed.

'What it would be like?' He could hardly hear her, she spoke so quietly. 'I always wondered. Even when I was in college, I had fantasies about a strong man, someone who would spank me and . . .' She broke off, unable to put it into words.

Flynn stayed silent, letting her find her own way.

'I know that it's silly. I'm a modern woman. I don't let men give me orders.' She broke off again and gasped when he give her a quick pinch on her bum. 'Ow. Don't get any ideas. Those stories about being tied up, they're just fiction. If someone tried to do that to me in real life, it would hurt and I would hate it.'

'Would you?' He continued to stroke. Did she realize how closely she was lying against him?

'Of course I would. Fantasies are just that. It's never the same when you do them in real life.' She sounded as if she was trying to convince herself.

'No. Sometimes it's better.' He waited for a few minutes, and then asked, 'Did you never get your boyfriend to spank you? Just to see?'

She shrugged. 'I didn't know how to ask him. And what if he told anyone? You can just imagine the headlines, can't you? "Summer O'Sullivan is into kinky sex". The tabloids would have a field day.'

She raised her head from its position on his chest. 'You do this stuff, don't you?'

He nodded.

'Do women really like it?'

He nodded again.

'How do you know? Adam thought I liked giving him blow jobs. Women probably just tell you what you want to hear.'

He laughed. 'Call it male intuition. There are certain subtle signs that tell me when a woman is really into it.'

Summer put her head back down on his chest. 'I still think they're just fooling you.'

But the quiver had left her voice and she relaxed into sleep. He grinned and expanded his plans for her education.

19

When she woke, Summer was still lying in his arms. Usually she liked guys who manscaped, but the light coating of hair on his chest felt nice. Masculine. Adam had always been ultra-conscious of his appearance and he had spent more time in the salon than she did. But Flynn was natural. Summer sniffed lightly, inhaling the scent of soap and something that was uniquely him.

'Do I smell?' The vibration in his chest rumbled against her ear and she giggled.

'No. I mean, yes. You smell nice.' She waited for him to make some excuse and leave. She would have, if their roles were reversed. How could she have dumped on him like that last night? A whole year of pretending that she didn't care, that Adam never happened and she had blurted it out like a teenager.

'Tell me your thoughts.'

'My thoughts? Why?'

'Because I'm interested. If I'm to protect you, I need to know everything that's going on inside your head.'

She stretched out her hand, and let it rest on his abdomen. Flynn had real muscles. They were rock hard. He was rather like one of the cover models from her favourite erotica.

'I'm waiting.'

Oh dear. Tarzan was back. 'I was thinking that you have abs like a cover model.'

Laughter rumbled through his chest. 'Is that so? I'll keep it in mind if I decided on a career change. What were you thinking about before then?'

There was no fooling him. How had he gotten inside her head so fast? 'That I'm sorry that I dumped on you last night.'

Flynn rolled over, pinning her against the pillow. 'You did not dump on me. I asked you to tell me.'

She could see the gold flecks in his eyes again. He gave an impatient sigh. 'How long has it been since you talked to anyone? I mean really talked?'

Summer bit down on her lip. She talked with Maya and Natasha all the time. About fashion, clubs, gossip but nothing serious. She and Molly had drifted apart over the past couple of years. Molly was different from the girl she had known in college. Only her cousin Sinead could see right through her. Luckily she didn't see her very often.

'That long, hmmm? How about a little wager – you promise to tell me the truth for a whole day. No evasions. No lies.'

Not a chance, she thought instinctively. She wasn't letting him inside her head again, but the challenge in Flynn's gaze made her hesitate. She could do this. Well, mostly. 'And what if I do? Will I get a prize?'

The smile he gave her had a tinge of wickedness. 'Maybe we'll explore some of those fantasies of yours.'

'What?' She almost rocketed out of the bed.

'You heard me.'

'But I thought you didn't sleep with clients.'

'You won't always be the client and I said nothing about sleeping.' Flynn released her and rolled off the bed.

'Wait. You can't just say something like that and walk away.'

But Flynn was already gone, whistling as he strode up the path to the spa. Summer battled the urge to run after him, or throw something at him.

When he returned, she was dressed and doing her best to get the fire going.

'I see you've never been in the boy scouts.' He busied himself at the fire while she laid the table and whisked the eggs in a bowl. In some ways Flynn was quite easy to be with. She didn't have to check her appearance in the mirror all the time, or worry that she had chipped a nail. It was almost comfortable.

They sat down to a breakfast of eggs and coffee.

'What is your earliest memory?' Flynn asked.

Summer paused, mid-mouthful. 'We're starting this already?'

'If you want one of your fantasies, yes. And remember, I get to ask the questions and I expect honest answers.'

Bugger. He was really going to do this. A whole day of truth for a single fantasy? Was it worth it? Looking across the breakfast table at him, his hair still damp from the shower, her neglected libido voted yes. 'I suppose it was hiding in a currant bush in my grandmother's garden. They weren't quite ripe and I had the worst belly ache ever afterwards.'

'Who was the first boy you kissed?'

'That's easy. It was Declan O'Malley during a game of kiss chase. I punched him on the nose when he caught me. His mother wouldn't let him play with me for months afterwards.'

'Have you ever stolen anything?'

He surely couldn't expect her to confess to a crime? 'Oh, now that's just mean. Come on, what happened to my favourite colour or what movie do I watch when I'm miserable?'

Flynn gave her a warning frown. 'Do I look as if I'm going to arrest you? Answer the question or we can stop this now.'

He was back in Tarzan mode again. 'Okay, I stole a lipstick, but it was a dare, part of a secret club thing at school. I never actually wore it.'

Flynn raised an eyebrow at that but didn't comment. He collected the plates and washed them at the sink. 'Come on, we have to catch something for lunch and given my luck yesterday, it might take a while.'

The surface of the loch was like a mirror. The morning mist had already cleared, and hardly a breath of wind moved the surface. Flynn helped her into the small rowing boat before untying the line. He rowed in silence, the oars making ripples in the water that spread out in expanding arcs.

Summer looked at the surrounding hills. The glen was a peaceful, beautiful place. No wonder Flynn liked to come here. She spotted a shadow on the horizon 'What's that up ahead?'

'It's a small island with a Culdees cell.'

When he saw her puzzled expression, he explained. 'Culdees were monks or hermits who practised healing. We can stop there for lunch if you like.'

'I'd like.' She smiled.

Summer sat back, cushioning her head against a sleeping bag they had taken from the cottage, watching as Flynn cast his line. She stared at the pale clouds scudding across the sky and allowed her eyes to drift closed.

'Have you ever done any kind of drugs?'

Oh god. Twenty questions was starting again. She stared at him through half closed eyes. 'No. As if.'

'How many sexual partners have you had?'

That one made her sit up in outrage and the boat rocked. 'You brought me out here to interrogate me? Would you answer a question like that?'

'I might, if you asked nicely, but I'm the one who gets to ask the questions.'

She wasn't sure if a single fantasy was worth it. If he was going to get this personal, she should have asked for half a dozen. One of which would involve torturing him. 'Just how many questions do you get to ask? This doesn't seem to be very fair. I only get one fantasy.'

'Perhaps you should have negotiated before you agreed.'

Summer stuck out her tongue at him. 'I didn't realize that I was dealing with such a devious, underhanded –'

His large hand closed around her ankle. 'One more insult and you can swim back to shore.'

Summer paused in mid-tirade and took a deep breath. 'I was simply pointing out that it wasn't fair.'

Flynn grinned shamelessly at her before releasing her ankle. 'Then perhaps you'll be more careful in future. We can put a limit on it if you wish – ten questions.'

'Ten?' Her shriek echoed around the hills.

'Aye, ten and I'm being generous – we can count the ones I've asked already. Now, where were we? Oh yes, sexual partners.'

Fine, if he wanted to play, she would play. She nodded her head as if she was counting and the seconds dragged by. After almost a minute the amusement faded from his eyes. She screwed up her face as if she was trying to remember and another minute ticked by. Flynn's steady gaze never faltered. She could almost imagine him counting along with her.

'Four,' she finally admitted. 'Including you.'

He huffed out a breath he had obviously been holding. She had finally got one up on him. 'You wee bitch.'

Summer giggled. It was such a good feeling not to be the one at a disadvantage. 'You shouldn't believe everything you read about me.'

Her sense of triumph was short-lived when Flynn asked, 'Have you ever had a sexual encounter with a woman?'

'No.' She snorted. 'Again – don't believe everything you read. I believe you're down to three more questions.'

A jerk on the line took Flynn's attention away from her. They had a bite at last. He played the line for what seemed like ages before he finally reeled the struggling fish in. The trout landed, its slippery body wriggling against the bottom of the boat. Flynn dispatched it quickly and baited another hook. After he cast out again, they sat in companionable silence.

'What country do you want to see before you die?'

That was an easy one. 'Argentina.'

He raised an eyebrow at that one. 'Why?'

'That's two questions,' she reminded him. 'Because Dad's airline doesn't fly there and I've never been.'

'What is your greatest fear?'

'The dark,' she announced without hesitation.

A look of disbelief crossed his face. 'You promised not to lie.'

Summer didn't answer. She had enough material to keep several psychiatrists busy for years. After Adam she had nightmares of waiting at the altar for him for hours. When she was a child living at her grandmother's, she was afraid of closing her eyes until her dad came home. Her greatest fear now? She honestly didn't know. Being chased by paparazzi down a dark alley? Stalkers? None of those things were as terrifying as loving someone and finding out that they were lying to you.

Flynn was having none of it. 'I'm waiting.'

He was using that voice again. The stern one he had used at *Noir*. The one that made her want to . . . She stared down at the wedding band on her finger and twisted it back and forth, hoping that the question would go away or that another fish might decide to bite. Water lapped against the side of the boat and a bird cried overhead. Flynn waited. He wasn't giving up. What had started out as a silly game had turned serious.

'I suppose it would be trusting someone and being let down,' she eventually answered.

She waited for his response. A few trite words of comfort, perhaps a teasing remark that she could always buy new friends. Flynn said nothing. Instead, he stowed his gear and picked up the oars again. They were heading for the island.

Summer trailed her hand in the crystal-clear water as he rowed. It was icy cold but the sheer beauty of the place made her heart ache. The glen was rugged, remote and brooding, just like Flynn.

'A penny for them,' he offered.

She shook her head. 'You've already had quite enough of my thoughts today.'

Flynn moored the boat at an old jetty and climbed out. 'Careful, it's slippery.'

She clambered up behind him and reached for his hand as she neared the top. Her foot slipped on one of the old iron rungs and for a frozen second, she fell backwards. She gasped.

'I have you.' Flynn shouted as his hand caught her arm.

Her free arm flailed, seeking something to grab onto and Flynn was there again. Grasping her by both arms, he pulled her onto the jetty. They landed in a tangled heap of arms and legs on the rough wood. Something about her proximity to him reminded her of the night at the club. She had a sudden vision of Flynn pressing her against the wall of the apartment, his jaw clenched, his eyes dark with passion. Embarrassed by the memory, she tried to laugh it off. 'I bet you don't often let the woman be on top.'

She could feel the warmth of his hands slowly caressing her through her thin T-shirt. His mouth was inches away from hers. If she bent her head she could be kissing him, tasting his mouth again.

'I could be persuaded. Why? Is that a fantasy of yours? Being in charge in bed?'

She scrambled off him, ignoring her racing pulse. The thought of Flynn lost in the throes of passion, helpless beneath her touch, sent the blood rushing to her core. But she would never admit it. 'You are such a bloody . . . Scot.'

Flynn grabbed his bag and hurried after her. 'Half-Scot. And I might remind you that you promised me the truth. You still have to answer one more question if you want your fantasy.'

Summer rounded on him, wishing he had never started this stupid game. Who did he think he was, prying in to her head like this for his own amusement? 'Stuff your fantasy. You know nothing about me and I'm not playing this game anymore. You've pushed too far.' She stormed away to the tumbled ruins of a stone building. It really was a small island. How could someone, even a hermit, have lived here? Summer did her best to ignore Flynn as he lit a fire and unpacked his bag. If he produced another tin of alphabet spaghetti she would beat him to a pulp with it and leave his body on the island for the crows.

The mouth-watering smell of char-grilled fish wafted to her nostrils. It didn't matter what Flynn cooked; she wasn't hungry and she wasn't speaking to him. Huddled on her boulder, she surveyed the rest of the island. It was hardly more than a rock sticking out of the loch. Whoever lived here must have gone barking mad with nothing to do all day and no one to talk to.

'Lunch is ready,' Flynn announced.

'I'm not hungry.'

Flynn came up behind her, but she refused to look at him. She shrugged in her best *I don't give a damn* gesture.

He put his hands on her shoulders and massaged gently, his skilled fingers finding every tiny knot, and easing the tension. 'You're right. I was pushing. But I do know that beneath the spoilt little rich girl is a passionate woman. That you adore your father and you want his approval, and that you're not half as wild as your reputation.'

Summer relented, relaxing into his touch. Whatever she had been expecting, it wasn't an apology.

'And one other thing. You can always rely on me. I will never lie to you and I will protect you, even when you're being a pain in the arse.'

Flynn planted a light kiss on her shoulder to break the suddenly serious mood. 'Now, come and eat with me. Tarzan has cooked lunch for Jane.'

She hated to admit it but Flynn could cook. On a remote rock sticking out of a loch, he had managed to produce a meal fit for a king, or at least a starving society princess. Fresh fish, some sort of artisan cheese wrapped in wax, and bread that was almost fresh. The feast was topped off with tiny wild strawberries.

Even if he looked like the back of a barn door, she would still have been attracted to him, simply for his abilities in the outdoors. His calm, can-do approach to everything was a refreshing change from the boy-toys Maya and Natasha usually hung out with. There was something intensely masculine about Flynn. Something that was capable and steady that she hadn't experienced before, and she wanted more, even if that meant exposing her innermost thoughts to him.

'Yes. I would like to be in charge in . . . in the bedroom. But not all the time,' she added, not wanting him to think that she was some kind of bossy boots.

His eyes lit up, the tiny gold flecks becoming more noticeable. 'Good girl.'

Somehow the phrase didn't irk her as much as it had done. If she had to admit it, she wanted to please Flynn.

'You're thinking about something.'

Summer shot him a sideways glance. 'Don't push it, Flynn. You've already had ten.'

20

Back at the croft, supper was over and Flynn hadn't said anything about his earlier promise. The more Summer thought about it, the less she liked the idea of exploring her fantasies. Yes, sure, she liked the notion of the stuff that was in her books, but faced with the prospect of actually doing those things, she was getting cold feet.

She bet that most of those things would hurt like hell, and not only that, they would be embarrassing and ridiculous. She hadn't realized how much she valued her dignity until now. She wondered if Flynn had changed his mind. Or forgotten. How humiliating would that be? She was quivering like a badly set jelly and he hadn't remembered his promise. She wasn't sure what she hoped for.

Flynn went outside, presumably to the spa, and she busied herself putting away the dishes. Those old-fashioned women who did embroidery had a point, she decided. At least it was something to make her look busy. Now she had nothing to do except wait for him to come back. Her stomach flipped and she realized her hands were shaking.

She sat down in front of the fire, holding her hands firmly in her lap. This was stupid. She was the infamous, notorious Summer O'Sullivan. She didn't shake just because a man had said he was going to make one of her sexual fantasies come true.

Flynn came back in, pulling off his boots at the door. 'Ready?' he asked, his eyes intent on her.

'I don't think this is a good idea,' she said, proud that her voice was steady.

'I was thinking we might start with a bit of bondage.' Flynn held up a length of rope.

Her stomach lurched. Bondage! She had a vision of herself tied to the bed upstairs, naked and spread-eagled. She'd be completely exposed to Flynn. She hadn't waxed or shaved since her trip to the salon the day before they left. Oh no, she couldn't do that. She'd be mortified. And what if her nose itched? She would be driven mad trying to scratch it. No, no, she didn't want to do this.

Flynn must have caught her apprehensive glance at the ladder. He laughed. 'Relax; I'm not planning anything terrible. I've only got one length of rope.' He held it up for her inspection.

Summer relaxed slightly. It was neatly coiled and tied, but it wasn't that long. Probably not long enough to tie her to the four corners of the big bed. 'What had you in mind?'

'I'm just going to tie your wrists. You can watch.'

'That's all?' It didn't sound too bad.

'That's it. And maybe blindfold you afterwards. No more than that. Can you cope?'

Before she could talk herself out of it, Summer nodded. This was a chance to try something she had always wondered about. She'd be a fool not to take it.

'Your safe word is red,' he told her.

Safe word. Oh my god, she had a safe word. She trembled, not sure if it was fear or excitement.

'Hold out your wrists,' he told her. She did it without arguing, telling herself it was mere curiosity that was propelling her. Flynn untwisted his coil of rope, letting it fall on the floor. To her surprise, instead of taking up one end, he took the bent-over middle part and looped it around her wrists a couple of times. It was loose on her and she relaxed. This was going to be a token bondage exercise. She'd get the feeling of the rope on her skin, but she'd be able to get free at any time.

He checked the loops were straight so that there were no twists against her skin and then looped the free end around the strands of rope between her wrists. It tightened up, going from loose to snug fitting.

'See if you can get free,' Flynn told her.

She wiggled and pulled. The bonds weren't tight enough to affect her circulation and weren't uncomfortable, but they were businesslike and efficient. She was tied up.

'What now?' she asked. She was trying to stay nonchalant, as if something primal hadn't stirred when she realized she wasn't going to be able to wiggle out of the rope. She was perfectly safe, he was her bodyguard, and he wouldn't hurt her. And she could still scratch her nose. It wasn't itching, but she rubbed it, just to assure herself that she could.

'I'm going to put a light blindfold on you. Come down here on the floor, it may affect your balance.'

Obediently, she stood and then got down onto her hunkers. Without her hands, it was more difficult than she had expected and she landed on her bottom with a bump. Flynn settled himself behind her.

'Here's the blindfold,' he said and held out a white piece

236

of material. It was so ordinary, so prosaic, compared to the sinister black hood she had feared, that she giggled. This would be okay.

'Okay. Do your worst.'

'Oh no, I'm going to do my best.' He folded the cloth and tied it around her head, taking care to make sure none of her hair was caught in the knot.

Summer's world plunged into darkness. She could make out only a faint glimmer of white and found it easier to close her eyes. Her breathing faltered.

'Good girl, take it easy. Breath with me,' Flynn murmured. His arms were around her, holding her, and she was intensely conscious of his warmth and distinctive scent surrounding her. There was a faint trace of mint. He must have brushed his teeth while he was outside.

'Breathe, breathe,' he told her. She obeyed, allowing herself to relax against him. Her world was reduced to Flynn breathing.

Something rough passed over her face. It wasn't Flynn's hand. She jerked.

'Easy, that's the rope.' Flynn pulled her back against him. The position felt decadent; she was stretched out in front of the fire and surrounded by Flynn, but she was off-balance. The rope moved down from her face to her neck.

She caught her breath. She hadn't realized how vulnerable she would feel like this. *It's Flynn, he won't hurt me.* His hand traced the curve of her cheek, causing her to lean into his caress. She wanted to purr at the feeling, even while his other arm pulled her sideways so that she was more unbalanced.

The rope moved again, this time across her breasts. She gasped. The sensation was unexpected. A quick jerk and she tipped over, to be caught by Flynn, but now she had no idea where she was. Still on the floor, still in front of the fire, she knew that, but now she wasn't sure which way she was facing.

It was stupid, such a little thing, but it made her feel helpless. 'Flynn.' She wasn't sure what she wanted to say, and was shocked at how thin and breathless her voice sounded.

'Shhh. Just go with it.' He brushed the bare skin of her stomach with the end of the rope. Summer jerked. She hadn't even realized her T-shirt had ridden up.

She was taken by surprise when her arms moved. Flynn was pulling the rope around her wrists, pulling it over her head. His muscles flexed around her as he tied it off, leaving her stretched out before him. She moaned, not sure if she was aroused or scared. Or both.

'All right?'

She nodded, not wanting to find the words to explain how she was feeling.

Flynn tipped her head back, stretching her neck, and kissed her. The brush of his mouth was gentle and tantalizing, but it was devastating. Knowing that she couldn't refuse it, that she was completely at his mercy, unleashed something inside her.

If she didn't think in words, she wouldn't say the word 'red' by accident, she decided, and gave herself up to the delicate exploration of his tongue. She didn't try to control him, just allowed him to do what he wanted.

She surrendered to the experience, vaguely aware that

her breath had shortened to pants and that moisture had pooled between her thighs.

Flynn gave a murmur of approval and traced a line of fire down her throat. He stroked a caress down the slope of her breast and over her nipple. She sucked in a breath. It had never felt like that before.

She heard his choked half-laugh. 'I can't resist,' he said. Then he pulled down her top and unclipped her bra. The air of the cottage was cool until his hot mouth took her by surprise. He licked and nuzzled at her nipple before he took it into his mouth and nibbled gently on it.

'Ah!' Summer's back arched. She had been half-propped against Flynn, though she wasn't sure if it was his thigh or arm, but she didn't care. She twisted, trying to get more of that contact.

'You have the most exquisitely responsive nipples I've ever seen.' Flynn pinched the other one, gauging the pressure so that she was left breathless. Her stomach had coiled into a painful knot which reminded her of that night when he had refused to allow her to come.

'Flynn?' She didn't know how to ask the question, but the thought that he might leave her trembling and needy was horrifying.

'Yes baby, it's okay, this is for you.' He continued to torment her nipples by pinching them while he nibbled his way up her neck to the lobe of her ear.

She twisted, trying to get more of the sensation. She was so close, so close. Her hips moved restlessly while she pressed her thighs together, trying both to bring more pressure to bear on her aching clit and hide the wetness between them.

'Naughty,' Flynn murmured. The next moment, the rope was looped around her right knee, pulling up and out.

She gasped. In this position, even though she was still wearing all of her clothes, she felt utterly open and exposed. And more aroused than she could ever remember being in her life before.

'No secrets, remember? What do you feel?'

She couldn't speak. All the air had left her lungs.

'Tell me. What do you feel?' Flynn's hand stroked her thigh, the edge of his nails making a delicious contrast to his questing fingertips. Summer wondered what it would be like to feel his mouth there, biting her.

He stroked the centre of her shorts; just enough to provide a tantalizing brush against her aching clit. She couldn't resist lifting her hips, offering herself to his teasing fingers. They moved away.

Oh yes, he wanted her to say something. What was the word? 'Aroused,' she managed.

'Good girl. Do you want to come?'

She nodded frantically. Was he even looking at her? 'Please,' she begged.

The rope slipped down and then she felt it tight against the seam of her shorts. The pressure was maddening. Flynn tipped her head back and kissed her deeply, possessively, while one hand pinched her excruciatingly sensitive nipple. She arched her back, giving herself up to his demands just as the rope tightened, bringing the perfect pressure on her clit.

It was too much. She exploded into orgasm, crying out as she twisted against the rope and into the caress Flynn lavished on her. For endless heartbeats, she forgot how to breathe, able only to ride the pulses shaking her body until she was left gasping and limp.

When she was able to think again, she was surprised to find herself still on the floor, still blindfolded and with her wrists tied. She felt as if she had been scattered over the Scottish sky.

'Good girl,' Flynn murmured and pulled off the blindfold. The sudden brightness made her blink and turn her face into his shirt. She was sprawled with her head in the crook of his arm as he lay in front of the fire. He was still fully dressed. It was too much effort to try to get untied; she would leave that to him.

He gave her a quick kiss. 'You're a natural. Just wait until you see what I have planned for tomorrow.'

21

Flynn stroked an errant strand of hair back from Summer's face, then stopped. That was dangerously close to a caress and he couldn't afford to get attached to his principal. Last night's encounter had already broken enough rules.

He might not have actually given in to his urge to bury his cock in her warmth, but he had come far too close. This business of holing up in his old croft to teach Ms O'Sullivan a lesson wasn't working out the way he had planned. Instead of taking the society princess down several notches, he was seeing her in a whole new light. One that made him uncomfortable and cranky.

Summer stirred, turning her head into his hand, like a cat begging to be petted. She gave a protesting murmur when he snatched his hand away.

She was the principal. His job was to protect her, and perhaps further her education a little. Not to have an affair with her. He knew what happened when bodyguards had affairs with principals. Dead bodies. He was not going to do that to Summer.

Even if she wasn't as spoilt as he had believed, they moved in different worlds, and always would.

Without his warmth to cuddle against, Summer burrowed down into the bed and pulled the sheet up over her head. 'Wake me when breakfast is served,' she muttered into the pillow.

Who was he kidding? She was a spoilt brat, used to being waited on hand and foot, and to getting her own way. Well, not with him.

Flynn pulled the covers off her. 'Rise and shine. Time for you to make my breakfast.' His voice caught when he saw how her teeny excuse for panties had ridden up during the night. Her buttocks were on display, and from the back, she might as well have been naked. He swallowed.

Summer didn't notice his reaction. She was too busy shrieking at him and trying to grab the sheet out of his hand. 'Give those back. It can't possibly be time to get up.'

'I'm hungry, and it's your duty to feed me. So up you get.' He jumped off the bed, taking all the bedclothes with him.

She sat up on the bare bed, twisting her nightclothes into some semblance of decency and glaring at him. 'If you knew all the horrible things I'm planning to do to you, you'd be running away, not standing there smirking,' she told him.

'Yeah, yeah. Talk is cheap. I want scrambled eggs and porridge for my breakfast this morning.'

Flynn was pretty sure that she would have ignored his command, but with no bedclothes, there was no point in Summer insisting on her right to stay in bed. She clambered down the ladder, muttering under her breath about 'Arrogant Scottish bollixes.'

By the time breakfast was over, Summer was in a slightly better temper. He was glad that she no longer obsessed about her lack of make-up and hair products and had pulled her hair back into a curly ponytail. That reminded him of something that had been nagging him.

'When you said you were afraid of the dark, you weren't lying, were you?'

She swallowed. 'No.'

'How bad is it?'

'The blindfold wasn't too bad, because there was a bit of light coming through it. But if it's really dark, or there is something solid over me, I'll freak.'

She picked up her empty coffee cup and seemed surprised to find there was nothing in it. She put it down again before she continued. 'When I was in college, I was out hiking with friends and we got caught in a downpour. They dashed into a little narrow cave. I couldn't make myself go in with them. I stood out in the rain for over an hour.'

'We'll work on that,' he promised her, then switched topics. 'What training have you had?'

'In what?' She recovered enough to give him a look that suggested he was a particularly backward toddler. 'I can speak four languages. I have an MBA in Transportation and Logistics. I can ride Western, classic and side-saddle. I can tell Beluga caviar from Sevruga, I can curtsy in a formal evening dress, and I know the correct form of address for any dignitary.'

Flynn sighed. He had really been fooling himself. 'Laudable as all that is, and no doubt essential to the good of mankind, but I was thinking of self-defence training.'

'I can dial 999 really fast,' she said, but she looked away and there was a trace of colour in her face.

'Not good enough. It's time you learned the basics of how to look after yourself. After all, a woman who knows how to ride side-saddle must be in prime demand by kidnappers.'

Her eyes narrowed dangerously at him, but with very little argument, she agreed to allow him to teach her self-defence.

'We'll start with a warm-up,' he told her, and led her outside. 'We'll go for a quick run to get the blood flowing.' He set off, leading the way along the paths he knew so well from his childhood.

He ran easily, enjoying the feel of his muscles working smoothly and the rush of his breath in the pure Highland air. Thank god that, bar the odd twinge now and again, he was back to full fitness. His physical strength and stamina were so integral to his job that he couldn't tolerate being injured. The thought of being permanently incapacitated bothered him far more than being killed.

At first, Summer jogged along behind him, keeping up for a while, then her steps began to labour and she fell behind. He slowed down to compensate. 'Having trouble?'

She glared, sweat pouring down her face and sticking the T-shirt to her back. 'You're doing this to torture me, aren't you?'

He suppressed a smile. 'We've only run two miles. If you were a rookie training with me, you'd be running carrying a 50 kilo rucksack and we'd be going for fifteen miles.'

She didn't have the breath to answer that, but her furious eyes spoke volumes.

He jogged along beside her. 'First lesson. Where is the croft in relation to us?'

She came to a shuddering stop. 'Are you telling me that we're lost?'

Flynn laughed. 'No. I know where we are. But the first

lesson is that you should always know where you are, and where safety is. Where is the croft from here?'

She looked around, a new awareness in her eyes, and pointed. 'Over there.'

'Good girl.' She flushed. 'You noticed that our path curved around, so the croft is not directly behind us. Remember this. Always know where you are, so you'll know how to get home.'

He headed back to the croft at a slow jog, aware that Summer was cursing him as she panted along behind him.

Back at the croft, he gave her a glass of water, and then began the first of a series of drills.

In some ways, it was good that Summer hadn't had any martial arts training before, so she wasn't tied in to some of the more elaborate patterns. But it was scary how little she knew about how to defend herself. Flynn was determined to teach her how to stay alive.

'Block, block and punch. Keep your thumb tucked outside your fist, not inside or you'll break it.' He showed her how to make an effective fist, curling her fingers down and tucking the thumb underneath. 'Keep your wrist straight when you punch. Use the first two knuckles and power it through your hips.' He held up his hands and let her punch them over and over again. 'Keep your feet on the ground and punch from the shoulder. You'll get one blow, so make it count.' He drilled her, making her do it over and over again.

'I'm exhausted,' she complained. 'Can't I have a rest?'

'You think the bad guys will only attack you when you are fresh and well-rested? Twenty more minutes and you can rest for a while.'

Her punch this time was the first one which he felt. 'Well done. Now you're getting it.'

He continued, 'First rule of self-defence. Don't be there. Listen to your instincts. Don't get into a situation where you have to defend yourself. Better to be rude than dead. But the second rule is that you are fighting for your life. No messing about trying to be nice. If you have to fight, you are the only one that counts. Do whatever it takes to get out alive.'

He showed her how to break an attacker's nose and possibly kill him before he let her rest. That was probably enough for the first day.

22

Next morning, when she was making her morning dash to the latrine, he checked out the box of provisions Niall had sent. Excellent, there was more food and a nice change from the usual scrumpy: a bottle of Baileys, nestled into a freezer box full of ice. It was his secret pleasure and he didn't give a damn that the guys of the Wing teased him about it. Hell, they could talk. One of them had a box of Tayto shipped by helicopter to some godforsaken place when they were stuck there over Christmas. Some of the other lads were worse than girls for chocolate, but no one gave them grief over that. Well, not without suffering.

As soon as breakfast was eaten and they were drinking their coffee, Summer announced, 'I've come to a decision.'

He put down his cup. 'Yes?'

'We're stuck here for the next couple of weeks, right?' He nodded. 'And I have no phone, no television, no internet, no Facebook, no Twitter, no Wii, no books to read, no access to a beauty salon, no gym, no yoga class, no shops and no friends. Have I got that right?'

He winced. It did sound bad. 'You've got a personal trainer,' he defended himself.

She waved that off. 'Basically, I have a whole lot of nothing to do. While that has a certain novelty value, and will no doubt do wonders for my stress levels, I'm already bored.'

'We could go fishing.'

She gave him the look he deserved for that. 'Fishing – the undisputed king of the boring sports. Yes, let's do that.' She shook her head. 'No, I have something different in mind.'

'Go on.'

She took a breath. 'While we're here, you're going to tell me everything you know about kinky sex.' She didn't wait for him to reply. 'The only advantage of this damned croft is that it's private. So I want to do all the stuff I can't do at home. And you can teach me.'

He had to admire her for being upfront. His resolve to keep her at arm's length had barely lasted through the first week. The prospect of teaching Summer, of doing all of those things he had fantasized about, was too much to resist. His treacherous cock was already awake at the prospect. It was an offer no sane man could refuse.

'After dinner, then. But first we have to find lunch.' They went out looking for wild herbs, as if she hadn't made that outrageous offer.

A change in the wind, bringing heavy black rain clouds in across the loch, sent them back to the croft for an early lunch. By the time it was cooked, the rain was beating down on the roof. They were stuck inside for the rest of the day.

The rain continued to drum against the windows long after they had cleared away the lunch things.

'You know, I think it's time we worked on one of your

weak spots,' Flynn said, but refused to tell her what he had in mind.

Summer waited for a hint of what he was planning. Whistling cheerfully, Flynn went to the jeep and when he returned he was carrying the bag from London. The one with the guns and other stuff that she didn't want to think about.

He set the bag down on the chair and unzipped it. From a small black case he produced a handgun. 'A Sig Sauer 9mm pistol.'

Flynn unclipped the magazine before offering it to her. 'You can touch it now. It's not loaded.'

Summer reached tentatively for the gun. It was heavier than she expected. She handed it back to Flynn, trying to hide her distaste. His search of the bag produced what he was looking for and he gave her a speculative look before he produced a coil of rope and some dark fabric. He set both on the table in front of her.

The fabric proved to be a finely woven bag with a drawstring at the end, like the kind of bag in which she would store shoes or handbags. She guessed that it wasn't for her Louboutins. Realization dawned and she knew how Flynn intended to use it. 'No. Absolutely not.'

'You need to do this in a safe environment. It means that you are less likely to panic if you ever encounter the real thing. And I promise to make it worth your while.'

Summer covered her ears. She didn't want to know.

'Look at me. There are four phases to a kidnapping: assault, transportation, captivity and release. The first and last phases are the most dangerous for a civilian. If you panic, you could be killed. I'm asking you to trust me.'

This was a dangerous Flynn, one that she didn't know, but his voice was steady and calm and her instinct was to do what he asked.

'What do you intend to do?' She hated that her voice shook. She wasn't a coward, but there were some things that scared the hell out of her.

'I'm going to tie you and then put the hood over your head. You won't panic because I'll be here with you. I won't leave your side for an instant.'

Summer bit her lip. Could she let Flynn restrain her? This wasn't the same as the rope. This wouldn't be playing. 'And you'll stop the minute I ask you to?'

'You have a safe word. All you have to do is use it.'

She couldn't say yes. That was the scariest word in the English language at this moment. Instead, she stretched out her hands to him.

'Good girl, but we'll get ready first.' He piled more wood on the fire until it was a hot, crackling blaze. 'And since this is going to be an experience you'll never forget, I want you naked.'

Naked? She swallowed. Did he have any idea what he was asking? She badly wanted to refuse, but the thought of appearing a coward in Flynn's eyes drove her on.

She stripped off and stood before the fire. The heat of the flames caressed her body.

Flynn's eyes warmed with appreciation and something more, but he was all business as he wrapped the rope around her chest and waist, then looped it around her elbows. When he was finished, her arms were pinned at her sides. Her hands were free, but she couldn't move them enough to do anything useful with them. He checked the tightness of the ropes, sliding in a finger here and there to make sure it wasn't too tight. He caught a knot at her back and pulled, and Summer had no option but to move back. She glared at him.

He grinned. 'I might keep this on you permanently. It's one way to keep you under control.'

She didn't get a chance to reply, because he pulled the black bag down over her head. She had a fleeting impression of the smell of gun oil and linseed.

Darkness descended.

For an endless, timeless, horrifying moment, Summer couldn't breathe. This was all of her worst fears coming together. She couldn't move, couldn't breathe, couldn't hear, couldn't even scream.

Then she was conscious of Flynn's warm hands on her skin, his strong arms around her, his voice in her ear. 'Good girl, I've got you. I'm here.' It was muffled by the hood, but she could hear him. 'Now breathe. Breathe with me.'

His chest rose and fell at her back, solid and reassuring. She made a heroic effort to quell her panic and concentrated on breathing in time with Flynn. She dismissed a random thought about how his lungs must be so much bigger than hers. Everything about Flynn was bigger. In. Out. In. Out. She could breathe. The panic receded.

'My brave girl,' said the voice in her ear. The hand on her stomach shifted and moved up to her breast. A sudden pinch on her nipple jolted her, igniting a spark of arousal in her pelvis.

'Oh yeah, that's my Summer,' he said. Both hands now skimmed up and down her body, setting her skin on fire and causing the bones in her legs to dissolve.

She didn't recognize herself. Here she was, naked and wearing a hood, in front of a fully dressed man with a gun. It should have been her worst nightmare, but all she could think of was getting him to continue to touch her.

'More,' she pleaded.

'Oh, there will be much, much more,' Flynn promised. 'Here, let me make you comfortable.'

His hands supported her while he helped her to her knees, then stretched her out so that she was supported by a stool. It wasn't what she had been expecting, but she did feel more secure than standing in the dark.

She turned her head, straining to make out what he was doing. It sounded as if he was rifling around the kitchen, searching for something.

'Now,' he said. 'We're going to have some fun.'

Something soft caressed her back. It was delicious, and she arched up, trying to get more of it. 'What is that, a feather?' she asked.

'You think?' he said, and she could hear the grin in his voice. 'It would be a strange bird grew this feather. Here, feel.' He put it against her hand, and she recognized the thin rubber strands of the little flogger she had bought in the hope that Adam would use it.

'I had no idea.' Her voice sounded muffled, but understandable. 'I thought it would sting.'

'Oh, it can do that too.' She had no warning before the flogger flashed down on her bottom, bright and sharp. 'But it doesn't have to.'

Flynn began to whisk the little flogger over her skin, from her calves up her thighs and ass to her back and shoulders. It started off light and teasing, causing little sparkles of awareness to flicker with each movement of his wrist. As the strokes got harder, the sparkles became hotter, each one a tiny sting, but she didn't want him to stop.

It seemed he heard her silent plea, because Flynn increased the intensity until she was consumed by the feeling of the flogger, and had forgotten about the hood. Eyes closed, all she felt was the hot, rhythmic sting. She sank into its embrace, allowing herself to feel without thinking.

Flynn's voice startled her. 'Of course, the beauty of a soft flail like this is that you can use it anywhere on the body.' That was the only warning she got before it stroked in between her legs, flicking her clit as it went.

'Ahh!' It wasn't painful, but the shock of it made her rear up. Flynn's hand kept her in position. Each tap of the little flogger against her clit was hot and sharp and arousing. She had no idea if she wanted it to stop or go on forever.

Flynn made the decision for her. He stopped and instead ran his hands up and down her body. Now his hands felt cool compared to her hot skin, but undeniably tempting.

Without even thinking about it, she parted her knees when his hands got to her bottom. She desperately needed those skilled hands where she was aching most. Knowing fingers explored her dripping pussy. Summer shifted her hips backwards, trying to impale herself on them.

'You're so wet,' he said. 'Which is good.'

She heard tearing, and hoped he was opening a condom. Please, please, let it be a condom. But no, those fingers were back at her weeping pussy, and she felt something being slipped inside.

For a few seconds, nothing happened, then she felt a change. Whatever it was, it was growing! It fizzed and pressed against the inside of her aching channel. 'What is it?' she gasped.

'Half an Alka-Seltzer.' There was no mistaking the grin in his voice. 'Like it?'

She tightened against the strange feeling, and it got stronger. 'I'm not sure.' She twisted her hips a little, but the fizzing got more obvious.

'Then I hope you'll like this.' He pushed something else inside her.

The cold of an ice-cube was almost enough to trigger her into orgasm. She gasped, hands uselessly clutching empty air as her focus was all on her pussy.

The ice melted, and suddenly the fizzing became so loud she could hear it even through the hood. A series of tiny electric shocks flooded her pussy. She was out of control, gasping and moaning and completely unable to resist the orgasm that swept over her.

Flynn's fingers on her aching clit made it deeper and stronger, until it finally passed, leaving her a boneless mass of satisfaction. She had a hazy thought that she could stay like that forever, then a vague astonished realization she still wore the hood. How amazing that she had forgotten about it.

She was still floating when Flynn lifted her off the stool. He hugged her tightly, allowing her to relax against his strength. She was mildly astonished to notice that he was still fully clothed. How remarkable that after all that, he was still dressed. She leaned against him, relishing the heavy thump of his heart under her cheek. Even through the hood, she could feel it.

'That was amazing,' she said.

'And we're not finished yet,' he told her. 'That was only the appetizer.'

Her lassitude vanished. 'That's good. I still have room for a main course.'

Flynn lifted her off her feet and settled her down on a pile of quilts in front of the fire. She was limp with pleasure, and not going to argue with anything he suggested. All those years of wondering what kinky sex would be like were being answered in a way that made her wonder why she had waited so long.

She sprawled shamelessly in front of him, uncaring that she was naked and hadn't seen a salon since she left London. With Flynn, she felt free.

'After the sweet, the sting,' he said, and before she could ask what he meant, something rough swept down between her breasts.

Summer jerked. 'What is that?'

He chuckled. 'It's your hairbrush. Like it? All natural bristle.' He brushed it across the tips of her nipples. It sent a miniature shock through her.

'I'm not sure.' Her over-sensitized nerves didn't know if they loved or hated what he was doing.

'Then try this.' This time, it was something soft and gentle that whisked down her body. Her flail again? She purred in reaction.

The hairbrush was pulled up the inside of her thigh, leaving a trail of fire in its wake, just before Flynn's mouth fastened on her neck. The heat of it twisted something deep inside her. She fought against the rope at her waist, frantic to touch him.

He raised his head. 'Naughty, naughty. I'm driving.' Without warning, something smacked down on her thigh, hot and stringing. 'A hairbrush has two sides, you know.' Then his mouth was sliding down her neck to her collarbone.

She gave herself up to his talented mouth, and was panting eagerly when he raised his head.

'Just one more thing,' he said. He moved down her body. She caught a hint of a new smell, one that overrode the gun oil of her hood, before something cold touched the hood of her clit.

It was only cold for a few seconds, then it got hotter and hotter. 'What is it?' she cried. Surely he wasn't going to hurt her.

'It's tiger balm.' She could hear the smile in his voice. 'Great for post-workout rubdowns. And for naughty girls.'

The heat expanded and blossomed. She twisted and moaned, trying to contain it. Her entire body was dominated by her clit. 'Ouch, that's hot.'

'It's supposed to be. Don't you like it?'

She hated to admit it, but she did. Her pussy was on fire, desperate for Flynn. His hand on her stomach stopped her writhing. 'Stay still and enjoy the feeling.'

'Are you kidding me?' she panted, struggling against him but unable to move away from that strong hand. Her clit tingled, driving her almost insane. She couldn't tell if she liked or hated it. Then Flynn's mouth on her breast decided her. She loved it.

His teeth closed on her nipple, the pressure just this side of pain. Despite herself, her pussy clenched and she lifted her hips, begging wordlessly for him to touch her.

'Fuck me. Please.' Nothing mattered in the world except what he was doing to her.

'You know better than that,' he said, but he moved again.

She heard a lid unscrewing, then his broad shoulders were between her thighs. She widened them more, giving him better access. At this stage, she didn't care what he did, as long as he did something to put out the fire blazing in her belly.

The coolness of the liquid over her clit was a shock, but before she could pull away, his hot mouth was there, licking and sucking. The heat of the tiger balm dissipated into a warm tingle, and the sweep of his tongue drove her mindless.

'Yes, yes, please, keep doing that,' she wept.

'Oh, I'll do more.'

Without warning, she felt long fingers sliding inside her, even as that relentless mouth kept up the delicious torture. She moved down, trying to increase the pressure, but his shoulders stopped her.

Then those fingers moved, opening and twisting inside her. Every pressure point Summer owned was under assault. She had forgotten how to breathe, how to speak. Her mind was incapable of words, but it didn't matter. Flynn kept up the suction even as his skilled fingers tormented her from inside.

It was too much. Her entire body seized in an orgasm that knocked out all thought. She was vaguely aware that she was screaming as she came again and again while Flynn urged her on for one more.

She convulsed, out of control, as her lungs emptied and the red behind her eyelids was lit by silver sparkles.

When she returned to earth, she was wrapped in Flynn's arms, the hood was gone and her body was still throbbing. He kissed her hot forehead. 'Still afraid of the dark?'

She smiled. 'What dark?'

23

Summer drained the last of her morning coffee. 'So, what's on the agenda for today? Hunting, fishing? Oh, please say it's shooting.' She batted her eyelashes at him in an exaggerated gesture.

'That attitude could get you into a lot of trouble.'

Flynn sounded as if he meant it and she was almost tempted to push him to see how far he would go. Would he restrain her again? What other games did Flynn like to play? A small shiver of excitement raced up her spine when she remembered all the things they had done.

'You won't be getting within twenty feet of a gun.'

Summer pouted at him and he scowled.

'I thought we'd discuss your current security profile and see how we can improve it.'

'Huh?' That wasn't exactly what she'd had in mind. Some fishing, maybe a short hike, but not a meeting. 'The security system at the house is pretty good now and –'

'I'm not speaking about the house. I'm talking about your own personal security. How you behave when you're out.'

'I know how to avoid the paps.' Before Adam, avoiding the paparazzi was the biggest complication in her life. But since the photographs were published she had encountered her fair share of weirdoes.

'How can you tell that they're paparazzi and not something more dangerous?'

She had no smart answer for that one. The incident last December had caused her father to install the new security system and for weeks afterwards he barely let her leave the house. Summer shifted uncomfortably in her chair. 'You mean what happened last Christmas? I don't remember much about it.'

She had no description, no licence plate number, nothing to show the police that she had been stopped except a damaged car and a few bruises. They probably wouldn't have taken her seriously at all, if it wasn't for the off-duty fireman who stopped at the scene. He had been too busy helping her to pay much attention to the van driving away.

'I read the report. You knew you were being followed, but you didn't go to the police, you didn't call anyone. You could have been kidnapped, or worse.'

There was no answer to that so she stayed quiet.

'I'll speak to Niall about organizing a defensive driving course when we leave. We'll also work on some counter-ambush and hijack drills.'

They were getting out of here? Summer's smile of delight was short-lived when Flynn added, 'But for now we'll work on what you should do if the worst happens. The most important thing to remember is that 80 per cent of abductions take place from your home, a hotel where you're staying or a friend's home.'

'So, the places that I feel the safest . . .'

'Are the ones where you're in the most danger,' he finished. 'You have a good security system in your home, but it's only good if you use it properly. Make sure that all of your household are security aware. Incidentally, you have a very high turnover of staff at the house. Why is that?

You can't be that difficult to work for – and the fringe benefits are stunning.'

The accompanying grin softened his words but Summer felt a small prick of guilt about the dark-haired housemaid. She hadn't seen her since the day she'd pulled that naked stunt at the pool with one of the bodyguards. 'I don't know,' she confessed. 'Malcolm takes care of all that.'

She didn't need Flynn's frustrated sigh to know it sounded as if she didn't know what was going on in her own home.

'Summer, you should know. Everyone new in your home is a potential threat. I'll speak to Malcolm when we return to London. Now, let's go outside. There's no reason why we can't get some exercise while we're talking.'

The man was obsessed with exercise. Her personal trainer wasn't as enthusiastic as Flynn. Grumbling under her breath, Summer pulled on her shoes and grabbed a sweater. Her muscles were still aching from the previous day.

Instead of heading towards the loch, Flynn took the path for the hills. She hadn't been in the forest since her escape attempt. The day was cooler and the cobalt blue sky had been replaced by misty grey clouds. She wouldn't be surprised if it rained. Bloody Scottish summer.

'We'll start with the dangers of social media.'

Summer almost giggled and stumbled on a tree root. Hearing Flynn say the words *social media* with such obvious disdain, was almost as entertaining as listening to a talking dog.

'Is that part of a series of lectures?' she asked innocently. 'Along with the dangers of drugs and alcohol.'

Flynn grunted. 'I am serious. How many friends do you have on Facebook and Twitter?'

'I've no idea, eighteen or nineteen hundred, I think.' It was probably a lot more but she couldn't remember the last time she had checked.

'And how many of them have you had coffee with in the past month?'

Ouch. Flynn had a way of getting right to the point. Lots of them were friends of friends of friends. How was she supposed to keep up with them? 'Maybe a dozen.'

'So, you regularly let a bunch of complete strangers know where you're going to be every evening and who you're going to be with.'

Put like that, she was a kidnap victim in training. 'But I need to –'

'Update your status after you get home safely. Not before. And don't go to the same place on a regular basis.'

'As if,' she said, rolling her eyes at the very idea of it.

'And remember, if anything ever happens to you, your kidnappers want to keep you alive. And I promise that I will find you. If I have to move heaven and earth, I'll find you and bring you home.'

She had no idea what to say.

It was barely dawn when Flynn woke up and slid out of bed. Each morning brought increasing reluctance to move away from her. What the fuck had he done? This was more than a physical interlude. Every day, every encounter brought them closer together. He wasn't acting like a Ranger any more. He was more like a love-sick puppy.

It couldn't go on. Checking that Summer was still asleep, he eased down the ladder and out to the Jeep. He opened the panel at the back which concealed his weapons. The Sat-phone was fully charged.

'Some of us have lives, you know,' Niall told him when he finally answered. In the background, Flynn could hear a female voice telling him to hang up.

'You have to get me out of here, man,' Flynn said.

Niall sniggered, now fully awake. 'What, one poor little rich girl is too much for you?'

'Of course not. She –' He broke off, not sure what he wanted to say. What the hell had happened to him? Summer O'Sullivan had tied him in knots.

'So what's the problem?'

'Do we really have to stay up here? She's going mad without her beauty appointments and crap like that.' Flynn knew he was being unfair. Summer had complained about a lot of things, but that wasn't one of them. But it was something Niall would understand.

There was a rustle on the other end of the phone. Niall was on the move. Flynn heard him opening his laptop. 'It's the safest place for you. Her father's still in Atlanta and there's no sign of that stalker. There's not a lot of sympathy from the local police. It seems your principal has a bad habit of driving too fast.'

'Fuck it, Niall. I can't take much more of this.' Flynn clutched the phone. The image of Summer writhing in orgasm was imprinted on his mind. He'd take that memory to his grave.

Niall laughed. 'Suck it up.' Summer sucking – No, he had to stop that thought, he already had a boner. 'But I'm

264

hearing rumours that there might be a job more to your liking coming up soon. I'll keep you posted.' And the phone went dead.

Fuck, fuck, fuck. Flynn put the phone back into its case carefully, trying to put off the moment when he had to go back inside and deal with his principal. The one who had become more than a client. Who could turn him inside out. Who gave him hundreds of ideas of things he wanted to do to her. And teach her to do to him.

The client.

Summer O'Sullivan was his principal. He was not supposed to be banging her. He'd already broken that rule, more than once. He was just going to keep his distance from now on. That was all.

He squared his shoulders and went back inside.

'Flynn?' Summer's sleepy voice came from upstairs. 'It's cold up here.'

Her voice echoed in a hollow spot inside him, filling him with desires he hadn't felt since he was a horny teenager.

'I can warm you up,' he said. He kicked off his boots and climbed up the ladder. Hell, the damage was done. He might as well be hung for a sheep as a lamb.

Summer was warm and tousled and he couldn't keep his hands off her. He climbed in and took her mouth in a devouring kiss. Damn it, so what if she was the client? She was still the sexiest woman he had ever met.

She squealed at the coldness of his hands, and he deliberately ran them down her back, making her wiggle in outrage. 'Ow! Get your hands off me.' But her eyes were inviting.

He pulled her hands above her head and held them there while he nipped at her neck. He wanted to mark her as his. The unexpected wave of possessiveness took him by surprise.

The image of Summer kneeling at his feet and wearing his collar returned to torment him. He tightened his grip on her wrists and nipped harder.

The alarm going off dragged his attention away from Summer's early morning scent. Fuck. There was an intruder.

Flynn bolted from the bed and leapt down the ladder, not even bothering to put on his jeans. He grabbed his gun, checked the perimeter readings and raced for the door. 'Stay down,' he shouted at Summer as he went.

Summer watched Flynn's very fine backside disappearing out the door, and caught her breath.

When he came back in through the door, it had been the most natural thing in the world to call down to him to get him back into her bed. She had been anticipating another bed-shaking orgasm when something had distracted him.

Flynn had bolted from the bed, flown down the ladder so fast he was only a blur, grabbed a gun and headed out the door. She barely registered his barked orders as he went.

Could the mad Scot truly be planning to run around naked? Outside, where anyone could see him? An unexpected burst of jealousy caught her by surprise. No, she wasn't jealous of the aggravating Scot. She didn't do messy emotions. Ask Adam. Ask anyone.

But he was her bodyguard, and running around in the buff like that reflected badly on her. They might be a long way from civilization, but all it took was one hill-walker with a phone to capture the sight of her employee with everything hanging out like that.

A naked Flynn on YouTube would guarantee millions of hits, all female. She hadn't realized just what a magnificent specimen of manhood he was until she saw him running out the door.

She winced when she remembered admiring Robert Fielding's physique. He might be taller than Flynn, well-built and more manicured, but there was no comparison. Flynn's body was fabulous, with those ruthlessly defined muscles flexing smoothly under his skin. That dusting of body hair, which had initially bothered her, now seemed all the covering he needed.

For a few minutes, she lay in bed, toying with the idea of introducing a bare skin policy for all the staff. Imagine having Flynn naked whenever she wanted. On the other hand, her father's secretary Brian was carrying about thirty pounds too much weight, and all in the belly. That was not a sight she wanted to see at the breakfast table. She couldn't even imagine Malcolm naked. Logically, she knew there had to be a body under those formal clothes he always wore, but she couldn't imagine it. He seemed to have been born in a white shirt. As for the new maid – Summer winced. The woman hadn't gotten over seeing Summer naked, so it wasn't likely she'd strip off.

She was giggling at the thought when the silence began to unnerve her. She held her breath, listening as hard as she could, hoping for any sound that would indicate what was going on. Her heartbeat drowned out any noise from outside. She sat up in bed and listened.

This was ridiculous. How long had he been gone? It must be hours now. The loft was much brighter than when he ran out. She stared at a shadow, convinced she could see it move.

Flynn hadn't meant her to stay here forever. What if something had happened to him? He had gone out there naked. He could have been bitten by a snake and be lying there dying. Did they have dangerous snakes in Scotland? She couldn't remember.

She climbed out of bed and pulled on a shirt of Flynn's. It smelled like him, a subtle musk which soothed her even as it aroused her again. She crept down the ladder, wondering if he would come back and catch her. Would he be more annoyed with her for disobeying, or aroused by her lack of underwear? She grinned. It could be interesting to find out.

The silence was unnerving. Surely there should be birds singing or something? She crept down and peeped out around the door. Nothing. No movement to break up the silence.

The sudden snarl and howl took her by surprise. She gasped. Flynn was out there, naked with whatever had made that noise. She rushed out to help him.

The perimeter had been breached on the mountainside. Who could be approaching from there? He would have bet money that any attack would have come from the lake or the road.

Once outside, he went into hunting mode, blending silently into the landscape. Even naked, he could make himself practically invisible. He slipped along through the trees, watching out for the intruder. There was no sound except the wind rustling the leaves and a distant motor on the lake.

There were no birds singing, he noticed. Whoever was out there had silenced the birds that normally serenaded the dawn.

Flynn reached the point where the perimeter had been breached without seeing anyone. There was no sign of any passage at all. He hunted around, letting his senses expand to take in any detail that would tell him who was out here. If it hadn't been for the silence of the birds, he would have assumed it was a malfunction of the electronics, even though they were top of the range and had been set to alert him to the passage of anything bigger than a fox.

He circled around and headed back towards the croft.

A sudden growl and howl came from the woodlands. He raced over and was just in time to see a feline shape disappear into the shadows. A mangled rabbit lay on the ground, blood still seeping from its wounds.

What the hell was that?

Flynn picked up the rabbit, which struggled weakly, and snapped its neck neatly to put it out of its misery.

A moment later, Summer emerged from the croft, wearing one of his shirts and a pair of sandals. 'Flynn? Are you okay? What's happening?' she called.

She saw the bloody corpse in his hands and screamed. It was the last straw. Rage and fear swamped Flynn. 'What the fuck do you think you're doing out here? I told you to stay inside.'

'What?' But she wasn't paying attention to him. All her focus was on the dead rabbit.

'You disobeyed me,' he bit out. 'I told you to stay inside, and instead you come out here, where there might be an intruder, and you're half naked and totally unarmed. You've just put yourself at risk, and by god, you are going to learn not to do this again.'

Flynn caught her arm with one large hand and pulled her into the croft. She stumbled after him, barely able to keep up. Once inside, he dropped the rabbit and turned to her. Those hazel eyes were dark, stern and focused. 'You disobeyed me. You put yourself in danger. Again.'

Summer tried not to shrink back from that steely gaze. God, he made her feel like a naughty schoolgirl. She didn't like the feeling. She straightened, thrusting her chin up, and forcing herself to meet his eyes. 'Big deal.' She managed to keep her voice breezy. 'I was in danger from a killer rabbit? Yeah right.'

His eyes kindled, narrowing dangerously. 'Last time you did something like this, I warned you that there would be consequences. Has anything given you the impression that I was joking?' He washed his hands at the sink, all without taking his attention off her.

She shrugged, determined not to be intimidated. 'Joking? You'd have to have a sense of humour for that, and you clearly don't.' She was aware as she said it that she was pushing it too far. He was right; she knew she had done the wrong thing. She should admit it and apologize. Instead she heard her own voice saying, 'Lighten up, for god's sake.'

The next moment, she was face down on the kitchen table. 'What?' she gasped, but there was a large heavy hand between her shoulder blades, holding her in place.

'You disobeyed, and now you'll be punished.' Flynn flipped the shirt – his shirt, damn it – up, revealing her bare bottom. She barely had time to register what he was doing when the first spank landed.

The blast of pain shocked her. For a moment, she could barely comprehend what was happening. The second blow restored her to her situation.

He was spanking her. Flynn Grant was spanking her.

The third spank landed in a blaze of pain that caused her to jerk against the table. The hand on her back held her in place.

'You bastard!' She finally found her voice.

'You bastard is masochist for "thank you",' he said, not bothering to hide the satisfaction in his tone. A fourth spank landed, this time on the other cheek. The sting was extraordinary. This was nothing like the club and definitely nothing like her fantasies.

'You can't do this.' She gasped the words out from her ignominious position.

'I can and I will.' Whap! Again.

'I'll have you fired.' He ignored her and kept going.

'You disobeyed –' another spank '– a direct –' another one, this time harder than before '– order.' This spank was harder again.

He was getting into a rhythm, hitting left and right, punctuating each spank with a lecture on her shortcomings, delivered in that maddeningly reasonable voice.

She yelled and cursed, trying to kick him, scratch him,

anything to break up that inexorable rhythm. He caught her wrists and held them in the small of her back.

She wanted to howl. This hurt. It was nothing like she had imagined a spanking would be. But there was something about Flynn's strength, his determination, that turned her to mush. When was the last time a man had just imposed his will on her? She couldn't remember. Despite herself, a flicker of arousal stirred. A tiny, primitive, cavewoman part of her gloried in his domination.

She was not going to get out of this. She knew it. He was going to punish her for breaking his rule. Something inside her softened, relaxed into the spanking. She continued to curse, but without any expectation that he would be affected by any names she called him or threats she made.

It was curiously freeing. The decision had been made. She was being spanked. She relaxed still more. Without her volition, her legs parted, allowing her to sink down more comfortably onto the table. This position made her more vulnerable even while she was more secure.

Summer wondered what would happen if she used her safe word. He might stop. She didn't want to risk it. 'Bully,' she hissed instead.

The spanking continued.

Now her pussy was exposed, and she could feel wetness down her thighs. She couldn't be aroused. This hurt. But the pain was merging into a different sensation, a bright sparkling prickle that surrounded her body. Unconsciously, she tilted her hips a little more, offering herself more fully to that rock-hard hand.

She needed something, but she had lost the ability to think. Words had deserted her. She could only feel, and she sank deeper; the table and Flynn's hard hands the only reality in her universe.

Close, she was so close. 'Mmm,' she murmured. That wasn't right. She was on the edge of something. 'Please,' she managed.

Everything stopped. The silence was shocking. Her ears had become accustomed to the steady smack of his hand against her bottom. What had happened?

She forced her eyes open and looked around.

Flynn was standing back from the table. His hands were steady, but there was a dark flush on his sharp cheekbones. 'That's enough. You've been punished.'

She shifted against the table. She was so close. Now she could recognize the rise to orgasm, and she was almost there. It would only take a touch to send her over. She pressed down against the table edge.

Then Flynn was there, helping her to straighten up, pulling her shirt down to cover her decently and holding her, as her unsteady legs were not up to the job. She was torn between begging him to continue and being mortified at the idea that he might know how close to climax she was.

She raised her head. Flynn's face was flushed and his nostrils were wide. He might claim this was a punishment for her, but he was affected too. Did he know what he had done to her? She caught the flicker of triumph in his eyes.

'You stopped deliberately.' She couldn't believe it.

His voice was steady. 'As I said, you've been punished.'

He turned away. 'I'll make breakfast this morning. You can set the table.'

Flynn kept a close eye on Summer for the rest of the day. She had needed that spanking but he wished it hadn't been a punishment. He'd much rather have given her a slow, sensual, over-the-knee spanking where he could warm her up and see how far he could push her.

She had surprised him. He chuckled silently. There had been nothing passive about Summer when she was being spanked. He hadn't realized she even knew some of the names she had called him. So much for a convent education!

It had taken her a long time to realize that she was going to get spanked, no matter what she said. Did she really think that she could ride roughshod over him the way she did with everyone else in her life? He hadn't missed the way her body had softened halfway through, when she accepted that he was in charge.

Something in Summer had responded to that giving up of control.

He made breakfast for her, fried eggs and mushrooms. It wasn't as elegant as Summer would have done but it was food. She winced slightly as she sat down and shot an accusing glance at him, but didn't complain. Not even when she found a bit of eggshell in her eggs.

He considered taking her out for some self-defence training, but decided she would be too sore to concentrate. Instead, they foraged for wild food, with Flynn keeping a wary eye for the wildcat that had killed the rabbit. Summer picked wild garlic, dandelion leaves and nettles. She determinedly didn't mention the spanking and concentrated on her hunt, but the edge that often sharpened her voice was gone.

She was full of energy and insisted on extending the search into the woodlands.

Later, she cooked dinner, showing off her ability to make a rabbit stew served with wild leaves. Afterwards she washed up without a single dig about lazy men. Until she pricked her finger on a sharp knife and burst into uncharacteristic tears.

Sub drop. Flynn had been expecting it and cuddled her while she cried herself out. He rocked her in his arms and fought against the desire to hold her like this every evening.

24

As he had expected, Summer crashed that evening. One minute she was arguing about the ethics of fur, the next she was yawning and slumped against him. She didn't even put up a fight when he sent her to bed. It always amazed him how much a spanking could take it out of a girl.

He climbed into bed when he was certain she was asleep, still unsure what to do. This was the perfect point to put a distance between them. After this morning, she wasn't filled with soft and fluffy feelings. It would take very little to have her really pissed at him.

She rolled against him in her sleep. Her sweetly rounded butt nestled into his groin with predictable results. On the other hand, he thought, could he really resist her?

That damned wildcat seemed to have found a new hobby – annoying him. At least once every hour, it tripped the perimeter alarm, sending him out to check that it was only the cat and not a tango.

When he came in from his fifth fruitless chase through the woods, he decided that he would have to reset the perimeter alarms to allow the cat to come and go as it pleased, or he would have to get rid of the cat. That wasn't an option he wanted to take. So he went out a sixth time, chasing after it again.

At least it had got Summer into the habit of staying put

when he told her. When she complained about being stuck indoors while it rained, he told her that they would be doing blow jobs 101 that evening.

As dinnertime approached, he could see her getting more nervous. For someone who was normally neat and competent in the kitchen, she was all thumbs and dropped two eggs. She stared at the smashed yolks on the wooden floor and looked as if she was about to burst into tears.

'Here.' He handed her a small glass of his favourite tipple. Niall had sent him a bottle and he had been saving it. This seemed as good an occasion as any.

'What is it?' she asked, wiping an unexpected dampness from her eyes.

'Baileys.' She took a sip and allowed the sweet, creamy taste to wash over her tongue. 'Don't laugh,' he told her. 'I get enough hassle from the guys about it.'

'You do?'

'Sure. It's not a macho drink. In fact, there was a case in the Cameroon where two guys were arrested for looking gay because they ordered Baileys in a bar.'

She took another sip. 'I can't imagine that anyone would look at you and think that.'

He grinned back at her. 'You're about to find out. Let's eat.'

After dinner, he stoked up the fire and spread all the quilts in front of it. He had been considering the best way to introduce Summer to the pleasures of a good blow job. The woman kneeling in front of the man was traditional because it was a great position, but he suspected it would set all sorts of alarm bells ringing for her. So he stripped off his clothes and lay down in front of the fire.

She was sitting at the table, determinedly holding onto her glass. He patted the quilt beside him. 'Come and join me. You can't reach me from over there.'

She squared her shoulders and rose. 'What do I do?'

'Whatever you like. Do what appeals to you, and I'll guide you as you learn.'

She sat down beside him, still fully clothed, and reached out a tentative hand to his chest. For someone who had already seen so much of him, she was surprisingly shy.

'Oh, one thing before we start,' he told her. 'I won't come in your mouth.'

That took her attention away from his nipples. 'Why not? I thought this was about teaching me to like the taste.'

'That comes later. You have to earn the right for me to come in your mouth.'

'WHAT?'

He ignored her outrage. 'Think of it as a sort of graduation ceremony. When you get really good at blow jobs, then I will.'

'It's great to be a Dom,' she grumbled but he could see the tension easing in her.

He allowed her to lick and kiss her way down his torso. His cock, always interested when Summer was around, was already erect and hard. She had started kneeling beside him, but when he didn't pounce on her, she lay down so that she was closer to him.

She laid her head on his abs, tracing the line of hair from his navel down to his groin, and examining the head of his cock from close quarters. The top of it was shiny with a drop of pre-cum. Summer leaned closer and licked it off.

'That's all you are going to get until you earn it,' he told her.

She glared at him, and then returned her attention to his cock. Visibly bracing herself, she took it in her hand. Her fingers were cool and he jerked. God, this was going to be torture.

'A little tighter,' he told her. 'That's it.'

She obeyed, and then explored the different textures of his cock and balls. Then she leaned down and sucked in the crown.

Flynn fought to keep his eyes from crossing. He would never get tired of her mouth. 'Good girl,' he said with an effort. 'No sucking yet. Just let it get comfortable in your mouth. Swirl your tongue over it.'

She did, and he had to take a deep breath to control the urge to thrust. Instead he lay back and allowed her to get used to the feel of him in her mouth. She moved her head to a different angle, so that she could explore the sensitive underside with her tongue. Unbidden, she began to suck.

Flynn threaded his hand into her hair and pulled her back. 'No, we haven't got to that stage yet. First, you're going to do a lot of licking. Make friends with it.'

'You're kidding me,' she said, but she did what he said. Her agile tongue danced up and down, making his cock wet and slippery. When she brought her hands into play as well, and caressed his balls at the same time, he had to fight to stay in control.

Seeing Summer like this did things to his insides, twisted them in complicated ways he didn't want to deal with. He had planned this little lesson to get back in the driving seat and remind Summer that she had to obey him, for now at least. But this was backfiring badly. Summer had the power to turn him into her slave if he didn't get a grip.

Summer was now more relaxed and clearly enjoying what she was doing. Flynn guided her down again, with her head on his stomach and her body aligned with his. This way, he could enjoy caressing her as she worked. 'I think you're ready to go to proper sucking now,' he said, proud that his voice still worked.

Without another word, Summer obliged, sucking the head of his penis deep into the hot recesses of her mouth. Again, he had to hold her head to slow her down. 'This isn't a race and I'm not going to come in your mouth.' Even if it killed him. And it just might. 'Forget that idea.'

He guided her into a slow, easy rhythm, one that she could maintain and which he loved. No doubt about it, having a beautiful woman sucking his cock was one of the best things in the world. Having Summer do it was mind-blowing.

For a while she was content to go at his pace, relaxing in the fire-lit dimness of the croft. Then she upped the ante and tightened her lips, sucking harder and speeding up. She had obviously decided that she could ignore what he had said.

Flynn allowed himself to enjoy the tightening of his balls and the feeling of his juices gathering itself for release. It would take very little to tip him over the edge.

Summer sucked harder and caressed his balls. So close. It would be so easy to come between her luscious lips. But as his orgasm swept over him, he pulled her head back and away from his cock.

He tilted his hips, and watched the semen pulse from the

end, spurt after spurt, and land precisely in the fire. It was a stupid trick, one he had perfected as a randy teenager, but it was effective. Summer's eyes were as round as saucers.

When the sixth spurt had found its mark, he allowed himself to relax.

'That was naughty,' he told her.

She had been watching the fire hiss, but that jerked her attention back to him. 'You're kidding, right? I just gave you a great BJ.' Indignation had flushed her cheeks and she looked adorable.

He shook his head. 'Now you have to start again. This time under my direction.' He poured her another glass of Baileys. She took a couple of sips. He stood up. 'We'll try it my way this time.' And he urged her to her knees.

His cock had softened, but just the sight of her kneeling in front of him, looking up with that combination of submission and rebellion, sent the blood surging to it again.

'Go on, lick it and get it hard again.' Her hands were so much softer than his, but he enjoyed the difference. She licked her way up and down, fascinated with the way it hardened under her touch. 'Pay particular attention to the point where the head joins the stem,' he told her and she obeyed.

God, this was so good. He locked his knees to make sure he didn't fall over.

He caught a handful of her hair. 'Now open your mouth and let it slide in.' He guided her as he moved, being carefully not to go too deep. He didn't want her gagging. He let her set the pace for a few minutes, and then stopped her.

'Have some more Baileys.'

'Are you trying to get me drunk?' Summer asked suspiciously.

'No, you're not allowed to swallow it.' He laughed at the expression on her face, but she took a mouthful. He slid his cock back between her lips. The coolness of the drink hit him first, then the tingle of the alcohol on his skin. The hair on the back of his neck stood up.

He held her eyes with his own as he moved slowly and gently. She tried to drop her gaze, but he told her to watch him. He wanted to see everything she was feeling.

Summer gripped his buttocks tightly. Her nails felt amazingly good digging into him. As he fed his cock into her mouth, controlling the speed and depth, he could not only see her face change but feel the way her nails dug into him. She was almost as aroused as he was. The knowledge made him want to howl with pride – and something else he didn't want to name.

He stopped, allowed her to take off her top, and to have another mouthful of Baileys. This time he went a little faster, but insisted on keeping control. Summer tried to make him go faster, urging him on with her nails, but he resisted.

He had lost track of time when the juice gathered in his balls. Summer felt it too, and sucked harder. 'Oh no, you don't.' She was going to beg before he'd let her swallow his cum.

He pulled back, out of her mouth. His orgasm hit, just as she grabbed his cock. He wasn't sure what she had intended, but jet after jet of cum ended up on her breasts.

She had never looked so beautiful as she did now,

kneeling in front of him, her lips shiny and wet, and pearls of cum marking her as his. He wanted to howl with triumph.

Summer looked down at herself, as if surprised. She raised her eyebrows and grinned. 'I'm pretty sure I read in *Cosmo* that this stuff is good for the skin.' She rubbed it in, circling around her nipple, and causing his blood pressure to rise again.

She got to her feet. 'I suppose it's bedtime now.' She smelled of him.

Flynn swallowed. How the fuck was he supposed to sleep beside her now?

25

Summer laughed as she got back to the croft before Flynn. Okay, she had surprised him with a sprint just as they were in sight of the door, but who cared? She had won. 'Loser, loser,' she crowed, dancing around the kitchen. She was fitter than she had been for years, and that was just her daytime exercise.

Flynn mock-scowled at her, but she wasn't fooled. He was delighted at her progress. As well he might be. If there was a degree in Creative Kink, she reckoned she deserved a Masters.

She had finally got her Kindle back and had read all the books she had downloaded. It was interesting to see which ones held up to the sensual education she was getting.

He nuzzled her neck. 'You smell delicious.'

'Are you mad? I'm sweaty and I stink.'

'As I said, delicious.'

'Pervert!' She pushed him away and looked to see what she could make quickly. 'How about a herb omelette instead?' she asked.

'Omelette first,' he said, but allowed her to cook. She broke some eggs into a small bowl and beat them. They were low on food again. Flynn would have to ring his mysterious source and have some more delivered.

'Penny for them.'

She hadn't heard Flynn come up behind her. The man

was as stealthy as a cat. Her arm jerked and she splashed her T-shirt with beaten egg. 'Now, look at what you've done. That's my last clean T-shirt.'

Summer stuck her fork into the eggs and flung some of the mixture at him. It landed squarely in the middle of his bare chest and Flynn gave her a look that told her she had made a big mistake.

He wiped it away with his hand and she giggled when the egg white clung to his fingers. 'I believe it's good for the complexion,' he said, with an edge to his voice that threatened retaliation.

Summer waved the bowl at him. 'Oh, yeah? You seem to forget that I'm holding the ammunition.'

Catching another dollop on the fork, she flipped it in his direction. He avoided the oozing missile easily and dived for her. Summer squealed as he put his arms around her and she struggled against him. Holding her against him with only one arm, he took the bowl from her and set it down.

Giggling helplessly, she continued to struggle as he carried her to the table. 'You brat. You're asking for another punishment.'

She was torn between letting him do his worst, and seeing how far she could push him. She kicked out in one of the moves she had learned from him during the endless self-defence training and landed a lucky blow on his shin.

Flynn hissed in reaction. Score one for the girl! 'You little wretch,' he said.

He deposited her on the table and turned to grab a rope. Summer swung her legs around and dropped to the floor, heading for the ladder.

'Oh no, you don't,' Flynn said and caught her before she had made it halfway up.

She struggled, knowing it wouldn't work, but enjoying the feeling of his strength holding her captive. 'I'll get away. I swear, you won't be able to keep me.'

Something changed. Flynn's eyes darkened dangerously and the atmosphere shifted. He was no longer playful and seductive. He was grim and determined. 'No, you won't.'

Without warning, Summer found herself face down on the table. Memories of the last time she had been in this position flooded back, and she looked around at him, wondering if he was going to do the same again. She wasn't sure what she hoped, but the hard slash of his mouth excited her as much as it made her nervous.

'You're staying with me,' he told her. 'Get used to it.'

His hand slid into her hair and grabbed a handful. He used it to pull her head back so that she couldn't avoid his eyes. They bored into her, fierce and demanding. The combination of that direct, commanding gaze and the hand in her hair did something to her.

Her breath caught as a twist of arousal tightened her insides. She wanted to do whatever he told her.

'Fuck me.' They weren't the words she had planned to say, but she meant them. Pinned down like this, her pussy flooded, and when she pushed back, she felt his erection straining the front of his jeans. It had been far too long since she had felt it inside her. She needed it or she would die. 'Please, fuck me.'

She heard a muttered, 'God help me', then the hand in her hair was released long enough for him to strip her shorts down her legs and open his own jeans. The sound of a condom packet ripping open was a further boost to her arousal. She widened her legs and tilted up her hips. Hurry, hurry, please hurry.

Flynn slammed into her without finesse or subtlety. A tiny part of her was astonished that the man who had been so self-possessed all through her lessons in kink was now so out of control, but she didn't have time to worry about it. In this position, his cock felt huge, and every movement in or out made her nerve endings shriek with excitement. At each hard thrust, she gasped and pressed back against him.

His hand was back in her hair, holding her head up so that her hips were more firmly planted against the table. 'You are not going anywhere. Do you hear?'

'Yes, Sir.' She had no idea why she said that, it just seemed the natural answer. And it was true, the last thing in the world she wanted to do now was leave him. His other hand held her hips anchored and her arousal ratcheted up another notch.

She was aware of wetness running down her thighs and the sound of flesh meeting flesh. But all her attention was concentrated on the feel of Flynn holding her hair and his cock slamming in and out.

Her gasps were getting louder and higher, but she didn't care. There was no one to hear, and she could not contain the ecstasy that tore through her with each stroke. The hand on her hips shifted, moved under her and brushed her clit, and she exploded. With a wail, she blasted apart, her insides doing something they had never done before.

Flynn roared as he followed her over and she allowed

him throbbing inside her to push her into another mind-shattering climax.

Summer lay on the table, gasping for breath with Flynn half on top of her, his big body shuddering in the aftermath, when a polite cough from the door alerted her.

The door of the croft was open and the shock on the stranger's face mirrored her own.

Flynn's reactions were startlingly fast. He pivoted, grabbing a chair as he moved and then swinging it at the intruder.

'David?' The chair dropped from his hand and clattered noisily on the flagstone floor. 'You almost gave me a heart attack.'

'Me? I came to check on the croft. I wasn't expecting to find a . . . to find you . . .' He darted another look at her, half-naked over the kitchen table, and his face flushed. 'I'll be outside.'

He closed the door again. Summer leapt up and was surprised to find her legs wobbled under her.

She had never felt so utterly exposed or humiliated. How could she have agreed to this? She scrambled off the kitchen table and grabbed her clothes. Her shorts were soaked with her pussy juice, her T-shirt was covered with beaten eggs and she desperately needed a shower. Ignoring his attempt to speak to her, she picked up Flynn's shirt from the chair and raced out to the spa, slamming the door behind her.

She scrubbed away the traces of her arousal and his, cursing men in general and Flynn in particular. When she returned from her tepid shower, the men were sitting at the table drinking tea. Flynn stood up, a sheepish grin on his face. 'Summer, this is my brother, David.'

David offered his hand. He looked like Flynn around the eyes, but there the resemblance ended. He was smaller and stockier and there was a hint of red in his hair.

'How do you do?' Summer spoke in the same polite tone she used for meeting her father's business colleagues as she offered her hand to David. His grip was warm and friendly.

'I'm sorry for earlier. I should have knocked, but we get the occasional squatter. You know how it is.'

Summer nodded, as if patrolling for squatters was something she did on a regular basis.

He released her hand and smiled. 'I was just telling Flynn that there's no way you should be staying in this place when his house is on the other side of the loch. Anyway, Mam will kill me if I come back without you.' He shot his brother a look of pity. 'And Flynn is in enough trouble as it is.'

Summer struggled, trying to digest his words. Flynn's family lived on the other side of the lake?

'I've packed your things,' Flynn said. 'I'll drive you there.'

Summer gave him a look that would have stripped paint. 'If you think I'm going anywhere with you, you need your head examined.' She levelled a look at David. 'I presume you have transport?'

Summer had a fleeting vision of Flynn picking her up, screaming and kicking, and attempting to strap her into the Jeep. That was *not* going to happen.

David was watching the scene with a wicked grin on his face. 'You tell him, Summer,' he encouraged her. 'Don't let him get away with anything. Come with me and I'll look after you.'

Flynn looked resigned. 'Have you kept your weapons training up?' he asked David.

His brother nodded. 'I can still hit the bull's-eye nineteen times out of twenty.'

'If Summer goes with you, I'll have to take the Jeep.'

Summer remembered the weapons and electronic equipment he kept there.

Flynn handed over his Sig Sauer. 'Take this and use it at the first hint of trouble. Make sure she gets there in one piece. Understand?' David nodded.

26

Summer picked up the bag Flynn had already packed for her. They were leaving the croft. She didn't know if she was more hurt by his deceit or the casual way he was ending their time here. All she knew was that she couldn't be near him.

Outside, the day was warm. The sun glittered off the waters of the loch. At the jetty a sleek motorboat waited. She remembered the days that they had rowed and fished in the old wooden boat and her heart dropped at the thought that those days were now over. Conscious of David's curious gaze on her, she linked her arm through his and gave him her best flirtatious smile. Flynn could go to his very own place in hell. 'Let's go. I'd love a boat trip.'

David took her past the island where she had picnicked with Flynn. A few miles beyond, she noticed a few houses dotted about the hillside. 'Turlochmor.' David raised his voice to be heard over the engine. 'It's not far now.'

A small forest swept down to the lake and around the next headland David turned the boat and headed for shore. The curved roof of the house was the first thing she noticed. This definitely wasn't a croft. The floor-to-ceiling windows ensured a panoramic view of the loch, and the local stone made it merge seamlessly into the rocky landscape. Large solar panels were positioned on the roof. Set slightly away from the house was a small wind turbine. Whoever designed it had taste and money. Summer whistled.

'Aye,' David agreed, 'but wait until you see inside.' He moored the boat and helped her climb out. 'Mam and Lorna are at church. I'll give you the tour.'

In the grounds, they passed a sunken tub, set to give the bathers a perfect view of the loch. Inside, the kitchen was filled with sleek, high-tech appliances finished in stainless steel. The glass walls and stone floors should have made the place feel cold, but they were balanced with cedar panelling. The low, comfortable chairs strewn with mohair throws made the place feel cosy.

David opened one door. 'I'm not sure where Flynn wants to put you, but I'll leave your things here for now.'

The king-size bed was covered in crisp white linen and looked out over the lake. One wall was covered with family photographs and pictures of men in dress uniforms. Another wall held a shelf covered with trophies. A door opened onto an en suite bathroom, with a king-size claw-foot tub and a picture window.

'It's a beautiful house,' Summer said.

'It's Flynn's dream home, but he doesn't get to spend much time in it. Niall keeps him very busy.'

'This belongs to Flynn?'

A puzzled expression crossed David's face. 'Aye, Mam's originally from Turlochmor. This house is built on our grandfather's land.'

A car pulling up distracted him. 'That'll be them back from the town. I'll leave you to unpack.'

When he was gone Summer sat down on the bed. Flynn owned this stunning house, but he led her to believe that the tumbledown croft was his home. There was something deliberate, something contrived and cruel about the whole thing. The spoilt little rich girl needed to be taught a lesson and he had taught her well. What would have happened if David hadn't arrived? How long would they have played house together before he came clean?

The worst thing was the realization that she would have been happy to stay at the croft, to live anywhere with him. She was in love with Flynn. Hopelessly, utterly in love with the arrogant Scot and he had played her for a fool all along. He had taught her to defend herself physically, but how could she defend her heart against Flynn, knowing that he didn't feel the same?

Summer heard voices outside. She couldn't hide in her room all day, even if she looked like a beggar, dressed in stained shorts and Flynn's shirt with no bra. She ran a comb through her hair, but nothing could make her look respectable. She took a deep breath before going to meet his family.

Morag Mackenzie was a petite woman with thick, dark hair shot with silver. She smiled as she came forwards to greet her. 'Well now, isn't this just like Flynn, to turn up without saying a word. You're very welcome, my dear, I'm Morag and this is Lorna.'

A slender blonde stepped forwards. She gave Summer a polite smile which didn't quite meet her eyes. She carefully avoided looking at Summer's clothes. Summer shook her hand, cringing when she compared her broken nails to Lorna's perfect scarlet manicure.

'Hi there. David says you've been roughing it up at the croft with Flynn.'

Her words were innocent enough, but Summer caught the emphasis on the word 'roughing'. Did Lorna think she was someone he had just picked up?

She squared her shoulders and looked Lorna straight in the eye. 'He insisted on somewhere remote. You know how paranoid bodyguards can be. I'm Summer O'Sullivan. Flynn is in charge of my security.'

'You're his client?' The relief in Lorna's eyes gnawed at Summer. Lorna was marrying his brother. Why would she be jealous that Flynn was with someone else?

'*The* Summer O'Sullivan.' Morag gasped and fluttered. 'Oh my dear, I didn't recognize you. Your hair and . . .'

She had almost forgotten about that. A month ago she had designer clothes and trademark long, blonde tresses that were a bit like Lorna's. No, come to think of it, they were a lot like Lorna's. The niggling doubt returned. Maybe she was just a physical type that Flynn liked. Summer ran her hand through her hair. She hadn't had a decent bath in a month. 'This was more practical, but I wouldn't mind cleaning up. The facilities at the croft were a bit . . .'

She allowed her voice to trail away and Morag took the hint.

'Why don't you go have a nice long bath and I'll start dinner.'

Relieved to make her escape, Summer returned to her room, ran a bath and stripped off her clothes. The bathroom was equipped with everything a girl might need. Toiletries, piles of towels and a fluffy white robe. She immersed herself in the warm water and sighed with pleasure.

Through the large window she had a perfect view of

the loch and the glen. There were no curtains, but then the nearest neighbour was miles away. It really was a perfect place. What a pity she didn't belong here. Summer closed her eyes and lazed in the bath, letting the stresses of the day drift away.

A tap on the window made her eyes fly open. It was Flynn and the hunger in his eyes was unmistakable. He could go to hell if he thought that he could pick up where they left off. Summer stood up slowly, allowing the water to drip down her body. She stepped out of the bath and reached for a towel. Flynn could look, but he could no longer touch.

The sight of Summer's wet, naked body made his cock twitch. She had given him a show deliberately, but he was betting that she had done it to spite him. She hadn't forgiven him yet for the shock and embarrassment she had suffered when David discovered them. And the hurt expression on her face as she left with his brother nagged at him like a festering wound.

He had fucked up badly. Now he had to face his mother and tell her that he had been holed up in the croft with a celebrity for the past month. He would never hear the end of it. How the hell was he going to make up with Summer while the others were here?

Flynn caught the aroma of food as he entered the house. His mother's Sunday roast lamb with garlic and rosemary was something he had missed. Morag would be beside herself at the thought of having a real live celebrity staying. He would have to warn her that she couldn't tell

295

the neighbours about Summer. Maybe he would have time for a quick shower before she noticed he was . . .

'Flynn Grant, and just when were you going to tell me that we were having visitors?'

Damn. He turned and followed his mother back to the kitchen. David had the good sense to make himself scarce but Lorna was there, watchful as a hawk. He nodded politely to her. 'Lorna.'

'How are you, Flynn?' There was an edge to her voice that he hated. She was marrying his brother but there was still so much between them. How could David not see it?

Trying to distract her, he dutifully admired his mother's orchids. He was away so often that he couldn't keep a plant alive in the house, but his mother was a different matter. He had known soldiers who weren't as tough and ruthless as she was when she entered a horticultural competition. Her latest prize-winning specimen took pride of place beside the window.

The pale waxy petals reminded him of Summer's creamy skin, and the touch of pink at the centre reminded him of how she had been earlier, laid out for his delectation like a feast. His cock twitched again. He had to stop thinking about her like that. As if she were his. As if there were any possibility that they had a future together.

He became aware of the silence. His mother had obviously asked him a question and he had no idea what she had just said. He guessed that it was about Summer. 'She's a principal, I can't discuss her. Sorry, Mam.' He kissed her cheek, hoping to soften his words. 'I'll just go check on her.'

Check on her. He wanted to devour her. Damn David

for walking in on them like that. He had a lot of making up to do. He ducked into the small guest bathroom and showered and dressed in clean clothes, telling himself that he wasn't putting off speaking to her, but he knew there was no avoiding it.

Flynn tapped on her door and stepped inside. Summer was lying on the bed, reading her Kindle. She sat up quickly and he could tell by the set of her shoulders that she was preparing for battle.

'I'm sorry,' he said.

She shot him a look that would terrify a regiment. 'Don't bother with the niceties. You've had your fun, but it's over. Tell Niall that I want out of here.'

The hostility radiating from her was a physical thing that he could almost touch. She had resumed her spoilt heiress persona again, but he knew the real Summer was hiding just behind it. Ignoring her frosty glance, he sat down beside her on the bed and pulled her into his arms.

She lashed out like a wild cat, wild eyed and furious. Both of them were conscious that they weren't alone in the house and their struggle was silent but violent, until the bed looked like a battleground and he had her pinned beneath him. His treacherous cock woke again, wanting nothing more than to be buried inside her. Summer was his. He knew that as surely as he knew his own name.

The hammering pulse at her throat told him that she wasn't immune to him, despite her anger. He pressed his mouth against it and was rewarded with a throaty moan.

'I hate you.'

'I know you do,' he murmured against her neck as he continued kissing her, using every trick he knew to give her pleasure. He pushed her clothes aside and feasted on her breasts, sucking her tender nipples into hard peaks while she writhed beneath him. He couldn't get enough of her.

A discreet tap on the door brought him to his senses. 'Dinner is in ten minutes.' David's voice came from the hallway.

'Hell,' he muttered. He looked at Summer's flushed face and parted mouth. How the hell was he going to sit through dinner? Flynn brushed his lips against hers in a tender caress. 'I never meant to deceive you.'

Dinner was a more torturous affair than he could have imagined. His mother had laid the table for a formal dinner and Lorna had changed her clothes and applied make-up. But even without her finery, Summer had a natural beauty that made Lorna look pale beside her, something that wasn't lost on Lorna. She raised her glass to David and he poured her more wine.

'I can't believe he made you stay at the croft.'

Flynn had a sneaking sense of pride when Summer smiled sweetly back at Lorna. 'Actually, I enjoyed it.'

'But you'll be going home soon, I'm sure. Once your father's *difficulties* are over.'

'My father is a businessman, not a crook. This inquiry has been blown out of all proportion by the media. He's in Atlanta as a businessman. He's not on trial.'

'Lorna,' David shot her a cautioning glare. 'I don't think that Summer wants to talk about that.'

She gave David a grateful glance, before returning her attention to her meal. His mother didn't notice that Summer only picked at her food while Flynn and David reverted to their usual eating contest.

'I see that Irish chappie, what's his name? has gotten married.'

David rolled his eyes. 'Mum, Summer has no idea who you're talking about. Give her a clue. Which Irish chappie?'

'The dark-haired one. The actor from that film. Oh dear, what's it called?'

'*Total Recall*?' Flynn offered, unhelpfully.

Morag gave him a scathing glance. 'That's Colin Farrell, dear. No, not him. The other one. You know,' her voice dropped to a theatrical whisper which could probably have been heard in Edinburgh, 'the spanking one.'

David choked on his food and Flynn pounded him on the back with more enthusiasm than was necessary. 'I think you mean Jack Winter.'

Morag nodded. 'That's the one. He married her, you know. That reporter girl.'

Flynn sighed. His mother might be as sharp as a tack about some things, but she found it almost impossible to remember names.

'Abbie Marshall,' Summer said. Occasionally it was useful to listen to Maya and Natasha.

'Yes, they were all talking about it at the Kirk this morning. They're coming here for their honeymoon.'

'To Turlochmor?' David recovered enough to shove Flynn away.

'Of course not, dear. Why would anyone want to honeymoon here? No. They're coming to Scotland before they go to visit his family in Ireland. I thought that Summer might like to see the wedding photographs. I have the magazine somewhere.'

David's lip curled with amusement. 'I'm sure she'd love to. The only alternatives are some of me and Flynn lying bare-arsed on rugs.'

After a frosty glare at her son, Morag turned her attention to Summer. 'Of course, you'll be used to a lot of media attention yourself.'

His mother's comment was innocent enough – Flynn knew she loved to read the latest celebrity gossip – but after Lorna's snide remarks he expected Summer to snap back.

Instead, she politely changed the subject. 'David mentioned that you're planning a wedding?'

Over dinner, his mother launched into a detailed description of dresses, bridesmaids and flowers while Summer nodded politely. Flynn could feel his eyes glazing over. He glanced across the table at his brother, who was stifling a yawn. Lorna poured another glass of wine.

'You look tired,' she said to David. 'You should have an early night. Why don't you show Summer the magazine, Morag? Flynn and I can clear up.'

In the kitchen, Flynn rinsed the plates and stacked the dishwasher. As he moved towards the cupboard to get detergent, Lorna blocked his path, wine glass still in hand.

'Not your usual type, Flynn.' Her eyes were bright and her speech was slightly slurred. That was all he needed to complete his evening – a lecture from a tipsy bride-to-be.

'That's none of your business. I'm sure I don't have to remind you that this is my home and Summer is my guest.'

'Oh, it's Summer now, is it?' Lorna took another sip from her glass. 'David said that you were . . . *busy* guarding her. You used to be a lot more choosy.'

Fuck his brother and his big mouth. The last thing he needed was Lorna mouthing off to her friends about Summer. He caught her by her upper arms and forced her to meet his eyes. 'Meaning you, Lorna? If I hear one word about Summer being here, you can go straight back to Edinburgh. And you can take your damned wedding plans with you.'

Her face crumpled and she wrenched herself free. She set the glass unsteadily on the table before running from the room. Damn. He shouldn't have said that. Flynn switched on the kettle. He was too wired up to go to sleep. He would make his mother a cup of tea before he went to bed. He dropped a tea bag into a cup and was pouring boiling water when David came into the kitchen.

'You couldn't leave her alone, could you? You had to go and make her cry.'

'Don't,' Flynn warned him as he removed the tea bag and poured in milk. He didn't need a lecture from his brother. 'You don't know what you're talking about. Lorna is . . .'

Flynn stopped. This was not the time to have a showdown with his brother, especially with his mother in the next room. He dragged in a deep breath to calm down.

David looked at him with scorn. 'I know exactly what Lorna is.'

Flynn didn't think his face betrayed his reaction but David gave a grim smile. 'What? You thought you were the only one with kinks? Lorna and I are a great match. And I don't disappear for months on end, leaving her on her own.'

'I was doing my job –'

'Fuck your job. It's a great excuse to screw up your relationships. You did it with Lorna and I bet you're all set to do it again with Summer.'

His brother's words hung in the air like the sound of a slap. Flynn lunged across the table and grabbed a handful of his brother's jumper. 'Don't you talk about Summer.'

David slapped his hand away. 'Then stay away from Lorna. She is mine.'

27

Summer rolled over, trying to fall asleep in her new bedroom but she couldn't get Lorna's words to Flynn out of her head. 'You used to be a lot more choosy.'

It wasn't unusual for people to make judgements about her before they got to know her. The constant attention of the paparazzi and her father's wealth saw to that. It was almost an occupational hazard, but tonight it hurt. These people weren't strangers, they were Flynn's family and she had wanted them to like her.

David was nice and Morag was a woman with a serious case of granny fever. But Lorna had looked at her as if she was something Flynn had scraped off the bottom of his shoe and it niggled at her. Was Lorna the type of woman that Flynn liked? A skinny blonde submissive? Summer punched her pillow and closed her eyes again.

The door opened and Flynn slipped into the room. She didn't want to talk to him so she kept her eyes closed and pretended to be asleep. To her fury, he climbed into bed beside her and spooned against her back. How dare he? She would kick him out in a minute. Just as soon as he had warmed her up. One more minute. Then she'd make him sorry. She fell asleep still planning what she was going to say to him.

The following morning she slept late and only Lorna was in the kitchen when she went in search of coffee.

'I suppose you'll be glad to get back to London? I can't believe Flynn took you to that dump.'

The croft might have been basic but she was missing it already. At least she didn't have to put up with Lorna. 'It wasn't too bad.'

Lorna gave a disbelieving laugh. 'I can imagine.' She stirred her coffee and then set the spoon down on the table with a clatter. 'Look, don't take this the wrong way, but try not to fall in love with Flynn.'

Summer sat back in her chair. What? It was barely nine-thirty in the morning and already the battle for Flynn had started. 'Thanks for the heads up but I don't –'

'You might find it exciting to be roughing it up here for a while but you're not what Flynn needs.'

'How do you know what he needs?'

A faint blush stained Lorna's cheeks and she shot Summer a look that was less than friendly. 'I've known David and Flynn for years. I'm almost part of the family. Take my advice. Don't make an idiot of yourself over him. When Flynn's working on something, it takes him over, but when this job is finished you won't see him for dust.'

Lorna rinsed her cup at the sink and placed it in the dishwasher. She closed the kitchen door behind her, leaving Summer alone.

Summer didn't like the woman one little bit. God help David being married to her. But what if she was right? What if she was just a job? She had seen examples of Flynn's ruthless focus. In many ways he was a bit like her dad. They were both single minded when they wanted something.

But what would happen when the want was satisfied? What would he do then? She had less than a week before her dad returned from Atlanta and they had to return to London. Once, the thought of it would have made her jump for joy. Back to her friends, the shops and the clubs, but none of that seemed to matter now. When she went back to London, Flynn could hardly share her bed again. The prospect of lying alone in the giant antique bed filled her with misery. She wanted to be back in the croft, in the bed under the eaves, lying against Flynn's chest, listening to his breathing.

'What's producing that expression?'

Flynn's voice startled her and she jumped. 'Are you trying to give me a heart attack?'

'And you're cranky. What's up with you? I thought you'd be pleased to be back in a proper house.'

'I am. It's just that . . .' She couldn't tell him the real reason: that every day they spent here was another day closer to going home and that they never seemed to be alone for a minute.

'Everyone's busy with the wedding. I'm in the way.' It was an easy truth, but not a complete one. She wasn't part of his family. She and Flynn came from two different worlds.

'Hey.' Flynn cupped her face and leaned in for a kiss. Barely a brush of his lips against hers but it made her shiver. She angled her head, seeking for pressure from his mouth. For a moment he obliged with a searing kiss that was as possessive and invasive as any he had bestowed on her at the croft.

Summer slid her arms around his neck and clung to him, returning his kiss as if it was the last she would ever have from him. A discreet cough brought her back to reality and she pulled away.

David stood in the doorway, a smug grin on his face.

'Don't let Mam see you doing that or she'll be planning another wedding.'

She expected Flynn to release her, but he kept his arms possessively around her. 'I don't suppose you'd like to take Mam and Lorna for a drive today? Maybe take them shopping?'

Summer wanted to giggle at David's expression. It was almost enough to make up for him bursting in on them the day before.

'Ach, Flynn. If I have to look at more dinner sets, I'll crack up. This wedding thing has grown out of all proportion. I don't know why we couldn't just go to the registry office.'

'Summer and I need to have a *business* meeting.' Flynn kept a straight face but the corner of his mouth twitched. The thought of some time alone with him was tempting.

David sighed. 'Fine, but you owe me, bro. You have until tea time.'

Flynn followed him out to the kitchen and after a while, Summer heard a car driving away. Through the bedroom window she heard footsteps on gravel. Flynn was firing up the hot tub.

He returned a few minutes later with a pile of fluffy white towels and a wicked smile on his face. 'Is madam ready for her bath?'

'Madam is,' she agreed and began to unbutton her top.

'Ah-ah.' Flynn shook his head and moved her hands away, taking over her undressing with strong fingers. 'After my shameless assault on your person yesterday, I'm going to make it up to you today.'

She liked the sound of that. 'What did you have in mind? A morning business meeting in the hot tub?'

Flynn tugged off her shirt and dropped it on the bed. 'It's not a hot tub, it's called an *ofuro*. The Japanese believe that sharing a bath encourages communication and builds better relationships between colleagues.'

Naked business meetings. She could imagine her father's face if she suggested that at the next AGM of O'Sullivan Airlines. Flynn unzipped her jeans, leaving her standing in her underwear.

'Do you need help with those?' The challenge in his voice was unmistakable, but if she let him get her naked now, they would never get to the tub. She shimmied out of them and stood naked before him. Flynn opened the door to the connecting room and she followed him inside.

The gigantic glass shower could have held six. 'I thought we were going outside?'

'We are,' he said as he tugged his shirt over his head and reached for the fastening of his pants. 'The idea is that you wash before getting into the bath.'

The image of the last time she had seen Flynn in a shower flooded her head. She sucked in a breath.

He kicked off his shoes and socks and stood unashamedly naked before her. Was it only twenty-four hours since they had made love?

'Did anyone ever tell you that you have a very expressive face? You're a very naughty girl.'

'So spank me.' She couldn't help wanting to provoke him, but Flynn resisted the challenge.

'First I'm going to wash you.'

True to his word, Flynn ushered her into the shower and turned it on. A torrent of water flooded them and Summer gasped. Flynn eased the pressure of the water and poured a dollop of shampoo into his hand. 'Turn around; I don't want to get soap in your eyes.'

She stood with her back to him as he massaged the shampoo into her scalp, working the tips of his fingers in a circular motion. He rinsed and repeated the pleasurable head massage before turning her and moving downwards.

With a damp washcloth, he tended to her arms and legs before turning his attention to her torso. Dispensing with the cloth, he used his bare hands to massage the suds into her breasts. She didn't know how much more of this she could take. She wanted his mouth on her.

As if he could read her thoughts, he dropped his head and placed a tender kiss on her left breast. The slow water torture continued as he soaped the cloth again and washed between her thighs. She squirmed beneath his touch and received a sharp tap and a caution to behave.

He was touching her but it wasn't the kind of touch she craved. Flynn turned off the water and, grabbing a large towel, dried her off and covered her naked body with a robe, before drying himself roughly.

Outside in the pebble garden, a cool breeze drifted in from the loch, but the steam rising from the bath water was tempting. She slipped off her robe and stepped into the pool, followed by Flynn. The temperature was perfect. They sat in silence. Around them, the air was cold, but somehow that made her feel more alive.

'The Japanese have an expression: *Hadaka no Tsukiai*,' Flynn said. 'It means "naked relationship" or "naked communication" because when we are naked, the barriers between us are gone and we are all the same.'

Summer nodded. She supposed that it did make sense,

but there were certain things that she wasn't prepared to communicate with anyone, especially Flynn.

'You were sad last night and this morning. Do you want to tell me what's up with you?'

Bugger. There were times she felt that Flynn could see right through her. He had gotten her alone and naked and now he was going to interrogate her. 'Nothing,' she said. 'I'm fine.'

Flynn snorted. 'It must be worse than I thought. When a woman says that nothing is wrong, a man is usually in big trouble. You're angry about being taken to the croft?'

'No, I loved –' She closed her mouth. She didn't want to acknowledge how much her time at the croft had meant to her. They had never spoken about having feelings for each other. Flynn would probably run a mile if she told him that she loved him.

The physical bond between them would break when they parted. It could never be anything more than that.

Flynn was waiting for a response, but she had none to give him. His eyes narrowed. 'I could always torture you,' he reminded her.

'Really? What did you have in mind?'

'Well, let's see, we could try Nyotaimori.'

Summer looked blankly at him.

'Body sushi,' he explained. 'Eating food off a naked body.'

She flushed at the idea. It was tempting.

'Or Shibari,' he continued. 'But I seem to remember that you liked being tied up.'

Summer giggled. 'You're so thoughtful. Anything else you learned in Japan?'

Flynn leaned back against the edge of the pool. 'Well there is this thing with live eels . . .'

It took a moment for the penny to drop. 'Flynn Grant! That is . . . Oh, you are so horrible.'

She stood up and splashed, sending a small tsunami in his direction. He moved more quickly than she expected and launched himself at her, so that they both ended up beneath the water. They surfaced again in a cloud of steam and spray and he took her mouth in a searing kiss that left her breathless.

'I think that bath time is over,' he announced in a husky tone that sent a shiver down her spine, despite the heat of the water. He clambered out and offered her his hand. The shock of cool air made her nipples peak, a sight that wasn't lost on Flynn. The look he gave her was one of pure hunger. 'You better run.'

Ignoring the damp robe, she raced for the house, with Flynn in pursuit. She shrieked as she hurried through the kitchen and into the safety of the bedroom where she threw herself onto the bed. Panting, she waited for Flynn to follow.

'I have something for you,' he said.

The orchid was beautiful. Its petals invited her touch. The centre was tinged with a flush of pink.

Flynn tucked the flower into her hair. 'It reminds me of you,' he said as he caressed her face before taking another kiss. 'The creaminess of your flesh and the pink at the centre, but it could never be as beautiful as you are.'

28

Niall rang him early in the morning. As soon as he heard the Tardis ringtone, he took the phone outside. Niall talked, and Flynn realized he had lost his enthusiasm for the job he was offering.

'What the fuck is wrong with you?'

'Nothing.' Flynn laughed, but it was forced. He should be over the moon. A new job. One that involved travel, danger and a chance for some real action. Except that it would mean leaving Summer.

'I thought you'd be pleased,' Niall said. 'You were the one who was moaning about the babysitting assignment.'

'Who's replacing me here?' He mentally ran through Niall's list of operatives. Summer needed a professional, not some retired guy that she would chop into mincemeat. And please not Andy McTavish. He was a charmer with an eye for the women. The thought of Summer alone in a safe house with someone else made him want to kill.

'Jamie McEntaggart.' It took Flynn a moment to place the name, and when he did, he choked.

'Are you crazy? That old fart. He can't do the job anymore.' Fuck, even Andy McTavish would be better than that old codger. He must be at least fifty.

'Fug, tell me the truth. Has anything happened that was out of the ordinary? Have there been any more attacks?' Niall's voice was deadly serious.

'No, nothing. It's been quiet.'

'Then I'm pulling you out and putting Jamie in. This is an urgent rescue job and I need you on the team.'

Flynn gripped the phone and said nothing. It was the sort of job he lived for, but everything in him rebelled at the thought of leaving Summer.

Niall's voice changed. 'Oh, has the brat beaten the Dom? Andy and I had a bet that she'd have you in love with her before the month was out.'

He choked. 'In love? With that spoilt wee brat? Are you kidding me? Never going to happen.' The bastards had been betting on him. He wanted to smash something. Preferably their faces. 'I just don't like leaving a job half done.'

His boss laughed. 'Are you sure? There's a lot of money riding on this, and there are a couple of days left before it falls due.'

'Get me out of here and keep your nose out of my business,' Flynn growled. He wasn't sure what was between him and Summer, but it was their business. The thought of Niall and Andy and god-knows-who-else betting on them made him see red.

'Okay, I'm sending a chopper to pick you up in about twenty minutes. You'll go wheels up as soon as you get to Glasgow.' Niall hung up before Flynn could protest.

Damn it. Flynn closed the phone and went indoors to pack. What the hell was he going to say to Summer?

Summer waited until she heard the front door slam before she emerged from her secluded corner of the conservatory. Whoever said that the truth hurt wasn't joking. She had never been so unprepared for the words she had overheard. Each one was like a knife in her heart. Everything that happened between them had been a lie. Spoilt wee bitch, he had called her. How noble of him to want to finish the job, even when he couldn't wait to see the back of her. How much he must have laughed while he pretended to care for her. How distasteful it must have been for him to fuck her.

And she had confided in him. Told him her deepest fears, her darkest passions, while he had played her like a fool. Encouraging her to believe that she was special, that he cared for her. She had almost begun to hope that they had a future together. It didn't matter that he wasn't rich. She didn't care if he hadn't got two pennies to rub together.

She had believed that he was an honourable man, but Flynn was worse than Adam. Much worse. At least Adam had wanted her for her money and her connections. She could understand that. Her dad often said that everything boiled down to sex or money.

How had she not seen it before? Flynn was just like her dad. They both compartmentalized their lives to the nth degree. Flynn would love her one day and hop on a plane the next without giving her a second thought. She would never know when she would see him again. Just like her father. She couldn't do that again, not with him.

She had to get out of here. As she crossed the hall she spotted the telephone. With shaking fingers, she dialled Molly's number. It was early, Molly was probably still in bed. 'Come on, please, answer the bloody phone,' she muttered.

'Yo?' a sleepy voice answered.

Summer closed her eyes. What was with the yo? Did Molly have to trend everything? 'It's me. Stop yo-ing.'

'Summer, is it really you? Where have you been? You've been gone for weeks and –'

'It's a long story. I'm stuck in Scotland and I need you to come and get me. The place is called Turlochmor. It's in the arse end of nowhere, so you'll have to look it up on sat-nav. Please, Molls.'

'Oh my god, are you in trouble?'

Summer bit down on her lower lip. It was good to hear a friendly voice, but she couldn't talk for long. If Flynn suspected that she would leave the moment he was gone, she would be in big trouble. 'I can't talk. I'll be . . .' She paused. She had no idea how big Turlochmor was or what was in the town. 'I'll be at the post office in Turlochmor at 3 p.m. tomorrow.' Everywhere had a post office; it couldn't be hard to find it.

'Don't worry. Of course I'll come.'

Shaky with relief, Summer replaced the receiver and hurried up the stairs to her room.

Twenty minutes later, the sound of a helicopter landing almost blew in the windows. Summer was used to choppers – her father used them all the time and she'd flown in her share – but this one was loud and mean-looking. It landed beside the house, the wind from rotors flattening the grasses in the pebble garden.

She debated staying in her room, but that would be admitting she cared. Besides, a tiny part of her hungered for one more glimpse of Flynn, even if he was walking –

no, make that flying – away from her. She joined the family in front of the house.

The door of the chopper opened and a red-haired man clambered out. Once he was on the ground, he lifted his suitcase out carefully.

Flynn emerged from the house, his battered rucksack over his shoulder, and approached the other man.

Summer couldn't hear what he was saying through the noise of the chopper, but Flynn brought him over to her. 'Summer, this is Jamie McEntaggart, your new body-guard. For god's sake, don't give him the sort of grief you gave me.'

Grief. She had given him grief. In that moment, Summer hated Flynn.

Flynn embraced his mother. Morag clung to him, tears running down her face. 'Please son, be careful. Don't take any risks.'

Then he punched David on the shoulder. 'Look after everyone. And don't get married until I get back. You're too young to rush into things.'

David shoved his hand away. 'For fuck's sake, Flynn, I'm not a baby. You're not in charge of me and you don't know what's best for everyone.'

Lorna threw herself into his arms. Flynn allowed her to weep hysterically for a few moments, and then pushed her over towards David.

He moved towards Summer. She took an instinctive step back. She didn't recognize this mood of Flynn's but she could see it was dangerous. He hesitated, then said, 'We'll talk when I get back.' He gave her one last look before turning and hopping into the helicopter. He was in it no more than a minute before it took off and headed upwards.

Summer stared at it as it got smaller and smaller, until it vanished altogether.

Morag dried her eyes, blew her nose and straightened her shoulders. The shocked mother was gone, and the gracious hostess was back. She inclined her head to the new bodyguard. 'Come along, Mr McEntaggart, we'll sort out some sleeping accommodation for you.'

It looked as if she had a new bodyguard – but not for long. After supper, she pleaded a headache and wished him goodnight. She wasn't lying, she did have a pain. A big aching one, where her heart should have been. On the way to her room, she ran into David.

He took in her ashen face. 'Don't worry. Flynn always comes back.'

'Why does everyone assume that there is something going on between us? I'm just a job to him.' She hadn't meant to snap at David but his sympathy was more than she could bear. She brushed past him into the kitchen, away from his perceptive eyes, and busied herself pouring a glass of water.

She wasn't prepared when he came up behind her and enveloped her in a hug. Summer put the glass on the counter and turned in his arms, burying her face in the warmth of his sweater.

He held her tightly and murmured against her hair. 'Just say the word, and the minute he comes home I'll drag him outside and let him beat the crap out of me.'

She raised her head and managed a half smile. 'Thanks for the offer, but no. I'll be fine.'

'Has he hurt you? Do you want me to speak to him when he gets back?'

Summer shook her head. 'There's no point. There's nothing left to say.' She made her way to her room and threw herself onto the bed. It was a long time before her eyes closed.

After a night of staring at the ceiling, she slept late and when she woke the alarm clock told her that it was almost noon. She tumbled out of bed and headed for the shower. There was no point in packing; it would alert her new bodyguard. Besides, she didn't want to see any of this stuff again. There were too many memories.

The house was quiet. There was only her and McEntaggart.

'You're awake then. They've gone to Turlochmor to do some shopping. They should be back late this afternoon.'

'Damn, I wanted to go with them. I could do with a break from the house. I don't suppose you'd like to drive me into town?'

McEntaggart raised an eyebrow. 'Not a chance. Niall said you were to stay here until the job was over.'

Bugger. She thought that because he was older, he would be a pushover. There was one thing she could try. 'You don't understand. I need to go to the pharmacy.'

He shook his head.

'I really need to go to the pharmacy. For some Tampax.'

A slow, red flush climbed up the older man's neck and Summer almost felt sorry for him.

She gave him her best pleading look. 'I only need to go to one shop. We can be back in less than an hour. No one needs to know.'

'Well, I suppose it is only the village.'

Summer hated lying to him, but she had to get out of here. By 3 p.m. she would be on her way home again. She hurried to her room; there were only a couple of things she could take with her. She shoved them into her pocket.

As they took the road out of the glen, she risked a final glance behind at the loch. In the distance she could see a small, dark shape near the water. The croft. Blinking away the threatening tears, she turned around and concentrated on the road ahead.

Turlochmor was a one-street town of dour grey buildings and cheerful shop fronts. It wouldn't take long to explore every inch of it. A red delivery van was parked outside the pharmacy and McEntaggart was forced to drive up the street to find a parking spot.

'You can drop me off here. I'll be back in a couple of minutes.' Without waiting for his agreement, she opened the car door and strode down the street, searching for the post office. As she crossed a side road, she heard a car horn.

The green jaguar looked out of place in the small country village.

'Summer!' Molly opened the passenger door.

Heart racing, Summer hurried down the side street and clambered into the car. Molly hugged her. 'Oh thank god. I had no idea where you vanished to and Robert was so worried about you. Weren't you, darling?'

Summer was almost afraid to turn her head. She glanced in the rear-view mirror. Lounging in the back seat was Robert Fielding.

29

The drive back to London was different to the ride north almost a month before. Molly kept up an endless stream of chatter all the way about Wimbledon, weddings and who was dating who in the party set. Summer couldn't remember which stick-thin blonde was which and she didn't care. All she could think about was Flynn. She tried to smile and appear interested, giving the occasional nod or monosyllabic response while parrying questions about why she had been in Scotland

They stopped at York for an early dinner, passing the car park where she had met Niall and the others. Summer felt a pang of shame when she remembered what a spoilt bitch she had been then. How much a month could change things.

Robert took them to the Blue Bicycle, a little restaurant near the canal. The exquisite fish starter was served on slates. It was the finest meal she had eaten for a month, but she would have given anything to be sitting at the rough table at the croft, drinking tepid scrumpy and eating trout fresh from the loch. She pushed her plate away.

Molly pressed her hand. 'You've hardly eaten anything. Are you feeling all right?'

She shook her head and tried to summon a smile. 'I'm fine. It's been a rough month.'

'It's over now. Don't worry. Everything will be back to normal when we get to London. You'll see.'

That was the problem. She didn't know what normal was anymore. Her old life of shopping and endless parties seemed facile and empty. Just how many pairs of Louboutins did a girl need, anyway?

'Has your father returned from America?' Robert asked. 'Will there be someone at the London house to meet you?'

She hadn't thought of that. Her dad was still in Atlanta, but some alone time would be good. She needed to think about her future. 'I'll be fine.'

Robert took over the driving when they left York and Summer took the opportunity to nap. When she woke they were outside Molly's apartment. Summer climbed out of the car and stretched.

'Are you sure you won't stay with me for a few days?' Molly asked. 'I hate to think of you being alone.'

'I'm fine, Molls,' she said, hugging her friend. 'Thanks for coming for me. I'll ring you in a couple of days and we'll catch up.'

'You better,' Molly whispered. 'And I want to hear everything.'

Robert opened the passenger door. 'Climb in, I'll drop you home.'

She was about to protest when she realized that she had nothing but the clothes she stood up in and no one to call. Summer slid into the passenger seat and waved to Molly. Robert was silent as he negotiated the late night traffic and she could feel her eyes closing again.

'So, you've finished with your little Scottish adventure?'

'What? Um yes. There's no need for me to stay there any longer. Dad is back in a couple of days.'

'He'll be glad to have his precious little girl back, hmmm? Although your *boyfriend* really should have seen you safely back to London.'

She didn't bother replying. Robert might be Molly's Dom, but that didn't give him the right to question her and there was no way that she would discuss Flynn with him.

He took his eyes off the road for a moment to give her a speculative glance. 'I think a month in the country has changed you.'

If only he knew. Each time she closed her eyes, her mind was flooded with images of Flynn and their time together. Late nights in front of the fire, the scent of his soap, the feel of his rough hands on her skin. She blinked the images away. It was all a lie. *Stop thinking about him.*

They pulled up at the gates to the house and Summer put in the code to open them. The house was in darkness and she doubted if any of the staff were still up.

Ever the gentleman, Robert stayed while she rang the bell and waited. Flynn hadn't thought to pack her keys and even if he had, they would still be in Turlochmor. No lights came on in the house. She rang again, keeping her finger on the bell and listening as it echoed in the hall. Why wasn't there someone on duty?

'Let's try round the back,' she suggested.

'I'll go,' Robert offered.

Just then a light came on in the hall and the door was opened by a bleary-eyed Malcolm. When he saw her, he stood to attention and pulled his woollen dressing gown around him. 'Miss Summer, we weren't expecting you until Wednesday.'

'Change of plans,' she announced.

'But, but you don't understand, madam. The chef is on a night off and . . .'

Summer followed him down the hallway into the sitting room. Despite her tiredness, Summer wanted to laugh. Chef? She had been catching and cooking her own food for the past month. She would manage to do battle with a well-stocked larder and a twenty-first century kitchen. A giggle escaped when she noticed the perfectly ironed crease in Malcolm's pale blue pyjamas.

'She's just overtired,' Robert assured Malcolm. 'We've had a long journey.'

'I see.' The frosty expression on Malcolm's face belied his polite response. 'Will you be staying, sir?'

Robert looked to Summer for her approval. The last thing she needed was a guest, but she couldn't really expect him to drive back to the other side of the city at this hour of the night. 'Of course, please stay. You've done enough driving for today.'

'One of the guest rooms on the first floor is ready, madam, or perhaps you'd like me to prepare the adjoining –'

'The first floor will be fine. That will be all, Malcolm.'

He inclined his head stiffly and left the room.

Even in a full-length dressing gown, Malcolm still managed to look disapproving. The cheek of him. Did he really think that she wanted Robert in the adjoining room, or that she would sleep with any male guest? She really would have to speak to her father about him.

As the door closed, Robert put his hand on her shoulder. She spun around, stumbling against him and Robert's arm slid around her waist. 'Of course, I wouldn't mind sharing with you.'

'What?' she shook her head, willing her brain to work. What was Robert up to? Did he really think that she would let him touch her? 'But you're Molly's –'

'Molly is mine. There is a subtle difference. Perhaps you'd like a demonstration.'

He propelled her backwards until her knees hit the edge of the couch and she struggled not to fall. Summer pressed her palms against his shoulders and shoved hard. Robert was stronger than she imagined. Her hands met solid muscle and he barely moved an inch. 'I said stop.'

'I know you don't mean that.' Robert grabbed a fistful of her hair and tugged her head back. His mouth slammed down on hers and he tumbled them onto the couch.

She struggled to breathe with the combination of his weight crushing her and his seeking mouth. Summer thumped her fists against his back, trying to dislodge him. He dragged his mouth away. 'What's the matter? You weren't so fussy with the Scot.'

Summer arched her back and lifted her left leg, trying to dislodge him, but her struggles only seemed to inflame him more. He tugged her hair harder and she cried out, 'Don't.'

'That's it, cry. But I doubt if dear old Malcolm can hear you from the servants' quarters.' Robert insinuated his hips between her thighs and rubbed his hard shaft against her. 'See what you've done to me. You're a very bad girl. I could tell that night at the club. You want someone to take charge, to dominate you.'

With his free hand, he grabbed the neck of her T-shirt

and pulled hard until the thin cotton tore, exposing her bra. Shoving the lacy fabric aside, he lowered his mouth to her breast.

The touch of his mouth broke something inside her. She struggled wildly and managed to free her trapped arm. Forming a fist, she struck him on the cheekbone and his head rocked back. 'Get off me,' she spat out the words. 'Get the fuck off me.'

Her fury made him hesitate. He rose to his feet and adjusted his clothing. 'Perhaps I've come on a little strongly. Molly told me about your fantasies. I was simply trying to give you what you needed.'

She pulled the edges of her torn T-shirt together and stared at him incredulously. 'My fantasies? You sick twisted . . . Get out of here. Get out.'

With a curt nod, Robert left the room. She heard the front door slam and his car roar down the driveway. Summer lay on the couch, unable to move. A tear splashed on to her cheek and she rubbed it away impatiently.

He wasn't worth crying over. She should call someone, but the only one she wanted was Flynn and he didn't want her. Summer continued to tremble. Outside, the first rays of sunshine peeked through a crack in the drapes. Feeling like an old woman, she climbed off the couch and made her way up the stairs to her room. She dropped her clothes into the basket beside her dressing table. She never wanted to see any of them again.

In the shower she turned the spray on full. The water pounded on her face and shoulders. She scrubbed her skin until it was red and every trace of Robert's touch had been washed away. She dried herself off and wrapped a towel around her hair. Wiping the steam from the mirror, she stared at her ashen face. She had never felt so utterly alone.

It was almost nine when she padded downstairs for breakfast. There was no sign of Malcolm. On the dining room table, beside a covered silver dish and a pot of freshly brewed coffee, was a note.

My apologies. I forgot to mention that I have a doctor's appointment in the city this morning. I should be back early this afternoon. I have taken the liberty of preparing breakfast.

It was signed M.

Bugger. After the previous night, she didn't want to be alone and even Malcolm's grumpy company would have been welcome. She lifted the lid of the dish. Croissants and preserves. She wasn't hungry, but she could probably manage coffee.

After the second cup, she began to feel better. Summer picked up the phone and hesitated before dialling Molly's number. What was she going to say to her? *Hi, your boyfriend tried to attack me last night.* Robert said that he was trying to fulfil her fantasies. Even if she did call the police, would they believe her? It would be Robert's word against hers.

She would be all over the papers again. Who would believe a party girl who had already been involved in far too many scandals? They'd take the word of a respectable property developer against hers. Summer dropped the receiver back in its cradle. It was better if she spoke to Molly in person.

She checked her messages. Tons of invites, interspersed with giggling calls from Natasha and Maya announcing that they were going to South Africa with Mike and Gavin. That one was only four days old. There was no point in calling them. A message from her cousin Sinead, apologizing for not turning up for the house party, but she'd been in Geneva for a job interview. Could they meet when she got back?

Two calls from a number in Scotland she didn't recognize, but no message. It must be Morag. She should ring her, apologize for running off like that.

Trying to delay the inevitable, Summer went back upstairs and opened her wardrobe. Ignoring the rows of designer dresses and expensive Italian shoes, she selected a pair of jeans and a long-sleeved pink cotton T-shirt. It would cover the bruises on her arm. She slipped her feet into a pair of pumps and went downstairs to face the music.

Morag sounded relieved to hear from her. 'Oh Summer, you gave us all a dreadful fright. Are you all right? Mr McEntaggart was very cross. He spent ages searching the town for you.'

'He did?' *Of course he did. Idiot. You're a job.* But some of her anger had already dissipated at the thought of him worrying and it gave her a pang of guilt that wouldn't go away. She hadn't meant to upset everyone like that.

'I'm fine, Morag. Tell him I ran into some friends and I'm back in London. I'll contact my dad. He'll square things with Niall.'

She hung up before Morag could answer.

Although she tried it several times, there was no response from her dad's private number. Typical. She left a breezy message saying that she was back in London and looking forward to seeing him.

Next up was Molly, and she was dreading it. 'Hi, Molls. Any chance we could meet for lunch? I really need to talk to you. Maybe I can take you up on your invite to hang out at your place for a few days?'

'Of course. But, can we make it dinner? I'm working on a proposal. You still have a key, don't you? Let yourself in and I'll see you as soon as I finish work.'

Summer flicked through her phone contacts. She couldn't stay here moping over Flynn, and her dinner with Molly was hours away. She needed to get out of the house. Maybe meet someone for lunch. Sinead was still in London. She dialled her cousin's number at the museum and was put through straight away.

'Summer, I thought I'd miss you again. I'm leaving next week for Geneva. I got the job.'

'Brilliant.' Summer didn't know Sinead had been looking for one. It had been so long since they had spoken. But that didn't seem to matter. They always seemed to slot back in whenever they met and they had a lot of catching up to do. 'I was wondering if we could meet for lunch?'

'Today? Let me see. I've a lunch meeting at noon, but I can sneak away after that for coffee. How about that little Italian place in Bloomsbury at two?'

'Sounds great.' She forced enthusiasm into her voice.

'Are you okay, Summer? What do you want to talk about?'

She couldn't fool Sinead for a second. Her cousin had a bullshit detector that was second to none. Half of the London art dealers were terrified of her. 'Promise you won't tell anyone, but I've met this guy and –'

Sinead cut her off. 'Sorry, I've got HR on the other line

trying to sort out my paperwork; you can tell me everything later. Gotta go.'

She replaced the receiver in the cradle. Bloomsbury wasn't that far from Molly's, she could drop her bag there first and then meet Sinead.

Molly's flat was still the same. She was relieved that Robert hadn't managed to dominate the untidiness out of her. Summer tucked her bag under the spare bed and flopped down. She had hardly slept a wink last night and she had half an hour before she met Sinead.

An insistent buzzer woke her and she hurried to the speakerphone in the hallway. It was the concierge. 'I've some gentlemen here with a delivery for Ms Ainsworth.'

Damn, trust Molly. She hoped it was a vacuum cleaner. 'Okay, send them up.'

When she heard a knock on the door, Summer opened it. Two dark-suited men waited outside. They didn't look like deliverymen.

'Miss O'Sullivan?' The taller of the two stepped forwards, his hand outstretched in greeting. His heavily accented voice was Russian or eastern European. His suit was tailored and his cuffs were pristine white.

Something about this didn't feel right, and how did they know her name? Summer remembered Flynn's instructions about personal security when he had been teaching her self-defence moves. *Always go with the gut. If it didn't feel right, chances were that it wasn't right.*

Summer took a step back into the apartment. 'I'm afraid there's been a mistake. Miss Ainsworth isn't here. You'll have to make another appointment.'

Ignoring her words, the dark-suited man covered the distance between them. He said something to his companion in a language she didn't understand. This definitely didn't feel right. To hell with being polite.

Summer tried to close the door, but he caught it easily and pushed back against her. Her leather-soled pumps slipped on the smooth wooden floor. There was no way that she could keep them out. She gave one final shove and was pleased when she heard a grunt of pain from one of the men as she caught his hand in the door. She turned and raced for the bathroom. She could lock herself in there.

She had almost reached it when she was caught in a low tackle. Summer crashed to the ground, smacking her head against the wall. The man managed to grab one of her ankles. She kicked out with her free leg, trying to get away from him.

He shouted over his shoulder. 'Uri, quick.'

The dark-suited man produced a syringe from his pocket. She had a flashback to the night when she had been run off the road. That man had held something in his hand too, but his voice was different. English. Summer lashed out again, making contact with his ribs. He roared and released her ankle. She rolled over and crawled towards the bathroom door.

'Bitch,' he grunted. 'Get her.'

As she reached for the doorknob, Summer felt something stab her upper arm and her scream was muffled by a blanket coming over her head. The scent of cleaning chemicals mingled with cigarette smoke and after that, nothing.

30

Afghanistan

Flynn climbed the mountain path, silent as starlight. He was the point man and knew his team were behind him, but he couldn't hear them. They were all good men, hand-picked by Niall for their ability in situations like this. Between them, they'd do the job and be gone before anyone knew they were there.

He filled his lungs with the night air, breathing in the scent of wood smoke, sweat and dust. It was a smell that always filled him with anticipation, one of the signs he was on the job, saving the world from the bad guys. And blowing stuff up, he admitted with a grin. He had no idea why he hankered after the cool air of a Scottish night.

His face was invisible under the dark robe he wore, which at first glance made him look like any other goat herder on the mountain. What was underneath it would get him shot at first sight. He was a walking arsenal of explosives and weapons.

The stars overhead were so bright that he didn't need his night vision goggles, but he kept his infrared sights handy. He knew they were getting close to the target and there were bound to be sentries keeping watch. If they were any good, they'd be able to blend in with the rocky cliff on which they stood.

Flynn was in the zone, absolutely calm, his heart beating so slowly he had time for a thousand observations and decisions between each beat. He could hear an insect skittering along a branch, the swoop of an owl, the passage of some night hunter. And he could smell the distinctive cigarettes that were all they could afford in this part of the world.

Thank you, he breathed to whatever god watched over knights errant. His job had just got so much easier. The cigarette-smoking sentry had given them an invitation and directions to the cave they were searching for.

Sneaking up on the sentry was easy. The man's attention was taken with keeping his fag alight, and the glow of the tip illuminated his face. Flynn hung back. It was unlikely that he was the only one. Sure enough, another man stamped back from the far side of the cave, adjusting his robes as he went. His gun was slung carelessly across his back, out of his immediate reach.

Those clowns deserved what was coming to them. What the hell was the Taliban recruiting these days?

Flynn waited to be sure there were no other sentries absent on pissing duty, and then he hand signalled the two men directly behind him. While Picard and Jones took care of the sentries, Flynn slipped inside the cave complex. He tapped his mic twice to let Niall know the op was on.

Although Niall was his boss, no one disputed Flynn's expertise in this sort of mission. For tonight at least, Flynn was God.

He suppressed a bubble of laughter at how Summer would react to that. She'd roll around the floor laughing.

He wrenched his thoughts away from her. Time to concentrate.

He knew the whole cliff was riddled with caves and that there were at least two dozen Taliban in the area. He'd been watching the area with a heat sensitive scope all day, and was pretty certain which of the various heat signatures belonged to the hostages. There were two bodies which had remained virtually stationary all day long. He'd bet his pay cheque for this op that they were the two reporters he was here to rescue. There were three active heat signatures in the cave with them, but plenty of others in the area. This would be a hand and knife op. With a bit of luck and a lot of expertise, they'd be in and out before the bad guys realized they were there.

Flynn slipped silently into the cave and had time to get a good look around before he had to take action. Yes, this was going to work.

The two reporters were sitting against the wall, misery bleeding from every pore. Their ankles were tied with thick rope, and they looked in worse shape than Flynn had expected, even after seeing the video of them being tortured.

Cheer up boys; you're on your way home now.

Flynn felt rather than heard his team behind him and he signalled the attack. It was four against four, but it was hardly a fair fight.

Two of them, Niall and himself, were former Irish Rangers. Jones was ex-SAS and Picard had been in the French Foreign Legion. Any one of them could have taken out the tangos on their own. In this situation, no one cared about fair.

Flynn had a brief impression of sweat and gun oil before his target realized he was under attack. He snapped his neck before he could make a sound. A grunt behind him signalled that Niall had taken care of his guy.

It was all over before the two reporters realized they had been rescued. They jerked upright, gasping, unable to comprehend that the lethal shadows in the cave had come to rescue them.

Flynn slapped a hand over the American's mouth. 'Shhh. We're here to take you home. But stay silent.' The man nodded, and Flynn pulled his hand away.

Breathing heavily, the blond asked, 'Who are you? Are you Navy SEALS?'

'Lucky for you, we're not. We're better than them.' Flynn untied the tarry rope around his ankles, while Niall did the same for the Danish journalist. 'Can you stand?'

The American, with Flynn's help, struggled to his feet and managed to remain upright, but he had been a prisoner for over a week now and had been tortured several times, and it showed. The Dane was in slightly better shape, but it was clear neither of them would be running marathons any time soon.

At a signal from Flynn, Niall and Jones slipped their arms around the American, while Picard did the same for the Dane. They headed out and started the trek down the mountain. Flynn would check over the cave and follow them.

Ignoring the bodies on the floor, Flynn investigated the cave. Sleeping bags, lanterns, half-cooked goat's meat, highly contraband beer, two battery-powered DVD players with more porn than cartoons, smelly clothes – and a stack of boxes pushed out of light. His internal clock was ticking. The other tangos in the area would be checking in soon, but his curiosity prodded him.

He opened one and swore. Opened another box. Another. Fuck, fuck, fuck!

Bombs weren't his area of expertise, but this had all the makings of a dirty bomb. He couldn't leave it here for the other tangos to assemble.

Aw well, a man's gotta do what a man's gotta do. Flynn dug out his C4 and timers and made sure no one would ever make use of this particular bomb. Unfortunately, the resulting bang would call attention to their getaway, but the guys were far enough ahead that it shouldn't be a problem. They must be halfway to the waiting helicopter by now.

He set the explosives and switched on the timers. He had three minutes to get out of the cave before it went off. He swept the cave with his heat-sensitive glasses one more time before he left – and caught a glimpse of red in the far corner.

A dog? It was too small to be a man. He leaned to check – and found he was looking into the eyes of a woman. 'Monsieur,' she breathed painfully. Her brown skin had blended in perfectly with the darkness of the cave, and she was far gone, in much worse shape than the two reporters had been. Who was she? She sounded French, but he hadn't heard of any French going missing recently.

It didn't matter. He had to get her out of there before the explosives went off. 'I'm here to rescue you,' he said. 'Permettez-moi de vous aider,' he repeated and tried to help her to her feet.

Fuck, she was chained. The padlock holding the chain in place was new and solid. With a little time, he could pick it, but he didn't have time. His internal clock warned him that he was already in the red zone.

He pulled out his Glock and shot the lock. It exploded into satisfying bits, releasing the chain holding the woman, but the noise was loud and unmistakable. They had to get out of here now.

He picked her up and ran for the mouth of the cave. The burst into night light seemed miraculous, but he knew they weren't safe yet. The angry shouts behind him told him that they were being chased, and with his hands full of abused Frenchwoman, he couldn't do anything about it.

Holding her as securely as possible, he belted down the mountain path. There was no question of silence or checking his footing. His only objective was to get the woman to safety as quickly as possible, and hope that his high-tech body armour was as good as it claimed. And that it would protect the woman in his arms.

He shifted her so that she was more protected from stray bullets by his body. Maybe it was lucky she was in such bad shape: she didn't seem to be aware of the significance of the shouts and shots coming from behind him.

The memory of the last time he had gone down a narrow mountain path carrying a woman rose to torment him. Was there anything he could do in his life that didn't bring him right back to Summer? The woman in his arms was a different shape, a different smell. Was every woman he met for the rest of his life going to be compared to Summer? And suffer in comparison, too.

Shut up and concentrate. This is no time to be thinking about Summer O'Sullivan. Focus! As if the words conjured it, his foot slammed down on a rock. His foot went sideways and his knee twisted.

Agony shot up his leg, stopping his breath. He was running so fast that his momentum kept him going, but his right knee was a blaze of agony. The woman in his arms was suddenly the weight of a baby elephant. He had to drag every last ounce of strength from his muscles to keep holding her. To keep running.

Keep running. Keep running. That was the only thought in his head. Everything else had gone. His world was reduced to the agony of putting one foot in front of the other. Dragging one more breath into his lungs. Holding onto the woman in his arms. Step. Agony. Step. Agony.

His knee was on fire. Every time he put weight on it, the pain increased. Now it was being stabbed by a dozen rusty knives. The knives were getting hotter. More of them.

Vaguely he wondered what he had done to himself. He knew he was running on adrenaline and sheer cussedness. Had he broken his kneecap, or just torn ligaments? he wondered. Maybe both. Was this the end of his career? Would he ever be able to walk again?

Somewhere at the back of his mind, a tiny vision of Summer egged him on. He ignored the pain that lanced through him and kept running. A bullet thudded into his back. Even through the body armour, it bruised him.

The boom of the explosion was a welcome change. The chase slowed up for a few minutes, but Flynn kept going.

The whirling rotors at the bottom of the mountain were the most welcome sight he had ever seen. With one last burst of speed, he flung the woman onto the floor of the chopper, and himself in after her.

'Who is that?' Niall demanded, but Flynn couldn't answer. He passed out before the chopper took off.

31

Summer blinked several times, trying to adjust her eyes to the darkness. The lumpy mattress beneath her was nothing like her own. *Okay, don't panic. Don't panic. Just breathe.* The memory of Flynn's words calmed her and she took several deep breaths.

She had a fuzzy memory of being carried down a flight of stairs and the smell of air freshener, which failed to mask the stink of cigarettes. A wave of nausea swept over her and she rolled over onto her side, kicking off the blanket. What the hell had they injected her with?

When the nausea passed she staggered unsteadily to her feet. Somewhere along the way, she had lost one of her pumps. She kicked the other one off and, arms outstretched, she moved slowly towards the crack of light at the far side of the room. She needed to see.

The chink of light was high above her head. Her hand hit something solid. The surface was uneven, like painted bricks. Where was she? A garage? Some kind of storage unit? Standing on tiptoe, she stretched towards the light, patting the wall lightly. There. Her fingers came in contact with something smooth, some kind of tape. She scratched with her nails until it came away from the wall.

More light flooded into the room and she looked around her. Apart from a bare mattress, the room contained no furniture. A cardboard box in the corner announced that it killed all known germs and a single light bulb hung from the ceiling. She squinted at her watch, trying to figure out how long she had been here. Four-thirty.

Late afternoon. She had missed her lunch date with Sinead – her cousin would be pissed. But her dad wouldn't be back until Wednesday. Would the men who took her know that? How would they convince her father that they had her? Would they chop off one of her fingers the way they did in horror movies and send it to him? Summer's heard pounded at the thought of it.

Stop it. Don't think like that. Positive mental attitude. Remember? Flynn had told her that if she was ever taken, she should co-operate. Kidnappers didn't want her, just the money she represented.

She took several deep breaths before she recommenced her assault on the layers of duct tape, pulling it away from the wall inch by inch. She winced as she broke one of her nails. Bugger. She bit down on it and removed what was left of the jagged edge. After what seemed like an hour, she was able to pull the covering away.

The small window had white painted bars. Through them, she could see a flight of stone steps with a wrought iron balustrade. She craned her neck and caught a glimpse of blue sky. 'Okay, Sherlock, what does that tell you?'

Focus. Just focus and stay calm. She had only been taken a few hours ago and already she was talking to herself. It was a basement, probably in a period house, and she couldn't hear any traffic, only birds' song, so definitely not in the city. Given the time lapse since they took her, she couldn't be too far away from London.

The sound of voices made her jump. She patted the

tape back into place around the window and jumped back onto the mattress, pulling the blanket around her. The lock clicked and electric light flooded the room. She held her breath and heard footsteps as someone approached.

He shook her shoulder roughly. 'Wake up. No more sleeping.'

Summer feigned bewilderment as she opened her eyes. 'Where am I?'

He wasn't one of the men who had taken her. His jet-black hair was flecked with grey and his swarthy complexion made him look like a gypsy. 'Up. Up. You eat now. Then I take you to bathroom.'

The rattle of crockery announced the arrival of the second man. The one who had been with Uri. At the smell of oxtail soup, her stomach gave a welcoming growl. She had eaten hardly anything since the day before. He placed the tray on the bed. One bowl with a plastic spoon, a bread roll and a bottle of water. It was better than nothing. 'Thank you,' she said.

Uri's friend grunted in response. As he stood up, his jacket moved and she caught a glimpse of a gun tucked into his belt. Any idea she had of making a run for it vanished at the sight of it. 'Why have you taken me?'

A flash of amusement crossed his face and he broke into a laugh. 'Why do you think? Your father will pay much to get you back.'

'My father is in Atlanta.'

That piece of information took him by surprise. He exchanged a glance with Gypsy who shrugged. 'No matter. He can take one of his own aeroplanes home. Be good girl and you will be free soon.'

With that, both men left the room. Summer heard the lock clicking back into place. At least they had left the light on. She ate the lukewarm soup slowly, trying not to gag. The door opened again as she scraped the last mouthful from the bowl.

'Come now.' Gypsy was back again, carrying a small plastic bag. Barefoot, she followed him into the corridor, glancing left and right from beneath her eyelashes, trying to establish where she was. She caught a glimpse of a row of brass pans in what appeared to be a kitchen, and an iron-gated wine cellar. At the end of the corridor, Gypsy opened a door that led into a toilet with a tiny sink.

He handed her the bag. 'You have five minutes.'

As if to warn her, he tapped the face of his watch. Summer nodded and closed the door behind her. It was too much to hope that the bathroom had a lock. The plastic bag contained a travel-size toothbrush and toothpaste.

Summer used the facilities as quickly as she could. She was still brushing her teeth when he pounded on the door. She spat into the sink and rinsed her mouth quickly. Gypsy didn't have a lot of patience.

When she returned to her room, Uri was waiting. 'We make a little movie, yes?'

She nodded. Somehow she didn't think that her dad would like this one any more than her last starring role.

Uri's friend returned, carrying a mobile phone and a newspaper which he placed beside her. 'You will sit on the bed and read from this.'

Summer took the paper from him. The prices of O'Sullivan Airlines shares on the stock market made her want to laugh, but the words on the page blurred before her eyes as her new reality came home to her. If something went wrong, she was going to die.

Flynn blinked his eyes free of the narcotics that were trying to hold him asleep. There was something driving him, something he needed to do. His head was still full of woodpeckers with pile drivers, but he couldn't stay unconscious any longer.

The soothing white ceiling and smell of a hospital greeted him. Fuck, not another one. He had spent far too long in hospital this year. He was getting old. It took a few minutes before the mission in Afghanistan came back to him. Ah well, not bad for an old guy.

He pressed the call bell under his hand. The nurse who answered looked tired, but smiled when she saw him. 'Herr Grant. You're awake.' Why did medical people always need to state the obvious, he wondered. 'I heard what you did. You're the hero of the hospital.'

'I'm a hero?' he repeated stupidly. He knew there was no way Niall would ever have leaked anything about their mission to anyone here.

The nurse checked his chart, examined the machines beeping beside him and finally handed him a beaker with a bendy straw. 'Yes, Doctor Blé told us all what you did, how you carried her down the mountain with a dislocated knee and torn ligaments.'

'Doctor Blé?' Flynn asked.

'Doctor Simone Blé of *Los Medicos Voladores*. She had been held captive for two months before you rescued her. She can't sing your praises highly enough.'

That explained who the French woman was, and why he hadn't heard about her capture. Flynn trusted Niall would look after her and return her home. He went back to the other part of the nurse's comment. 'What's wrong with my knee?'

He held his breath while she checked his chart again. One of these days, he would have an injury he couldn't recover from, and he had no idea how he would cope. His mind shied away from living as a cripple.

'You've got grade three tearing on your ACL and medial ligaments. It's a miracle you were able to move at all, never mind run. If Simone hadn't told us herself, we wouldn't have believed you could have done it. We've operated on you, but I'm afraid you're out of action for at least six months.'

'No way. I have a wedding to go to. I am not going on crutches.'

The nurse looked at him sternly. 'If you don't want to regain the use of your knee, that's fine. I've seen your record; you've already used up all your luck when it comes to injuries. Abuse your knee and it will never work properly.'

Flynn flopped back against the pillow. Six months on crutches? It wasn't possible. He couldn't stand that. He'd be a laughing stock at the wedding.

And Summer? Somehow things had rearranged themselves in his mind when he was unconscious. Summer was HIS. So she wasn't the perfect little sub that Lorna had been. So, she was high maintenance, headstrong and bratty. He loved those things about her. And even more, he loved her willingness to explore, her loyalty, her vulnerability, her sensuality, her big heart. And it didn't hurt that she had a body like Venus, he admitted.

Summer wasn't his principal any longer. He wasn't exactly the sort of man she usually dated, but to hell with that. He knew what she wanted. He'd shower her with kink from night to morning if that's what it took to make her happy.

He had hoped to make a more athletic entrance but to hell with it, he couldn't wait. His phone was gone, so he demanded the hospital phone and stuffed his credit card into it. 'Hi Niall, put me through to Summer. I need to talk to her.'

Niall laughed and told him to hold on. The wait dragged on and on. The numbers on his phone cranked up and up, and were over a tenner when Niall came back on the line. 'We don't know where she is. She gave McEntaggart the slip.'

Despite the heat of the hospital, Flynn's skin chilled. 'When?' His lips were stiff.

'No one has seen her in several days.'

'Find her, Niall. I'll be with you soon.' He hung up and jammed his finger on the call button.

When an annoyed nurse arrived, he told her, 'Get me my clothes, a knee brace and a wheelchair. I'm discharging myself.'

She gave an impatient sigh. 'I can't stop you from leaving, Herr Grant, but I must remind you if you don't give yourself time to recover, you may be limping permanently.'

Try to keep track of time and establish routines – item nine or whatever it was on Flynn's list. She was lucky that she had

344

a watch, although unsticking the masking tape around the window to read the time was a pain.

She hadn't managed to sleep much. The room was cold and the thin blanket did little to keep her warm. She had seen no one for almost eight hours. Were they still in the house? Had the ransom been paid? Maybe something had gone wrong?

That thought prompted her to climb off the mattress again and make her way to the door. The silence was broken by footsteps. Someone was coming. She stood on her abandoned shoe in her hurry to get back and had to stifle a yelp of pain.

The light was switched on and the door opened. It was Gypsy. 'Bathroom, then food.'

She walked slowly down the corridor, trying to stretch her legs. She would have to exercise, maybe do some circuits of the room. Anything to stave off the boredom and stop her thinking.

'You slept?' Gypsy asked her.

She shook her head. 'Not a lot. It was cold.'

'Five minutes.' He tapped his watch and Summer scurried inside. This time she checked the tiny room thoroughly. There was a window but it was too small for even a child to climb through and there was nothing here that she could use as a weapon.

She washed quickly and opened the door a crack. There was no sign of Gypsy. Could she make a run for it? The kitchen door swung open and she heard voices. Summer stepped back inside and closed the door.

'You come now.' It wasn't Gypsy, but the sidekick. She had heard Gypsy call him Andrei.

He propelled her ahead of him back to her room. On a tray in the middle of the mattress was a bowl of cereal and a small carton of milk. Best of all was the smell of coffee coming from a red mug. Summer's mouth watered. She devoured the cereal quickly and finished off the milk, not sure when they would feed her again. She wrapped her chilled fingers around the mug and sipped it, grateful for the warmth. Andrei stood in the doorway, watching her every move until Gypsy re-appeared carrying a plump bed throw.

'Hey, Uri said no touching stuff from upstairs –'

'Pfff,' Gypsy shrugged. 'Do you want her getting sick?'

'I suppose not,' Andrei replied, but he looked on with disapproval clearly written across his face as Gypsy laid the throw on the end of the mattress.

'Thank you.' Summer smiled gratefully at him. She drained the last of her coffee and placed the mug back on the tray. Gypsy picked it up and headed to the door. 'Could you leave the light on? Please?' She hated sounding anxious, but the thought of another endless day here in the dark was more than she could tolerate.

The door closed behind them. The lock clicked into place and then the room was plunged into darkness. She heard voices outside, and almost immediately the light came back on again. She pulled the throw around her, thankful for light and warmth.

32

Flynn fumed as he limped into the terminal and switched on his phone. Bloody plane. It was bad enough that he had been stuck on a commercial flight for hours. Niall would have a cow when he got the bill for the three first class tickets he'd bought so that he could stretch out his leg. The client would probably end up paying for it.

When he reached the arrivals hall, a tall figure sloped away from a pillar and came to greet him. Andy McTavish could wear a dishrag and still look elegant. The joke at the agency was that Andy made 'tall dark and handsome' sound like an understatement. Niall often used him as bait for missions involving women.

'What are you doing here?' Flynn demanded.

'I'm your driver. I hear you're all injured and delicate and we have to look after you.'

'Fuck off, Andy.' It didn't help Flynn's temper that it was true. His leg was encased in a giant plastic and metal brace that make him look like RoboCop, and he had a long list of things he was not to do if he ever wanted to use his knee again.

He directed Andy to drive to Dunboy House. Chances were that there would be some clue there as to where Summer had gone.

The butler was his usual disapproving self, but to give

him his due, Malcolm seemed genuinely upset by Summer's disappearance. He wrung his hands with uncharacteristic agitation when he told Flynn that he had gone to the doctor's the last time Summer was here.

'That nice Mr Fielding gave her a lift home. I did offer to make up a room for him after the drive, because it was late at night, but his bed wasn't slept in.' He gave Flynn a pointed look, which he ignored.

'When did you see her after that?'

Malcolm shook his head. 'I didn't. I had a medical appointment that morning, and I missed her. She was gone when I returned.'

No matter how much he probed, Flynn couldn't get anything else out of the butler. He left Malcolm polishing silver and checked the rest of the house. Summer's room had been tidied, but still smelled of her.

Was it really less than a month since he had been here? He lifted the bottles on her dressing table and sniffed them. None of the scents were half as exotic as the smell of her skin or her hair or the taste of her as he buried his face between her thighs.

Down boy. Keep your focus on the mission. A small tissue-wrapped parcel caught his attention and he opened it. A pebble from the loch, the one with the pattern that looked like a star; he had found it for her. A small pinecone like the ones that littered the forest floor where he had found her the night she ran away. A pale orchid with a touch of pink at the centre, a little battered around the edges. All memories of a Scottish summer.

Tiny objects that marked their time together. The only things that she had taken with her when she walked away from him. The truth was so blindingly obvious that only a fool could miss it.

Summer was in love with him.

Flynn sat down heavily on the bed. He had never run away from anything in his life. He had fought in every dangerous corner of the planet, but nothing had been as dangerous as spending a month alone with her. Oh, she was spoilt, wilful and demanding. But she was also sweet and tender and he had never met a woman who challenged him more.

Flynn lifted the pillow from the bed and pressed it against his face, catching the faint scent of her. He was turning soft. Tim O'Sullivan would never let his only daughter marry a man like him. He was a soldier. A well paid one, but he couldn't keep her in designer shoes for a month, never mind keep up with the lifestyle that her father provided for her.

Flynn wrapped the souvenirs back in the tissue. Somehow, when he got her back, he would find a way for them to be together. Summer O'Sullivan belonged to him. But he had no time to think about that now. He heard cars outside on the gravel drive. The rest of the team were arriving. It was his fault that she was gone. His job was to get Summer back. No matter what it cost.

He continued to search the room, and in the rubbish bin found clothes which he recognized. Summer had worn them at the croft, but now the pale pink T-shirt was torn at the neck. He doubted that she had done it. Rage boiled up inside him at the thought of someone hurting her.

He held onto his temper with an effort. He rang Niall

and asked for a forensic sweep of Summer's room. This was the last place she had been, as far as they knew; it was the logical starting point.

Downstairs, he listened to the messages on the answering machine. There were reminders about yoga class, a dental appointment, a message saying, 'Read the paper, bitch. And she's not looking for a pre-nup.' Probably Bayliss, Flynn thought.

There was an irate message from someone called Sinead.

'Thanks a million for that, Summer. You were the one who wanted to talk to me, and instead you leave me hanging around for two bloody hours waiting for you. You'd better have one hell of a good explanation, or you can deal with Tim on your own the next time you're in trouble.'

Flynn dialled her number right away. 'Sinead O'Sullivan, Jewel Collection, how can I help you?'

The hint of an Irish accent reminded him painfully of Summer. 'Summer is missing; I need to talk to you.'

There was a brief pause, and then the efficient voice said, 'Of course. I see from the number on the display that you're at the house. I'll be there as soon as possible.'

Flynn and Andy interrogated the other servants, hoping that one of them had a clue about where Summer could have gone. They were barely finished when the main gates opened and a sedate Volvo came up the driveway.

The driver got out, and Andy whistled. 'Well, look at that.'

Flynn looked. The woman in the dark grey car was buttoned down and conservative, in a tailored suit with a white blouse. Her hair was pulled back into a neat chignon, and she wore glasses with silver frames. She moved like a young woman, but the clothes made it impossible to tell how old she was. 'What?' he asked Andy. 'She looks like she wears granny pants.'

Andy shot him an incredulous glance. 'Did you not see the arse on her when she got out of the car? That is one world-class arse.'

Flynn couldn't summon interest. The only arse he was interested in was Summer's.

The woman introduced herself as Sinead. Something clicked. 'Oh, you're the cousin who was at school with Summer and –' He stopped.

'Plain Jane Superbrain?' she said evenly. 'Yes, that's me. What makes you think Summer has disappeared?'

'No one has seen her for six days.' Put like that, Flynn was aware it sounded thin. There was no law that said Summer had to tell anyone where she went. She was rich enough that she could have hopped on a plane to Argentina without telling anyone. Except that her well-stamped passport was still in her room, and all his instincts were screaming at him that something was wrong.

'I spoke to her last Monday. She said she wanted my advice about a man.' Sinead stopped, and a knowing expression crossed her face. 'I'm guessing it was you.'

Flynn nodded.

'She was supposed to meet me for coffee, but never turned up. Summer's often late, but this was the first time she didn't show at all.'

Flynn questioned her but she didn't know anything else. 'That's fine, thank you, Miss O'Sullivan. You can go now.'

'That's Ms O'Sullivan. And there's no way I'm leaving

here until Summer is found. I'm not leaving her recovery to a man who can barely walk and a bunch of goons.' This was said with such a polite voice that it took a second for the words to sting Flynn.

'You can't stay here,' he said.

'Of course I can. I'll tell Malcolm to have a room made up for me.' She rang the bell and as she waited, she asked, 'Is there any way that he's involved in this? He's such a creepy little man. I wouldn't be surprised if he's hiding something.'

Flynn darted a look at Andy; the last thing they needed was a civilian getting in their way.

The light was still on when Summer woke. 'Okay, time for exercise.'

Great, now she was talking to herself. She got up and stretched. There wasn't a lot of room to walk and after ten circuits of the room she was bored stupid. Press ups. She could do some of them against the wall. Three sets later she was feeling warmed up. She tried some kicks, aiming at a shadow on the wall that looked like Flynn's hand.

Flynn. *Kick*. She was trying not to think about him, but now she could think of nothing else. It irked her to admit that if she had stayed in Scotland, none of this would have happened.

Kick. Kick. If he hadn't lied to her the whole time they were together, she would still be there. She aimed another series of kicks at the shadow. 'Lying. Scottish . . .'

How could she have been so stupid as to fall for him? *Kick. Kick. Kick.*

If Flynn was within ten feet of her she would punch

his lights out. Summer kicked again and again until sweat trickled down her spine. She bent over, trying to catch her breath, then peeled off her top and threw herself down on the mattress, panting.

Despite the exercise, the memory of the nights lying in his arms in the croft refused to go away. But it was his mouth that she missed most of all. The warmth of it on her skin, the rough drag of his stubble against her neck, the nip of his teeth on her ear lobe.

Flynn did more than just kiss. When he took her lips, she felt that he owned her mouth. She had never expected that she would enjoy the sharp bite of pain with her pleasure. Flynn had taught her that. The way that he twisted the strands of her hair between his fingers, angling her head for his kiss, still made her shiver.

It was curious how such a small display of his strength could make her dissolve into a wanton puddle. Even now, trapped in this godforsaken hole, she couldn't dispel the memory of his touch and how he had made her feel. How could she hate him and want him at the same time?

Her hand slid to her neck, remembering his fingers there as they traced a path along her jaw and parted her lips with his thumb. She had licked it, sucked it into her mouth, watching the heavy lidded expression on his face.

Summer caressed her breast through the thin lace of her bra and her nipples peaked at the memory of Flynn touching her with his hand and mouth. Worshipping her with calloused fingers, driving into her wetness and licking his fingers afterwards. Or Flynn, buried between her thighs, with her heels digging into his back, her nails scoring his shoulders as he rode her hard.

The ultimate pleasure for her was knowing that whatever happened next, she couldn't do anything to stop it, and she didn't want to. She had wanted someone to watch over her; instead, Flynn had possessed her, body and soul. And despite everything, he still did.

A key in the lock startled her. She reached for her discarded top and fumbled with the buttons. It was too early for another meal. Maybe it was a bathroom break. Gypsy had left a plastic bucket in one corner of the room, but she would cross her legs all day rather than use it.

The door opened. It was Andrei, carrying a bottle of water and a newspaper. He tossed the water bottle onto the makeshift bed.

'Thank you.' Summer looked at the doorway, waiting for Gypsy to appear, but Andrei was alone.

He gave her a speculative look. 'Your picture is in newspaper.'

Her picture? Summer's stomach flipped. Did the press know that she had been kidnapped? That wasn't a good sign. That meant the police would become involved and Uri had said, no police.

Fear must have shown on her face because Andrei laughed. 'Not kidnap picture. Sex picture. See.'

He thrust the tabloid at her. The lurid headlines screamed *Bayliss Bags Babs*. The nudge nudge wink wink reportage crowed that *'Former London city dealer and fiancé of Summer O'Sullivan has just become engaged to hotel heiress Barbara Silverwood.'*

She couldn't read any more. Plastered beside the image of a smiling Adam and a platinum blonde was one of the infamous photographs he had sold to the tabloids.

Sickened, she threw the paper onto the floor. Adam had finally got his heiress, but the photographs he had taken would haunt her for the rest of her days. Despite the hair and heavy make-up, his new fiancée looked young. She wondered how long it would be before Adam tired of her or bled her dry.

Laughing, Andrei picked it up and smoothed the page. 'Would you like to get out of here for a while? Perhaps see rest of house?'

His eyes flicked from her photograph to her and back again and he licked his lips. She could guess exactly what a tour of the house would involve. Summer tried to mask her revulsion at his suggestion. 'No, thank you,' she said in a frosty tone.

Andrei shrugged. 'Pity. Perhaps you will change mind later.'

Not in a million years. Summer held her tongue with an effort and kept her eyes cast down. There was no sense in aggravating him if she could avoid it. She heard his footsteps as he walked to the door and locked it behind him. Then the room was plunged into darkness.

For what seemed like hours, there was silence. Summer couldn't sleep. She was too unsettled by Andrei's visit to close her eyes. Flynn had told her to co-operate as far as possible, but she drew the line at getting up close and personal with her kidnappers.

Summer squinted, trying to see the face of her watch. Eventually, she made her way across the room and began the laborious task of removing the masking tape around the window again. A chink of light emerged from behind the barrier. Electric light. It was night and no one had come for hours. She glanced at her watch. Almost ten o'clock.

Her stomach rumbled loudly, protesting the lack of food, and she desperately needed to use the bathroom. They couldn't leave her here like this, locked up like an animal. She stuck the tape back into place and made her way slowly across the darkened room. Someone had to come. She raised her fist and banged on the door. 'Let me out. Let me out of here.'

When no one came she pounded the door again. That made her feel good for a while, until her fist screamed in protest and then she had to stop. No one was coming. Sliding one foot in front of the other, she made her way to the corner of the room until her foot encountered the plastic bucket. She fumbled with the fastening on her jeans and used the 'facilities' before making her way back to bed.

Summer poured a small amount of water into her hands to wash them, wiping them off on her shirt, before taking a deep mouthful to quench her thirst. She didn't know when they would bring more. Her water would have to be rationed. Dragging the quilt around her, she shut her eyes tightly, trying to ignore her grumbling stomach. If they weren't taking care of her, that meant that things were not going well. They should want to keep her alive, otherwise how would they get paid? No one would pay for a corpse, least of all her dad.

Stop thinking like that. You will get out of this. Flynn will come for you.

But what if he doesn't? Flynn was on a mission somewhere else. There was no reason for him to come. The first tear slid down her cheek, then another. She rubbed her eyes with her fist. 'Stop. You're wasting water.'

Her words sounded loud in the room and she giggled. She was finally losing it, talking to herself like a madwoman. *Have to calm down. Have to think of a way to get out of here.*

Flynn was annoyed to find that Sinead insisted on coming with him when he interviewed Fielding. 'You can't drive with that thing on your leg. Besides, I'm good at telling when people are lying,' she told him.

'And you think I can't?' What was it with these bossy O'Sullivan women?

'You're a man. Men are shite at stuff like this.' And she climbed into the driver's seat. Damn it, Flynn hated being driven. There was something about letting other people be in control that put him on edge, unless they were part of his team. But his knee was still weak enough that it wasn't worth insisting on.

Sinead drove confidently and smoothly and always one mile per hour below the speed limit.

'Not tempted to go a bit faster?' he asked idly.

She took her eyes off the road for a half second while she flicked him an unreadable glance. 'That would be illegal.' She didn't say anything for the rest of the trip.

Robert Fielding was at his office, a glossy marble and glass edifice with thick carpeting and espresso machines in the reception. He glared at Flynn and made time for them with a bad grace. 'I have no idea why you are wasting my time like this. There is nothing I can help you with.'

Flynn noticed that Sinead hadn't moved, she continued to sit silently on her leather and chrome chair, but she had gone on the alert. 'We're just trying to confirm when Summer was last seen,' he told Fielding.

'I have already told that uncouth boss of yours. I dropped Summer at the house last Monday, then I went home.'

'What time did you get there?' Flynn asked.

'About 3 a.m. My concierge can verify that.' He flicked through several sheets of paper, as if bored with the conversation.

Sinead entered the conversation for the first time. 'Malcolm said that you spent some time with Summer. What did you talk about?'

'That's private.'

'Not when she's missing. I need to know,' Flynn told him.

Fielding considered for a moment, measuring them with his eyes before he spoke. 'I'm telling you this in confidence; please don't repeat it to anyone.'

Flynn nodded tightly. He had a feeling he wasn't going to like what he heard.

'If you must know, Summer made a pass at me. She said she wanted to know what a real man was like.' Flynn's muscles tightened in protest, but he forced himself not to react. 'I was flattered, of course, but I had to turn her down. You know I'm involved with Molly.' He shrugged. 'She seemed upset. Perhaps she went off somewhere to get over her disappointment.'

Sinead's hand on his arm kept Flynn from exploding off his seat and throttling him.

Fielding handed him a card, telling him to phone at any time, and that he would be delighted to tell him any other details.

As soon as they were in the street again, Sinead told him, 'He's lying. I'm not sure about what but he's lying. Summer wouldn't do that. I know she wouldn't.'

Flynn wondered if he was trying to convince himself or Sinead. 'Probably not.'

Sinead insisted. 'I know that snake was lying about something.'

33

Flynn stood in the sitting room and stared at Adam Bayliss with the pitiless eyes of an executioner. Whatever he knew about Summer's kidnapping, he would get out of him. But inside he wondered what Summer had ever seen in him.

Adam was tall and soft. There was no other word for it. His shoulders were broad enough, Flynn supposed, but the muscle was undefined. He moved like someone whose most energetic activity was dancing. Or making love. The thought of Adam making love to Summer caused a red mist to descend over Flynn's eyes.

He took a breath, forcing himself to calm down, and caught a whiff of expensive cologne. Adam's hair was cut in a style which vaguely reminded him of some pop star. His clothes were all designer, and all with logos of strange animals on them.

What the hell had Summer ever seen in this man milliner?

Adam shifted from foot to foot under Flynn's relentless gaze, and then seemed to force himself to stay still. He couldn't succeed in disguising his fear. 'Look, whatever it is, I'll be glad to help, but I don't know anything,' he said.

'Then why are you sweating?' Flynn asked. He had to force himself to keep his fists unclenched, but fury filled him. The thought of Adam anywhere near Summer enraged him.

Adam wiped his temples with an embroidered linen handkerchief. 'It's been a hot day.'

'And you're in hot water, aren't you, Bayliss?'

Adam failed to conceal a wince. 'I have no idea what you are talking about,' he said unconvincingly.

Flynn produced a piece of paper from his pocket. There were a few scribbled phone numbers on it, but Bayliss had no way of knowing that. 'You owe a lot of money. And not just to the banks.' It was a safe bet, considering what Summer had told him about this weasel.

Bayliss swallowed. 'I admit I may have over-stretched my credit limits recently but –'

'And you wanted to get revenge on the O'Sullivans. They deserved it for the way they treated you, right?'

He nodded. 'What sort of girl doesn't trust her fiancé and demands a pre-nup? I knew she wasn't the right girl for me when that happened.'

Bayliss kept going. 'Do you know what O'Sullivan did to me when I said that a husband and wife should trust each other? He did his best to ruin me. Those jumped-up nouveau-riche paddies have no idea how to behave.'

Flynn held onto his temper with an effort. 'And you decided to teach them a lesson.'

Adam moved a step closer to Flynn, apparently warming to his subject. 'He should have been grateful that someone was willing to marry that frigid tart. She might look like she's a goer, and she takes a good photo, but she's a bloody icicle.'

Flynn had no idea how it happened. One moment he

was standing on the other side of the table, the next he was holding Bayliss by the neck. 'You little prick,' he hissed through clenched teeth. 'I'm going to wring your fucking neck.'

Bayliss clawed frantically at Flynn's hands, desperate to relieve the pressure on his throat, but Flynn wasn't letting go. This worm was the one who had taken photos of Summer at her most vulnerable and posted them all over the internet. And who had almost broken her pride. His fingers tightened. He ignored the clawing, even when it drew blood, and enjoyed seeing his eyes bulge with terror.

What was he doing? The worm didn't even know Summer was missing. Flynn dropped him in disgust.

Adam landed on the floor, panting for breath and scrabbling away frantically. His eyes were red and bloodshot and the marks of Flynn's fingers showed clearly on his neck. 'I'll have you arrested. Who the hell are you anyway?'

'Haven't you guessed? I'm Summer's husband.' Well, he would be, if there was the slimmest chance that she would have him. As soon as he found his orchid girl safe and sound they would have to talk.

The smell alerted him. He looked down and saw that Adam Bayliss had pissed himself. The scent of urine pervaded the room and showed up clearly against his light coloured pants. Flynn couldn't resist. He whipped out his camera and took several shots. 'See you on YouTube,' he told Bayliss before he left the room.

The noise level of the entire mansion rose as soon as Tim O'Sullivan walked in. Even though he was just off a long flight from Atlanta, he radiated energy and temper. 'Where the hell is my daughter?' he roared as soon as he came in the front door. 'What sort of an arse-feckin outfit are you running that you could lose her like that?'

Niall took a breath before he replied. 'Summer deliberately gave her bodyguard the slip. She came home, spent the night here, phoned people, apparently had a romantic disappointment and drove herself away. She's an adult; she can make her own decisions.'

'Adult?' Tim spat. 'She's an idiot. She needs someone to mind her. And that was supposed to be you.'

Flynn couldn't take any more. 'Summer is not an idiot,' he said coldly. 'Don't speak of her like that.'

'She's my damned daughter; I can call her anything I like.'

The only thing which kept Flynn from throttling the bombastic little tyrant was the faint tremble in his hands and the pallor of his skin.

Tim demanded updates on all their efforts to find Summer, and occasionally put in a sharp, helpful comment. He looked up from sheets of computer printouts when Malcolm came in with an envelope on a silver salver. 'Why are you interrupting me? Give that to Brian,' he barked.

The high turnover of staff was no longer a mystery. Flynn wondered idly why Malcolm put up with Tim. He hoped he received a very high salary.

'I'm sorry, sir. This was delivered with instructions to give it to you personally.'

It was a padded envelope, with no stamps. Tim ripped it open before anyone could stop him. The only content was a cheap USB stick. Flynn stuck it into his laptop and Summer's image flickered into life.

At the sight of her scared and dirty face, Flynn forgot to breathe. God no, his orchid girl was hurt. She was in danger. The fury that roared through him at the thought of anyone hurting her made it hard to hear what she was saying. He forced the rage and terror deep inside him, assuming an icy mantle so that he could concentrate on the details.

The picture was shaky, probably taken with the camera on a phone. He focused on the silent, unsmiling girl sitting on a mattress in a bare room. Beside her was a copy of the *Financial Times*, ironically featuring news of Tim O'Sullivan's latest multimillion-dollar deal.

The muscles in Flynn's stomach clenched when he saw the bruise on her left temple.

Summer raised her eyes to the camera, as if waiting for instructions. Then she read an extract from the stock exchange prices for the day before picking up a piece of notepaper. 'If you want me returned, the price is one million pounds in diamonds, payable tomorrow. If you don't pay, I will die. You will receive instructions about payment. Follow them exactly. If you don't, I will die. Do not contact the police, or I will die.'

Her voice faltered over the last words, but then she raised her chin and stared at the camera. She seemed to be looking at him. He resisted the urge to reach out and stroke her face. She was trying her best to be brave but he could tell that it was hard for her.

Tim groaned.

Beside him, Sinead whimpered. 'Oh Jesus,' she whispered as she sagged against him.

Flynn squeezed her hand. 'We will get her back. I promise you.'

While Andy took her to the kitchen and made some tea, Flynn sat in front of the laptop and watched the brief clip half a dozen times. Scanning the room for any clues to her whereabouts, listening for background noises, watching Summer's face for every minute change. Before she started reading, she glanced in one direction, obviously at the camera man and then a little to the right? Was there more than one man? It seemed likely.

Tim stood up. 'Where are you going?' Niall asked.

'To get the money. You heard them. They said a million pounds in diamonds. I need to get that from the bank. No matter what it costs, I'm going to get my little girl back.'

Despite the weight of the quilt, she couldn't seem to keep warm. Summer reached for the water bottle and then remembered that it was empty. Voices outside made her sit upright. Gypsy was back. Maybe they were going to let her go. She rolled out of bed and hurried to the door. With as much force as she could muster she banged on the wood with her fists, throwing in a few kicks for good measure. She wouldn't stop until someone came.

The lock clicked open. Summer stepped away from the door as Gypsy pushed his way inside. A string of words, which Summer guessed were curses, streamed from his mouth when he saw her shivering in the darkened room.

'We need another picture. The negotiator has demanded further proof that you are still alive.'

A picture? He hadn't come to set her free. She could

just imagine what she looked like by now. Her dad would be worried sick. 'Alive? I won't be alive for long without food or water.'

Gypsy's eyes narrowed. 'You have had nothing since I left?'

'A small bottle of water,' Summer grudgingly admitted.

He looked around the room, noting the crumpled quilt and the bucket in the corner and she caught a little flicker of sympathy in his expression. He wasn't the worst of them. Well, he wasn't as bad as Andrei.

'You wash now.'

His words were a demand rather than a request. She was tempted to refuse, but the prospect of warm water was too appealing. Summer followed him along the corridor to the tiny bathroom and closed the door behind her.

The image in the mirror was worse than she had expected. Her hair hung in lank clumps around her face and her pale skin contrasted with the dark circles beneath her eyes. Even in the awful days after Adam's betrayal, she hadn't looked this bad.

Outside, the shouting began again. English mixed with whatever godforsaken language they usually spoke. Summer opened the door a crack and peeked out. The kitchen door was closed and the corridor was clear. Dare she?

Summer slipped out and hurried along the corridor, holding her breath as she passed the kitchen door. Her bare feet were silent. The men were still arguing. She pushed open a door at the end and hurried up the narrow staircase, until she reached the landing. It wouldn't be long before they discovered that she was gone. Another door beckoned and she stepped into a marble-floored hallway. She caught her breath.

She knew this house. She had attended a cocktail party here several years before. The family were in the Far East now. What was their name? Roxton? Floxton? She couldn't remember. It didn't matter. What mattered now was that she knew where she was. She couldn't be more than ten miles from home.

Summer hurried to the front door. It was locked. Too much to hope it would be open. She had a vague memory that the dining room had French doors which led out to the garden. She would break out of here if she had to.

The furniture was covered in dust cloths and the curtains were drawn but the room was still the same as she remembered. Summer jerked on the handle. The door was also locked. There must be a spare key around here somewhere. She reached for the ledge above the door and ran her fingers along the dusty edge. Yes. She breathed silent thanks.

Her fingers curled around the key. Trembling, she pushed it into the lock and turned. The door opened with a protesting creak. She was free. Now, all she had to do was make it to the road and flag down a car. She closed the door behind her. The longer she could delay her pursuers the better.

Heart pounding, Summer raced to the front of the house and down the driveway. She winced as her feet found every tiny stone along the way. Behind her, she heard a roar. Gypsy or Andrei was following her.

She could hear a car. Yes! She'd be rescued. She increased her speed. Almost there. Ignoring the thudding footfalls closing behind, Summer clambered over the gate and stepped out onto the road, waving her arms at the oncoming vehicle.

Relief washed over her when a dark blue BMW screeched to a halt. 'Thank you. Oh thank you.'

She hurried to the driver's side of the car. 'You have to help me. I've –'

Summer stopped in mid-sentence. It was Uri. The car door opened and he climbed out. His face was a model of cold fury.

'What are you doing out here?'

This couldn't be happening. Not when she had come so close. She backed away, desperate to get free. A breathless Andrei vaulted the gate and cursed when he saw who she was with.

'Take her back to the house. Now,' Uri shouted.

'No!' she screamed. She kicked out as Andrei tried to grab her. It was useless in her bare feet, but she'd try anything to stop him. Surely another car would come. Summer landed a punch on his nose and was rewarded with a grunt of pain.

'*Pizdă.*' Andrei's mouth curled in a vicious snarl and the last thing she remembered was his fist flying towards her face.

The second message was delivered by a helmeted courier to O'Sullivan Airlines HQ. Tim O'Sullivan was to carry the diamonds in a bag to St Pancras train station where he would receive further instructions. Once the diamonds were picked up and verified, Summer would be released.

If Tim was followed, or the police were involved, she would die.

Niall had tried to convince Tim to let the agency handle it. But he had refused. He was determined to do this alone. There was no way that he was risking his baby.

But Flynn couldn't give up. They still had twenty-four hours to try to find a lead. Someone had to know something and he would start with Molly.

Her flat was a lot like her, a mixture of the weird and wonderful and impractical. There were mismatched scatter cushions, all in startling colours, a leather and horsehair sofa, an elegant mahogany table with rings bolted into the legs. A collection of old teddy bears occupied one armchair, and a rainbow of small fish darted around an aquarium filled with castles and model forests. Lavender oil was burning in a small incense burner.

Molly looked out of place, wearing a smart suit and dressed like a grown-up. She was nervous and agitated. 'Please tell me you've found Summer.' She clutched Flynn's arm, ignoring Sinead.

He shook his head. 'No sign of her yet.'

Molly gulped back a sob. 'I knew there was something wrong. She was supposed to come and stay with me, but she never showed up.'

'When was she supposed to arrive?'

'On Tuesday. She said she had something important to tell me. I should have stayed home to meet her,' Molly sobbed. 'I just told her to let herself in, and I'd meet her after work.'

Tears leaked down her cheeks. 'She never arrived. Now, I'll never know what she wanted to tell me. It's all my fault.' Flynn questioned her for a few minutes, but it was obvious she had nothing more to add.

'Girl, girl.' The voice seemed to come from very far away. 'You eat now.'

Someone put an arm under her back and lifted her to a sitting position. She opened her eyes and closed them again quickly. The light was too bright and her face hurt like hell. Summer pressed a hand to her cheekbone. Her skin felt painful to the touch, but she didn't think that anything was broken. That side of her face was stiff and swollen, but it was nothing compared to the knowledge that she'd lost her chance.

Her escape attempt had failed. The men would watch her like hawks now.

On a tin plate beside the bed was an apple, a small packet of crackers and a bottle of water. She took a mouthful of water before she pulled open the plastic wrapping and ate the crackers two at a time, licking the salty crumbs from her fingers. The apple, she approached like a feast, relishing its scent before she bit into the dark red skin.

A sudden vision of the croft came into her head, of Flynn licking honey from her skin while she squirmed helplessly under his seeking hands and hot mouth. Was this the last man with whom she would feel a lover's touch? Despite everything that had happened afterwards, she was glad that it had been Flynn. She couldn't imagine wanting to spend her last night of passion with any other man.

Summer smoothed the page of the newspaper. At least

they had left her that. She flicked through the pages, smiling wryly at the gossip column. Maya and Natasha were planning a double wedding. She wondered if they had even noticed that she was gone, or did they still think that she was in Scotland? She closed the newspaper and tossed it on the floor. 'Stop being maudlin. You're not dead yet.'

34

Summer drifted in and out of sleep, losing track of time. Raised voices came from outside and she heard a car driving away, but still no one came. Sometime during the night she reached for her water bottle to find that it was empty. She lay there shivering until she fell asleep again.

The sound of Andrei tearing down the blackout tape from her window brought her back to consciousness. He crammed it into a rubbish bag. Daylight flooded the room and she blinked.

He eyed the plastic bucket with distaste. 'Go to bathroom and empty it. You look a mess.'

She struggled to her feet before staggering towards the corner. There was no sign of Gypsy and no familiar scent of morning coffee. Where was he?

Andrei dragged the quilt from the mattress and tossed it into the hallway. The tin plate and sheet were shoved into the black refuse sack. A sudden flare of hope made her ask, 'Has the ransom been paid?'

'Yes,' he replied in a clipped tone as he scanned the room. He dragged the mattress from the floor and stood it against the wall behind the door before putting some of the cardboard boxes in front of it. 'What are you waiting for? Move it.'

Summer grabbed the bucket and fled down the corridor. It was over. They were going to free her. She wanted to jump in the air and scream her delight but Flynn's words about the stages of kidnapping flashed into her head. Release was a dangerous time. They would be on edge. She emptied the contents of the bucket into the toilet and flushed it.

Andrei came up behind her and pointed at the stairs. She went up obediently, keeping an anxious eye out so that she could tell where she was. He gestured her into a room off a bare corridor. It was a utilitarian bathroom, complete with towel, shampoo and soap.

Why would they care what she looked like when she was free? She didn't care. It had been almost a week without washing; it was too good an opportunity to miss. She started to strip off her sweat-stained clothing until a chuckle reminded her that Andrei was still there.

'I guard you,' he said, grinning. 'You wash or I do it for you.'

With horror, she realized that he intended to watch her shower. She shuddered as she stepped out of her jeans and into the shower. She determinedly kept her back to Andrei while she scrubbed her hair and body as quickly as possible. As soon as she was clean, she wrapped herself in a towel. He made a disapproving noise but didn't move from his position lounging against the door. His eyes made her feel dirty.

Summer dragged her fingers through her hair, trying to untangle it. In the tiny scrap of mirror over the sink, she stared at her face. A pale, hollow-eyed reflection stared back at her. She was bruised where Andrei had struck her, but she was alive and determined to stay that way.

She reached for her clothes, but Andrei was there first.

He pulled her T-shirt out of her hands and his eyes raked her body. 'Pretty little *pizdă*. How 'bout we make sex pictures together? You like that. Yes?'

'N-n-no,' she stammered. 'I would not like. My father has paid the ransom. You have to let me go.' She said the last words with more confidence than she felt.

Andrei flashed her a look of impatience. 'Uri is very angry. He told them no tricks, but your father put tracker in diamonds.'

He dropped his hand to his cock and stroked it slowly through the fabric of his jeans. 'Now, you be nice and maybe I will make it quick for you. Yes?'

A boiling rage swept over her. Andrei was going to kill her. They never had any intention of doing otherwise. They had beaten her, starved her, and lied to her. But she was damned if she was going to let Andrei touch her. The rage disappeared as quickly as it had arrived and a cold calmness descended on her as she drew on her memories of Flynn's lessons in self-defence.

He was bigger than she was. He was probably armed, but Andrei was thinking with his dick and that was the only advantage she had. With more confidence than she felt, Summer let her towel drop to the floor and forced herself to smile at him.

She only had one shot at this and had to make it count. Smiling, she stepped towards him, conscious of his eyes on her breasts, the cold-hardened nipples simulating an arousal she didn't feel.

'Why don't you let me help you with that?' she purred in her best imitation of a sex kitten.

Taking advantage of his distraction, she punched

upwards, palm flat into the underside of his nose. It made a sickening crunch as her blow broke his nose.

She had practised the move with Flynn dozens of times, but nothing could have prepared her for the reality. The sudden spurt of blood and the crack of Andrei's head as he fell against the shower cubicle and slumped to the floor. Oh my god, it worked. She had actually knocked someone out.

Summer stared down at him, shivering from shock, mixed with exhilaration. Her hand ached from the blow. The stinging warmth reminding her that she had to escape in case one of the others returned. She grabbed her T-shirt and pulled it over her head, before dragging on her blood-flecked jeans. Barefoot, she raced up the corridor towards the stairs.

The kitchen door swung open. 'Andrei, is it done –'

It was Robert. Her heart leapt. Somehow they had found her. Summer looked over his shoulder expecting to see others behind him but he was alone. Cold dread squeezed her gut. How had Robert known where to find her? How did he know the kidnapper's name? The shock of realization must have shown on her face.

'Summer, I . . . look, I never intended to . . . a deal went bad and I needed to raise some money. After the house party I realized that you were the solution. It wasn't supposed to end like this.'

Robert had been involved all along. He must have known that she would be at Molly's flat that day. He had been part of it. Uri and Gypsy were gone. The ransom had been paid. She was the final loose end. 'Then don't. Just let me go. I swear that I will never breathe a word to anyone –'

Robert shoved his hand into his hair and she saw that it was shaking. 'I can't do that. I'm sorry.'

Summer walked towards him, hands outstretched. 'I know you're a lot of things, but you're not a killer. Please listen to me. This won't be over just because I'm dead. How can you face Molly, knowing that you killed her best friend?'

Robert hesitated and the doubt in his eyes gave her hope. She pointed down the hallway to where Andrei's body lay slumped in the doorway. 'There's nothing to link you to this. I promise you I will never tell a living soul.'

She knew that she was babbling but she didn't care. She was too close to freedom to give up now.

'Stop,' he snapped. 'I need to think.'

Sweat trickled down her spine as she watched Robert approach Andrei's body and nudge it with the toe of his shoe. Satisfied that he was still unconscious, he turned to face her. 'Damn it. He'll be out for hours. I can't leave him here. I've got someone coming to view this place tomorrow.'

'I'll help you. I swear on my life I will never tell anyone.'

'You'll co-operate? Do whatever I say? And there will be no prosecution?'

Her heart thudded like a bass drum as she waited for him to make his decision.

Robert nodded. 'Then grab that quilt, we need to get him out of here.'

Flynn slumped in his chair. His knee hurt like hell and he hadn't slept in more than twenty-four hours. He couldn't.

Not while she was still missing. He stared at the computer screen again. The frozen image of Summer continued to haunt him. This was the reason why he didn't get involved. The reason all of his relationships were short term. He was afraid that someone else would have to face the pain and uncertainty of knowing that the one they loved was in pain, or maybe dead.

He should be the one who was in danger, not Summer.

Sinead arrived carrying two mugs of tea. There was no one on duty in the kitchen. Niall had insisted on questioning all of the staff again, personally. They didn't call him 'The interrogator' for nothing. If they had missed anything, no matter how small, Niall would find it. 'You okay?' she asked.

'As well as could be expected,' he admitted bleakly. 'I keep thinking that we're missing something. She can't just disappear like that. Someone had to know where she was going.'

Sinead gave him an arch look. 'I bet that Malcolm knows more than he's saying. Creepy fecker.'

She sounded so like Summer for a moment that Flynn was tempted to laugh. 'Are you saying that the butler did it?'

She glared at him over the rim of her spectacles. 'No. I'm saying that he knows something and if you won't check it out then I will.'

Putting down her mug, she left the room. Flynn heard her footsteps in the hall and then going up the stairs. Malcolm had worked in the house for the last ten years. According to the employment agency, the O'Sullivans were lucky to have him. Niall had run a background check on him and all the other staff. Malcolm had no criminal record, not even a parking ticket, and he had been at the doctor's for a check-up on the morning that Summer had disappeared.

'Bloody woman,' he muttered as he limped after Sinead. His crutches clattered on the stairs.

The butler's apartment was on the second floor. It was self-contained, with a small sitting room that led to a bedroom with an en suite. Everything was neat and tidy, just like Malcolm. Sinead was already in the bedroom, riffling through the rows of starched shirts and carefully pressed charcoal trousers which made up Malcolm's wardrobe.

'I hate neat men,' Sinead said. 'There's something wrong with a man who's tidy.'

Flynn leaned against the desk for support, admiring the efficient way she searched through Malcolm's belongings. If she had any physical skills, she might be good for the agency.

Over the desk was a neat row of keys. Pantry, wine cellar, garage, all labelled, except one. He picked up a key fob for a HiAce van. He was willing to bet a month's salary that it wasn't parked beside the Aston Martin. Flynn called Andy. 'Run a trace on the butler for me. See if you can find a van registered in his name. Thanks, man.'

Sinead pivoted. 'If you've nothing better to do, you can check the drawers.'

To humour her, Flynn opened the top drawer. Socks, all black and packed in neat rows. The next drawer was no better. Underwear, white and probably starched. Poor Malcolm. A flash of colour at the back of the drawer caught his eye. He had almost missed the cream, barely-there panties with the pink bow, but he knew who they belonged to.

Sinead snatched them from his hand with a triumphant look. 'Told you.'

They searched the rest of the quarters but there was nothing. Trying to be reasonable, he said, 'It could have just been an error with the laundry. We've found nothing else.'

'There must be something.' Sinead scanned the room before focusing on the battered antique desk.

'I've already searched it,' Flynn said. 'Nothing but household papers.'

Sinead picked up a paper knife. 'I've seen one of these in work. Some of them have a hidden drawer.' She pulled out the drawer and used the tip of her knife to reach into the gap. 'Oh, you beauty,' she breathed when she heard a click.

The notebook looked exactly like the household books – except for the newspaper cuttings that tumbled from it. Summer smiling, Summer laughing at a party. Summer . . . oh, shit. The photos. The ones with Adam.

Sinead snatched them from him before he could study them. 'If you care about my cousin, don't look at them.'

She flipped open the notebook. The fine, neat hand-writing was legible, even reading over Sinead's shoulder. The first entries were almost reverent. How pretty Miss Summer looked in her new dress. What a charming, sweet girl she was. Then came a few references to Adam. After that, the words leapt off the page. *Bitch. Tart. Whore.*

Well, at least he knew what Malcolm thought of his employers.

379

Almost caught her last night, one entry in December noted. *I ran her off the road like a dog. Played afterwards.*

Flynn wanted to punch something. Preferably Malcolm's face.

Another entry read: *New bodyguard. A Scot. Another mangy mutt to entertain her, probably because of my little message on the car. Since the crash, they're so easy to scare. Stupid paddies.*

Sinead thumbed through the latest entries. *Had a lively little play last night. The whore almost got what she deserved. She screamed, but I could tell she was gagging for it. What a pity Mr Fielding didn't have the guts to finish what he started.*

Flynn wanted to kill him and he could think of a number of very creative ways to do it. Sinead turned her head and looked up at him. 'Odious little man. What does he mean, "playing"?'

He ground out the word through clenched teeth. 'Masturbation.'

'Oh.' Sinead blushed to her roots and returned her attention to the notebook.

There were no more entries. Probably because Summer had been missing since the last one. He took the book from her hands. It was time to talk to the butler and after that, he was going to have a lengthy conversation with Robert Fielding – one that Robert wouldn't enjoy.

35

Robert took off his blazer and hung it on a doorknob before wiping his forehead with the back of his hand. 'He's heavy. We have to get him outside.'

That didn't sound good. 'But –'

Robert's annoyed glance silenced her. 'I'll take his shoulders, you grab his legs.'

They half dragged, half carried Andrei to the staircase and then stopped to catch their breath. Summer was beginning to wish that she hadn't hit him so hard. Robert took the lead and dragged the quilt-clad bundle up the stairs as she lifted from below; wincing each time she heard Andrei's body thump against the steps.

Finally, they got him to the top of the stairs and Robert opened the door and dragged the body onto the tiled floor of the lobby. 'Wait here,' he said before disappearing through the door again.

She heard his footsteps on the stairs and then silence. Left alone in the dim hallway with Andrei, the adrenaline which had been pumping through her system finally ran out. She still wasn't out of this. She had actually hurt someone, and badly from the look of things.

Rationalizing that she was defending herself, that Andrei had been about to kill her, didn't make it any better. How did Flynn do it? How did he kill someone and live with himself afterwards? No wonder he never spoke about his work.

The door to the basement swung open again. Robert was wearing his blazer and carrying a refuse sack, which he thrust at her. She heard the clink of her tin plate inside it. 'Stop moping about. Open the front door and take this outside.'

Summer hurried to do his bidding. The bright sunlight outside hurt her eyes, making her blink. She drew in several deep breaths of fresh air. She had never felt so glad to be alive.

Robert dragged the body outside into the stone portico. He locked the door behind him and then hurried to open the rear door of the car. Andrei groaned. 'Quickly, we don't have time for this. Let's get him inside and we can drop him at a hospital.'

The gravelled driveway hurt her feet as she helped Robert carry him. Grunting, Robert swung the body into the back seat of the car. What would Andrei do if he came around? He was going to kill her. The realization that she was still in danger suddenly hit her. She had no guarantee that Robert would let her live. *Co-operate with their demands.* She could almost hear Flynn's stern order.

'Get the refuse sack,' Robert ordered.

She hurried back to the house and grabbed the plastic sack while Robert unlocked the boot. He took it from her and shoved it inside.

Robert gestured to the car boot. 'Now, get in.'

She eyed the dark, cramped space. There was no room. She couldn't possibly get in there. 'Please, no. Robert, I . . .'

He clenched his jaw and reached into his pocket to produce a snub-nosed pistol. Andrei's gun. His thumb slid the safety off. 'Don't make me, or I swear . . . Just get into the fucking car.'

She clambered into the trunk, wriggling to fit in as best as she could. Her last glimpse of daylight was Robert's face and the blue sky above his head as he slammed the lid shut.

The car started with a roar and she was thrown against the floor. She yelped and tried to hold on, clutching blindly at the inside of the boot, but each bump, each pothole in the road threw her around like a rag doll. After a few minutes the car screeched to a halt. They couldn't have gone far. She screamed and kicked the carpet-covered panel. The boot jerked open.

Robert's face was a mask of rage. He waved the gun in her face. 'If you make another sound, I will use this. Do you understand?' He reached into the boot and pulled out the refuse sack. He was probably dumping it, destroying the evidence.

She couldn't tell if the safety was off, but the sight of the pistol was enough to silence her. The door of the boot slammed shut. She heard a car door opening and closing, and then the engine started again. He was going to kill her. No one would ever know that she had been in the house or that Robert was involved.

She sniffed. There was a faint smell of petrol and in the confines of the boot she began to feel nauseous. Trying to distract herself, she began to count, anything to focus her mind and stop the rising panic that she would suffocate on petrol fumes. *Stop thinking like that.* Flynn would . . . She sighed. Flynn would do nothing. He didn't even know that she was missing. She couldn't depend on anyone turning up to help her. If she wanted to get out of this, she had to do it herself. Think. Think. There has to be something.

The car hit another bump on the road and Summer was thrown against the hard wall of the interior. Another jolt, this one more powerful than the last, and she cried out as her skull bumped against the panel, which popped open. She rubbed her head. She would have a lovely bruise there tomorrow. If there was a tomorrow. She managed to shove the panel away and reach in to explore the cavity behind. She could feel wires.

The last time she had a blinking tail light, the mechanic had done something with them as a temporary fix. Could she do it? If Robert had a problem with his rear lights, would he be stopped?

It would be one way of getting out of the car. Her sweaty fingers couldn't get a grip on the wires. When had it gotten so warm in here?

With a determined grunt, she grabbed a handful of cables and pulled hard. Something popped and the cables came away in her hand. Yes! She had definitely broken something.

The road beneath the car became smoother and Summer could hear heavy vehicles rushing past. Motorway. But which one and where was Robert taking her? The car increased speed and she was thrown against the metalwork. Robert was driving like a lunatic.

Calm down. Calm down. The more out of control he was, the more likely that he would be noticed. The car jerked and turned. He must be weaving in and out of lanes. Please God, they wouldn't crash. A vision of the car mangled in the middle of the motorway made her heart race again.

She could hear a siren, faint at first, then louder. Oh please, oh please, let it be the police. The car slowed down and stopped. Oh, thank god. She heard a car door thunk followed by muffled voices. Robert's voice and another, deeper one. They were talking?

Beating her fists against anything she could reach, she screamed. 'I'm here, I'm in here.'

She grabbed the discarded panel and banged it against the lid of the trunk. 'Help me. Please, someone help me.'

Then, with a squeal of rubber, the car took off again. She clenched her eyes shut tight and recited every prayer her grandmother had drilled into her. A host of images crowded into her mind. Flynn. Her mother laughing and swinging her in the air on the beach near Castletownbere-haven. Flynn. Her father at her graduation, smiling. Flynn . . .

Flynn drummed his fingers on the antique wood, and then stopped himself with an effort. He hated being on desk duty, but Niall was right; he was the best person to co-ordinate the search of Fielding's properties. Intellectually, he knew he could help Summer best that way, but it still drove him mad.

He rolled back the office chair and stood up, letting his left leg take his weight. His knee throbbed with a jabbing pain that he could ignore from long practice. The loose-ness of the joint was harder to ignore. He walked a few steps, and only the strength of the heavy brace kept the knee from collapsing under him. Some hero he was. Couldn't even walk properly without crutches, and was reduced to riding a desk.

Somewhere out there, Summer needed him. He knew it.

He popped another couple of pain pills and spent a painful quarter of an hour doing the physio exercises to get his knee working again. By the time Sinead put her head around the door, he was sweating.

'Here, let me get you a glass of water,' she offered and disappeared before he could snarl at her. He checked his Sig for the third time that day before putting it back in its holster. It would be very useful if Fielding decided to come visiting.

'So what happened?' he asked Sinead when she returned.

She shrugged. 'Malcolm is under arrest, but so far he's only charged with stealing Summer's panties. They're going to hold him on that and decide what to charge him with later. He was the one who stabbed her bed that night, but he knew she was out. He wanted to scare her.'

The memory of Summer's terrified face that morning was still fresh in his mind. 'He did.' She had been almost as frightened that night as she looked in the ransom demand video. He pulled up the clip again. There must be something in that video somewhere that would give them a clue. He set it to play again.

Sinead looked around. 'Where is everyone?' She put on the television on the news channel.

'Out searching Fielding's various properties. Summer has to be in one of them. But they're scattered all over the city.'

'You're certain it's Fielding who has her?'

He tore his attention away from Summer's scared eyes.

'I'm not certain of anything, but Niall says he's in deep money trouble and he knew that Summer was going to Molly's apartment.'

He forced himself to ignore Summer's image and looked at the background. It was just a blank wall, but there must be something. He listened again, trying to hear any background noise. Nothing. There must be some clue. He examined the background again, inch by inch.

There was a blur in one corner. He zoomed in, trying to make out details. It looked like some sort of bell. 'Why would there be a bell so high up?' he muttered. Something about it looked vaguely familiar.

'Oh, Christ.' He had seen a bell just like that in Malcolm's apartment. It was for calling a servant in a big house. Summer was in some sort of old-fashioned mansion.

Hardly daring to breathe, he thumbed through the computer printouts of Fielding's properties. One of them was a Regency period house near Hampstead Heath. They had put it to the bottom of the pile because it was so close that it seemed the least likely.

Flynn picked up the phone. 'Niall, I think I know where she is.' He ignored Sinead tapping him on the shoulder until she pulled the phone out of his hand and pointed at the television.

It was an aerial view of the main road into London. '. . . *And the Eye in the Sky can confirm that the green Jaguar which fled from a police checkpoint only minutes ago is still driving erratically on the motorway. Unconfirmed reports suggest that the car belongs to property developer Robert Fielding and that the man driving the car was armed. Police are trying to block off the road. Over to the studio . . .*'

The reporter's helicopter clearly showed Fielding's car recklessly dodging in and out of traffic.

'I have to go after her,' he said, grabbing his crutches and swinging his way out of the house as fast as he could.

'Are you mad?' Sinead panted after him. 'You can't walk or drive. What are you going to do?'

He had reached the Venom. 'No, but I can still ride a bike. I'll catch her, trust me.'

As he pushed the bike to its fastest speed, he prayed that he could make good on his word. His right knee wasn't actually painful on the bike, except for the vibration that rattled through it, so he could concentrate on weaving in and out of lanes, saving precious seconds by driving up the wrong side of the road to pass traffic. Summer. Summer. Summer. Her name echoed in his head with every turn of the wheels. He had to find her in time. It couldn't be too late. Surely he would know if it was too late. Summer. Summer. Summer. He swerved around a tractor pulling bales of hay without dropping speed. Summer. Summer.

The screech of tires and the endless weaving between lanes made Summer lose track of time. It could have been minutes or hours. Everything jumbled into one gigantic, bruising pain. More sirens. Louder this time. She could do nothing but hold on.

The good times, the special times in her life flashed by like a series of photographs. Her dad, travelling with Molly, but most of all Flynn and the croft. The nights she had lain in his arms. The feel of his mouth on hers. The rough tug of his hands in her hair as he pleasured her. Owned her.

Was this what happened when you knew you were going to die?

She would regret none of that. Not one single night. And if she had her life to live over again, she would change nothing. Because everything she had done, every aimless, stupid, spoilt action she had taken had brought them together. For the briefest of times, for a single summer, she had felt truly loved.

And nothing else mattered.

The car stopped and the lid of the boot opened. Robert grabbed her arm. His other hand held the gun. 'Out. Get out now. This is all your fault. Bitch.'

He dragged her out of the boot and put one arm around her neck, holding her in a headlock. Only then was she conscious that the motorway was eerily empty. A helicopter circled overhead.

Flynn was suddenly in the middle of a honking mass of stationary traffic. He dodged around, barely slowing, and found himself facing two police cars blocking the road. It was clear they were sealing off the motorway. They were not going to stop him.

He aimed his bike at the tiny gap between the two cars, and opened the throttle. It was a tight squeeze but he got through with no more than bruises.

He was out on the motorway, flying along in search of a green Jaguar with a broken tail light. He was vaguely aware of police motor bikes in pursuit and the traffic helicopter above him in the sky. The radio told him that they were following the Jag, waiting for a suitable place to stop it.

Flynn raced along, so concentrated on finding Fielding that the other traffic appeared to be stationary to him. All he could think about was finding Summer before it was too late. If it wasn't already too late. No, he couldn't think that. He had to find her. He would find her in time. There was no alternative.

He kept riding.

A snarl of stopped cars ahead alerted him. He flew along until he could see a green car surrounded by police vehicles, and a familiar fall of dark hair. His lungs seized for a moment. Summer was still alive. He was in time.

He braked sharply and dropped his bike in the shadow of an overpass. His knee wobbled as he got off, but he ignored it. If both his legs had been broken, it wouldn't have mattered. He was in time. He would save her.

Someone shouted through a loudspeaker, but Summer couldn't make out his words. All she was conscious of was the sleeve of Robert's blazer, the stink of his sweat and the tarmac scraping her bare feet as he dragged her along. She was afraid to acknowledge the cold press of his pistol against her bruised face.

Everything seemed to slow down; every breath was torn from her lungs and felt as if it was her last. Her pulse pounded in her eardrums like a jackhammer, so loudly that she couldn't make out the words that the police were shouting. The helicopter moved behind the overpass, the rotors keeping time with her racing heart.

The helicopter moved further away and in the aftermath, there was a silence so complete and so surreal that she could have been in a post-apocalyptic zombie movie. The thought made her giggle hysterically. Her chest heaved and she coughed against Robert's arm.

In the distance, a motorbike screeched to a halt and a lone man emerged from beneath the bridge. She couldn't see his face, but even from this distance she knew him. She blinked, trying to focus, hardly daring to believe her eyes.

It was Flynn. He hadn't abandoned her. Flynn had come.

Flynn's stomach twisted. Fielding was holding Summer in a brutal grip. He had his arm around her and was holding her head back by grabbing a hank of her hair. She was doing her best to stay calm, but he could imagine her panic. Fielding was holding a pistol to her head.

Flynn's hand tightened around his Sig.

The police were talking to Fielding through loudspeakers, telling him to let her go and it would be all over. As if anyone believed that. Fielding's grip tightened.

'Let me go or I'll shoot her,' he shouted. 'Back off.'

One of the cops moved closer. Fielding yanked Summer's head back, making her gasp with pain. 'Move that car out the way or I swear, she's dead.'

The cop moved closer.

Flynn watched as Fielding's finger tightened on the trigger.

He took a step out of the shadow of the overpass, raised his Sig and fired.

Time slowed down. It seemed that the bullet took forever to reach Fielding, and for a horrible moment, Flynn thought Fielding would see it coming and move out of its path. But the shot was clean. It took Fielding straight in the mouth, severing his spinal cord as it exited the back of his head.

Fielding dropped, Summer's hair still tangled in his hand. She tumbled down with him. It only took a few strides for Flynn to reach her and pull her up.

She fit into his arms as if she had never been out of them. She was shivering, barely able to breathe, and to his surprise, Flynn found he was shaking too.

In the background, people were moving, vehicles got out of the way, and someone hovered over Fielding. None of it mattered. No one would ever take her away from him again. She was his, she would be his forever.

He raised his head to tell her so.

She whimpered. 'Flynn, Flynn, oh god, I was so frightened.'

He tightened his arms around her. 'It's okay, you're safe now.'

'Ahem.' A polite, and obviously fake, cough alerted him a moment before a policeman tapped him on the shoulder. 'Sir? You need to come with us.'

Flynn raised his head and glared at the young officer. 'What do you want?'

'We need to question you, sir. You discharged a firearm and shot a suspect.'

'Suspect?'

The officer had the grace to look embarrassed, given that his colleagues were staring at what looked like a body in the rear seat of Fielding's car. Flynn quashed a murderous rage that threatened to flare out of control at the thought of Robert locking her in the boot of the car. He had done that to his precious Summer. He wished that Fielding was still alive so that he could shoot him again.

'I'm sure it will be fine, sir. But we need to interview you.'

36

Flynn scrawled his signature on the last of the police paperwork and pushed the clipboard across the desk to the middle-aged detective. 'That the last of it. You're free to go now,' she told him.

'Great,' Flynn muttered. He was stiff and sore from sitting in an interview room for hours. He hadn't seen Summer since the motorway and the need to be with her gnawed at his gut. He stood up, eager to find his orchid girl. Despite the support brace, his leg wobbled like jelly and he almost missed his crutches.

He pulled his collar up as he exited the building, ignoring the reporters hanging around outside and hoping that they hadn't seen him. Flynn stepped into the street and tried to hail a passing taxi. As soon as he did, a swarm of reporters thrust microphones and cameras in his face. 'Are you the man who shot Robert Fielding? Would you care to make a statement, sir?'

One of them tried to shove a business card into Flynn's face. Damn it. This was why Niall insisted on a low profile. Flynn refused to answer them. Just as he was about to curse his boss, a dark limousine pulled up and the rear door opened. 'Get in and stop making a show of yourself.'

'I hope you didn't dress up for me,' Flynn said as he climbed awkwardly into the back seat beside Niall, who was wearing a tailored suit instead of his usual jeans.

'Fuck you,' Niall said and punched him on the arm. 'We got out of this one by the skin of our teeth – from zero to hero in an hour. I thought O'Sullivan would have my nuts for sure.'

'Where is she?'

'If you mean the principal, she's installed in a penthouse in Claridge's. The last time I saw her, she was surrounded by personal shoppers, and Teflon Tim was cracking open the champagne.'

Flynn shook his head, remembering his last encounter with Summer's personal shopper. Was that only a month ago? Now she was back in her own world. The enormity of it hit him like a punch in the gut. The job was over. The bad guy was dead. There was no reason for them to be together any longer. But the memory of her kiss on the motorway made him ache with hunger.

'She wants you delivered ASAP.'

'What?'

Niall grinned. 'You heard me. Ms O'Sullivan has requested your presence and you know it's unforgivable to let a lady down.'

Summer glanced around the suite. Where had all these people come from? Sinead was deep in conversation with Flynn's friend Andy. The phones were ringing off the hook with reporters looking for an exclusive. The police were still here and her dad was pouring champagne as if there was no tomorrow. The couch was littered with dozens of bags from her favourite stores, but none of them held a scrap of interest for her. She was still wearing the same grubby clothes she had worn for the past few days and all she could think about was Flynn. She had to see him.

Niall promised that he would collect Flynn and bring him here, but she didn't want to see him with all of these people here. Surely it couldn't take this long to deal with the police? As if sensing her distress, Sinead abandoned her companion. 'I just got a message from that arrogant ass, Niall Moore. He said to tell you that the package is on its way.'

'Oh thank god. Sinead, can you, um . . .'

'Get rid of them?' Her cousin gave her a conspiratorial wink. 'No problem.' In her best impersonation of a schoolmistress, she clapped her hands loudly until she got their attention. 'Can we take this downstairs please? Summer needs to rest. I'm sure you'll appreciate that it's been a very difficult week for her.'

Within minutes, the suite was hers again. She caught a glimpse of herself in the mirror. Flynn was on his way, and she looked like she'd been dragged through a hedge.

She washed quickly in the glass-walled shower and hurried back to the lounge. The shopper had thought of everything. Moisturizers, serums, lingerie. The Scot was in for a surprise seduction. She pulled on an aubergine-coloured corset, heavily embroidered and decorated with lace. Someone had helpfully provided a matching dressing gown and length of silk ribbon. Maybe she could use it on Flynn. Digging further into the pile, she located some hold-up stockings. Another bag contained a pair of sky-scraper heels.

A month in the croft had given her some insight into his tastes. *Operation Flynn* was under way. She would make him hers again and this time she wasn't letting him go. Summer closed the curtains and switched on a bedside lamp before hurriedly shoving the bags out of sight. She had almost finished drying her hair when a knock on the door announced his arrival. Her stomach fluttered like a dozen butterflies as she opened the door.

The tall, blond man from the car park at York Minster leaned nonchalantly against the doorframe and beside him was Flynn. The delight in his eyes didn't hide the pallor of his skin. Why hadn't she noticed that earlier? Summer stepped back to allow them inside and winced when she saw Flynn limp to the nearest couch, where he sat down heavily.

She looked to Niall for an explanation.

'He has a few scrapes from his last outing. Don't be too rough with him.'

A dark cushion sailed across the room and bounced off the door. 'Watch it. Even with one working leg, I could still beat the crap out of you.'

'Temper, temper.' Niall laughed. 'If the lady decides she wants a real man, I'll be downstairs in the bar. I'll be back with your crutches later.' He dropped a kiss on her cheek and closed the door behind him.

Summer turned nervously, unsure what to say to him. After the kiss on the motorway, she had foolishly thought that they would fall into each other's arms and things would be exactly as they were at the croft. But there was a nervousness about Flynn, a reserve that hadn't been there before.

She had dressed up like a femme fatale for him. Why didn't he react? Flynn did care for her. He had to.

'Nice place you've got,' he said, glancing at the barrel-vaulted ceiling and sumptuous pale furnishings.

'It was Dad's idea.' Summer shrugged as she crossed the room. 'He wanted to celebrate and he's organized dinner for later, to thank you.'

'A farewell dinner?' The edge to his voice made her uneasy. Flynn might be resigning himself to not being her bodyguard any more, but she was damned if she was giving up on them.

She had missed him so much. The awful time when she had been trapped in Robert's car, thinking that she was going to die, had made her realize that Flynn was the only man for her. She had to break through his reserve tonight or she might never see him again. She couldn't risk that.

If Flynn wouldn't make the first move then she would. She had to convince him that they had a chance together, even if it meant stepping outside her comfort zone. She pressed on before she lost courage. 'I had a lot of time to think about things while I was . . . while I was away,' she said. 'You know me better than anyone else. I've never felt so close to another person in my life. But you don't know everything about me yet. So maybe we should keep exploring.'

'Exploring?'

Summer perched on the edge of the couch, relieved when his glance strayed to the lace at the top of her stocking. 'And I believe you have something that belongs to me.'

'Oh? And what would that be?'

She took a deep breath. 'You owe me a fantasy.'

'Is that right?'

The hint of danger in Flynn's tone made her swallow. 'Tonight, I want to be in charge.'

His expression barely changed, but his eyes warmed. 'In charge?'

'Yes. You know, you do what I say, when I say it. That kind of in charge.'

The dancing amusement in his eyes was tinged with something else and Summer couldn't decide whether it was anticipation or lust. 'You really are . . .'

'A kinky wee bitch?' she mocked. 'Oh, but you knew that already. You've always known.'

'Summer, I have a brace on my leg that makes me look like RoboCop, and I doubt if I can make it as far as the fireplace without help. Niall wasn't joking about the crutches.'

Disappointment mingled with relief. He did want her, but Flynn was afraid. This might not be the reunion she had longed for, but the only thing she was certain of was that she wanted Flynn now more than ever before.

A tingle of anticipation fluttered low in her belly. *You're the notorious Summer O'Sullivan*, she told herself. *And it's not as if he can run away from you.* She stood up and offered him her arm. 'That's okay. I can move for both of us.'

Flynn whistled when he saw the four-poster bed. If he wasn't injured, she was willing to bet he would have found some creative uses for the wooden posts. Her nipples peaked with excitement.

Flynn sat on the edge of the bed. His hooded expression gave her little confidence. She brushed her mouth against his in a teasing kiss. 'Haven't you missed me? Even a little bit.'

'My little bit missed you a lot,' he admitted grudgingly. 'But I warned you what would happen if you ran away again. If I weren't injured, you'd be in for a punishment spanking right about now.'

She nipped at his jaw, tiny biting kisses as she opened the buttons of his shirt one by one. Encouraged by his murmur of approval, she tugged it down his arms and dropped it to the floor.

'Your turn to take something off,' he ordered.

She let the silk dressing gown fall to the floor, relishing his hungry expression when he saw what she wore beneath. 'Your turn.' She gave a throaty laugh.

'I think you'll have to help me.' Flynn unstrapped the brace on his leg, then lay back on the bed and opened his pants. Summer pulled them off and gasped when she saw his leg. He hadn't been kidding about being injured. 'Holy hell. What happened to you?'

'Afghanistan. Somebody didn't want me there.'

'Does it hurt?' she asked.

Flynn shrugged. 'The only thing that hurts more than my leg right now is my cock. Now, come here and kiss me.'

Conscious of his injury, she straddled his hips, enjoying the feeling of his hard shaft rubbing against her clit. The kiss turned open mouthed, hungry. Her tongue duelled with his and he dragged one hand through her hair while the other gripped her hip, holding her in place as he raised his hips and ground against her. He reluctantly broke the kiss and ran his finger along her lace-covered breast, leaving a trail of goose bumps in his wake. 'Much as I appreciate the thought, take the damned thing off.'

She scooted off the bed and wriggled out of the corset, watching Flynn's eyes narrow when he glimpsed the hard pebbles of her nipples and the tiny triangle of silken thong.

His nostrils flared as if he was scenting her. 'Leave on the stockings and the heels.'

'Just whose fantasy is this?'

Summer cupped her breasts as if she was offering them to him. 'Like them?' she purred in her best imitation of a sex kitten. 'If you're a good boy, I might let you touch them later. Now place your hands behind your head.'

Flynn stretched his arms up as if he was yawning before folding them behind his head, the very picture of insouciant indolence.

Conscious of his eyes on her, Summer played with the lacy edge of the thong before shimmying out of it. Ignoring the heat in his eyes, she looped the thong around each of his wrists as he had once done with rope.

'Was there something particular you had in mind? I might need my hands free.'

'No hands.'

She knew the scrap of lace wouldn't hold him for a minute if he was really determined, but symbolically she wanted him to surrender. Flynn had to know that he could trust her, even when things were bad. Standing before him, Summer surveyed her naked and bound prize. Despite the injuries on his leg, Flynn was still beautiful.

'Do you like what you see?' he drawled.

She ignored his attempt to rile her. Instead she climbed onto the bed and crawled up his body with the slow, stealthy pace of a tigress hunting her prey. 'Do you?'

Summer hovered over him, allowing her erect nipples to graze his chest. She lowered her head and nipped his neck with small, biting kisses that turned slow and languorous. Trailing along his jaw, she sucked lightly on the sensitive spot just beneath his ear. The muscles of his shoulders turned rigid. Poor Flynn. She kissed a path along his collarbone and licked delicately around one nipple before turning her attention to the other one, delighted to discover that he was sensitive there.

Flynn stifled a groan as her hair slid along his chest. Summer made her way slowly down his abdomen, determined to stretch out the erotic agony. Flynn's cock was now fully erect but his eyes were squeezed shut.

With a regretful glance, she ignored her prize and instead she nipped at his hip, licking a path towards his balls before moving away again.

'Are you planning on torturing me for long, woman? I could always go back to Afghanistan for that.'

'Would you like me to torture you?' she said innocently. Flynn liked to give pain, but did he also like to receive? There was one way to find out. She kissed a spot on his inner thigh before biting down hard.

His hips jerked and he gave a strangled groan. That appeared to be a yes, but she didn't quite know what to do with it. Summer sat back on her knees. His engorged cock looked terrifyingly large. She gazed up at Flynn. The heavy-lidded expression was back.

She licked the length of his shaft and was rewarded with a hiss of pleasure tinged with frustration as he fought for self-control. Poor Flynn, she almost felt sorry for him. Opening her mouth wide, she closed it over the head of his cock and swirled her tongue around the sensitive tip. His hips bucked involuntarily.

'Don't,' he gasped. 'I'm not sure how long I can last. How about I return the favour?'

Summer caressed his balls and licked again, unwilling to release her prize. It wasn't often that Flynn let her be on top.

'I bet that I can give you an orgasm in less than three minutes.'

Her libido screamed at her to take the wager. She inched her way up his body, not sure how to handle this. She was already so turned on by the idea that she wasn't sure how long she could last. Should she release him or not? Would he be able to do this without using his hands?

Sensing her confusion, Flynn whispered, 'Come closer. I'm good, but not that good.'

She felt awkward, hovering above his face, feeling his warm breath against her leg, and had to brace herself against the wall.

'Closer,' Flynn said hoarsely.

The stubble on his jaw rasped the tender skin of her inner thigh as he nuzzled her gently. Then the wet heat of his tongue flicked across her clit, setting her nerves on a jangling edge. 'Yes, just like that.'

His mouth closed over the sensitive bundle of nerves and his tongue swirled slowly back and forth. With her arms straight against the wall in front of her, Summer threw back her head. The throbbing pressure on her clit eased as Flynn's tongue licked a path along her lips, tasting her. The vibration of his groan of pleasure made her squirm. Flynn kissed her with the same ruthless attention that he gave her mouth, as if every part of her belonged to him.

'Oh god,' she gasped when his lips focused on her clit again, sucking the tiny bud into his mouth. Her breath came in panting gasps. She was close, so close. She was going to come. Nothing could stop it now. Every nerve ending was poised on a spiralling path to pleasure. 'Please, oh please, don't stop.'

He bit down. The pleasure-pain sent her over the edge and she screamed his name. A maelstrom of sensation washed over her. Exhilaration mingled with ecstasy as she rode the wave. She rested her forehead against the wall as the last trembling aftershocks took her. Her legs were still shaking when she climbed off him and down to rest her head on his chest. Flynn's heart raced in time with hers. She wasn't the only one who was affected. 'That was. That was . . . amazing.'

'Two minutes and forty-nine seconds.'

'What?' Summer lifted her head in disbelief. 'You were counting?'

'Well, we did have a bet.'

'And what do you want for a prize?' Her eyes roved down his muscular torso, watching the rise and fall as his breathing returned to normal. His cock was so stiff and engorged that it looked painful. Poor Flynn. She would have to do something about that.

'Condoms?' he asked hopefully.

Bugger. How had she forgotten something so basic? She very much doubted that whoever had shopped for her had thought to buy any. Rolling over, she punched in the number for housekeeping into the bedside phone.

It said a lot for Flynn's self-control that he had lasted this long, but she noticed that his hips bucked when she rolled the latex sheath over his hard length. Straddling his hips, she grasped his cock and teased him, rubbing it back and forth in her wetness. Flynn's face contorted as he desperately fought for control. Just what would it take for him to lose it?

She lowered herself down, taking the barest inch of him inside her before rising again. God, he felt so good. 'Do you like that?'

Flynn's pupils were so dilated that his eyes were black. 'No more games.'

He grasped her hips and Summer squealed in surprise when he pulled her down hard onto his shaft. 'You may be on top, but that doesn't mean I'm at your mercy. Does it?'

The sternness in his tone made her quiver. 'No, Sir.'

'Good girl.' He captured her wrists and drew himself towards her until they were face to face, exchanging ragged breaths. His kiss was like the first time, outside the club. A hard and merciless domination, an invasion of his tongue into her mouth. He possessed her, owned her. Gripping her hair tightly, Flynn slanted his head and plunged deeply again.

She was helpless against the onslaught. She had thought she would be on top, in charge. For once, she wanted to be the person in control, the one who made the decisions. Every time with Flynn was mind-blowing in its intensity, but the fear was always there that she would lose herself in him.

She'd convinced herself that if she were on top, it would be different. She'd dominate him. Flynn had turned the tables once again. She was the pupil and he would always be the master. His brutal claiming of her mouth was an exercise in showing her exactly who was in charge. Summer moaned against his mouth, desperate for more.

Flynn could kiss her for a thousand years and she would still be hungry for him.

Flynn pulled his mouth away from hers. She had never felt so exposed or so wanton.

'Who's driving here?' Flynn asked, his voice strained with passion.

'You are.' She whispered. 'You are.'

'Then ride me.'

She clenched her inner muscles around his cock and he groaned as she began to move, slowly at first, enjoying the exquisite feeling of him inside her. The ache between her thighs was almost painful. If she didn't come soon she would die. She rocked against his hips, grinding her clit against him at each downward stroke. *So good.*

Flynn grasped her hips, setting the pace. Holding her in place. He raised her up, the head of his cock nudging the entrance to her slippery sheath before slamming her down hard again. 'Touch yourself,' he ordered.

Summer cupped her breasts. Her nipples were painfully hard. She sucked her index finger into her mouth and traced a circle around her clit and she almost came just from a single stroke. 'Please. Don't stop.'

With a grunt, he arched his hips and slammed deeper, his pace increasing in speed and ferocity. Each hard thrust, every heady gasp of her breath, drove all thought from her head and she cried, 'Oh god, Flynn. I love you.'

There was nothing in the world but them. Her and Flynn, Flynn and her. Her orgasm slammed into her like a tidal wave, obliterating all rational thought. Flynn groaned as she clasped her inner muscles around him, but still he pounded, lost in his own passion.

A second climax hit her before the first had faded, and she screamed his name. Flynn stiffened and shuddered, until with a final series of thrusts he joined her in ecstasy and she collapsed onto his chest. Their unsteady breaths mingled in the silence until his limp cock slid from her. With a hoarse sigh, he kissed her forehead. 'Jesus, woman, I think you killed me.'

'I did?' Summer giggled. 'How would you feel if I killed you every night for the rest of our lives?'

She hadn't intended to ask him. Not like this. Although the thought of being apart from Flynn again was more than she could bear. Her heart thudded as she waited for his response.

Flynn stroked her face and raised her chin. The golden flecks in his eyes had never been so prominent. 'I love you, Summer. I think I've loved you from the first moment I saw you coming down the stairs wearing that excuse for a towel. I almost went crazy when I thought I would never see you again.'

'Then it's yes?'

He brushed his lips against hers. 'It's always been yes.'

37

The first thing that he realized when he woke was that his leg was throbbing in agony and the second was that he was now engaged to Summer, who was nowhere to be seen.

'Dinner is in thirty minutes,' she announced, as she came into the bedroom carrying a freshly ironed shirt. 'Do you need help getting into the shower?'

'No, I'm fine,' he said as he eased off the bed.

It was bad enough letting her be on top without having her wash him too. Although he might let her do that later, when they had more time. Flynn watched as she disappeared again, giving him a flash of bare shoulder in a strappy evening gown.

'Damn,' he muttered. He was hardly dressed for dinner and he wasn't sure how Tim O'Sullivan would greet the news that his only daughter was going to marry her bodyguard. Emerging from the shower ten minutes later, Flynn discovered that his trousers had been sponged and pressed and that the shirt had a price tag on it that would make Niall wince. Who the hell spent £450 on a shirt?

'You'll need a tie with that.' Summer returned, her hair was now pinned up in an elaborate style and her eyes were shaded with a smoky silver shadow that made her look sexy as hell. He wanted to drag her back into bed again and maybe they could find another use for the tie she was carrying.

She looped it around his neck and tied it with expert hands, before planting a kiss on his mouth, giving him a flick of tongue that sent the blood from his head.

Flynn cupped her hips and pulled her against him. 'I think I'll have to impose a no panty rule.'

'Don't start that again, or we might miss dinner. Come on, Dad's waiting.'

All eyes were on her as they entered the restaurant and Flynn went straight into bodyguard mode, checking out the entrances, exits and their fellow diners. His instinct would always be to keep her safe.

Tim O'Sullivan stood up and clapped him on the shoulder. 'It seems I've you to thank for getting her back safely.'

Flynn tried not to wince as O'Sullivan's voice boomed across the restaurant. 'I was just doing my job.'

'Speaking of which . . .' O'Sullivan reached into his pocket and produced an envelope which he thrust at him. 'A little bonus for you for a job well done.'

'There's no need –'

Flynn shot a glance at Summer and she shook her head. She obviously hadn't told her father. She nodded in the direction of the restrooms, a clear signal that she needed a few minutes alone with her father. He stood up. 'Excuse me for a moment.'

He walked slowly from the restaurant, trying to ignore the interested glances from the other diners. In the restroom, he splashed his face with cold water. The contents of the envelope nagged him like an itch he couldn't scratch, so he opened it and peeked inside. A cheque for £100,000 stared back at him. Fuck. That was a serious bonus and not one he could accept. He stuffed it back into his pocket.

When he returned to the restaurant, O'Sullivan had ordered more champagne but the look he gave him was less than welcoming. Flynn hadn't expected anything else. Only a madman would want his daughter to marry a man who put his life on the line every day of the week.

'I have to return this, sir. There's no way that I can accept it.'

O'Sullivan waved his hand. 'Keep it. It will barely keep her in shoes for a year.'

Summer darted her father a vicious glance. 'Dad . . .'

'I'm joking.' He smiled indulgently at her before turning his attention to Flynn. 'Summer tells me you have a place in Scotland?'

Flynn forced a smile. This was suddenly beginning to feel like a job interview. 'Yes, Turlochmor. I built a house up there four years ago.'

'I'm sure it's grand, but she'll need a place in London, too. Can't have her alone up there while you're away. How long do you think you'll be at that racket? I'm sure we can find you something in security down here instead.'

The rest of the meal was torture. Flynn couldn't remember what he ate. O'Sullivan's voice grated on and on. By the time coffee was served, Flynn felt that his life was no longer his own. He was almost relieved when his phone rang. He hurried from the dining room, ignoring the disapproving glares as the sound of the Tardis blared.

'Are you carrying?' Niall asked him without preamble.

'Always,' Flynn responded.

'Good. That vehicle check you requested came back. One blue HiAce van registered in Malcolm's name.'

'Fuck.'

410

'Tell me about it. It's stored in a rented lockup along with some other nasty stuff – chains, knives, you name it, including some bullets for an old Luger pistol. Our Malcolm has made quite a little shrine to Summer. Photos, clothes and CCTV footage from the house.'

'Where is he?'

'Sorry, Flynn, but Malcolm made bail this afternoon.'

Flynn glanced around him. Everyone was a potential threat. Someone who could harm Summer. He had to get her out of here fast.

'Stay where you are,' Niall said. 'Get her back to the penthouse. Andy and a few of the team are already on their way.'

Flynn disconnected the call. He loosened his tie and shoved it into his pocket as he hurried back to the restaurant. He grabbed Summer by the arm. 'We need to go back to the room. Now.'

'What the –' Tim said.

'Malcolm is out on bail. Niall found his lockup – it looks like he was behind the threats all along.'

Summer's face blanched and she closed her eyes.

'Now!' Flynn snapped while he scanned the restaurant again. There were no new diners and most of the ones that remained were drinking coffee or enjoying after-dinner drinks. There was no visible threat here, but they would have to go through the lobby to reach the lifts.

The kitchen doors swung open again. The uniformed waiter kept his head down but Flynn recognized him immediately. Malcolm. Instinctively, he swung Summer behind him. She jarred into Tim, who crashed against the table. 'Everybody down,' he roared.

Like a slow motion clip from a movie, Flynn was conscious of movement all around him – shock, screams, the sound of glasses breaking – but he kept his eyes on the target. He drew his weapon and flicked the safety in a single motion.

Malcolm's eyes were dark with rage and all of that rage was focused on one person. Summer.

'I say. You can't –' A grey-haired man stood up, trying to protect his wife who was cowering in her chair.

'Get out of the way,' Flynn shouted. Bloody civilians.

Malcolm grabbed the man by the collar and pulled him in front of him, using him as a shield.

Fuck. He couldn't get a clean shot at the target. This was going to get dirty. More screams. The kitchen doors opened and closed again.

Malcolm raised his arm and pointed the gun at the upturned table where Summer and her father were crouched. It wouldn't be enough to protect them.

With every nerve end screaming, Flynn threw himself in front of the table. This was going to hurt.

Two gunshots sounded in quick succession. Malcolm fell to the floor, dragging his hostage with him.

Flynn was aware of a blinding pain. One that was horribly familiar. For a single moment he was back in Afghanistan, the night sky above his head and the tang of blood heady in his nostrils.

Then Summer was there, her face pale and shocked, and Andy and Jamie were pulling her away. His vision blurred and faded. Cold sweat bathed him as pain radiated from his battered leg and he had to clench his teeth not to roar from the blinding pain. The last thing he remembered was someone shouting about an ambulance.

When he opened his eyes again it was dim. A siren wailed overhead. He couldn't move his arms or legs and it took him a moment to realize that he was immobilized on a stretcher in the back of a speeding ambulance.

'You're awake,' the paramedic stated the obvious. 'You've certainly made a right mess of that knee.'

Fuck. The nurse in Germany had warned him. He could still hear the words coming from that prim, disapproving mouth of hers. *If you don't rest, you could lose the use of your knee.*

Fuck fuck fuck. He had really done it this time.

'We're almost there. Are you in much pain?' the paramedic asked.

'No.' Flynn shook his head. The pain in his leg was nothing compared to the raging ache inside him. How could he marry Summer if he was crippled? What sort of a husband would he be to a woman like her if he couldn't walk?

It was bad enough that she was filthy rich and he was only a soldier, but how could he support her if he was pensioned off? He was thirty-five not sixty-five. He wouldn't be able to keep up with her physically. He would be Summer O'Sullivan's crippled husband. Dependant on her financially and otherwise. Almost as bad as Bayliss.

No, he would be worse than Bayliss.

Cold realization started in Flynn's gut and spread upwards until it engulfed his chest and strangled his heart.

He couldn't do that to her. Not to his Summer. He couldn't marry her now and he didn't know how he was going to tell her.

The ambulance slowed and stopped and the doors opened. A second paramedic climbed in and they transferred him onto a gurney. Rows of ceiling lights flashed overhead as they hurried down the corridor and through doors marked 'X-ray'.

Niall's anxious face hovered over him. 'Don't worry. They've called in the best surgeon. You'll be –'

'Give me a phone.'

'Sir, you can't use a phone in here,' the paramedic said.

'Then get me outside, but give me a fucking phone.' He couldn't wait until after the surgery. If Summer found out that he was badly hurt, she would be here ASAP and he didn't want that. He didn't want her staying with him out of pity. He wouldn't take that chance.

'Niall man, I have to talk to her.' Flynn hated the edge of pleading in his voice but already the pain was threatening to overwhelm him. He had to do it now.

Niall clapped him on the shoulder and, ignoring the protesting nurse, pushed the gurney outside and handed him a phone. 'You have five minutes.'

The phone rang again and Summer checked the display before answering. 'Flynn? Oh, thank god. I've been so anxious. They wouldn't let me go in the ambulance.'

'Better off there,' his voice slurred.

'But I want to –' How could she leave him alone in a hospital when he had just saved her life? Her father hadn't stopped praising him, saying that he was the bravest man alive.

'No. Summer, you have to listen to me.' Each word was distinct, as if Flynn was forcing them out. 'You have to realize . . .'

She waited. Something was very wrong here. A chill washed down her back.

'Summer. I will always care for you. I want to be your friend, but . . .'

Her friend? Flynn wanted to be her friend?

He continued. 'But we can't get married. I'm not like Adam Bayliss. I'm not willing to live off your money.'

How could Flynn think about money at a time like this? He had saved her life. He had said yes. He had told her that he loved her. Surely he hadn't changed his mind? 'I know you're not like Adam. I love you, Flynn. Why are you talking like this? It's only money.'

'To you, maybe.'

'Are you worrying about my father? He'll insist on a pre-nup, of course, but that's almost standard these days when one person –'

'Is richer than the other,' he finished. 'Can't you see? Marriage would ruin what we have together. And that's not the only thing.'

Flynn's voice faltered and that gave her a small glimmer of hope. 'Can't we just talk about it? We needn't have Westminster Cathedral if you don't want to. We can –'

'You're not listening to me. Believe me when I say that I have thought about this. I've thought of nothing else.'

She heard him draw a breath and then there was silence before he added, 'I don't want to be Mr Summer O'Sullivan.'

One month later

Her body remembered before her brain, her stomach clenching as the first wave of pain hit her. Flynn was gone. She lay in the tangled sheets, wishing that she had something to throw at the bird who was chirping on her window ledge.

'I don't want to be Mr Summer O'Sullivan.' His parting words were her first thought each morning and the last thing she remembered before she went to sleep. If she could sleep. Flynn had left the hospital by helicopter following surgery and despite putting pressure on Niall, she couldn't find out where he had gone. He had just disappeared.

She wandered to the bathroom to survey the latest damage. Her eyelids were purple from crying. Par for the course. Summer returned to the bedroom to dress.

The new butler – Andrew from Perth – was probably waiting for her to come down for breakfast. He was under orders to report to her father what she ate. Some days she barely managed coffee and could swallow nothing solid. She glanced at her phone, squinting at the display through tired eyes. Lots of emails, some text messages from the girls wishing her well and hoping that she would fly to Australia for their weddings.

Someone from the publicity department at her dad's office had forwarded a request for an in-depth interview about her and Flynn. 'Keep that up and you're definitely getting fired,' she told the phone.

Flynn. Even reading his name hurt. How could he have done this to her? It wasn't her fault that she was rich. But to break up with her because of it was more than she could bear. She had tried to forget him. Over the past month she had bought an entire new wardrobe and partied until she dropped each night, but nothing took the edge off the pain.

There was a tap on the bedroom door and Andrew entered. 'I apologize for disturbing you but your father sent this by courier from his office. He said that you may want to see it.'

He approached her with the same trepidation as a tourist who had fallen into the lion enclosure during feeding time at the zoo. 'It seems to have been mixed up with your father's business papers by the previous incumbent.'

By incumbent, she presumed he meant Malcolm. 'What is it?'

'I believe it's a wedding invitation. From Scotland, ma'am.'

'Scotland?' She snatched it from his hand and tore the cream parchment envelope open.

Mr David Mackenzie and Ms Lorna Bell cordially invite you to celebrate with them on the occasion of their wedding at Canongate Kirk on July 31st 2013 at 3.30 p.m. and afterwards at The Witchery, Royal Mile, Edinburgh. RSVP.

There was something familiar about the date. 'What day is it?'

'It's Friday, ma'am.'

'No, not day, date. What date is it?'

'The thirty first of July, Ma'am.

'Holy shit.' Summer leapt off the bed.

'Time?'

'Twelve forty-five.'

'Shit, shit, shit.'

'Will that be all, ma'am?'

Summer stopped halfway across the room. A flight on

one of her dad's aircraft wouldn't get her there on time. 'Tell Dad I need a helicopter on the front lawn in one hour. I'm going to Edinburgh.'

After a quick shower, she riffled through her wardrobe and emptied some of her recent purchases onto the bed. She needed something that would wow Flynn. Something that would make his mouth water and the blood rush to his cock when he saw her. She selected a dramatic red shift dress. Well, she wouldn't want to clash with the bride and Flynn would be able to spot her from a mile away. Teamed with a killer bag and a pair of fuck-me heels, she prepared for *Operation Flynn*. She would have to wear sunglasses to hide her eyes, but hopefully the swelling would have gone down before she saw him.

She would make Flynn see that she had changed. Hell, she would give up being an heiress and go live in the croft with him if he wanted her to. All she wanted was him. Nothing else mattered.

Despite the swift flight to the helipad at the Prestonfield Hotel, she knew that she would miss the arrival of the bride. But when her car arrived at the Canongate, the wedding party were still waiting outside and Lorna's limousine was pulling away. Something was definitely wrong.

'Summer.' An anxious David waved to her. 'Is he with you? Is Flynn here?'

'No, I . . .' Her heart dropped. Flynn was the best man. Surely he wouldn't let his only brother down? 'I haven't seen him since the night . . . I have no idea where he is.'

Morag arrived, resplendent in lavender. 'I'm sorry David, but the minister says that he can't wait. He has another wedding booked for half past four.'

'Damn. I can't believe Flynn has just vanished like this.' David turned away, shaking his head, and she was left alone with Morag, who pulled her phone from her neat handbag and rang the chauffeur. 'You can bring her back now. We'll have to start without him.'

The rest of the ceremony went without a hitch and behind dark glasses, Summer brazened out the pointed stares. Her foolish dreams of being reunited with Flynn had turned to dust before the wedding was over. It wasn't hard to imagine what they were saying about her. The arrival of the infamous Summer O'Sullivan at an intimate Scottish wedding had almost upstaged the bride. She guessed that the invitation hadn't come from Lorna. David must have insisted on it.

After the photographs had been taken, she followed the wedding party up the Royal Mile and into the dim interior of the Witchery. She had never eaten there, but knew of its reputation for sumptuous gothic interiors and fabulous food. It would have been the perfect place for a bout of glorious make-up sex with Flynn. In her fantasies, they would have stayed in one of the suites for a week and not gotten out of bed the whole time. Now she felt foolish and uncomfortable.

Lorna sent her a few dagger glances during the drinks reception. Apart from Morag, the only ones who spoke to her were two pimply youths with questionable taste in neckties and no tolerance for alcohol.

At last they were shown to their tables. She guessed there had been a last-minute re-shuffle of the place settings when Flynn failed to arrive. She shared a table with a few of David's bachelor friends and an elderly uncle from the Orkneys who was deaf as a post. Judging by the amount of time he spent staring at her cleavage, there was nothing wrong with his eyesight.

'So you're Flynn's wee girl?' his voice could be heard on the other side of the room and she saw Lorna's head shoot up.

'Not exactly,' Summer murmured as she took a mouthful of her starter.

'Have ye plans for a wedding yourselves?'

Summer caught a sympathetic smile from a middle-aged woman at the next table. She had been hoping to have a quick dinner and return to London. Now, she was proving to be the evening's entertainment. She gave her interrogator a polite smile. 'Not at the moment. No.'

The grey-haired man sitting on his other side tried to distract him. She overheard the words 'broken up' and cringed. He turned to Summer again. 'That's a shame. Still, I suppose he must have had his reasons.'

And now my evening is complete. There was no way in hell that she was going to sit there and be pitied by Flynn's relatives. 'Actually, we broke up because I'm moving to South America.'

Her statement provoked more attention from the top table and she pressed on. 'I just came to say goodbye to Morag and David. I'm leaving for Argentina at the end of the month.'

Summer left quietly as soon as dinner was over. At reception, she scribbled a quick note on the front of an envelope addressed to David containing a voucher for two tickets to a destination of their choice, courtesy of O'Sullivan Airlines.

38

The following morning, the London house seemed bleaker than before. Yesterday she had a tiny sliver of hope that she would see Flynn again. Today was the first day of the rest of her life, and what an aimless, stupid life it was turning out to be.

The unopened designer shopping bags that littered the bedroom floor mocked her. The last month had proven that she couldn't be Summer O'Sullivan any longer. That airhead heiress had been lost somewhere in the Highlands and she wouldn't be returning. Flynn had seen to that. How could one man have changed her life so much and then just walk away? She couldn't spend the rest of her days wishing for something that she couldn't have. Maybe South America wasn't such a bad idea after all.

Her father greeted her news with the same enthusiasm he had for the announcement of fog at Heathrow airport on a Friday evening. 'South America! Are you out of your feckin mind?'

Summer laughed when she saw the expression on his face. 'No, Daddy. I think it's the first time I've been sane in years.'

'Sane, me arse. Stop mooning over that Grant chap and get on with your life. You didn't see me moping about the place after your mother died.'

She couldn't listen to his lecture again. How he had

thrown himself into his work a week after the funeral and never stopped since. 'Well, maybe you should have. If you had taken time to grieve for Mum you wouldn't have been such a miserable git for the past fifteen years.'

A wash of scarlet rose from his neck and covered his cheeks. 'Don't you speak to me like that about your mother.'

That was the problem. They never spoke about her mother, or about the years that Summer had cried herself to sleep at one school after another while she missed both of them. Her dad thought that money could cure everything. But it had caused a rift with Flynn and nothing could ease the pain of that.

For the first time in her life, Summer wished that she was ordinary. 'I will speak about her. Why did we leave everything behind when we moved here? We don't have a single thing from the old house. Why don't we have photographs of her?'

She gestured to the gilded portraits that had come with the mansion. 'Do you know who any of these people are? Name one of them.'

The dark flush had now reached the tips of her father's ears. 'You ungrateful little bitch. I work a seventy-hour week to give you this. Who do you think pays for the cars and the credit cards and all the other stuff you spend your life buying?'

Tears prickled behind Summer's eyelids, but she wouldn't cry in front of him. Her father hated tears. 'I don't want *stuff*. I need something else. I'm leaving, Dad and there's nothing you can do to stop me.'

'If you step outside that door, I'll cut you off without a

penny. How long do you think you can arse around Brazil without your credit cards and your five-star hotels?'

He gave her the look he used when he was at a board meeting and was determined to get his own way. If she worked for him, she would have been quaking in her Jimmy Choos by now, but she wasn't going to back down.

'It's Argentina, Dad, and this time I'm leaving the credit cards at home.'

Summer stepped away from the check-in desk and put her passport and boarding card into her small rucksack. She had two hours to kill before departure. Time enough for coffee and some last-minute phone calls. The envelope containing her precious letter from *Los Medicos Voladores* peeked up at her.

She wasn't useless after all. Some places in the world still jumped at the chance of a volunteer worker with language skills and aircraft logistics experience. The money in her savings account would be enough to rent a place to live until she had wages coming in.

In the duty-free shop, she picked up a bottle of Baileys. Maybe some day when the memories of their time together at the croft didn't hurt so much, she would crack it open, play her favourite Melody Gardot songs and remember Flynn without wanting to cry.

'I wouldn't recommend drinking that alone.'

Flynn's voice. She was going crazy. Summer blinked and turned in the direction of the sound. He was taller than she remembered, or maybe it was because she was wearing flat pumps instead of her usual heels. The top buttons of his shirt were undone and she caught a glimpse of tanned flesh. Flynn had been travelling again, on some secret mission he would never speak about.

Summer clutched the bottle, wondering if she should replace it on the shelf or put it in her basket. It wasn't his business what she drank. If she put it back she would look as if she cared what he thought. She put the bottle in her basket and added a bar of chocolate for good measure before she managed a half smile. 'You look good.'

His eyes roamed her face. She was aware that all the sleepless nights of the past seven weeks showed. 'It's more than I can say for you. What have you been doing to yourself?'

Missing you, more than you can imagine. That would be too humiliating to admit. He had walked out on her; she didn't owe him a thing. She shrugged, trying to play it cool. 'Nothing special.'

His mouth tightened. 'Moving to South America is nothing special? What were you going to do, send me a postcard when you got there?'

'If I knew your address and didn't think you were a complete bastard, I might think about it. And you can tell my father that I don't need a bodyguard.' She tried to pass him, only to have him catch her arm in an inescapable grip.

'Your father didn't send me. I haven't spoken to him since I left.'

Summer rounded on him. 'So why are you here? Do you think you can just drop in and out of my life whenever you feel like it? Stop torturing me, Flynn.'

He released her arm. Standing this close to him she could see the gold flecks in his eyes, catch his familiar scent. 'Summer, don't. I tried to stay away, but I just can't stop thinking about you. Nothing works, not even C4.'

She laughed at the thought of him blowing up stuff to get over her but then heard the announcement that her flight would be boarding shortly. 'That's me,' she said.

Summer picked up her basket and paid for her purchases. She would get to say goodbye to him after all. The thought made her stomach flip. How could he do this to her? A few minutes in his company and already she was beginning to melt.

Memories of the croft flooded her. Flynn laughing. Flynn holding her. Flynn making love to her. It shouldn't hurt this much just to see him again. 'I have to go. Why don't you walk me to the gate?'

He slid his arms around her waist and it was as if the past few weeks had never happened, that they had never been apart. 'What if I don't want you to go? A woman like you can't travel around South America on her own. God knows what kind of trouble you'd get into.' Flynn bent his head and whispered in her ear, 'What if I wanted to go with you?'

Summer closed her eyes as he nibbled his way down her neck, not caring about the amused glances they were attracting. The thought of them being apart again was more than she could bear. But Flynn had already turned her down once. She couldn't take that chance again. 'I thought you didn't want to be Mr Summer O'Sullivan?'

The kisses stopped. Flynn captured her ear lobe between his teeth and nipped. The pleasure-pain shock sent a jolt through her, setting her pulse racing as she waited for his answer.

'I don't. I was hoping that you might want to be Mrs Flynn Grant.'

Only Flynn would wait until the very last minute to show his hand. Bloody international man of mystery. She tilted her head back and stared at him, but there wasn't a hint of amusement in his face. If anything, he looked unsure.

'What makes you think that I'll say yes?'

The lines around his eyes creased with laughter. 'Because I'm crazy about you. And I'm hoping you might feel the same way. I'll give you until we get to the gate to think about it.'

'You arrogant. Scottish –'

'Half-Irish,' he corrected her.

He was serious about this. They were in the middle of a busy airport. All around them people were racing in every direction, while Flynn acted as if he didn't have a care in the world. What way was that to propose to anyone? If he thought for one minute that he could treat her like that when they were married, he was sadly mistaken. 'Ask me in six months' time and I'll think about it.'

'That's good enough for now. Come along, Mrs Grant, we have a flight to catch. I just need to make a quick phone call first.'

He punched a speed dial code into his phone. 'Niall, man, I need a favour. Summer and I are on the Heathrow to Buenos Aires flight departing in thirty minutes. Any chance you can upgrade us to first class?'

Epilogue

Flynn strolled up the jacaranda-lined street and into the cool interior of the former biscuit factory which was now their home. Under his arm, he carried a brown paper bag containing steaks and salads. Ignoring the lift, he took the stairs two at a time until he reached the top floor. His knee was finally back to normal and he was glad to be working again.

O'Sullivan was still having a conniption that his precious daughter was roughing it in a loft in La Boca, instead of a fancy apartment in a better neighbourhood. Rumours had been circulating that 'El Teflon' Tim O'Sullivan was considering expanding his intercontinental routes to include several South American cities. Summer rolled her eyes every time it was mentioned. No one associated the Irish señorita with the international airline magnate, and that was just how she liked it.

He laid the table, placed a single white orchid in a tiny glass vase, and put the Baileys in the fridge to chill. Summer had surprised him. He hadn't expected her to last a month out here, but she had taken to her new job like a duck to water, planning, begging and bargaining with suppliers for the best deal they could offer. She was shameless about using her connections to raise money for the medical charity, and thanks to her, they now had the use of two more light aircraft and a warehouse. Sometimes he wondered if she wasn't more like her father than she realized.

He hadn't asked her to marry him again since the day at the airport. She had asked him to wait six months. Tonight, whether she was ready or not, he was going to ask her again. It was six months to the day since the first time they had met on the stairs of her father's house. There hadn't been a day since then that he hadn't wanted her or loved her. He was through waiting.

Flynn wandered into the bedroom and changed the bed linen. It wasn't every evening that he got to seduce his wife-to-be, but tonight had to be perfect. He took a shower, shaved and pulled on her favourite shirt. It was dark cotton and fitted him like a glove. Unfortunately there was nowhere to hide a weapon so it mostly hung in the wardrobe. Summer had bought it for him the day after they had gone to their first tango show.

She had plagued him to take tango classes with her after that, but he had refused. Irishmen didn't dance. Full stop. Period. Unless they were Michael Flatley. He might be willing to negotiate on a lot of things, but dancing wasn't one of them. He would wear the shirt to please her and they could tango all she wanted in bed.

Flynn opened the doors to the tiny balcony and let the warm air drift into the room. It was nothing like Scotland. At this time of the year, he and David would have been sealing off the croft in preparation for the winter. Sometimes he had a hankering for the old place, for the bed beneath the eaves, for the sweet scent of the air there.

Buenos Aires was a different place entirely and it was only his home because Summer was here.

He heard voices on the stairs and her cheerful words as she exchanged greetings with Maria Elena, their elderly neighbour. Even when she spoke Spanish, Summer's Irish lilt was something which she couldn't disguise. Just as he heard her key turning in the lock, he turned on the music.

Coming home to Flynn always made her smile. Her whole life had changed since they moved here. The city was a vibrant, sensual place and she had learned to live her life as she wanted. But best of all was Flynn. He still took jobs which he didn't speak about. Short, dangerous episodes, when he was gone for several nights and she kept her phone beneath her pillow with Niall's number on speed dial, just in case.

One thing she had come to know was that Flynn never took chances. What they had together was too precious. She had learned to relax about it – almost.

Summer tucked her bag under her arm as she turned the key in the lock. She couldn't wait to tell Flynn about the text from Molly – she had finally got over Robert and met a kinky Cork man called Gabriel.

She forgot all about it when she noticed the table was laid for a special dinner and that her favourite tango music was playing. Then Flynn was moving towards her with the slow, deliberate stride of a dancer who was intent on taking the lead.

Without speaking, he took the bag from her and put it on the table. She loved it when he was like this, when she could simply surrender. Summer took a step back. The game had begun.

Flynn took her hands in his and raised them above her head, before pressing her back against the door. He insinuated his thigh between hers and, almost without thinking, she raised her leg and slid it along his hip. He lowered his head, seeking her throat and she gave a little whimper as his mouth fastened on her skin. Hot and insistent, he kissed her neck, releasing her wrists only long enough to pull the straps of her dress down over her shoulders. Then he captured them again.

'I do believe I've missed you, Mrs Grant.' His voice rumbled just below her ear lobe, sending a delicious shiver through her. 'It's been almost ten hours.'

'You have?' Her voice shook as she tried to concentrate on what he was saying. Flynn had managed to unzip her dress and he was busy exploring her bare skin. Her breasts were now bared to him and with slow, deliberate focus he blew a breath on one erect nipple. She almost came on the spot.

Flynn bit down, sending a thrill of pleasure-pain through her. 'Naughty, Mrs Grant. You don't get to come until I say so and you know what happens to bad girls. Now, keep your hands above your head.'

With both hands now free, Flynn pulled her dress down to her waist. He cupped her breasts in his hands, rubbing his thumbs back and forth against her nipples, driving the sensitive peaks to distraction. She was ready to plead with him to stop, when he released them.

Flynn tugged her zipper down fully, and her dress slid to the floor and pooled at her feet. She stepped out of it and kicked it away, standing before Flynn in nothing but two triangles of pink silk held together with ribbon.

'I see you've been shopping,' he murmured as he dropped to his knees and planted a kiss on her silk-covered mons, 'but I don't think we'll be needing these.' He tugged on the ribbons, leaving her bare, and he pocketed the scraps of silk.

'If you behave, you can have them back later,' he said in a tone that made her heart race. Sometimes he tortured her by taking her to one of the fancy hotels and demanding that she go to the ladies room, remove her panties and then give them to him. Then they would sit and sip a cocktail while Flynn spoke to her in a low voice, telling her in explicit detail what he was going to do to her when they got home.

The sensuous music rose to a crescendo as a plaintive Spanish voice begged her errant lover to return. Summer closed her eyes, dragging her fingers through his hair as Flynn used his mouth and tongue on her to bring her to the point of orgasm. Nothing else existed. The planet spun on its axis. She was so close. There was nothing but his mouth, his hands holding her thighs firmly apart and the tiny pulses of pleasure that were racing out of control.

'Oh god, Flynn. Oh yes, yes. Just like that.' She twisted her hands in his hair, panting his name over and over in an incoherent litany. Then everything stopped.

Summer opened her eyes and stared down at him. His mouth was wet from tasting her; his smile was heavy lidded with passion. 'Why have you . . . ?'

'Stopped? Well, it just so happens that I have you in the perfect position for what I have in mind. Wet, needy and just at the point where you'd agree to anything I want.'

She trembled with excitement at the thought of what he might have in mind. One evening, he had taken her from behind on the balcony, knowing that he was hidden from view, but that she couldn't make a sound because the balcony door of the next apartment was open. There was a part of Flynn that would always court danger.

Summer gave a throaty laugh. 'What did you have in mind?'

Flynn reached into his pocket and produced a ring box. 'Marry me?'

The music drifted away, leaving the room in silence. But for the support of the door against her back, Summer would have keeled over. His affectionate teasing, calling her Mrs Grant, had become a joke between them. Now, there was nothing but Flynn and her. In the distance, she could hear the sounds of the city that had become home to both of them. She wouldn't change a minute of their lives here or contemplate a time that they wouldn't be together. Flynn was forever.

With one hand, he flipped the box open. Nestled in the black velvet Cartier box was a ring shaped like an orchid. Its intricate diamond petals cradled a larger pink diamond at the centre. Her favourite flower and colour.

'I didn't think you'd want something traditional, but I can take it back, if you don't like it.'

'Like it? Oh Flynn, it's beautiful. It's the most perfect ring I've ever seen.' She stretched out her left hand eagerly.

Relief and joy mingled on his face, and then his mouth

curved in a wicked smile. 'Ah ah, who's doing the driving, Mrs Grant? You haven't answered my question.'

She flung herself at him, sending them both tumbling to the floor. 'Stupid man,' she said as she kissed him soundly. There was only one answer she could give. 'It's yes. Yes. Yes.'

Acknowledgements

Caroline and Eileen wish to thank:

Our beta readers, Claire, Mary, Silje, Ger and D, for their encouragement and for pointing out the obvious.

Patricia Deevy and everyone in Penguin.

Our agent, Madeleine Milburn.

Website designer Seoirse MacGabhann for the IT support and endless pots of coffee.

Our wonderful tutor, Patricia O'Reilly, who continues to inspire and mentor us.

Mircat, special advisor on archery.

John Colgan, special advisor on weapons and military.

Ian O'Reilly for information about London.

Our unshockable friends on FetLife for their kinky suggestions.

And all those, too numerous to mention, who answered our questions – no matter how strange – during the writing of *The Pleasures of Summer*.